CROSSROADS

Nancy Moser

TYNDALE

CARO

D0967354

Visit Tyndale's exciting Web site at www.tyndale.com

TYNDALE is a registered trademark of Tyndale House Publishers, Inc.

Tyndale's quill logo is a trademark of Tyndale House Publishers, Inc.

Crossroads

Designed by Beth Sparkman

Edited by Kathryn S. Olson

Published in association with the literary agency of Janet Kobobel Grant, Books & Such, 4788 Carissa Avenue, Santa Rosa, CA 95405.

Scripture quotations are taken from the *Holy Bible*, New Living Translation, copyright © 1996, 2004. Used by permission of Tyndale House Publishers, Inc., Carol Stream, Illinois 60188. All rights reserved.

Library of Congress Cataloging-in-Publication Data

Moser, Nancy.
    Crossroads / Nancy Moser.
        p. cm.
    ISBN-13: 978-1-4143-0161-7 (pbk.)
    ISBN-10: 1-4143-0161-8 (pbk.)
    1. Older women—Fiction.   I. Title.
    PS3563.O88417C76 2006
    813′.54—dc22   2005024352

Printed in the United States of America

11   10   09   08   07   06
 9   8   7   6   5   4   3   2   1

Many blessings to the small towns
that hold a special place in my heart:
Allenspark, Dawson, Dexter, Laurie, and Minden

PROLOGUE

A person standing alone can be attacked and defeated,
but two can stand back-to-back and conquer.
Three are even better,
for a triple-braided cord is not easily broken.

ECCLESIASTES 4:12

September 1, 1936

"Do it!"

Hearing the command, Madeline McHenry shoved Augustus
Weaver away, sending him sprawling into her other bosom buddy,
Web Stoddard. Both boys fell onto the grass. She *would* do it.
When *she* wanted to.

She leaned on the rear steps of the town gazebo and took aim
at the back of Mayor Ganfield's legs as he gave the Founders Day
speech. Though there were potted ferns in the way—which also
served to give her cover—she knew she could meet her mark.
At the last minute she changed her method from overhand to the
sideways flick she used skipping rocks. With one last glance at the
boys, she flicked the pebble toward its mark.

Poing!

The mayor flinched and looked behind him. Madeline did not flee, but sat up proudly on the step, adjusting her blue voile dress as if waiting in rapt attention for the next words of his speech. She gave him the innocent smile she had perfected when dealing with adults. The mayor looked skeptical but turned back to his audience. "As I was saying, in this era of tensions in Europe and struggles at home . . ."

The boys held in their laughter and pulled her down the steps and away. But as they skimmed the outer edge of the crowd, something made Madeline slow down.

"Come on!" Augustus said, pulling her hand.

She shook his grip away, her eyes riveted on the scene.

"What's with you?" he said. "I don't want to hang around here with *them*."

She felt rather than saw Web at her other side. His voice was soft. "What's going on, Maddy?"

She hated when he called her that. It was so . . . common. And she had no answer to his question. Something *had* made her stop. Something *had* detoured her from running away to play with her two best friends.

She scanned the crowd, trying to figure it out. The town square was filled with people she knew. Neighbors, shopkeepers, relatives. Yet it was as if she were detached from them, as if she were watching a scene played out in a newsreel before a Shirley Temple movie. But it wasn't exciting like Bonnie and Clyde being ambushed, or sad like seeing people in bread lines, or scary like news of drought and war; it was . . . nice. And good. And more than anything, hers.

Augustus grabbed her arm again. "Come on! This is boring."

Madeline stood her ground and shook her head. The banner behind the mayor flapped in the breeze: *Weaver's 30th Birthday!*

1906–1936. Thoughts turned into words that came out unannounced. "We have to stay here."

"No, we don't. Our parents are going to be busy with all the birthday stuff. They won't notice we're gone."

He didn't understand. She wasn't sure she did either. "We have to stay here—live here. Forever." She looked at the boys on either side of her. "Promise me we'll live here in Weaver. Promise we'll never leave."

Augustus took a step away. "I'm not promising any such thing. I'm going to be rich and run a big company. I can't do that here in—"

"I'll promise," Web said. He took her hand, his eyes sincere. She could always count on Web.

Augustus threw his hands in the air. "Holy cammoly, you two. This is dumb."

Web shook his head, his eyes locked onto Madeline's. "No, it's not. We *should* always stay here. We're a team. The Fearsome Threesome."

Augustus rolled his eyes and once again, Madeline knew he didn't see what she saw, didn't feel what she felt. She wasn't sure Web did either, but at least he was nice enough to try. Augustus could be so stubborn. . . . She held out her hand to him, knowing that the fact Web was holding her hand and he wasn't would goad him into the circle. Jealousy could be useful sometimes.

With an exaggerated sigh, he gave in.

She squeezed both their hands. Hard. "Let's say it out loud."

"This is double dumb."

She ignored him. "I solemnly promise to stay in Weaver forever and ever."

"That's a long time," Web said quietly.

She looked back at the Founders Day celebration, at all the

people of Weaver gathered together as one. "I'm going to be at the one-hundredth birthday. That's what I'm going to do." She looked Web in the eye. If only he'd agree . . . "Are you in?"

Web hesitated a second. "I'm . . . I'm in. I promise."

They both looked at Augustus. "Your turn," she said.

"Come on, Gus."

"If I agree can we get going?"

"Absolutely," she said.

"Fine. Then I agree."

"You promise?"

He spit on his right hand and raised it. "Promise."

Madeline felt a surge of satisfaction—and relief. For in this one moment of commitment it was as if her life had gained meaning and focus. Purpose. She knew who she was and where she would spend her life.

And she knew two of the people who would be there with her.

ONE

Be strong, and do the work.

1 CHRONICLES 28:10

September 2005

Eighty-one-year-old Madeline stormed into the middle of Weaver's main intersection, positioned herself directly beneath its only traffic light, spread her arms wide, and screamed, "I will not allow it!" Just to make sure every atom and chromosome of every person within range heard her proclamation, she turned one hundred and eighty degrees and did it again. "Do you hear me? I will not allow it!"

The light guiding the traffic traveling along Emma Street turned green, but there was no need for Madeline McHenry Weaver to move out of the way. The light could show its colors from now until Elvis returned and she would not have to move—for safety's sake anyway. Yet the truth was, she couldn't stand out here all day. If the heat of their Indian summer hot spell didn't get to her, her arthritis would. Annoying thing, getting old.

"You done yet?"

Web Stoddard sat at the corner on a bench that skirted the town's only park, with one arm draped over its back, his overall-clad legs crossed. The shoelace on his right work boot was untied and teased the sidewalk. He slowly shooed a fly away as if he didn't have anything better to do.

Which he didn't.

Which brought Madeline back to the problem at hand.

She waved her arms expansively, ignoring the light turning red. "No, I'm not done yet. And I won't be done until people start listening to me."

His right ankle danced a figure eight. "No people to hear, Maddy. It's too late."

She stomped a foot. "It's not too late! It can't be."

Web nodded toward the Weaver Mercantile opposite the bench. "Want to go sit at the soda fountain? I have a key."

"You have a key to every empty business in town. Don't abuse the privilege."

He nodded slowly, then grinned. "Want to go neck in the back of the hardware store?"

She crunched up her nose. "It smells like varnish and nails in there."

"Not a bad smell."

"You're obsessed with necking."

"When was the last time I mentioned it?"

She hated to be put on the spot. "But you *think* about it a lot."

"Last I heard, thinking 'tweren't a bad thing. And don't act like I'm pressuring you. The last time we kissed was 1942."

She looked past him toward the gazebo that sat in the middle of the town square. Even from here she could see that the floor was covered with the first sprinkling of gold, rust, and red leaves. Dead

leaves. Blowing away, just like the town. Yet that's where she and
Web had exchanged their last kiss. "October 22, 1942."

He smiled. "You remembered."

"You were abandoning me, going off to war."

"You were supposed to wait for me."

Ouch.

She took two steps toward the bank that she and her husband,
Augustus, had owned. Yet proximity or distance from Web
wouldn't make the past right itself. But how dare he bring it
up at a time like this? She put her hands on her hips and glared
at him.

"Gracious day. What a look. What did I do?" Web said.

"Here I am worrying about Weaver and you . . ." She let her
head wag like a disappointed mother.

He sat up straight and his loose lace became sandwiched
between shoe and sidewalk. "You need to let the town go, Maddy."

She shook her head.

He patted the bench. "Come over here."

She crossed her arms, hugging herself. She didn't want to be
scolded, or worse yet, placated. "I will not let Weaver die on me."

His voice softened. "It already has."

Her arms let loose, taking in the expanse of the main street.
"The town's going to turn one hundred next year. We can't let it
expire at ninety-nine. It's . . . it's sacrilegious."

He squinted his left eye.

"Scandalous?"

"You're overreacting, plus taking it way too personal."

"It *is* personal. I'm a Weaver." As soon as she said the words
she wished she could take them back. Her becoming a Weaver
was directly related to her not waiting for Web's safe return from
World War II.

He was charitable and let it slide. "Nothing lasts forever. Not even a family line," he said.

Ah. Sure. Rub it in. If only she and Augustus had had children . . .

"It's just you and me, kid," Web said, doing a pitiful Humphrey Bogart imitation.

But he spoke the truth. They were the only lifers left in town . . . which made her remember, there used to be another. "I can't believe the Sidcowskys left. We went to high school with Marabel."

"You can't blame them for moving to Wichita to be closer to their grandchildren."

Madeline strode to the curb in front of Sidcowsky's Hardware and kicked it. The scuff in her shoe and pain in her toe were worth it. "They're traitors, the lot of them. Abandoning their lifeblood, their hometown that needs them. They are selfish beings, thinking nothing of the greater good, only thinking—"

"The Sidcowskys are good people, but they, like others, came to a crossroads and had to make a choice. The Sidcoswkys held on way beyond when others left."

Madeline would concede the point—privately. She did a lot of conceding in private. Although she hadn't let others see her panic, that *was* the emotion holding her in a stranglehold this past year. What had Queen Elizabeth called her horrible year when Windsor Castle burned and she endured the scandal and divorce of her wayward children? *Annus horribilus.* So it was.

Actually the demise of Weaver had not come about in a single year's time. The disease that had eaten away at its foundation had come slowly, like a cancer cell dividing and eating up the good, only making itself known when it was too late. Townspeople finding jobs elsewhere. People moving out; no one moving in. People getting greedy or panicking when business slowed. Closing up shop. Forgetting in their quest for more money, more success, and more happiness, all that Weaver stood for: family, tradition, safety, security, continuity.

Where was that continuity now? Where was the loyalty? It wasn't strictly a Weaver problem. People did not stay employed with one company their entire lives anymore. They didn't even stay in one neighborhood, but hopped houses and even spouses as if all were interchangeable and acceptable on the frantic road to happiness. The truth was, Weaver's demise had killed her husband. The doctor may have said it was his heart, but Madeline knew frustration and despair were the real—

"This town isn't the only town going through hard times, Maddy. People need to eat."

She pointed at the Sunshine Café on the opposite corner. "People could've eaten right there, until those quitters, the Andersons, moved out."

"Moved on, Maddy. People have to move on when they aren't making enough to live on. Big towns with big stores and big jobs. That's what people need."

She watched a squirrel scamper diagonally from the park to the bank just a few feet in front of her. It didn't even hesitate. Even the rodents knew there was no need for a traffic light in Weaver anymore.

Her shoulders slumped. What she *needed* was a long soak in a lavender-scented bath. What she *needed* was time—more years to accomplish what she wanted to accomplish. "They don't *need* those things they're after, Web. They *want* them. Big difference."

He came toward her, right there in the street. She let him come. She could use a hug. In the three years since Augustus had died, she'd relied on Web's arms to make her feel better when the world was uncooperative. Her cheek found his shoulder. The clasp to his overall strap bit into it, but she didn't care.

"It's not your responsibility, Maddy." He put a hand on the back of her head, and she closed her eyes to let the years slip away. Many, many years . . .

But then his words—instead of falling away as they gave comfort—hung back and started to jab like a bully offering a challenge.

Yes, she and Web had lived a lot of years here, shared a lot of history, but it wasn't time to rest on those laurels yet. There were too many years between them to brush off as being past and over. She may be old, but she wasn't dead yet.

She suddenly pushed away from him. "It *is* my responsibility, Web. You don't know . . ."

His faded blue eyes looked confused, as if he'd forgotten he'd just said those very words.

She repeated herself, growing impatient. "Weaver *is* my responsibility." She pointed at the street signs. "Emma Street is named after Augustus's great-grandmother, and Henry Avenue was named for *her* father. Every street in this town is named after a Weaver. They claimed it ninety-nine years ago and we've been here ever since. I'm the last Weaver standing and I will not go down without a fight!"

She noticed her arm was raised in a give-me-liberty-or-give-me-death position. She kept it there for effect.

"Ever hear of retirement, Maddy? Enjoying your golden years?"

She lowered her arm. "Oh, pooh. Use it or lose it." She started walking toward the Weaver Garden on the far edge of the park, right across from the Weaver mansion. She often did her best cogitating among the flowers.

When she didn't hear footsteps coming after her she turned back and found Web still standing in the middle of the abandoned street. "You coming?"

He put his hands in his pockets. "Depends. Exactly *what* are you planning to do?"

"I'm going to save Weaver, silly. And after I do, we're going to have the best and biggest one-hundredth birthday celebration this town has ever seen." Web's shaking head riled her. "I *will* save Weaver, Web Stoddard. The question is: will you help me?"

Web's sigh was eaten up by the drone of the cicadas overhead. "What do you have in mind?"

Madeline had never let technicalities stop her before, and she certainly wasn't about to start now. She put her hands on her hips. "Are you in or out?"

"You need to explain—"

She took a step toward her best friend. "I don't need to do anything of the sort. I need a yes from you. Now."

"Before I even know the question?"

"Exactly."

"You're not being fair, Maddy."

She planted her feet dramatically and waited. *Come on, Web. Do this for me. For Weaver. For us.*

Web's head shook no even as he said, "Yes. Yes, I'm in."

Bravo.

It was a start.

Madeline grabbed hold with both hands and shook the chest-high, wrought-iron gate leading to the Weaver Garden. "Put this on your fix-it list, Web. Lately, I can't open this thing."

"I've fixed it multiple times." He moved to give it a try.

Presto. It opened.

She stood back, incredulous, and watched as he swung it back and forth. "How do you do that?"

He rubbed his fingers together. "Finesse. You should try it sometime."

From what she could figure, there was no reason she shouldn't be able to open the gate herself. Yet lately she never could. And he couldn't leave it open for her unless they wanted dogs to dig up the bulbs or a stray deer to munch at the leaves.

He let her go in first. She strolled along the circular path with purple asters on her left and pink roses on her right. He caught up with her and duplicated her stance, clasping his hands behind his back. The asters gave way to a strong stand of mums and orange tiger lilies bowing in the breeze.

"So. What are you going to do?" he finally asked.

Though she wasn't sure, she shared the idea that was centermost on her mind. "Buy it up. All of it."

"You're going to buy up the entire town?"

His doubt fueled her. "You betcha. Every single property that's for sale—and maybe a few that aren't."

"But that will cost—"

"Millions."

"You have millions?"

Her stomach did a backflip, but she simply shrugged and walked away. "A few."

He came after her. "A few million?"

"Give or take."

"What are you going to do with all that property? The few who've stayed behind already have homes, and as far as I know there's no line of people at the edge of town wanting to move in. And *I* certainly don't have the inclination to take care of all those properties. Keeping up with all the to-dos of the public areas is enough for these old bones."

She hated when he got all practical on her. If only he'd let her finish. "I'm going to buy it up, then give it away."

"What?"

She pointed to a honeysuckle bush, long past its flowering stage. "You need to trim that up. It's gangly."

"Yes, yes, I'll add it to the list. You can't mean you're planning to give away property, Maddy. Really give it away?"

She raised her chin. "I most certainly do."

He eyed her, then sighed. "Unfortunately, I know that look. Your mind is set in stone with deep foundations that can't be moved. Not that I haven't tried a few thousand times."

"Then stop trying."

He shoved his hands into his pockets and gave her his aw-shucks smile. "Actually, I'm proud of you."

She looked at him warily. "What's the catch?"

"Jesus told the rich man to give up everything and follow him. By giving away the town you're doing what he said, giving up the things that stand between you and him. That makes me proud. Jesus too."

She raised a hand as a stop sign. "If you know what's good for you, you and Jesus better back away and keep your veiled compliments to yourself. I'm not following him; I'm following me. What I give up, I give up for my sake, not his. Because *I* want to."

Web sighed. "You always have done what you wanted."

But not always gotten what I wanted.

Web bent over and plucked a weed from between the lilies and slipped it in his pocket. "But come on, Maddy. Think this through. If anything, buy it up and sell it again—even at a loss. That way you'd get some of your money back and still get people to move here."

"But that negates my purpose."

"Which is?"

She faced him head-on. "To revitalize Weaver. My way. Not just attract people looking for a bargain but—"

Web laughed. "You don't think *giving* property away will attract people looking for a bargain?"

She leaned toward a golden mum and pinched wilted blooms. She straightened and took a deep breath, raising her face to the breeze. And suddenly, she didn't feel like the elderly matriarch of Weaver anymore, but like a young Madeline, cheeks flushed, wind whipping through her auburn hair, her eyes flashing with life, an attentive man at her beck and call. . . .

With a shake of her head she left such romantic memories aside. "Pay attention to me, Web, because what I'm going to say . . . a lot of it is going to fall on your shoulders because I can't do it alone. Just like it's always been, it's you and me." She started to pace the path, her hands accentuating her words. "I'm not going to give Weaver to just anybody. This will not be an Oklahoma Land Rush without the rush. No, indeed, I'm going to take applications."

"Like a job application?"

"Exactly like a job application. In fact, I will make a list of specific positions that need to be filled. We don't want a town populated with twenty lawyers or a dozen ditchdiggers, do we? We don't want people to have to look elsewhere for employment. We want them to work here, right?"

"Yup. Suppose so."

"I've told you not to say *yup*. It makes you sound uneducated." She started to pace again. "I'm going to make a list of professions: a doctor, teacher, peace officer, grocer—"

"Pastor."

"If there's room. And we'll put ads in national newspapers and get on national television, on talk shows."

"Television? Who's going to go on TV?"

She pinched her lower lip and thought out loud. "I suppose we could get some pretty model to draw the younger crowd, but honestly, is that our target? Though we need a mix of ages to move here, the more mature candidates will be best. And *they* won't be put off by maturity—by me. I'll do it. So I'm old? I'm rich. I'm—"

"Bossy?"

"Since when is that a bad thing? At any rate, they'll listen to me. And they'll apply. You mark my words; they'll apply in droves."

"What will we ask them on the application?"

She turned back the way they'd come. "Come to the house. We have work to do."

"But the mailbox at the police station needs fixing. Somebody drove over it."

She paused amid the vivid splashes of color. "You want to save Weaver or not?"

He sighed. "I'm coming."

As if he had a choice.

TWO

Watch and be astounded at what I will do!
For I am doing something in your own day,
something you wouldn't believe
even if someone told you about it.

HABAKKUK 1:5

January 2006

Crash!

Lavon Newsom ran toward his son's bedroom. Four-year-old Malachi looked up from his toppled tricycle. He'd run into his Lego tower.

"Sorry, Daddy." He didn't look sorry, but grabbed two chunks of the tower, rolled onto his back, and made them clash until no two pieces hung together.

Lavon took the surviving pieces away. "Shh. Mama's sleeping, remember?"

"Oops."

Lavon took the trike into the hall where there was a clear shot next time Malachi felt like riding. Yet how far could he really ride in their sixth-story apartment on the Upper East Side? Sure, they took the trike down the elevator and to the park when it was nice out, but that was always a chore, an expedition.

Enough mental complaining. Lavon returned to the bedroom and whispered, "Come help me with breakfast, Chi-Chi. I want to make something special for your mama." They made a big deal out of tiptoeing into the kitchen, where Lavon turned on the TV and switched to a morning talk show.

Malachi found a shoe and, holding it like an airplane, flew into the living room. That kid had an imagination that could turn everything into anything. He returned to base and landed the shoe on the counter.

"The runway's on the floor please."

He moved it.

Lavon stirred some orange juice. "So what'll it be? Pancakes or dirt?"

"Dirt!"

"Dirt it is." It was a silly daily exchange, but neither one of them seemed in any hurry to change it. Lavon thrived on such silly moments. The thought of going back to work full-time and not being home with Malachi made his stomach turn in a way that was not conducive to either pancakes or dirt. Getting laid off from his consulting job was the best thing that had ever happened to him. Them. Lavon knew God did it. God got him out of the office and home where he belonged. Sure, it made money tight, but they were getting by.

Until Patrice quit her job.

He couldn't blame her. She'd been employed at the bank seven years, working toward a vice presidency. Two days ago, when she'd been passed over, she quit. Now they were an ex-banker and an ex-consultant. At least one of them needed a job—and soon. Privately, he hoped Patrice got one first. He didn't want to relinquish his Mr. Mom role. Besides, it wasn't as if she was going to ever accept being a stay-at-home mom. Patrice's homemaker abilities would make Martha Stewart, Heloise, and Mr. Clean quit in total frustration. She was a whiz at business and banking but a klutz at cooking and cleaning. In a way, Lavon had saved her and Malachi from herself.

Malachi wasn't his son—by blood anyway. When Lavon had first started dating Patrice, Chi-Chi was only six months old and his biological father was long gone. Not that the creep had ever truly been around. It was a good thing Patrice hadn't married the bum, but the choice to remain unattached had left her in the diffi-cult role of a struggling single mother. Actually, she struggled more than most because Chi-Chi had acute asthma, plus Patrice possessed a mind that was more focused on career than home.

In truth, she was a piece of work. "High maintenance" his buddies called her. "Get outta there and don't look back" had been their advice when Lavon had told them he was serious about her. In truth, it would have made life easier. But after much prayer and many sleepless nights, he'd made the choice to stick around. And in the process had fallen in love. With the mother—and the child.

Even as a baby Malachi had been able to make Lavon glow from the inside out. Every time he'd looked at the boy, every time he'd held him in his arms and put his cheek to baby-soft cheek . . .

It hadn't taken long for Lavon to realize that marrying Patrice—and becoming Chi-Chi's father—was his destiny. He hadn't regretted it a day since.

Well, maybe a day. Things hadn't worked out exactly as he'd hoped. He'd thought that with a little help Patrice would soften to the mother role. But she hadn't, and Lavon had been forced to surrender his image of a traditional family. But since he'd started

staying home with the boy . . . he was good at it now. He even took
a bit of pride in the fact that he'd proven himself good in both the
business and domestic worlds. Sure, he got flack from his friends,
but he could handle them, and purposely kept a few domestic
details to himself. They didn't need to know how he jumped out
of bed each morning, looking forward to the day in a way that was
unthinkable when he worked outside the home. Who knew he'd be
good at kid rearing, kid talking, kid thinking, and kid wrestling?

Speaking of . . .

"Syrup run for the pancakes!"

Malachi lifted his arms and Lavon scooped him up, setting him
like a bedroll against his hip. They moved to the refrigerator,
where Malachi opened the door and grabbed the syrup. With a
quick angle of their bodies, his feet shut the door. A few steps
more and the syrup was on the counter. "Syrup run complete!"

As soon as Malachi's feet hit the floor Lavon saw Patrice in the
hallway, her pj's disheveled from sleep.

Malachi ran into her arms. "Morning, Mama!"

"Hey, bud."

"I was being real quiet so you could sleep."

"Mmm. I heard you being quiet."

"We're having dirt for breakfast."

"Again?"

Lavon met her halfway, giving her a kiss. "You look wiped out."

She fell into a kitchen chair and ran a hand over her head. She'd
cut her hair short and looked a lot like Halle Berry—but prettier.
"It's hard to sleep when my entire future has been ruined."

"It's not ruined; it's just taken a detour." But Lavon had to
admit he hadn't slept well the past two nights either. Their life had
been pushed off-kilter.

While Malachi ran off to play, Lavon poured his wife some

coffee and started making the pancakes. He glanced at the TV. A stately, elderly white woman sat on a couch next to Chad Ames, an ever-smiling talk-show personality.

"Today our guest is an extraordinary woman who has an extraordinary offer. You'll probably see her ads in newspapers across the country this week, and today she's here in person. Madeline McHendry Weaver, of Weaver, Kansas." He turned toward her. *"Welcome."*

"Glad to be here. But it's McHenry. No D."

Chad glanced down at his cheat sheet, his façade broken. *"McHenry. Sorry."* The smile returned. *"Tell us about the ads, about what you're offering our listeners."*

Patrice leaned forward. "I've never seen Chatty Chad falter like that. I like this woman already."

"Shh," Lavon said. "I want to hear."

The woman tried to lean forward but it was evident the couch was too cushy for her frame. She put her hands on her knees. *"I have lived in the town of Weaver, Kansas, my entire life."*

"Your name is Weaver. Are you from one of the founding families?"

"By marriage. But even before marrying, Weaver was my home. It's still my home. It's a home I want to share with the world. By giving it away."

Lavon fumbled the pancake turner.

Chad displayed an ad for the camera. *Free Land!* screamed from the heading. *"You're giving away a town? By placing ads?"*

Lavon hadn't seen any ads.

"That's how it will begin. Weaver was once a thriving town of eight hundred and thirty-two. But due to economic and societal changes, it's emptied out."

"How many live there now?"

"Forty-two."

"Forty-two?" Patrice said. "I can't imagine."

Lavon was glad she didn't say more. He didn't want to shush her again, but he had to hear. He took the griddle off the burner and shut off the heat.

The woman's head shook back and forth. *"Forty-two is not enough. Not enough. In October Weaver will be one hundred years old and I don't want it to die. It will not die. I've dedicated myself to making it thrive again by buying up all the empty properties. I've had them parceled into homesteads—similar to what was done for our ancestors one hundred and fifty years ago. I am offering these homesteads free to settlers who apply and qualify."*

"She's giving away free land!" It had burst out of him.

"So?" Patrice said.

"Listen!"

Chad continued. *"You said the word* qualify*? How do they qualify?"*

"We have a Web site where people can find more information, including a list of the positions available and—"

"Positions?"

"Indeed. Remember, I am repopulating a town. There are certain needs that must be met."

"Such as?"

She counted off on her fingers. *"Teacher, peace officer, postmaster, café owner, banker, maintenance manager—"*

Lavon pointed at his wife. "A banker!"

"Again I ask, so?"

Chad smiled. *"Rich man, poor man, baker man, thief?"*

Mrs. Weaver made a face, not amused. *"The thief need not apply."*

"But the rest?"

"They can fill out an application, write the required essay, and send it in. We will interview the finalists in person."

"So work experience is a determining factor."

"In regard to skills, yes." She again tried to get comfortable, but seemed unsuccessful. *"Yet an applicant's past is only important as much as it helped create who they are now, and who they'll strive to be in Weaver. I'm giving the town to new 'settlers' who want to be there— need to be there. They will fill a need in the town and we will fill a need in their lives—the need to start over and put down roots."*

As the woman talked, Lavon held the edge of the counter. His legs were weak, his heart racing. He absorbed every word.

"I'm searching for people with the pioneer spirit who are willing to leave their old lives behind to work hard and rebuild Weaver to its previous glory. In return for homes—plus storefronts or businesses— the winners will have to sign a contract to stay put for five years. If they give up before that time—I despise quitters—they will lose their prop- erty, including any improvements they've made. Such a no-turning- back obligation will weed out the weak or indifferent."

Chad's eyebrows raised. *"You seem to have it all worked out."*

"No 'seem' about it. I am determined."

"I'm sure you are." Chad's smile was condescending. Lavon had the feeling the interviewer was *not* the kind of person this woman wanted to move to Weaver.

Chad turned to the camera and gave the Web site address. Then he thanked her. A commercial for lemon-fresh Lysol came on.

Lavon tried to collect the thoughts that were ricocheting through his mind.

"Can I talk now?" Patrice said.

He realized he'd been rude. "Sorry, but——" he pointed at the TV—"did you hear what that woman offered?"

"Land. Property. In Kansas."

"They need a banker."

She put down her coffee mug. "Lots of places need bankers."

"But they *need* bankers and they're offering free homes and—"

"Uh-uh. Surely you don't—?"

"Why not? You just quit your job. You want to be the vice president of a bank."

"Not in a town that only has forty-two people."

"It's going to have more. That's what she's doing with the giveaway. Bringing people in."

She shook her head. "But it's Kansas. We're lifelong New Yorkers. We've never been west of Ohio."

"A huge oversight on our part."

"We're city people. Big-city people."

Lavon spotted Malachi's trike in the hall. "We could have a house with a yard and a place for Chi-Chi to ride and play. . . ."

"You've been watching *Leave It to Beaver* again."

Guilty as charged. He loved that show.

She nodded toward the window. It was snowing outside. "It snows in Kansas. A lot, from what I've seen. There would be no riding trikes outside in the winter there either."

"That's when they go sledding and make snow angels and snowmen and—"

"Sledding and snow . . . you can romanticize anything. We should never have watched *It's a Wonderful Life* last Christmas."

He smiled. "It *would* be a wonderful life . . ."

"You're impossible."

Maybe. And he *was* mesmerized by shows depicting small-town life. Hometown settings. Hometown values. Hometown problems. He thought of something else. "You wouldn't be dealing with big corporations and bank politics, but loans to help people start over. You'd make friends with your customers and—"

"Oh yeah. A black female banker in a tiny town populated by 99 percent whites. Don't be naïve."

"There are blacks in small towns in Kansas."

"How do you know?"

He didn't. But surely with a project like this, there would be an air of community that would transcend the normal ethnic and racial issues.

And then the most important reason hit him. "The doctor said Chi-Chi would benefit from clean air, from moving out of the big city. Kansas is full of clean air." He thought of something else. "Just last week Dr. Brown told me about a specialist who's done a lot of work on the kind of asthma Chi-Chi has, but I discounted it because the doctor is based so far away."

She gave him a look. "Don't tell me. His office is in Weaver, Kansas."

Now *that* would be a God thing. "No," Lavon said. "He's in St. Louis. But that's close to Kansas. Closer than we are here."

She pointed to the stove. "I'm hungry."

He stood and turned the heat back on.

"What would you do in a tiny place like Weaver?" she asked.

Good question. "I'd do what I'm doing now. Or maybe I could start my own consulting firm. Have a home-based business with our computer." He was glad she didn't comment. A commercial came on showing a car zooming down an open highway edged by fields of waving wheat. He pointed with the pancake turner. "Open spaces. Clean air for Chi-Chi. Big-sky country."

"That's Montana."

"I'm sure they have big sky in Kansas too."

She fingered the handle of her mug. "We don't even own a car."

"We could get one. A minivan."

"Get yourself a minivan," she said. "I want a Porsche."

Since she'd cracked open the door, he stepped in. "I'll get you any car you want—any car we can afford."

"So I'm just supposed to hold off looking for a job until this fantasy of yours miraculously happens?"

She had a point. Even if they entered the contest, there was no guarantee they'd win. "Of course not," he said, without much conviction. "Go ahead. Apply for jobs."

"Thanks for your permission. But what if I get one?"

He felt his hope deflate, but pinched it shut. He couldn't give up yet. "I'm not sure."

She spread her arms. "This is where the jobs are, Lavon. New York. Or at the very least, the East Coast."

He had no argument. Then he realized what always became the bottom line. "If God wants us in Weaver, he'll get us there."

Patrice shook her head. "Husband, sometimes your faith drives me crazy. You and God have this pipeline going and neither one of you cares to know my opinion."

Actually, there was no question about Patrice's opinion.

She sighed deeply a second time. "But you're serious about this, aren't you?"

He faced her and put a hand to his gut. "I know it doesn't make sense, but it feels right. Deep-down right. At least let me look into it. Where's your pioneer spirit?"

"I don't have any. And neither do you. Our ancestors emigrated from who knows where and stayed put. They never felt the need to move west. Why should we?" She got up to get more coffee. "We probably wouldn't get accepted anyway."

Lavon turned back to the stove. *But maybe we would*.

Joan Goldberg hated the way her husband, Ira, spread the morning paper across the kitchen table as if he owned it—which of course he did, but that wasn't the point. His total disregard for the space *she* needed, the mere inkling that *she* might want to sit at the table in the morning and read *her* part of the paper never crossed *his* mind.

She knew such trivialities shouldn't bother her after nearly forty years of marriage, but they did. Or they did now that they were retired. During the thirty-one years Ira had run Goldberg Five & Dime in Los Angeles he hadn't had time to read the paper. Up at five, home at nine. Headlines. He'd read the headlines of the papers he sold on the rack beside the checkout counter—until he and Joan had retired to Surprise, Arizona, three years ago. No annoying "snowbird" tag for them. They were full-time residents of the gated retirement community of Desert Acres. Now he had time to read four newspapers every morning, spreading them over the table in this totally obnoxious way.

Joan was sure she had developed a few obnoxious habits too—though she wasn't in a hurry to pinpoint any of them. Her habits stemmed from the fact she'd spent twenty-eight years teaching junior high, so the things she craved most were silence and the company of humans who could sit still for more than thirty seconds, didn't chatter incessantly, and didn't ask repeatedly to go to the restroom. The first and second wish she'd had answered in Surprise. The third . . . getting old could be the pits.

Surrendered to *not* sitting at the table to read the paper, she took a section along with a cup of minty-smelling tea into the living room where she sat in her favorite chair by the window. She never read the paper cover to cover like Ira did, but was a scanner. Lately she found herself looking out the window a lot. She wasn't sure what was bothering her and sometimes wished she could discuss her unease with Ira, but he wasn't a talker. "People talk too much," he often said, meaning *her; she* talked too much. He saw nothing wrong with just sitting there, close but not too close, saying nothing.

Joan looked up from her reading just as Ira looked down. A second sooner and their eyes would have met. Their glances were off, mistimed.

It was nothing. It meant nothing. And yet . . .

She went back to the paper. Such lapses in communication—small though they were—happened more often of late. Joan wasn't sure who or what to blame. Maybe to find the proper one-mind connection a couple had to receive the impetus and stimulus of work, the constant ebb and flow of other people. After work was done for the day, the couple would seek a common center by being together. They'd ache for it. Need it. It seemed that the too-much-togetherness of retirement had caused a misfiring in their lives, as if Ira's path was always a half step away from hers, just out of reach.

Yet life here *was* wonderful. Calm. Relaxing.

Too calm. Too relaxing.

Even when she had activities—and there were plenty to take up the minutes and hours of her life—it was almost too . . . too . . .

Perfect.

Joan shook the thought away and rubbed the space between her eyes. What was wrong with her? She was an ungrateful nudzh.

She adjusted her reading glasses, determined to read the paper. At times of such discontent it was best to expand one's horizons beyond me, myself, and . . .

FREE LAND!
Start over, start fresh,
and ignite your pioneer spirit!

She devoured the ad, then felt guilty for it. Who was she to want *more* at this point in their lives? They were settled. She had no right to rock the boat and change—

But when she saw that the ad mentioned the need for a grocer . . .

She clapped a hand to her mouth, stifling a laugh. Ira, having another store? Although she was involved with the activities available in Desert Acres, Ira didn't do much of anything but read and mess around on the computer. He wasn't even into golf—which in the Phoenix area was nearly traitorous. He was definitely the *tired* in *retired*, both in body and mind.

"What're you laughing about?" Ira asked.

She was about to say, "Nothing," when she found herself standing, then walking toward him, newspaper in hand. "Look at this."

He adjusted his glasses on the tip of his nose and read the ad. He handed it back to her. "So?"

He *would* make it difficult. "Would you consider it?"

Off came the glasses. On came his are-you-crazy? look. "We have a great life here. We're done with working. We're too old to start over. And nothing's free. It's a gimmick. A con."

"Don't you dare say we're too old!" She moved a chair and sat close.

When he leaned away, she realized she had violated his personal space. A big no-no. She sat back and tried to sort her thoughts. "Do you really think our life here is so great?"

His left eyebrow answered for him, arching in a way she'd memorized and had often tried to imitate.

"Don't you ever get tired of the sameness of it all?" she continued. "The same weather, the same people who are the same age? Do you realize we rarely see anyone who isn't retired?"

"Our son comes to visit."

"Once. He's come once. And grandchildren—if we had any—are only allowed to visit for one week—for pity's sake; it's a rule of the neighborhood. Don't you think that's strange, that we retirees are so selfish in preserving our own little world that we have to have a rule to keep younger people from staying too long? They're not the enemy."

"They disrupt the flow."

Her steam was rising now and propelled her out of the chair. "The flow of what? The flow of our golf carts? The flow of our dinner parties?" *And it's not as if you do much of anything anyway, you old stick-in-the-mud.*

"Those aren't bad things."

"You're right. They're good things, fun things. But I'm not sure they're enough." She took a breath. "I'm bored, Ira. Bored out of my shorts, sandals, and rhinestone-studded sunglasses."

He looked away and tapped his fingers on the table. Joan knew when it was best to remain silent—though it *was* difficult.

Finally, he spoke. "The whole land thing is ridiculous. It's a small town—a miniscule town. We're big-city people."

That did it. She pushed her chair back and stood. "You're a big-city person. I grew up in a small town in Indiana."

"That was eons ago."

Low blow. "I've always wanted to go back. Small towns can be magical. They're safe, calm, and full of everything good."

"Mom and apple pie."

"Exactly."

He looked at her incredulously. "You've wanted to move back to Indiana? I never remember you saying such a thing."

True. "But I have asked to move to a small town. More than once. Surely you remember that?"

He finally graced the moment with a subtle shrug. She jumped on it. "When you and I met in college and first decided to get married, where did I want to live?"

He blinked twice. "But my first grocery job and your first teaching job were in LA."

She tapped a finger on the table. "But I wanted to live in a small town."

Another shrug.

"And when we retired, where did I want to go?"

"Surprise is a small town."

"That's virtually engulfed by Phoenix. We're surrounded by over a million people." She thought of something else. "Besides, I'd love to live somewhere that has all four seasons. I miss snow."

He stared at her. "Since when?"

Okay, so that was a weaker point. She began to sing. "'I'm dreaming of a white Christmas. . . .'"

"We're Jewish."

He was totally missing the point. "I'd like to live in a place that doesn't string jalapeno-shaped lights at holiday time. There's something wrong about that."

"I don't want to go back to work."

Actually, that was no surprise. "Fine. Then I'll work. I'll teach again or—" she put a hand to her mouth as an absurd thought came to her—"I'll open a soda shop."

"A what?"

"A soda fountain. A place that serves ice cream and root-beer floats."

"What brought this on?"

She hadn't had the thought in years, but now, probably because of her dip into memory lane . . . "Back in Indiana, when I was growing up, all the kids used to congregate at Swenson's Soda Shoppe—two *P*s."

He shook his head. "That was then; this is now. Kids don't go to soda shops—two *P*s or one."

"But they could. They would if I made it a fun place. And their parents would go too, grabbing on to a piece of nostalgia. People long for what was good in the past and will buy into anything that reinforces that in order to build a better future." She put a hand to her chest. "That was rather eloquent; don't you think?"

Ira shrugged. He was impossible.

"Family values are big again, Ira. People would flock to such a place."

"You're way out of touch, Joan. Way out."

I'm out of touch? She smacked him on the arm. "It would work. I know it."

He adjusted the newspaper and began to read again. How dare he dismiss her idea!

She snatched the paper away, crumpling it at her chest. "Listen to me, Ira Goldberg. We've done things your way for forty years. It's time I get a turn. Don't squelch my dream just because you don't have any. You can sit around and do nothing in Weaver just as well as here."

He pointed to the newspaper. "Soda jerk is not one of the jobs listed, Joan. They don't want a soda fountain in Weaver."

"They may not know they want a soda fountain. But I'll convince them."

He rolled his eyes. "This makes no sense. None. I mean . . . Kansas."

Indeed. Yet Joan had such a strong feeling about all this. Women's intuition, instinct, gut feeling . . . she knew that whatever it was wouldn't leave her soon. She had to act on it. She had to give it her best shot.

Toward that end, Joan knelt beside her husband and put a hand on his arm. She offered him her best smile. "Just let me try, okay?"

He looked down at her, the wrinkles around his eyes prominent. "But we're old, Joan. They'll never choose us *because* we're old."

She whacked him on the arm and stood. "Stop saying that! I, for one, am not ready to give up on a productive, hardworking existence. For three years we've had our vacation, our leave of absence from life. It's time to reengage the gear into Drive and gun the engine, full steam ahead!"

He sighed, beaten. "You make me tired."

She turned on her heel. "Oh, honey, you ain't seen nothing yet."

It was tough being shot at.

It had happened only twice before today, but Officer Seth Olsen knew he'd never get used to it. Shooting *at* criminals wasn't any easier. *Shots fired. Need backup* . . .

This time it had been a liquor-store holdup. Nothing that hadn't been portrayed a dozen times on TV cop shows. But the reality of how it played out was far less neat and clean, less cut-and-dried than anything you could watch on a screen that blurred the distinction between pretend and real. When a bullet had hit the door of the police cruiser Seth had been using for cover, he'd known that a few centimeters of metal had stood between him and death. And when he fired back and hit the robber in the shoulder, he'd heard the bullet tear into flesh. He'd heard the scream, seen the pain on the man's face, and watched him stumble and fall. Checking on the perp, Seth had stepped in a pool of blood.

Sickening sounds, horrible sights. All in a day's work. All in the line of duty.

Line of duty . . . they were words of glory that had initially drawn him from the family farm to the police force with the noble goal of ridding the world of crime—and having a few adventures in the process. How naïve he'd been.

Back at the police station, Seth opened his locker. He started to unbutton his shirt but found it took too much energy. He sank onto a bench and leaned his arms on his thighs, his head too heavy to hold erect.

Hearing another officer come into the area, he sat up straight. He relaxed a bit when he saw it was his partner, Tom.

"You okay?" Tom asked.

"Fine." Seth stood and finished the work of his buttons.

"You don't look so good."

"I'm just tired."

"Paperwork does that."

Though Seth hated the paperwork that followed every incident, they both knew *it* wasn't the source of his weariness.

Seth was glad they changed into their street clothes without talking. He and Tom were good at reading each other. When to talk. When to shut up.

They said their good-byes and headed home. The rush-hour traffic made Seth long to be back on the night shift. He used to drive home against the traffic, but now . . .

Denver might sport the lofty distinction of being the Mile High City with the Rocky Mountains enticingly close, but in the midst of stopped traffic, or trying to keep calm while zooming through six lanes of cars going 70 mph, Seth might as well be living in the middle of anywhere. Although the precinct was downtown, he'd moved to a suburb to be closer to the nature he craved. By driving thirty minutes due west he could shrug off the pressures of the job and be awed by God's creation instead of flummoxed by man's.

He'd thought about moving closer to work, but the idea of moving deeper into the city made his chest tighten as if he were starving for air while strong arms held him down. At least being a beat cop let him get out and about. He was not an office kind of guy.

Brake lights. Lots of them. His chest tightened.

Seth sighed and followed the traffic to a complete standstill. He switched on the radio and pushed buttons trying to find a song he liked. Commercials for mortgage companies, cell phones, and a song by Barry Manilow. Three strikes, you're out.

Then the banter of a radio host caught his attention. *"Who wouldn't want free land?"*

The DJ's crony said something witty and they parried back and forth a few times, but Seth's mind had latched on to the words *free land*. What were they talking about?

Finally, they stopped trying to be cute and got to the point. *"It's true, folks. If you want to get a free house and a free business, all you have to do is enter the contest."*

The tightness in Seth's chest altered from traffic frustration to excitement. Free land? A free home? A free business?

"You entering, Joe?" the DJ asked.

"Nah. If it were in Honolulu, maybe. But Weaver, Kansas? I'll pass."

Seth's heart nearly stopped. The place in question was Weaver? Weaver, Kansas? They were giving away land in his hometown?

He put a hand to his chest and concentrated on breathing deep. He'd left quiet little Weaver eight years ago to be a cop in the big exciting city. Now he longed for the wide, quiet streets he'd left behind, the Norman Rockwell downtown strung with thousands of Christmas lights, the rows of hundred-year-old trees that canopied grassy yards edged in tulips, lilacs, and swing sets, and sunsets that took your breath away. The mountains blocked the sunsets here.

He'd given up a chance to run the family farm in order to run after creeps, crooks, and clods. If he hadn't been so arrogant he'd be farming right now. His parents had offered him the farm and he'd refused. Then just a year ago Dad died and Mom had been forced to sell the farm and move to Kansas City. His dad died because Seth wasn't there to help. His mother had suffered a broken heart because of him: *"You're breaking my heart, Seth."* She'd said those very words to him in an argument when he'd told them he was leaving the farm. Leaving home.

There were no more Olsens in Weaver.

But maybe . . . if he went back . . .

He gasped at an idea that topped all ideas. What if he got the farm back? Was his family farm some of the land being given away? Surely as a hometown boy he'd have an in. And getting the farm back might go a long way toward making things right. His mind skipped ahead to the thought of standing before his mother in her dull, little, ranch-style house in Kansas City with a yard too small for even a minimal garden. "I got it back, Mom. We can move home. You and me." She would look at him incredulously, then rise from her chair and hug him. All would be forgiven.

No more Olsens in Weaver?

Not for long.

The traffic started to move again. Seth silenced the radio.

But not the dream.

The pop-up ad on the computer got Kathy Bauer's attention:

FREE LAND!
Start over, start fresh,
and ignite your pioneer spirit!

Before she even had time to dissect her decision to do so, she found herself going to the Web site. She was greeted by pictures of Americana: a white gazebo in a park; a main street free of parking meters but lined with wide sidewalks that held planters of red geraniums and pink impatiens. A smiling couple sitting on the porch swing of a Victorian house. Kids parading in Halloween costumes. The more she saw, the more she read, the faster her heart raced. Free land in Kansas? A house? A business? And the Web site said the town needed a doctor—her husband, Roy, was a doctor. She was an artist—a painter. She could paint anywhere. Only recently had she taken up the brush again. . . .

But what really got her attention was the underlying theme of starting over. That sounded good right now.

Sixteen-year-old Ryan shuffled into the kitchen.

"Morning, hon."

"Mmm." He made a beeline for the bag of bagels and put one in the toaster.

Kathy was glad he was dressed and ready for school. She'd add an *as usual* to her thought except that in the last six weeks she'd often had to force him out of bed. And to school. They'd all had to do a bit of forced living since Lisa had died. Daily living made little sense when a vibrant fourteen-year-old was ripped from life and thrown through death's door—at ninety miles an hour.

Although it had been beyond traumatic for all of them, the effect of Lisa's death on her big brother was disturbing and went beyond the usual grief—yet, *was* there a "usual" grief? In the past six weeks Kathy's perfect, godly, sensitive son had changed. Her son, who at age eight had changed the poster above his bed from the Arkansas Razorbacks football team to a picture of Jesus, had tossed aside his Bible reading, praying, soft-spoken ways. His normally meticulous room was now a mess, he'd shunned his slightly geeky plaid shirts for T-shirts and baggy jeans, and he'd started to play video games. He'd even been brought home in a police car because he'd been with a group of kids who'd painted graffiti on a bus-stop shelter.

In short, her spiritual prodigy had turned into a typical kid—and it scared her to death. She'd had the typical-kid experience with Lisa, her perky pop-tart who'd thrived on fads, friends, french fries, and friction.

And fast older boys with too-fast cars.

They'd taken Ryan to a psychologist. Kathy and Roy had gone too and it had helped *them*. But Ryan remained elusive, sullen, and . . . oh so angry.

Kathy swiveled her chair toward her son. "You get your homework done?" She didn't used to have to ask that.

"Enough of it," he said. He opened the refrigerator and drank milk from the carton.

Kathy started to object, but squelched the comment. The psychologist had said, "Pick your battles," though at the rate they were going, she'd need to hire a military strategist. She turned toward the screen to put the computer on hibernate while she did the carpool thing. Although Ryan was old enough to drive, she let him do so with great reluctance and much worrying. If only she could keep him from driving until he was at least . . . thirty. Thirty would be good.

She thought about asking her son's opinion about the free-land contest. But maybe not. No way would he want to move—not even if it was for his own good. She hit the Sleep button and sent the Web site for a nap.

She'd wake it up later.

Kathy planned to tell Roy about the contest for free land. Eventually. She'd fill out the application first, *then* show it to her husband.

What she didn't expect was Roy coming home from the hospital over lunch. She was in the basement finding a box for a wedding present when she heard his voice in the kitchen above. "Hell-o-o? Kath? Where are you?"

"Down here. Just a minute." She rummaged through the gift boxes in the back room.

She heard Roy's voice swell and fall as his footsteps moved through the house. "I'm just home for a quick break. I need the charger for my pager. You got anything I could grab for lunch on the go?"

She'd already eaten the leftover lasagna. There was tuna in the pantry. She turned off the lights and headed upstairs. "Is tuna all—?"

Kathy stopped on the top step when she spotted Roy standing over the pages from the free-land application that were spread across the kitchen table.

Hoping to create a diversion, she opened the refrigerator door. "I also have some bologna if you want a sandwich. Or there's lettuce. Are you up for a salad?"

He held the papers in his hands. "What's this?"

"Just a contest."

"For free land?"

She closed the door and moved to save the rest of the papers from his eyes. The application was multifaceted and not an easy entry. It involved essay questions such as *I propose_____. I'll provide_____. I'll prove _____.* "It's nothing. I was just dinking around."

Though she tried to take the papers away, Roy stopped her. "This is in Weaver, Kansas, right? That elderly lady on the news?"

Kathy was taken aback. "This is on the news?"

"One of my patients had it on during my rounds." He held the papers between them. "You're interested in this?"

"Not really. You know I'm not a risk taker. I was just curious. I—"

"You think this, *this* would make you happy?"

She hated the undertone of his words, yet she couldn't deny their root. She was the one who most openly expressed her grief and discontent, while Roy was the family's foundation, the one who went out of his way to keep things on an even keel. Sometimes she privately ascribed the sales pitch of a car salesman to her husband: "What do I need to do to sell you this car today?" By inserting "make you happy" for "sell you this car" she had an apt description of the rock that was Roy.

"Kath? You think moving to another town would make you happy?" His voice was insistent, wanting an answer.

She showed him her back and got out the bread and bologna. "It's not about me." *Not just about me.* "It might be good to get Ryan away from here. He sees that Matt kid every day at school. Twice a day we drive on the road where Matt crashed, where Lisa . . . maybe it would be good to start over."

"Away from here you're hoping Ryan will snap out of it."

Unable to fully gauge the nuance of his voice, she glanced over her shoulder to see his expression. He was serious. She faced him, the package of bologna in hand. "Though bluntly said, that's exactly what I hope. I want my son back."

"He's here in body. Maybe that has to be enough for now."

"It's not." She went to him and took his hand. "Ryan used to be so special, so close to God, so full of promise and purpose. He's lost that."

"God's here just as much as he's in Kansas, Kath."

"But maybe Ryan can't find him here. Anymore."

He pulled away from her, opened the pantry, and stepped inside. He emerged eating from a bag of chips. Then he sat at the table, shoved her papers aside, and began reading the newspaper.

It took Kathy a moment to realize he'd left their discussion behind. They were in the middle of a conversation about a contest that would move them from Eureka Springs, Arkansas, to Weaver, Kansas, and he was reading the paper?

She yanked it out of his hands.

"Hey! I was reading that."

Kathy pointed to a page of the application. "This is serious. This is life changing. I need your input."

"I gave it to you."

She blinked slowly. "Did I miss something?"

He finished chewing, then swallowed. "If you think moving to Weaver would make you and Ryan happy, go for it."

"Just like that?"

"You want me to argue?"

Oh yeah. She thrived on conflict. She lived for it.

He ate another chip. "Just remember, you can't make people into the image *you* want, Kath."

She hated this discussion. "Don't even start."

"You're the one who encouraged Lisa to be with that crowd, to be popular, to be what you considered normal—because Ryan wasn't any of those things."

"Ryan is exceptional. I love him for who he is." *Was.*

"But he's different. Which for some reason made Lisa's normal-kid routine so important to you."

"I encouraged her to have friends, to have fun. I just wanted both kids to be who they are. I wanted Lisa to be herself."

"Being herself got her killed." He stood, closed the bag of chips, and left it on the table. "I gotta go. Enter the contest, or don't. It's up to you."

As soon as he left, Kathy sank into a chair and looked at the application. She *did* want to enter. It felt right. And maybe it *would* make them happy. Yet what would really make her happy was if both men in her life would find normal again—whatever *normal* was to them. As it was, each of them was walking through life on cruise control: Roy complacent, and Ryan angry. In their own ways, they were like the straight line on a heart monitor indicating that life was gone and there was no activity present. All that was missing was the piercing scream of the machine saying life as we know it was gone for good.

The sound of the machine—Lisa's monitor—came flooding back to her. She squeezed her eyes shut and pressed her hands against her ears. *Make it stop! Make it stop!*

She opened her eyes and saw the application papers strewn before her. She picked up a pen.

THREE

When doubts filled my mind,
your comfort gave me renewed hope and cheer.

PSALM 94:19

July 2006

Madeline sat at the kitchen table, took a loud sip of her coffee, and addressed her to-do list—which seemed as long as Santa's. As of yesterday, the winners of the Weaver land rush had started to arrive. There were twenty-five families already in town or on their way. She liked the image of moving vans converging on this tiny dot on the map like modern-day covered wagons carrying pioneer dreams.

The response to her initial free-land promotion had been heartening. She'd received over ten thousand applications, proving the rampant desire of many to start over, and also proving that the pioneer spirit that had initially created this country was far from dead. Web had begged her to get some help reading the applications, but she'd refused. This was her town, her contest, and her philanthropy, so she was not about to let some eight dollar-an-hour peon have control over who was worthy and who was not.

Even Web's opinion was not considered in the initial weeding out of applicants. Madeline had read them all—late into the night. Web had often come over first thing in the morning to find her with three piles sitting on the dining-room table: a Yes pile, a Maybe pile, and a To-Be-Read pile. The floor around the table was littered with the No's.

Web had asked Madeline what she looked for, what *the* determining factor was in whittling the ten thousand to fifty finalists. Madeline had answered, "Gumption and creativity—and the ability to put five words together in a sentence." Plus, neatness counted. "Strikeouts and messiness on the page indicate strikeouts and messiness in a life."

Once Madeline had pared it down to fifty finalists it had been Web's responsibility to make arrangements for the next phase of the contest—the interviews. Madeline had insisted on in-person interviews with all the finalists—and their spouses, if applicable. That had turned into ninety-five airline tickets and fifty rental cars and motel rooms. They'd had to stagger the interviews because Weaver's only motel, the Sleep-EZ, only had six rooms.

It had been up to Web to whip the homes into shape—twenty-five homes that had been left in various stages of disrepair. At first he'd attacked the challenge as if each were a piece of art, but at Madeline's insistence, had pared back his ambitions. A complete remodel would be up to the new tenants. Web's job was to make sure everything worked and the place was tidy. The rest would be up to the winners' imaginations and elbow grease.

The interviews Madeline had conducted over the last two months had been exhausting and enlightening. Web had worried about the sheer variety of the backgrounds. After all, Weaver's previous minority inhabitants had consisted of a Cajun family from Louisiana and a lone Jewish family. The rest were white-bread America, their ethnic origins of German, Italian, or Czech having long been blended until being from Weaver had been the source of their identity. Madeline had found the diversity of the finalists remarkable, a sure indication that the roots that had origi-nally been planted in Weaver would grow and blossom different fruit. There was nothing wrong with that. Fruit was fruit.

She heard a clearing of the throat and turned to see Web in the kitchen doorway. "Daydreaming again?" he asked.

"I do *not* daydream," Madeline said. "I plan."

"Plot is more like it."

She got up for more coffee. "Don't you have a thousand things to do?"

"I came by to get my latest to-do list."

She retrieved it from the counter.

"It's long."

"Don't complain."

"Oh, I'm not," he said, folding the list in half. "I like that you need me. Really need me."

She waved the sugar spoon at him. "Dream on, old man."

He moved close, "Come on, Maddy. Admit you need me."

"I will do no such thing." She licked the spoon and tapped his nose with it. "Now git."

He kissed her forehead and left.

Ira sank onto a stack of boxes in the living room of their new circa 1919 Craftsman-style home, a hand to his chest. "You're killing me, woman."

"Don't be dramatic," Joan said. Actually, drama had never been Ira's style, and since winning the contest he'd moved even further into the land of the preoccupied. He'd often stop in the middle of unpacking a box and ask, "Where does this go?" even though she'd just told him, and even though common sense said that a measuring cup went in the kitchen not the garage.

She cut open a carton of vases and began unwrapping them. "I wasn't going to tell anyone, but killing you off is my intent, dear one. More elbow room. So quit yer bellyaching or I'll use up all the hot water when I take a long soak tonight for my own aching muscles."

"I wish we still had a Jacuzzi," he said. "No Jacuzzi, no double sinks, no walk-in closets . . ."

She moved to the divider between the living and dining rooms. "But look at these oak pillars. Six-panel doors. Oak floors. This is craftsmanship at its best."

"It's old."

"It's classic. Just like us. We're getting a new start, just like this house." She moved toward the front window. "We have a yard and there's room for a garden out back. Plus, I saw a kid's tricycle down the street—there are children here. Imagine that."

"I don't like children."

He was such a grump sometimes. "Of course you do." At the window she saw an old Cadillac pull up front. "Well, well. We have company. It's Mrs. Weaver."

He pushed on his thighs to stand. "I don't know her."

It was an odd comment. "Of course you don't. We don't know anyone. That's the point. Starting over, meeting new people." She saw Mrs. Weaver near the front porch. "Now be nice. The only reason we have the house and the business are because of *her*, Ira."

Joan ran a hand through her hair out of habit more than an

assurance that it would do any good. She opened the door. "Welcome. Our first visitor."

Mrs. Weaver came inside, smelling of gardenias. "I'd say I don't mean to intrude, but I do. Truth is I'm checking up on you." She stepped around some boxes, her arms behind her back like a drill sergeant.

"We really love the house," Joan said. "The woodwork is exquisite."

Mrs. Weaver put a hand on a pillar and gave it a stroke. "They don't make 'em like they used to. That's why I gave away the old houses, because they're the ones that have the most potential, the ones that deserve a second chance."

"Kind of like people?" Joan said.

It took her a moment; then Mrs. Weaver nodded. "You're not so old. You're only sixty-four." She nodded toward Ira. "And you're sixty-eight. You have plenty of good years left. Appreciate 'em." She held up a finger. "Age is a state of mind."

Ira arched his back with a groan.

Joan didn't want Mrs. Weaver to think they were weak. "Nothing that a good soak and a little Ben-Gay won't take care of."

"Exactly," Mrs. Weaver said. "Enough of this. I want to see that soda shop of yours. I want to hear your plans for it."

"Now?" Joan asked.

Mrs. Weaver took a step toward the door.

Now was good.

Ira stayed behind at the house, so Joan had to face Madeline Weaver's scrutiny on her own. Not that Ira would have been any help. Yet Joan hated being put on the spot, hated to be pushed. And Joan could tell Mrs. Weaver was a pusher.

The older woman strode into the store as if she owned it. Which, technically, she still did for five more years, but still . . . Joan hoped her initial show of power was just that—initial. After the town was full, surely Mrs. Weaver would have other things to do, other people to pester.

When Joan switched on the lights, one of the hanging fixtures didn't come on.

"Web was supposed to fix that," Mrs. Weaver said, pointing.

"It's not a problem."

Mrs. Weaver shook her head. "Though subsequent improvements are the responsibility of the new tenants, Web was supposed to make sure the basics were in good working order."

"Really, it's no prob—"

She turned and glared at Joan. "He'll be over to fix it."

Okay then.

Mrs. Weaver walked the length of the store between the aisles of empty shelves. She turned left at the back wall and came toward the front again, running her hand along the long oak counter. "As you can see by the shelves, this was the Weaver Mercantile. I assume you'll want all these shelves out of here?"

Joan swept between two rows. "Actually, I might have a few shelves for candy and the like—but not these awful metal things. I've had my eye out for some antique display cases. Oak with glass."

"That would be nice." Mrs. Weaver said. "I hated when the mercantile started using the soda-fountain part of the building for a cosmetics counter. The fountain used to be the heart of Weaver, a place where children gathered, where teenagers took their dates.

Important events happened here. *I* had dates here." Her hand stroked the counter.

"Your husband?" Joan asked.

Mrs. Weaver blinked. "Him too."

"I've been boning up on recipes for malts, banana splits, and sarsaparilla."

"I haven't had a sarsaparilla in decades. But you realize the kids won't know what that is."

"I'll educate them," Joan said.

Mrs. Weaver nodded, then headed to the front, stopping short of the exit. "When can we expect the doors to open?"

Joan felt a stitch in her stomach. There was so much to do. "I didn't think there was a deadline."

"There isn't. But with people moving in . . . they'll have needs you can fill. We don't want them to get into the habit of driving elsewhere, do we?"

"We'll do our best."

"We? So your husband *is* going to help?"

"Of course." How much was another question. Ira had been to the shop only twice since they'd moved in and seemed distracted—by what, she couldn't imagine.

"The sooner you can open the better," Mrs. Weaver said. "What have you decided to name the place?"

"Swenson's Soda Shoppe. Two *P*s."

"Swenson?"

Joan shrugged. "It's the name of the soda shop back in Indiana, where I grew up."

Mrs. Weaver thought a moment, then said, "It's as good a name as any." And she was gone.

Joan strolled behind the counter and pushed the white porcelain

plunger on one of the ice-cream-topping containers. Soon she'd
be doing it for real.

A dream come true.

She headed home. She was hungry. For so many things.

"I'm back," Joan called out as she returned home from the shop.

Ira answered from upstairs. He was setting up the computer in
the office that would second as a guest room for the rare appearance of their very successful but too-busy-to-visit son, Jacob.
No problem—with Ira wanting to work upstairs. But big problem
with the infrequency of Jacob's visits *and* his lack of a wife at age
thirty-three. But it was a problem for another day.

With Ira busy, Joan returned to work on the living-room boxes.
But twenty minutes later, when she noticed a lack of commotion
filtering down from above, she went to the bottom of the stairs
and listened.

She heard only the faintest sound. The swish of pages being
turned? Magazine pages? The thought that Ira was perusing a
magazine while she was working up a sweat galled her. Her first
inclination was to storm up there, swing the door open until it
bounced off the wall, and demand, "Working hard, or hardly
working?" Yet . . . the alternative of stealthily catching him lazing
off held more appeal. And more fuel for future compensation.

She tiptoed up the stairs and down the short hall.

The door to the office/guest room was open. The mattress to
the double bed held up the wall to the right. Ira sat in front of the
computer desk that faced the adjoining wall, his back angled
toward the door. Sure enough, he was flipping pages in a magazine. He held a scissors in his right hand. Cutting out coupons?

That was not Ira's style. Suddenly, he must have seen something
he wanted, because his shoulders slumped over the magazine in
work mode and he cut something from a page. A small something.
The size of a quarter.

What *was* he doing? He took the small cutout and gazed at it as
if it were something precious. Then he slipped it into the pocket
of his shirt and put his hand against his heart, staring into space.
Even from this angle Joan could see the hint of a smile on his lips.
Obviously whatever he was daydreaming about gave him pleasure.

She'd fix that.

She strode into the room. "What have we here?"

He looked at her, then away. "You caught me off guard. I was
thinking."

"Two times in one day. Don't make it a habit." She moved to
the desk and noticed a pile of magazines. She picked up the top one
and he grabbed it away, putting it back on the pile.

"My, my. Getting a little possessive of *Good Housekeeping*,
are we?"

"Leave them be. I'm going through them. They're in order."

Too many questions begged for answers. "You're going through
the magazines for what reason?"

He slipped the scissors between his thigh and the chair, clearly
trying to hide them. She looked right at them, but he put a hand
on top of their edge and didn't say anything. For a moment he
reminded her of a child, ineffectually hiding a no-no from parental
eyes.

Forget the scissors. Joan decided on an end run to the goal line.
She moved close and put a hand in his shirt pocket to retrieve the
treasured cutout. Ira slapped her hand away and stood, sending
the wheeled chair into gyrations that ended against the edge of
the desk.

"Leave it alone!" he said.

"Goodness, Ira. The look in your eyes. You're practically frenzied."

He blinked a couple times and the frenzy left him. He looked down at his hand, still protecting his pocket. He moved his hand to his side, though the act seemed to take effort. "We have work to do." Then he walked past her, out of the room, and down the stairs. "You coming?" he called.

Joan glanced at the magazines. This wasn't over. "I'm coming."

Joan clutched her pillow as she would have loved to clutch her husband. But he was unavailable, lying on his side of the bed, turned away from her. She could tell by his breathing he wasn't asleep— but was pretending to be.

Which was worse. Far worse.

After almost forty years of marriage she was used to his moodiness and his sudden silence. Despite repeated attempts to get used to it, not let it bug her, and not take it personally, it still drove her bonkers.

Why couldn't he just tell her what was bothering him? At least give her a hint.

He started to snore. She turned over so they were back-to-back, yet she doubted sleep would come.

Not until she knew . . .

She carefully lifted the covers and slid out of bed, easing her weight to the floor one leg at a time so as not to disturb him. Then she went to the laundry basket and plucked out the shirt he'd been wearing today. She clutched it to her chest and moved into the hall and down to the office. She flipped on the light, closed the door until it touched the jamb, then felt in the chest pocket.

And felt again. There was nothing there.

Her fingers dug deep, but it was empty. Whatever he'd cut from the magazine had been placed elsewhere—which increased her curiosity quotient a good fifty points.

She looked at the desk. The magazines were no longer piled on top. She opened drawers but found them still empty. The room was littered with unopened boxes from the move, but none looked promising.

The closet.

She opened the door and found it, too, was empty of everything save taped-shut moving boxes. But as she was closing it, she stopped herself and opened the door wide. There was a high shelf above the hanging pole; her fingers barely curled over its edge. At five foot one she often needed Ira's help getting her own shoe boxes down.

She'd make her own help. She shoved a box close and stood on it.

Bingo.

There, pressed into the far corner of the shelf, was the pile of magazines. She had a sudden stab of anxiety that she'd find more than *Time* and *Good Housekeeping* in the mix. Ira had never been one for dirty pictures . . .

Yet the fear made her hesitate. Ignorance could be bliss, yes?

And curiosity killed the cat.

Meow. Hiss.

Getting up on her tiptoes she pulled the magazines to the edge and then, climbing off her makeshift step stool, moved them to the floor. With a fresh breath she looked at the titles. The most racy was a copy of *Sports Illustrated*, but it wasn't even the swimsuit issue, so it didn't count.

The titles answered no questions. From what Joan could see there was no reason Ira should be hiding these magazines that had always been around the house in full view.

She sat on a box and looked through the top one.

Odd cuts from the pages flapped awkwardly, bending every which way during the flipping. She opened to a cut page. It was an ad for Ivory Soap showing a woman with flawless skin nuzzling her face against that of a baby. The only thing cut from the page was the *S* in the word *soap*. Why would Ira cut out a single letter?

Images of criminals carefully creating ransom notes from cutout letters came to mind—but was discarded as ridiculous. Ira? A kidnapper? It was laughable. Half the time he didn't know what to do with *her*, much less a kidnappee.

She turned to another cut page. This one was for shampoo. The *S* was missing. Another was for Safeway. Again, the *S* was gone. The next magazine held more dissected *S*s. Just *S*s. No other letter.

It made no sense at all.

Joan had the notion to wake him up and demand an answer, and yet . . . this was not the usual husband-wife question. She really doubted Dr. Phil had ever dealt with this problem on his TV show: Husbands Who Collect *S*s and the Wives Who Love Them.

Curiouser and curiouser.

Joan put the magazines back on the shelf, moved the box, and headed back to bed. She would try to be patient. She'd keep her eyes open.

But she *would* get an answer.

FOUR

Trust in the LORD with all your heart;
do not depend on your own understanding.
Seek his will in all you do, and he will direct your paths.

*S*s. Joan dreamed of *S*s. Slithery, slimy, secretive, scintillating *S*s.

Why was Ira cutting out *S*s? She got out of bed again and staggered into the bathroom, trying to wake up completely, hoping with her eventual cognizance would come logic—and a different reality. For certainly she'd dreamed the whole thing. Certainly her husband wasn't cutting out *S*s.

After going through her morning routine she felt a little better, a little more with it and able to handle what life would throw at her—as long as it didn't start with the letter *S*.

No such luck. The first incident involved *shirt*. She came out of the bathroom to find Ira searching through the laundry basket. "Where's the shirt I wore yesterday?"

Oops. Joan had left it in the office.

He stood up from his rummaging. "Did you take my shirt?"

She moved to make the bed. "Why would I do that? And why do you want that shirt anyway? Aren't you planning to wear a clean one today?"

"Sure, but—"

"Then put one on. You have a closetful." She yanked the comforter up over the pillows, tossed the two throw pillows toward the middle of the bed, and left the room.

On the way downstairs, she detoured into the office, snatched up the shirt, and shoved it under her UCLA sweatshirt. Through the living room, through the kitchen, and into the addition off the back that housed the washer and dryer. Up went the lid; in went the shirt.

Out of sight, out of mind. Ira was handled.

She, however, was not so easily sidetracked.

The mystery of the *S*s remained.

Seth Olsen, the new police chief of Weaver, Kansas, stood on the cracked sidewalk leading up to his house. His home. His first home. How many times had he driven by this house—the Anderson house—going to and from the farm while growing up? Shouldn't he have had an inkling that someday it would be his? Wasn't that how life worked? Weren't there clues along the way if only a person saw them?

He scuffed the toe of his sandal against the edge of the grass. Who was he kidding? He was Clueless Seth. If he'd had a clue he wouldn't have rejected his parents' offer to take over the family farm. He would have seen how much it meant to them that it stay in the family. For him to move away had been death to his father and sorrow to his mother.

Like he said: clueless.

He walked around the house to the back of his property. How nice of Mad Madeline—that's what the kids around town used to call her—to give him this particular property on the edge of town, with land that butted up to his family's farm—which unfortunately had *not* been available as part of the free-land contest. Close . . . so close. His initial disappointment had evolved into gratitude. Being anywhere in Weaver was a good beginning. He'd get the farm eventually. He'd position himself. He had a plan. . . .

Speaking of . . . Seth pulled out his cell phone and called the one person who would appreciate where he was standing. His mother answered on the third ring, sounding out of breath.

"You'll never guess where I am, Mom."

"Seth. I . . . isn't it kind of early?"

Seth looked at his watch. "It's after ten, Mom. Surely you aren't still in bed."

"No, no, of course not." He could hear her fumbling with some-thing. "I was just . . . so . . . I'm guessing you're in your new home?"

"Better than that. I'm standing on the back edge of my property, looking out on our farm."

"On what used to be our farm."

A technicality. He hadn't shared the details of his larger plan with her. It would be a surprise that would change both their lives. "I was given the Anderson place."

"That ugly green house on Theodore?"

With effort Seth kept his frustration at bay. "Nothing some paint won't fix. But it's mine, Mom. And I'm here. Back in Weaver. Everything's in place."

"That's nice, honey. I'm really glad you won the contest. You've been so obsessed with it."

He pulled in a breath. "I was not obsessed, Mom, I—"

"Obsessed. Ever since you entered you haven't been very open to think or even talk of much else. And I have some good news of my own I've been trying to share with you for months and—"

"You should see the corn, Mom. It's doing great."

"Good. Good. Seth? I think I'm going to be moving."

He blinked. Moving? Yes, she was going to be moving. To the farm. With him. But she didn't know that yet. "What are you talking about?"

"I've put the house up for sale. I—"

"I know you're not happy there in Kansas City, Mom. It's a nothing house, but—"

"The house is fine; it has nothing to do with the house. I'm moving because—"

Seth heard a truck pull up out front. It was Web Stoddard in his old clunker. "I have my first visitor, Mom. I have to go."

"But I've been trying to tell you—"

"I'll call you later. Promise."

"You really need to work on your listening skills, Seth. You're—"

"Love you. Bye."

Seth started to go around to the front of the house, but Web saw him, waved, and headed toward the backyard.

"Hey ya, Seth." Web pointed at the field. "Corn's doing good; don't you think?"

Seth sang a line from *Oklahoma*: "'The corn is as high as an elephant's eye. . . .'" He stopped the song. "Dad would be pleased."

Web chuckled. "I'm glad Maddy chose you. Makes sense to have a hometown boy come back and get this town lively and living again." He put his hands in the pockets of his overalls. "And I'm proud of you for being willing to come home without harboring any hard feelings against the Bowdens."

"The who?" Seth knew very well who.

Web looked surprised. "The people who bought your place. Sorry. I thought you knew their name."

Seth looked at the ground, keeping up the ruse. "How are they doing? With the farm."

Web reached out and touched a stalk of corn. "They don't complain. Seem happy enough."

"They have any kids to help?" Seth tapped into his memory bank: *One daughter, Bonnie, age twenty-four. Kind of cute, with short blonde hair, a degree in agricultural engineering. No boyfriend*—at least none that Seth had seen or heard about when he was in town for the contest interview a few months earlier.

Web answered his question. "They have a grown daughter, Bonnie. She just got a degree in agriculture something-or-other from K-State. She's back home now and is keen on farming."

As was Seth.

They stood a minute, looking out over a field of green. A fly buzzed Seth's ear.

At the sound of a car, they both looked toward the street. "Well, well." Web made a beeline across the grass. "Maddy. What are you doing here? Are you the welcome wagon?"

Mrs. Weaver held out her hand. "Quit the inquisition and help me out of this thing."

Web helped her out of her silver Cadillac, and she smoothed her dress over nonexistent hips.

"Good morning, Mrs. Weaver," Seth said.

She gave him a nod.

Web pointed at him. "Seth here appreciates how you let him have this place that backs up to his family farmland instead of some other place farther in town."

"It's not what you think no matter how Web tries to spin it,"

Mrs. Weaver said. "There's no sentiment involved. I figured being able to see what you gave up, being able to touch what you ran away from——" she offered a curt nod—"it builds character."

"Yes, ma'am." Whatever her reasoning, he was glad for it.

Mrs. Weaver strode toward the front of the house. She stopped short of the porch steps. "So. What are your plans for the place?"

Web let out a laugh. "Maddy, let him get settled first."

Mrs. Weaver scanned the yard. "I don't see any boxes out here. Looks like he is settled."

"I don't have much," Seth said. "It didn't take long."

She turned toward the car. "Then we'll expect big things of you, Mr. Olsen. Big things soon. This yard needs weeding."

"Yes, ma'am. I'll get right on it."

Web helped her back in the car and she pulled away.

"Well then," Seth said as he and Web watched the car turn at the end of the block.

Web chuckled. "That's Maddy for you. A cyclone in comfortable shoes. Always has been—though the shoes used to be a bit more fashionable."

"You've known her forever, haven't you?"

"My whole life. She used to live next door to me over on Martha Lane. We've been best friends ever since."

By the way Web was still looking down the street, Seth guessed there was more than friendship between them. When he was a kid growing up here, he'd never seen it, but now, back as an adult . . .

Interesting.

Within seconds of standing in the doorway of their new home, Patrice's heart sank. Gone were the high ceilings of their New

York apartment. Gone was the bank of glass that gave her a sixth-story view. Present were oak floors in dire need of refinishing, wallpaper from some indistinguishable era, and over the fireplace, a cheap print of a surf-ridden beach. Beach. Ha. She was in the middle of nowhere Kansas. The middle of middle America. The nearest surf was thousands of miles away.

Lavon closed the door and their world was enveloped in silence. Patrice wasn't used to silence and felt it close around her like a shroud. "Great. Just great," she mumbled.

Malachi pushed past her and ran to the front stairs. "Look, Daddy! Stairs!" He clomped up each one, making as much noise as possible.

"Don't be an elephant!" Patrice yelled. The four-year-old turned his stomp into an exaggerated tiptoe.

She felt Lavon's hand on the back of her neck and the breath of his whisper in her ear. "Take it down a notch, lovey. We're in Kansas now. You need to learn to relax."

She stepped into the living room that had small windows framed with heavy mauve drapes that blocked the light. "Relax here? It's going to take months to turn this place from pitiful to livable."

Lavon took hold of the oak casing that delineated the foyer from the main room. "It's got great potential." He let go of the wood and spun around. "And room. Just look at the room. This house has twice the space of our apartment in New York. Now we have space to grow."

She gave him a pointed look. "If you're talking about me having another baby, I'm outta here. We went through this. Since I'm a working mom, one's enough."

His face fell and Patrice knew she'd hurt him. Again. Although Lavon loved Malachi as his own, she knew he longed for another child. He loved kids and was a kid magnet. Lavon could take Chi-

Chi to swing at the park and end up with four other kids swinging in midair as he ran back and forth among the lot of them, keeping them going while they squealed and giggled. He was a fantastic father.

And she . . . she was a fantastic banker. She wasn't being arrogant, just honest. Recognizing and making the most of one's strengths was the best way to attain the highest level of success. And though Patrice wouldn't mind having another child in theory, in reality she knew she wasn't up to it. She had only so much love to go around. It didn't do any good to try to be something she wasn't.

Lavon had moved on into the kitchen and she heard Chi-Chi running around upstairs. When would that boy learn some grace? He could trip over air.

"Come in here, Patrice. Come see this fabulous breakfast nook."

The kitchen was marginal. The cupboards were painted white, the stainless-steel sink and faucet distressingly generic. And worse, the laminated countertops were a horrid shade of aqua. Patrice ran her hand on their surface, stopping to scrape a piece of ancient food with a fingernail. "We really need to install Corian or granite."

She heard Lavon sigh. "Don't change things until we move in, okay? Look over here. Here. At the breakfast nook."

She gave him her attention. In the corner of the kitchen was a booth beneath a window, like a booth in a diner.

"Isn't it fantastic?" He slid along the aqua vinyl bench seat and patted the place next to him.

"I'll pass," she said.

His shoulders dropped. "Since when did you get to be such a snob?"

"Since we left behind a modern apartment in Manhattan. This whole house, this whole town is so . . . so . . ."

"Charming."

"That's not the word."

He extracted himself from the booth and faced her, his height intimidating. "Look, Patrice. *We* agreed to do this. *We* filled out the application, *we* wrote the essay, *we* came here for the interview. We saw what Weaver was like, and though we didn't know the specific house that would be ours, we knew what we were getting into. No, this is not New York—thank God. While New York is fine for some, and was fine for us for a while, it's all about busyness, bad air, high walls, and rushing through life toward society's idea of success. Weaver isn't like that."

She snickered.

He took her hands in his and pulled them to his chest, forcing her to look into his eyes. "Weaver is lazy evenings on the porch, wide lawns blending into our neighbor's, and taking long walks toward . . . toward . . ."

She pulled her hands away and stepped back. "Toward what? And lazy days? They'll drive me crazy. Just because we moved here doesn't mean we don't want to succeed. I didn't take the job at the bank to fail, to *not* make money. And you . . ."

His lack of a job was a tender subject. "While you're at work, I'll get us settled. Then I'll see what needs to be done around Weaver and fill the need."

"Just like that?" she asked.

"Just like that."

She strode to the flowered café curtain on the back door and adjusted the spacing of the brass rings. "I don't see Weaver overflowing with high-powered jobs. So you'd be satisfied sacking groceries, waiting tables, or clerking in a store?"

He nodded. "If I felt I was helping and I enjoyed the people, sure."

"Whether or not you're bringing in a decent paycheck?"

He opened the refrigerator, which was on but empty. "Living in Weaver is not about money, Patrice."

"Don't be naïve. Living anywhere is about money." She pointed at him. "And don't you dare say, 'God will provide.'"

"Which he will. But I also know we have to do our part. 'Be strong, and do the work.'" He leaned against the fridge, cushioning his tailbone with his hands. "But here in Weaver, it's finally more than just busywork. It's about discovering why we're *here*."

"Here, here, or—" she spread her arms dramatically—"*here* here."

"Don't make fun of me, Patrice."

Then don't make yourself such a good target. She walked into the dining room. "Our Angoli table will look atrocious in this room."

"We never should have gotten an all-glass table. With a child it's impractical. But it'll be fine. For now." Lavon was back-stroking the woodwork. "It'll be eclectic. Isn't that in style?"

What her husband knew about style could fill a crack in the baseboard. Not that she had the time or inclination to focus on such things. If it wasn't on the Internet, she didn't buy it.

Chi-Chi stomped down the stairs. "Can I ride my trike? Outside?"

Patrice shook her head. "We need to unpack, bud. We have work—"

"Ah, come on, lovey," Lavon said, heading to the front door. "What help can a four-year-old give? And I purposely put his trike at the back of the truck so our little racer could get to it first thing." He held the door open for Malachi. "Come on, Son. Let's get you on the road."

Patrice followed them onto the porch. "You spoil him."

Lavon unlocked the back of the moving truck. "He's the only son I've got, so I don't have much choice, do I?"

Nice. Real nice.

Within a minute, Lavon had Chi-Chi's tricycle on the sidewalk and the boy was steaming by full speed with a long stretch of side-walk before him. He made ferocious engine noises. *He never could go full speed back in New York . . .* "Don't go far!" Patrice called.

"He'll be fine," Lavon said. He removed a leather dining-room chair from the back of the truck. "He's finally free. Don't fence him in."

Double meanings abounded.

A car drove by and slowed. "Hello," said an Hispanic man from the driver's window. His wife leaned down to wave from her side of the car. Patrice could see the heads of two little girls in back.

Lavon went to the side of the car and chatted.

Patrice stood her ground. She wasn't in the mood.

When the car pulled away with a honk and a wave, Lavon approached her. "That was rude. Why didn't you come say hello?"

She shrugged. "There's plenty of time for that." *Too much time.* "Who are they?"

"Maria and Diego Lopez and their twins, Paulina and Constanza. They're running the café. It was called the Sunshine Café, but they're changing the name to Salida del Sol."

"Goodie. Taco City."

"Patrice!"

She shrugged again, though she *did* partially regret her lack of tact. Then, before she could stop her words, she heard herself say, "So they're the token Hispanic family, and we're the token blacks. They probably have a Jew, an American Indian, and an Asian too."

Lavon looked at her, incredulous. "Where did that come from?"

She plucked a dead bloom off a potted geranium. "Face it; we've just entered white-bread USA. Their attempt at being politically correct is woefully transparent."

"You'd be complaining even louder if they didn't make the effort."

"I don't like quotas."

"No one does," Lavon said as he removed more chairs. "But so what if they've filled the town with a sampling of ethnic groups, a sampling of America? I like Mrs. Weaver. I didn't witness any hint of prejudice in her. You're showing more prejudice than she did."

"We're black, honey. In case you didn't notice."

Lavon set a chair down hard and took hold of its back. "Can't we just *be* here? Maybe for once it won't matter."

"Maybe it will."

"If you make it matter."

She was tired of arguing. She walked to the truck and grabbed a chair.

"Ryan! You get back here and help!"

Ryan continued walking away, his hands deep in his pockets. Kathy turned to Roy. "What's wrong with that boy?"

"He doesn't want to be here. Cut him a little slack."

She knew he was right. Ever since they'd been notified they'd won the contest, Ryan had been the prince of moodiness, spending even more time with the boys and activities Kathy disliked. But now . . . Weaver was a safe place. It was a lovely summer afternoon. There were no snow, no ice, no curvy roads, no fast cars. . . .

Roy grabbed another box and headed in the house. "Face it, Kath, you've been harboring the dream that upon crossing the boundaries into Weaver, Ryan would become your little boy again—a five-foot-eleven little boy."

"Not true," Kathy said, holding the door. *Not entirely true.* She went out to the moving truck, but ended up leaning against the opened door rather than taking a new box. She looked in the direction Ryan had gone.

Ever since her son was a little boy he'd had the ability to command attention in a group of children *or* adults. Ryan had an air about him that made people take a second look. And once he had their attention—and *they* were trying to figure out why—they couldn't help but notice a serenity that capped off an intensity beyond his years. He felt deeply, thought deeply, yet exuded a peace that could only come from somewhere most people never tapped into.

And that somewhere—that some*one* was God. Jesus to be exact.

Ryan had had a special connection with the Almighty. Though he'd always been a sensitive kid, she hadn't really noticed anything that special until he was eight. It was two years after Kathy's estranged husband, Lenny—Ryan's father—had died in an awful fall, and soon after she and Roy had gotten married. Ryan was watching the evening news. Lisa, being a normal six-year-old, wanted to change the channel. Ryan insisted it stay where it was, saying he *had* to watch the news so he knew who needed his prayers.

Then there'd been the time she'd celebrated the first gallery showing of her paintings by giving each of the kids one hundred dollars to spend on toys. Lisa had been the normal kid, spending all the money on toys for herself. But Ryan had spent his money on toys for a family who'd lost their house and possessions in a fire.

In truth, her son shamed her with his heart for others and for God, and sometimes she found herself experiencing the not-very-maternal emotion of envy. Why couldn't she feel so godly? act so godly? Why did she struggle with doing the right thing, feeling the right thing, even thinking the right thing? As the mother, shouldn't she have a stronger faith than her son?

Help him, Lord. Help me.

At the realization she'd just prayed she snickered. Maybe she did have the stronger faith.

For now, anyway.

When Ryan realized he had no idea where he was going and that it might be possible to get lost even in tiny Weaver, he slowed, walked a couple steps, then stopped. He looked behind him, half expecting to see his mother running after him, out of breath, just checking to make sure he was safe, obsessed with keeping tabs on him. Since Lisa had died he'd practically smothered under her attempts at protection. Going to the psychologist had helped. She'd laid off a little after that.

And she hadn't followed him now. *Thank God for small favors.*

Actually, if Lisa had been around, Mom would have sent her after him. And vice versa. Although they'd been as different as red is to blue, he and his sister had been a team. He'd been Lisa's confidant and she his protector. Protector from whom? Ryan had been a Jesus freak, and because he was more interested in prayer, JC, and doing the right thing rather than parties, J-Lo, and doing the fun thing, he had been bully bait. Most of the time he'd handled it. The key was becoming as invisible as possible. *"Love your enemies. Do good to those who hate you. Pray for the happiness of those who curse you. Pray for those who hurt you. If someone slaps you on one cheek, turn the other—"*

Ryan shook the verses out of his head. He didn't want to hear them. Know them. Not anymore.

He moved to the curb and sat, turning his thoughts away from
God and back to Lisa. One time, when he'd ended up with a plate
of goulash in his lap—thanks to Joey Fillerton—Lisa had crossed
the lunchroom wielding a very large American history textbook
and had smacked Joey on the back of his shoulders. She'd suffered
a one-day suspension for that. *"God blesses those who are hungry and
thirsty for justice, for they will receive it in full."*

He'd been so proud of her.

Ryan sat forward, rested his hands on his knees, and leaned his
head against them. When he closed his eyes he could imagine her
here, sitting beside him. He could hear her voice: *"Come back to the
house, prodigy child. You know Mom never really gets mad at you so
I'll take the brunt of it."*

It was true. His parents had always treated Ryan as if he were
special. They enjoyed Lisa. They revered him. It didn't make
sense. All he was doing was having a little faith, praying a little,
focusing on what God wanted.

In many ways it had been a lonely life. There weren't many people
he could talk to about faith stuff. His mom and dad tried to understand, but the more he mentioned feeling the presence of the Holy
Spirit, or hearing God's direction, or getting the answer to prayers,
the more they—his mom especially—stopped really listening and
put him on a pedestal, like some idol to be admired and worshiped.

Like a freak. Set apart. If he heard his mom quote the book of
Jeremiah one more time, he'd run away for good: *"I knew you
before I formed you in your mother's womb. Before you were born I set
you apart and appointed you as my spokesman to the world."*

"It's your life verse, Ryan," she'd said a hundred times. "God's
talking about you."

He didn't want to be set apart anymore. If he'd been a regular
kid like Lisa, he might have been hanging around with her the

night of her accident, and he might have been able to stop her from going in Matt's car. Loser Matt, who was three years older than she was and stinking drunk at the time.

That's why Ryan had stopped wearing the geek clothes after her death, and had jumped headfirst into the land of normal. Maybe his mom would enjoy him rather than idolize him. The unexpected product of his retreat into average teenhood was that the bullies had backed off. For the first time in his life Ryan had friends. He'd taken advantage of the opening. Sure, he'd gotten in trouble about that graffiti thing, but in a way, it had been cool to get caught and brought home in a police car. Didn't *that* prove to his mom that he wasn't Saint Ryan?

But even that she'd blamed on Lisa. If Lisa hadn't been killed, Ryan wouldn't have written a bad word on a bus shelter? Give me a break.

Yet that's the way it always went. If there was blame to be given, Lisa got it, and had usually taken it with a shrug to her shoulders, a wink of her eye, and a toss of her hair. Oh, the unfair burdens she'd taken so he could remain pure in the chosen-child role. Lisa should have hated him, but she hadn't. Sometimes he wondered if that, more than anything, was at the source of his lingering grief. In so many ways she'd been the better person. She had loved him so *well*.

He tossed a pebble and it banked off the far curb before falling still.

He needed one of Lisa's pep talks now: *"Come on, Ry, reclaim Jesus for the Gipper so we can get on with things."*

If only it were that easy.

Ryan extended his legs into the street. There was little chance he'd ever need to move them for a car. He could lie in the street and be perfectly safe.

He thought of Lisa lying in the street after the accident. . . .

To dispel the image, he forced himself to remember there was no ice here now, no snow. It was July, not December. There was no curvy road. The streets of Weaver were straight, flat, and crossed like a big tic-tac-toe board. Most were canopied by trees heavy with green. It seemed safe. It seemed cozy and good.

And yet . . .

He looked across the street, then behind him. The town had its own level of weirdness. It was odd being surrounded by so many vacant buildings, almost like being in a cemetery with the physical present, but the spiritual gone.

Which was pretty much how he felt lately. . . .

Ryan would admit to putting his relationship with God on hold. He had no idea how he could ever feel close to God again. It used to be that all he had to do was crack open the door of his brain and an incredible peace and feeling of communion flowed in. But now, he didn't want communion with a God who would take Lisa away, so he kept the door locked. Double bolted. *Just try to get in. I dare you.*

The dare was made with a certain trepidation. God was, after all, God, and if he wanted to smudge Ryan out under his celestial thumb he could.

The truth was, God *hadn't* flung the door open yet. And he *wasn't* talking to Ryan like he used to. The line of communication had been broken and Ryan's biggest—though unspoken—fear was that he wouldn't be able to get it back. Not even if he wanted to.

And so, here he was, hundreds of miles from home in a town that was being populated by other losers who felt the need to start over—and who would probably fail.

He was doomed. A right and just fate, all in all.

FIVE

You can make many plans,
but the LORD's purpose will prevail.

PROVERBS 19:21

Madeline carried her morning cup of coffee to the dining room. The table was spread with to-dos for the one-hundredth Founders Day celebration coming up in less than four weeks on the first Saturday in September, plus the Meet 'n' Greet tonight. She planned to make it a requirement that all newbies pitch in for the birthday celebration. No exceptions. After all, she'd already given them a week to get settled. Now it was time to get down to living. And giving.

As she passed the side window, she spotted a red car in the driveway. She hadn't heard anyone drive up and it was too early for visitors. She pulled aside the lace curtain to see better. There was no one inside. Where was the occu—?

Suddenly, a head popped up in the backseat. She assumed by the small size it was a female. The woman stretched. Had she been

sleeping in there? The car hadn't been there last night when
Madeline had gone to bed at eleven.

Madeline would not have her driveway used as a rest stop. She
stormed out the front door and moved to the corner of the porch.
"You there! You in the car!"

The woman—a young woman in her early twenties—had
seen her coming and had exited the car on the driver's side. She
smoothed her short dark hair. "I'm . . . I'm sorry to surprise you
like this."

"Then don't. Just leave. This is private property, not a parking
lot for stragglers."

The girl's hand froze in mid-smoothe, moved to her chin, then
to the pocket of her jeans. "I'm sorry. I'll go. I never should have
come." She opened the driver's door and started to get in.

Her words implied there was premeditation to her parking in
this driveway in the middle of the night. "Hold on a minute,"
Madeline said. "State your business."

The girl stood between the car and the opened door. "I'm not
surprised if you don't remember me. It's been three years."

Remember her? Madeline looked closer. There *was* something
familiar about the girl. Something about the eyes. Then she made
the connection. "Are you Jenna? Barb's daughter?"

The girl put a hand to her chest. "Yes! That's me."

Madeline hadn't seen her great-niece since her high school
graduation. "Come on up here, child."

Jenna closed the car door and hurried up the front steps, where
Madeline greeted her with a hug before holding her at arm's length.
"You're too skinny. All bones and angles. And that hair . . . all tousled
like a little boy's. You're not one of those anorexic girls, are you?"

Jenna looked down. "I've just been . . . I haven't felt like . . ."
She shrugged, but even that seemed like effort.

Madeline decided now was not the time to mention that she was still waiting for a thank-you note for the graduation gift she'd given the girl. Kids. No concept of proper etiquette. Not that Jenna had received any proper training from her mother, Barb. If Madeline thought about it long enough, she was probably waiting for some thank-you notes from that generation of Camdens too.

She put an arm around Jenna's shoulders and led her inside. "We'll take care of your skinniness right this minute. I make a mean omelet."

"Don't go to any trouble, Auntie."

"Nonsense. You came here for help. It's as obvious as these blasted wrinkles on my face. Unless you always sleep in your car."

Jenna stopped in the foyer, her head down as if she could go no farther. Madeline put a finger under her chin and lifted it. "Don't be studying the floor, child. My housekeeper wouldn't appreciate you checking the quality of her work. You came to me; you look at me. In the eye. You and I will handle whatever's bothering you. I promise you that."

Jenna's chin quivered and she began to sob.

Oh dear. Oh dear. Oh dear.

Madeline decided she'd give Jenna a reprieve from discussing her problems until she'd had a proper breakfast. So as she made the ham-and-cheese omelet, toast with orange marmalade, and poured apple juice and coffee, she rambled on about Weaver's contest. She was shocked to find that Jenna hadn't heard a thing about it.

"So much for our advertising dollar," Madeline said as she placed a plate of food in front of her great-niece.

Jenna picked up her fork but only poked at the omelet. "I'm sure most people saw it. I haven't been watching the news much. Haven't been reading the paper either."

Madeline took her own seat and dug into the eggs. "Shame on you. It's every citizen's responsibility to keep up with what's going on in the world."

There went the downcast eyes again. Apparently, the lecture on civic responsibility would also have to wait. Madeline ate a few bites in silence. She glanced at the clock on the microwave. Her to-do list for tonight's Meet 'n' Greet was extensive. It was time to dive in and find out what was wrong. She set her fork down. "So. Out with it. What brought you to my driveway in the middle of the night?"

Jenna started to look down but, seeming to remember her aunt's earlier admonition, raised her chin. "I *had* to leave. I can't live around . . . can't be near Mother anymore. Actually, I moved out a month ago and have been staying with friends, but when I found out . . . I couldn't impose on them indefinitely. So I came here."

That was *it?* A mother-daughter spat? "I know your mother isn't the easiest woman to—"

Jenna snickered.

Having never had children, Madeline had no experience in this area. She knew Barb was a flighty thing, and ever since she'd divorced her husband a good decade earlier, she'd run through a string of boyfriends, but as far as Madeline knew she had a decent job. Finances had never been a problem. And Jenna had made things easier by getting a scholarship to—

"You still in college?"

Jenna tore off a corner of her toast but didn't eat it. "I was. But I'm not going back."

"I always thought you did well in school. You're a bright girl."

"I did okay. As and Bs. One C."

"So?"

"I just can't. I'll go back later."

Madeline knew such detours were often permanent. "You shouldn't let a spat with your mother affect your entire future. Back at school you're away from her—or did you live at home?"

"At home."

"Then move into a dorm. Better for both of you."

Jenna shook her head, her forehead tight.

The mother. The key was Barb. "Is your mother still dating that accountant? Joe something?"

"Oh no. That ended ages ago. There've been tons since." Jenna brought the coffee to her chin, close enough for the steam to give her a facial.

"So she has a new flavor of the month?"

Suddenly, Jenna stood. "Could I lie down awhile?"

All righty then. Madeline had obviously hit a nerve. "Go up to the blue bedroom. Take a shower if you want. Then climb into bed and get caught up on your sleep. I have to go out, but after I get back, we'll talk again."

Jenna hugged Madeline from behind. "Thank you, Auntie. I feel so safe here."

Her niece was looking for "safe"? Now that was a different kettle of fish.

Joan felt like a detective, a private investigator—or at least Nancy Drew. All week long while pretending to lead a normal life, she'd been secretly trying to decipher the mystery of the *S*s. Meeting with Web about her remodeling plans for Swenson's plus getting the house in some semblance of order were by-products that had occurred almost unconsciously—though her muscles were *very* conscious of the progress she'd made.

Ira had done his share of the unpacking, but she noticed every time there was a lull in the to-do list, she found him holed up in the office bedroom. Most of the time he was in front of the computer, like a junkie needing a fix. She'd never actually caught him cutting up any more magazines, but she was at the shop as much as she was home, so who knew what he did when she was gone. And *he* was never gone. She'd repeatedly asked for his help at the shop, but he'd refused. She wasn't sure he'd even left the house in a week. Which was another issue that bothered her . . .

Back to the *S*s . . . since there'd been no further evidence, maybe she'd imagined the whole thing.

Yet she knew she hadn't. The pile of magazines she'd found in the closet with only *S*s missing was proof—of something. Joan was determined to find more clues to the mystery, or at this point, she would even accept a red herring that would confuse the issue. This not knowing anything, not finding anything beyond the magazines, was driving her bonkers.

Which begged the questions: Why *S*s? What was Ira doing with them?

And why did she care? Some men collected beer cans, some had rooms filled with sports paraphernalia from their favorite team, and some spent thousands on toy trains or antique tools. Her husband liked *S*s. So what? It was harmless.

And yet . . . there were larger overlying questions attached to his odd choice—which certainly made him one in a few trillion—that ignited her need to know *something*.

Toward that end, this morning, while reading the Sunday paper—Ira having spread it across the kitchen table while she read a section in a chair by the window—she decided it was time for a showdown. She set the paper on her lap, folded it over, and stood. "Honey? You seem to really like your new office. Why don't you give me a grand tour of all you've done in there?"

He looked up. "It's *my* office."

Why did he remind her of a two-year-old saying, "Mine!" "Of course it is. But you've worked so hard. I'd love to see what's consumed so many hours."

"It's just a computer room with a bed in it. You don't do computers."

True. She knew the basics, but had resisted learning any more than what had been necessary for her teaching position. She found the idea of a global Internet overwhelming, and people's penchant for e-mail alarming. What happened to talking to each other face-to-face—or at least phone to phone? or writing a letter?

She decided to lie. "I'd like to learn. Maybe we could share the space and—"

He looked up from the paper. "I don't think so."

"Why not?"

He waved an arm around the room. "You have the entire house at your disposal—plus the shop. All I want is one room for myself. To myself. Is that too much to ask?"

Actually . . . "It's our house, Ira. All of it. I don't ban you from a single corner."

He looked down at the paper. "Why the sudden interest in my office? in computers?"

"Can't a wife show interest in her husband's interests?"

"Some wives do."

Fiddle. Held captive by her previous apathy. "Fine!" She threw the paper on the table, directly on top of where he was reading.

"I don't want to see your office. You couldn't make me see it." She went to the sink and got a glass of water.

But when she turned around she saw he'd moved her paper out of the way and was engrossed in one of the headlines: "Senator Questioned."

His interest in the news didn't bother her. But the way his fingers traced the *S* gave her chills.

As Madeline crossed the park on her way to the bank she spotted a young man, stooped over, plucking plants in the Weaver Garden. What was he doing destroying the flower bed?

"Hey! You there! Stop pulling up those flowers at once!"

He stood, a plant with long dangling roots in his hand, and Madeline recognized him as the Bauer boy. His eyebrows touched and his mouth was formed in the beginnings of a question.

"You there, Ryan Bauer. Look at what you've done."

He looked where she was pointing, then at her. "I hate weeds."

Weeds? She took a closer look at the pile. Yes, sirree, they were weeds, all right. Not a blooming bud among them.

"I'll clean it up," he said.

"Yes, you will." She tried to regain her authority even though the teenager was nearly a foot taller than she.

He wiped his dirt-encrusted hands on his jeans. "I didn't mean any harm. I'll clean it . . . is there a bigger garbage can around here? I don't want to go filling up those little things by the gazebo with all these weeds."

Which brought them back to the original point. "Why are you pulling weeds here in the park?"

"They needed pulling."

"Did Web—did Mr. Stoddard tell you to do this?"

"Nobody told me. I just saw them and picked them. I hate weeds."

Madeline zeroed in on the potential. "You want to pick weeds for pay?"

"A job?"

"You bet. There are plenty of empty houses here in Weaver, properties with lawns and flowers. Grass to mow and weeds to pick."

His face brightened. "I like to mow."

"Then you're hired. And if you're willing, I can keep you plenty busy with other fix-it, errand-boy-type jobs."

"Sounds great."

She stepped out of the garden and looked toward the main inter-section. She saw Web's truck in front of the Sunshine—the Salida del Sol. "See that truck? It belongs to Mr. Stoddard who can direct you to a mower and tools. He'll be your boss. You go in there and tell him I sent you."

"What's he look like?"

"An old man who's eating biscuits and gravy, unless the Lopez family has gotten him to try a breakfast burrito. Don't worry. You'll spot him."

Ryan closed the gate behind them, then shook her hand. "Thank you, Mrs. Weaver. I won't let you down."

"You'd better not." She looked back at the garden and saw the weeds on the path. "Hold up, boy. . . ." She went to open the gate but it wouldn't budge. She pointed past it. "Before you go any-where, you need to clean up those weeds." She shook the gate. "Stupid gate. Lately, I can't seem to get it open."

"Here, let me try." With no effort at all, Ryan opened the gate.

Madeline slapped his arm. "How did you do that?"

Ryan closed the gate and replayed his movements. The gate opened a second time.

She pushed him aside. "Let me try."

But try as she might, the gate would not open.

"Here, let me show you again," Ryan said.

Madeline hated being shown up by a mere boy. The gate could wait. "I can't be bothered with stupid gates; I have work to do at the bank. And you have work to do cleaning up your mess and talking to Web."

She strode toward the bank leaving the boy and the ornery gate behind.

Ryan spotted the man who must be Web Stoddard even before he went into the Salida del Sol Café. Two old guys sat at a table by the full-length window facing the street, one wearing jeans and a polo shirt, and the other, overalls over a plaid shirt. The latter looked like a fix-it man. Their eyes met. The man winked.

Ryan went inside. A lady with black hair met him at the door. "Table for one?"

Ryan spoke softly and discreetly pointed to the overall man. "Is that Mr. Stoddard?"

Before she could answer, the man stood and came toward him. "You want to talk to me, Son?"

Ryan held out his hand. "I'm Ryan Bauer. I was talking with Mrs. Weaver and—"

"Near the garden. I saw you." He smiled. "Maddy's commandeered you to work, hasn't she?"

"How did you know?"

"Maddy's a pro at delegating. Come sit and tell me about it."

He started to pull an extra chair to the table, but the polo-shirt man finished the last of his coffee, stood, and said, "Have my seat. I gotta get back to the hotel. The toilet in number 2 needs replacing."

Ryan took his chair and a waitress quickly cleared the dirty plates. "What can I get you?" she asked.

"Nothing," Ryan said. "I'm fine."

"Don't be silly," Web said. "Get him a big plate of biscuits and gravy."

The waitress changed her weight to the other foot. "It's not on the menu, Web. This is a Mexican restaurant now. Diego only makes those special for you and——"

"And I appreciate it."

"And maybe the boy doesn't like biscuits and gravy."

Web looked at Ryan. "You like biscuits and gravy?"

"Actually . . ."

Web slapped the table. "See, Maria? Go get 'em."

As she left, Maria shook her head and Web called after her, "A big milk too."

Ryan wasn't that keen on milk, but didn't say anything. This man was so eager to please he couldn't bear to offend him in any way. Besides, it was kind of nice having someone order things for him.

"So then," Web said, cutting into the final half of a biscuit, "which one of the newbies are you?"

"I'm Ryan Bauer."

"Ah. You belong to the doctor and the artist."

Ryan didn't like the word *belong* but said, "Uh-huh."

"You okay about moving here?"

Ryan shrugged.

"Can't blame you for not being excited. Weaver takes some

getting used to, and the Weaver that's happening now isn't the Weaver that used to be. . . ."

His voice faded away, and Ryan sensed a sadness there. "You lived here a long time?"

"Nye past forever."

"Wow."

Web laughed.

Ryan felt himself redden. "I didn't mean it bad."

"Old is old, son, and I know I'm one of the oldest of the lot. And though I miss the Weaver that used to be, I'm glad for all of you newbies moving here and making it into something fresh. Twenty-five new families. That's exciting."

"You've met them all?" Ryan asked.

"I will tonight. Everyone will."

Ryan wasn't sure what he was talking about.

"The Meet 'n' Greet. It's tonight."

"Oh yeah." *Whoopee*.

Web laughed. "It won't be that bad. It'll be a chance for you to meet some other kids."

Ryan's milk came and he took a sip, then wiped his mouth. "I don't care much for other kids right now."

Web's fork stopped in midair between his plate and his mouth. "Why not?"

"Don't feel the need, that's all."

"Feeling it or not, the need's there, boy. People need to connect with people."

Ryan didn't want Web to think he was a weirdo hermit. "Oh, I like people. But I've always felt more at ease with adults."

"Old for your age?"

"Something like that."

Web put his fork down and studied him.

Ryan felt uncomfortable, so he looked out the window while searching for something to say. He grabbed onto the garden and the weeding. "Mrs. Weaver wants me to help mow and clean up yards and—"

"What's got you hurting so much, boy?"

He looked back at Web, who was still studying him as if his face were a painting in a gallery. "Excuse me?"

Web wiggled a finger toward Ryan's eyes. "I see hurt in you. A mighty hurt."

Ryan looked toward the kitchen. Was there a way to cancel his biscuit order?

Web reached across the table and tapped the place near Ryan's arm. "Don't bolt on me. I mean no harm, and if you don't want to talk about it, that's fine by me. But hurt is halved by sharing."

Ryan forced his shoulders to relax. The man meant no harm.

"'For my yoke fits perfectly, and the burden I give you is light,'" Web said.

"Matthew 11:30." As soon as Ryan said it, he wished he could take it back. He didn't want anyone to know this side of him.

Too late. Web sat back in his chair. "My, my. You a Bible-knowing boy?"

"I've dabbled."

Web let out a guffaw and slapped the table. "Dabbled. That's a good one." He lowered his voice and leaned close. "People do not dabble in the Bible, boy. Once you've seen its power, it's got you—heart, head, and soul."

Ryan shrugged.

Web studied him a second time, and Ryan could tell his attitude had changed slightly, like he was seeing Ryan in a new light. He'd hoped to live in Weaver and not be known as the Jesus freak, not be set apart because of his faith. Now that Web knew that *he* knew some of the Bible, he was toast.

Forget the biscuits and gravy. Web could eat a second helping. Ryan pushed his chair back. "I gotta go."

"But your breakfast . . ."

"Sorry." Only when he was halfway across the park did he realize he hadn't talked to Web about work. Some employee he was.

It couldn't be helped. He was not going to make the same mistakes twice. He was not going to let faith take over a second time. He couldn't.

Kathy carried a pile of empty boxes out to the porch where they'd built themselves a mountain of cardboard. Roy had just added his own contribution to the pile and held the door for her as they went back inside.

"We'd better stop and get cleaned up for the Meet 'n' Greet," he said.

Which reminded her. Kathy retrieved a yellow notice they'd received from the table in the foyer. "Did you see this? Mrs. Weaver says it's mandatory we all help with the Founders Day celebration that's happening the first weekend in September."

"Sounds reasonable."

"I don't have time to be on any committee."

Roy picked up some stray wads of packing paper. "Everybody's busy, Kath."

"But I detest committees."

"Which is your real objection. But if I can do it, so can you. Since the house is nearly done, you know I have to focus on getting the clinic in running order. I have hours and hours, if not days and days of work ahead of me."

She folded the announcement in half and gave it to him to add to the trash. "Same with my studio." Hours and hours. But not days and days.

He shrugged, pressed the trash back into her hands, and started up the stairs. "I'm taking a shower."

The shrug infuriated her, and she was tempted to run after him and argue about his gesture and all that it implied. Sure, Kathy's art wasn't life-and-death like a medical clinic. But she did have a deadline. Although she'd been lax about producing since Lisa died, she did have a showing in St. Louis in six weeks.

It was all due to the prodding of her dear friend Sandra Perkins, who was opening a new gallery. Sandra had done a lot of prodding in Kathy's life and had been Kathy's art mentor and friend. It was Sandra who'd first sold Kathy's paintings in her gift shop back in Eureka Springs. It was Sandra who'd urged her to paint her heart and find her own art, not copy someone else's. And more recently, it was Sandra who'd urged—no, yanked—Kathy out of her grief and gotten her to paint again.

Kathy was well aware the gallery showing was all but charity and both of them would be lucky to make a dime, but she also had to admit that getting back to her art *was* therapeutic. Between that and moving to Weaver, Kathy could see a small light of hope on the horizon, tiny but visible if she looked real hard. She was somebody. She was Kathleen Bauer. All in all, not bad for the mother of two from Arkansas, who'd gotten pregnant in high school and married the wrong man.

Lenny. Poor Lenny. She *had* loved him once. And though having the baby—Ryan—was a choice she praised God for daily, marrying Lenny had been a mistake that had caused both of them many years of pain. And yet Lisa had also come out of that union . . . good out of the bad. But now to have Lenny *and* Lisa dead?

Kathy tossed the trash—and memories of her first husband—into an empty box near the couch. She adjusted a stack of books near the fireplace as she adjusted her thoughts.

The bottom line was that Roy needed to treat her art with respect. She was producing again, and would produce even more here in Weaver. Adding to her momentum was the fact that she finally had a decent studio above their garage behind the house. It was a room that had been used as an apartment once, and contained a bathroom and a kitchenette. She'd get a great new start there. Anything was better than the basement studio she was used to. She'd show Roy she was a real artist. He wouldn't dare shrug.

She heard the shower turn off and headed upstairs to get cleaned up. If Roy wanted her to be a committee-going Weaverite, so be it. But Kathy was much more than that.

She was an artiste. So there.

Seth Olsen checked out the food table at the community hall where the Meet 'n' Greet was being held. There was a chocolate-frosted sheet cake with the words *Welcome to Weaver* written in bright yellow, a lemonade punch, coffee, mints, and nuts. The community center was dotted with round tables set with centerpieces of yellow and orange asters. It looked kind of weddingish but was nice, just the same.

The new—and old—citizens of Weaver filed in. There appeared to be over a hundred people present. Those with blue name tags were the old-time Weaverites, and those with red name tags were the rookies . . . there seemed to be an equal sprinkling.

Seth wondered what each new person was going to do in town. What position had they filled on Madeline Weaver's list? It reminded him of the children's rhyme "The butcher, the baker, and the candlestick maker." There were some necessary adjustments for the job openings of the twenty-first century, but the essence was the same. All in all, it was pretty cool.

Less cool were the reporters hanging around. Seth had already given one interview this evening, but sure didn't want some camera crew hanging outside his house, checking his every move. He'd said something to Web, who had assured him the media had been invited only for this one event and then would be gone. Seth hoped it wasn't wishful thinking. The fact that Weaver was small-town America, a bastion of normal life the press generally ignored, was in their favor. Surely some big-city event would grab their interest sooner rather than later.

With each new addition to the community center, Seth looked for a family with a twentysomething daughter. He looked for Bonnie Bowden. Finally, they arrived. The father had the ruddy complexion of a heat-of-summer farmer; the wife was obviously used to her own good cooking. And . . . then there was Bonnie. She alone was the subject of his interest, as well as the subject of more than a few scenarios that he'd played out since winning the contest. Everything depended on this smiling girl across the room.

Fortunately, Bonnie was cute. Not a beauty, but cute enough. Her hair was cut chin length and had a Meg Ryan tousle to it. She wore a denim skirt and a yellow knit top that revealed an athletic body. When he'd first come up with the plan to get the farm back, he'd hoped for someone stunning, but had long since accepted that sacrifices might have to be made. And now . . . finally seeing her . . . it could have been far worse. Plus, because she wasn't a stunner, maybe she was eager for male attention, making her an easy mark.

His mother had often gotten after him for using his charm and
good looks to get what he wanted. "Don't abuse it, Seth." But why
shouldn't he use it? Women did all the time. And didn't everybody
use what they had to get through life? to grab on to some happiness?

His charm and boy-next-door good looks had certainly come
in handy on the police force. Many a time he'd cajoled a perp, or
enticed a witness to give a little more information by using his
smile and wit. As far as the dating scene? He'd had his share of
girlfriends, but there'd been no one who'd reached past the surface
to touch him down deep. He wanted that. He really did. Yet now
. . . that lofty goal *might* have to be sacrificed. He couldn't lose his
focus. Getting the farm back had to remain top priority.

The Bowdens put on their name tags and looked around the
room for a table. It was time to make his move. He walked toward
the father, knowing *he* was the proper way to gain entry to the
daughter. Their eyes met. Seth smiled and extended a hand. The
older man glanced at his name tag, seemed momentarily taken
aback, then shook Seth's hand.

"You're the Olsen boy?"

"Yes, sir. Seth Olsen, at your service."

"Bill Bowden. I heard you were back in town."

Seth scanned his face for some hidden nuance but found nothing.

The wife stepped forward. "Amelia Bowden. You're running the
police force?"

"I am now your chief of police. If you ever need a villain appre-
hended, contact me." Seth turned to the daughter. "And you are?"

The girl offered her hand. "I'm Bonnie. Nice to meet you." Her
handshake was firm. Her skin was flawless and her eyes sharp in their
blueness. He'd judged her too harshly. Up close she was *very* cute.

"How's your mother doing?" Bill said.

She'll be doing better in a few months, thank you. "Pretty good.

She lives in Kansas City now." He leaned forward to make a joke about one of Kansas City's attributes. "And all that jazz."

Mr. Bowden did not smile. "Your father's death . . . we're really sorry about that. It's a horrible thing to have to sell because of something like that, but I was glad we were able to step in. It's a good farm. Good land. Even better than the land we had in Iowa. And with Amelia's mother living in Emporia, it was ideal to get a place close by."

"We love it here," Amelia said.

"The farm's a good one," Bonnie added.

It should be my farm. My land. "Let me know if you ever need anything or have any questions," Seth said. "I lived there my whole life."

"Until you moved away," Bonnie said.

He had to pause for a breath and in the pause found a smile. "But as they say, there's no place like home." He looked around the room. "Mrs. Weaver's contest gave me a second chance here in Weaver." When Bill cocked his head, Seth hastened to add, "I'm looking forward to my job at the station, and I've got a great house on Theodore Lane."

"It backs up to the farm, doesn't it?"

Careful now . . . "Mrs. Weaver thought it would make me happy."

Amelia snickered. "That doesn't sound like the Mrs. Weaver we've come to know."

"Now, now, honey," Bill said. He looked toward the door. The place was filling up. "We'd better find ourselves a table or we'll have to eat standing up, and I'm no good at that."

Seth waited for an invitation to join them, but it didn't happen. Oh well. It was best not to push. He had all the time in the world. "If you'll excuse me," he said. "But Bonnie? Maybe we could get

together sometime? Eat something decadent, chitchat, play in the
dirt . . ."

"Maybe."

Fine. At least the stage was set. Let the games begin.

Ryan ran a finger along the dollop of chocolate frosting left behind
by what *had* been a large piece of cake, licked his finger noisily,
then shoved the plate away. He pushed his chair back and stood.

"Where are you going?" Kathy asked.

He glared down at her. "To meet people. Isn't that what we're
supposed to be doing?"

He was gone before she could answer.

"He got you on that one, Kath," Roy said.

But I want him here, with us. Yet "here with us" wasn't necessarily a pleasant experience. Ryan's sullen silence reigned. Trying to
get her son engaged in a normal conversation exhausted her. Several months of moods, attitude, and arrogance. Yet she couldn't
give up. He was her son. They'd come here for him.

So why did it gall her to see him chatting and laughing with
Web Stoddard and that police officer, Seth?

"You're glowering."

Kathy blinked but knew Roy was right. "How can he be so
charming and nice to other people yet treat us like he hates us?"

"We're his parents."

She shook her head vigorously. "Don't give me that. Teenagers
don't have to hate their parents. We had a good relationship with
him—and Lisa. Before."

"But this is *after*," Roy said. He mumbled, "It will always be after."

Suddenly, he stood, pulled out her chair, leaned close, and

whispered in her ear. "Time for us to join the Meet 'n' Greet shuffle, my dear."

That was fine—for now. But what did come *after?*

Lavon hated to admit it—admit that Patrice had been right—but they were the only blacks in Weaver. And other than the Lopez family, the rest of the winners were various shades of beige. Everyone acted friendly enough, but a familiar feeling returned: the feeling of being conspicuous when he would have preferred to blend in.

Patrice had been gracious enough not to say, "I told you so." Maybe they should have stayed in Manhattan where diversity was the norm. Though there was excitement in starting from scratch, this new demographic factoid was another hurdle to overcome.

Luckily, Malachi didn't care about race and skin color. He was off playing with a half-dozen kids ranging in age from three to eight. Kids were great. Why couldn't people hold on to that innocence and acceptance? Why did naïveté have to change to harsh knowledge?

Lavon's gaze was drawn away from the kids, past his wife who was talking to Mrs. Weaver about bank business, landing on a nice-looking man and woman coming toward his table.

The man held out his hand. "Hi, I'm Roy Bauer, and this is my wife, Kathy."

They shook hands. "The doctor and the painter, right?"

They sat down. "You have a good memory," Kathy said. "When Mrs. Weaver made everyone stand and say something about themselves, I lost track. I'm sorry; I forgot what you do."

"You probably don't remember because I currently hold the ambiguous title of consultant." He leaned forward confidentially.

"My wife made me say that. In truth, I'm unemployed and have been staying home, taking care of our son, Malachi. Not very glamorous, I'm afraid."

"But worthwhile," Kathy said. "That's what I like about painting. I can do it at home, from anywhere."

A woman named Georgia, who was the new town librarian, stopped at the table. "Excuse me for interrupting, but Dr. Bauer? My family, along with the McDonalds, who are going to run the gas station; and Marilyn Cady, who's opening the beauty shop while her husband handles the post office, we—" She took a fresh breath. "Would you come over to our little group and tell us about the clinic you're opening?"

Roy looked at his wife and Lavon. "If you'll excuse me?"

They watched him go. Lavon smiled at Kathy. She had pretty hazel eyes that complemented her shoulder-length blonde hair. "So. What's your medium?"

Kathy raised an eyebrow. "The way you ask . . . you must have some art background."

"Why do you say that?"

Kathy shoved a used plate aside so she could lean on the table. "Most people ask *what* I paint. Few ask the medium."

"Which is?"

"Acrylics. I've dabbled in watercolors, but I like the texture of acrylics better."

He nodded. "Have you had . . . are you . . . ?"

She made it easy for him. "I *have* attained a certain measure of success. I've been very blessed."

Blessed. Not lucky. He perked up at the term of faith. "It's good to utilize the gifts God hands out. That's what frustrates me now. Since I'm not working, since I'm not using much of anything I would call a gift . . ." He shrugged.

"But being a stay-at-home dad is a gift in itself, isn't it?"

"You'd think so." He glanced across the room at Patrice.

Kathy turned around to see whom he was looking at. "Your wife doesn't agree?"

"She'd like me to have a real job."

Kathy laughed, then put a hand to her mouth. "Sorry, but it's odd hearing those words said by a man."

"Try living it."

Her face softened. "With the new house not costing anything . . . now should be the time you *can* stay home. Financially, I mean." She shook her head and waved her hands in front of her mouth. "I'm being quite the busybody. Forgive me for intruding into your private affairs."

"No, it's fine. It's nice to talk to someone about it."

Her shoulders relaxed. "You're very gracious. But maybe we should talk about something safe. Tell me about Malachi."

Lavon was glad to oblige and when he was done, he asked Kathy about her kids. A dead child. How horrible. And another teenager who'd withdrawn. . . . Those teen years were in the future for him and Patrice, and he doubted they'd get through them unscathed.

He was glad to see his wife coming over to join them. He wanted her to meet Kathy, and held out his arm as she neared. She took his hand. "Is Mrs. Weaver ready for you at the bank?"

"I start tomorrow. It'll be good to get back to work." She looked at Kathy.

"Patrice, I'd like to introduce you to Kathy Bauer."

Kathy shook her hand. "So nice to meet you. I'd love to hear about life in New York City sometime."

"Where are you from?" Patrice asked.

"Eureka Springs. Arkansas."

Patrice's right eyebrow raised. "Oh."

Kathy laughed. "I know. Not too exciting. Nothing like New York. It has more trees and rolling hills than people. It's in the Ozark Mountains. It's a beautiful place."

"I'm sure it is." But Patrice's voice implied otherwise.

Kathy looked away, then pointed toward her husband who was motioning her over. "It seems I'm being beckoned." She stood. "It was nice to meet both of you. We'll talk again soon."

Patrice sat in her vacated space. "Her husband's the doctor, right?"

"He's opening a clinic."

"Doctor, artist . . . they must be rolling in money."

"Not necessarily. Ever heard of 'starving artists'?"

Patrice looked after Kathy. Her eyes were in their critical mode, not missing a thing. "She doesn't look starving to me."

Lavon wasn't in the mood for one of Patrice's instant character assessments. Sometimes it was fun playing along, guessing about people's lives from just a glance or quick meeting, but other times it made him uneasy. Like now. He didn't want to hear anything negative about Kathy Bauer. He liked the woman and didn't want her dissected by a pro like his wife.

Luckily, Patrice was distracted. "I see Joan Goldberg over there. No one's talking to her but some teenager." She stood and smoothed her skirt. "I'd better go say hello. I hear she's starting a soda shop. She might need a loan."

Lavon hated to admit it, but he was glad to see her go.

Coming home after the Meet 'n' Greet, Madeline intercepted Jenna coming down the stairs. "Well, well. I was beginning to think you were a figment of my imagination."

Jenna pointed toward the kitchen. "I was going to get a Coke."

"I don't have any."

Jenna was still wearing the same grungy jeans and T-shirt she'd been wearing this morning. Obviously she hadn't partaken of a bath. "I'll take whatever you've got," she said.

I'm sure you will. Madeline shut the door and hung her purse on the hall tree. "We missed you at the Meet 'n' Greet."

"Sorry. I didn't feel up to it. Besides, there's no one I want to meet. Nor greet," Jenna said.

"That was rude, young lady."

"Oh. Sorry." Jenna's shoulders slumped as if she'd been slapped.

Two sorries in the span of fifteen seconds.

"I'll just grab something to drink and be out of your way."

Madeline took her arm. "Whoa there, child. You're not in my way, and as far as drinking anything, I'm betting a cup of hot tea would do you better than anything."

"I've never had hot tea."

"Then you're in for a treat."

They entered the kitchen where Madeline put the kettle on. She pulled down a plastic container of tea bags. "I've got quite an assortment from ginger-orange to mint."

Jenna took the closest bag. So much for offering a tea smorgasbord. Speaking of food, Madeline looked around the kitchen. Everything was as she'd left it this afternoon when she'd headed over to the community center to supervise the setup. Either Jenna was a clean freak, or . . . "Have you had anything to eat today?" *Other than picking at your omelet?*

Jenna fingered the tea bag and shook her head. "I wasn't hungry."

"Pooh. Hungry or not you have to eat."

"My stomach's a little upset."

"Why didn't you say so?" She plucked the Lemon Zinger tea

bag out of Jenna's possession and replaced it with a soothing chamomile. She heard the water on the stove begin to roll. Good. The sooner the better. She went to the cupboard and got out a can of chicken-noodle soup.

"You don't have to make me anything. I'm fine."

"Nonsense. Call me a vain old woman, but I make it a rule never to have anyone around who's skinnier than me, and as it is now, you're stretching my rule. So you're going to eat. No arguments." She opened the can and poured it into a pan on the stove. Then she thought of something. "Are you sick enough for a doctor, because we have a doctor in Weaver now. Dr. Bauer."

"No!" Jenna's eyes widened. "I mean, there's no need for a doctor." She stood. "I'm tired. In fact, I think I'll call it a night."

Not again. After experiencing two short dialogues, and two quick exits in one day, Madeline's patience was shot. She intercepted Jenna at the kitchen door. "That's fine—for now. But in the morning I have some filing I'd like you to do, and then I'd like you to call the printers to make sure the programs will be ready for Founders Day."

Jenna looked overwhelmed, as if Madeline had asked her to write the Declaration of Independence. "I . . . I suppose I could do that."

"I don't take to freeloaders, Jenna. A family visit is fine, but even with that, I'd think you'd want to stay busy. Am I right?"

"Uh . . . yes."

"Glad to hear it. Now go. Have a good night's rest."

Kids.

Seth tried to not get spooked out, but it was eerie walking through the cornfield in the middle of the night. The leaves of the stalks cut against his arms as he passed, the corn so high he couldn't see anything but its silhouette against the moonlit sky. There was total silence except for his own footfalls and breathing, the swish of his arms parting the leaves, and the soft hopping sound of grasshoppers jumping out of his way. Too soon the harvest would take away this cover.

It's not that he hadn't walked through fields many a time. But rarely at night. There had been no reason for such a thing when he was a farmer working the land.

Not a policeman sneaking onto someone else's land.

There was no huge agenda for this night's trek. He'd simply come home from the town gathering, gone to bed, and found sleep impossible. He didn't remember making the decision to get dressed and head out toward the Bowden farmstead, and because of that, the whole thing felt a bit surreal. Like a scene in a horror flick where bad things popped out of the corn and ate people who were stupid enough to be walking through the rows in the dark in the middle of the night.

Dumb. Dumb. Dumb.

Yet even as he called himself names, he didn't turn back. He was almost there. Almost home.

He saw the end of the row lit by artificial light and knew he was coming to the clearing that held the outbuildings and house. He slowed, more concerned with the possible bark of a dog than his presence being found out by any human inhabitants. Most farmers went to bed early in order to get up early. It was nearly one in the morning. The coast should be clear.

Clear for what?

Seth stood at the boundary between field and yard and looked at the Olsen family home. His bedroom on the northwest corner was dark. Was that Bonnie's room now? A dim light glowed on the

first floor, probably from the hall light near the closet beneath the
stairs. They'd often kept that light on at night. He'd had a club-
house in that closet when he was seven, until his mom got tired of
the winter coats sitting in the corner by the couch.

Feeling the need to be bold, Seth stepped out of the field one
giant step and waited for a reaction from pet or people. Nothing.
Their old dog, Rex, would have been at his heels by now, yapping
and dancing around. A farm without a dog? It was unheard of.

But it *was* to his advantage. He skirted the edge of the yard and
found himself heading for the barn. The ancient door, which hung
crooked on old hinges, couldn't close all the way if it wanted to,
and so with just a nudge to widen the gap, he slipped inside. The
pungent smells of hay, manure, and dust were like perfume to his
soul. Two slices of moonlight gained entry at the door and at the
high window near the loft. Seth didn't need more. He knew this
barn better than he knew his old room—for he'd spent more time
here. Working, playing, dreaming.

How ironic. How many hours had he spent in the barn's loft
dreaming impossible dreams, and eventually planning his getaway?
During his middle teens he'd decided life would be better in the
big city. He'd find adventure there, and be away from the daily
tedium of chores and back-breaking work. He'd find a job where
he didn't have to sweat, get sore muscles, or worry about the vari-
ables of weather, disease, and a fickle economy. That was the life
for him.

The ladder to the loft beckoned and he paused to trace the carv-
ing of his name on the fourth rung from the bottom—a wooden
scar left by an unappreciative kid who hadn't known what he had
until he lost it.

He reached the top and out of habit moved toward the corner of
the loft where some old tarps were still piled along the wall on top

of some empty crates. The crates had been used as chairs, a boat, and even a spaceship for many games of his imagination. A stray stick sat at his feet and he picked it up. It immediately became a sword and he took an en garde stance.

Take that, Robin Hood!

The voice of his best friend, Davey, sounded in his head but seemed real enough that he turned around to see if Davey—as the sheriff of Nottingham—was hiding across the loft, behind another stack of crates they'd often used as a castle.

Davey. Seth had become a police officer because of Davey. When his friend had been twelve, he'd gone on a family vacation to Los Angeles. But Davey's hopes of seeing Disneyland had been dashed when an act of road rage had left him dead.

And Seth devastated.

Seth's mother had consoled him, but his father . . . *"Buck it up, Seth! Be a man!"*

He dispelled the hurtful memory with a shake of his head and focused on thoughts of his mother. On impulse he extended his arms, moved his feet in a one-two-three pattern, and turned round and round. Before his first junior high dance, his mother had taught him how to dance up here. She'd looked so pretty as she'd laughed and shook the hair back from her eyes. Of course the waltz she'd taught him had been useless since the music played at the dance had nothing much to do with one-two anything, but the memory still made him smile.

Speaking of smiling . . . his eyes strayed back to the bales of hay. Melissa Ramos. Long red hair and dazzling green eyes. How close they'd come to losing their virginity together, right there in the corner. Luckily, they'd both chickened out, and within a month their romance had faded of its own accord, but . . . it continued to be a hallmark moment in his life.

Seth turned in a slow circle. Much about this loft made him smile. So many memories. So many milestones. No wonder he'd braved the walk through the field in the moonlight to come to this place.

He walked to the tarp-covered crates and stretched out on them, letting the tarp's sturdy roughness bite his cheek. He cushioned his face in his arms and closed his eyes. *Help me. Please help me get it all back.*

That was as far as his prayers progressed before the oblivion of sleep took him away.

SIX

*In everything you do,
stay away from complaining and arguing,
so that no one can speak a word of blame against you.*

PHILIPPIANS 2:14-15

"*Be a man, Seth!*"

Seth turned over in his sleep and groaned at the words.

"*It's good he's gone, Seth. You two playing stupid games? Cowboys, Robin Hood. Cops and robbers. I never had time for games. Real men don't play make-believe games. Davey was a bad influence on you, Seth.*"

Davey. Davey.

Seth's back hurt. It was hot. Having the sun in his eyes didn't make sense. The bedroom in his apartment got evening sun, not morning—

His eyes shot open and it took him a good ten seconds to realize that not only wasn't he in his Denver apartment, he wasn't in his house in Weaver. He was in the barn—the Bowdens' barn.

And he'd been dreaming about Davey. And his father. He stood and stretched as he moved to the edge of the loft and looked down to the main part of the barn where the argument had occurred. It had been right after Davey had been killed. His father had found Seth crying in the barn, and had ordered him down from the loft. Front and center.

That's when his father had let out his tirade against their imaginative games. His dad had made it sound like there was something wrong with their friendship. But there wasn't. Davey was Seth's best friend and he'd been killed at the ridiculous age of twelve. His father had no right saying anything against him.

So Seth had fought back—verbally. The first time he'd ever taken a stand against his father.

But not the last.

Years later, when Seth had made the decision to become a cop, he'd made sure his father knew he'd first thought of it that day in the barn. *Be a man* had merged with his desire to avenge his best friend's death. A way to do that had been to go into law enforcement. Perhaps Seth should have kept the source of his decision to himself.

But he hadn't.

And the rift between father and son had grown deeper.

A bird fluttered in the rafters, drawing Seth out of his memories. He looked at his wrist to check the time but his watch wasn't there. Time had not seemed important last night when he'd made his trek through the field toward the family homestead. But now, he really needed to know the time. He was supposed to start work at the station this morning. He couldn't be late—not that there'd be anyone there to clock him in.

He moved to the loft window. The sun was still low, the shadows long, and the color of the morning more blue than golden. Six-thirty? Maybe seven?

He saw movement at the kitchen window and saw Mrs. Bowden at the sink. People were up. He had to get out of here before chores were started. He did a scan of the rest of the yard. The coast was clear. He hurried down the ladder. The door was still nudged to his slink-in/slink-out position and he did just that. He gave a quick glance to the kitchen and was glad to see Mrs. Bowden was gone. He had to make a run for it.

But just as he thought he was home free, only twenty feet from the edge of the field, he heard the wail of the hinges on the kitchen's screen door. He didn't dare look.

"Hey! Hey you!"

It was Bonnie's voice. He took another step toward the corn, but she didn't give up. "Seth? Is that you?"

With a fresh breath and a smile he faced her. "Morning."

She came off the back stoop and walked toward him. She was wearing shorts, a T-shirt, and running shoes. "Don't 'morning' me, as if we just met on the street. I saw you coming out of the barn. What are you doing here?"

He was speechless and mad at himself for even being here.

"Well?" She stopped a few feet away.

"I . . . oh . . . shoot. I got nothing." He braced himself for her reaction.

She laughed. "I'd say, 'How refreshing. A man without excuses,' but I'd like one. The truth, preferably."

The whole truth was not an option. He put on a stricken face and looked sheepishly at the barn. "Let's just say I was suffering a bout of homesickness and felt an intense desire to fill my lungs with the smell of straw, manure, and tractor oil."

"In *our* barn."

Seth dropped his head and nodded forlornly. "Sorry. It won't happen again. I'll get my own manure."

He didn't dare look up, but he could feel her eyes.

"You love this place."

It was a statement, not a question. He shrugged. "Most people feel strongly about the place where they grew up."

She nodded, but her eyes were still wary. "Since you're here . . . care to go running with me?" she asked.

He shook his head and pointed toward the field, toward his home. "I have to get back. There's only so much aromatherapy I can take in one day. I start work this morning. At the station."

"I could drive you."

He felt himself redden. "No thanks. I think I'll leave the way I came."

She looked toward the corn and nodded. "You plan to do this often?"

"Hmm?"

"You plan on taking early morning strolls through cornfields to visit other people's property?"

His throat was dry. "Not unless I'm welcome." He raised his right hand. "Promise."

She nodded and began jogging in place. Then, with a wave of her hand, she ran away from him, down the long driveway toward the road.

Seth turned toward the field and spotted Mrs. Bowden leaning toward the kitchen window, looking at him.

Great, just great. But what could he do? He gave her a wave, then kept walking, disappearing into the rows of corn like a phantom baseball player in *Field of Dreams.* Nothing like making a dramatic exit.

But no more sentimental trips down memory lane.

He couldn't risk it.

Madeline awakened and shot to sitting in a single movement. *The papers! They're at the bank!*

She looked at the time: 6:43. It wasn't that she was late getting up. She had plenty of time to get to her eight o'clock meeting with Patrice Newsom at the bank. It was Patrice's first day. Madeline was going to show her around and get her settled into being the new vice president of Weaver National Bank.

There was no problem with any of that. Madeline was happy to be handing the day-to-day reins to someone else. She just didn't have the energy anymore. Yet, she wasn't giving in. She'd never give in.

The problem had to do with the papers that were in Madeline's office. Records spanning sixty years of past dealings and deals that were private—that had to remain private. Up until now there'd never been anyone of authority present on a daily basis, so there hadn't been any reason to worry about their discovery. But now, with Patrice in residence at the bank more than Madeline . . .

It was a risk she had to address or her entire plan could be ruined. She'd come too far and sacrificed too much. And too much was at stake.

Madeline got dressed, then power walked across the park toward the bank, determined to get there before Patrice. But as she approached the park's bench on the corner, she was shocked to see her new employee sitting there, dressed in a tan suit and heels, ready for work. Such enthusiasm was usually commendable, but not today.

At the sound of Madeline's footfalls, Patrice turned. Madeline reluctantly set aside her original agenda in order to greet her. The rest would have to wait. But not for long.

Brownie points were essential in the world of business—a piece
of wisdom Patrice Newsom had discovered during her first job
as a waitress, and one she had carried to her last job at the bank in
Manhattan. A good employee never did *only* what was asked of
her, but always more. And—since it was difficult to toot one's
own horn gracefully—the more visible the *more* was, the better.

Like today. Patrice and Mrs. Weaver had agreed to meet at the
bank at eight. Although Patrice had not known for certain, she had
guessed by Mrs. Weaver's personality that she was also an early
person. And early people appreciated other early people. So, to
make sure Patrice beat her to the starting gate, she'd been sitting
across the street from the bank since six forty-five.

She rose as Mrs. Weaver approached. "Good morning."

"My, my. Early bird, worms, and all that," Mrs. Weaver said.

"I'm eager to get started."

"A commendable approach." Mrs. Weaver strode across the
intersection, completely ignoring the red or green of the traffic
light. Patrice had to scurry to keep up.

Once inside, with the lights switched on, Patrice let Mrs. Weaver
give the grand tour. Apparently, the bank's lobby had been completely renovated in the eighties, and the oak woodwork, tin ceilings, ceramic-tile floors, and original brass light fixtures gave the
place a feeling of stability, as if it had always existed and always
would. The bank still had the original vault, but a new one had
been added, along with a new safe-deposit-box area.

There were three teller cages that were actual cages, with shiny
brass rails that Mrs. Weaver said needed polishing once a week.
Patrice wondered who did this work and assumed—or at least
hoped—it *wasn't* herself.

Patrice was impressed by Mrs. Weaver's knowledge of computers, but realized it made sense. *Adjust* and *adapt* were key words in the climb up the ladder of success. As were *determination* and *gumption.*

Patrice was adept at all four—if she didn't say so herself. Which she would if pressed, stressed, or depressed.

The only thing that bothered her were the vast number of storage boxes and files taken up with old records. These were unnecessary and went beyond regulation. She decided to mention it to Mrs. Weaver. "It seems you have records here that could be discarded." She pointed toward boxes dated from the 1930s that were piled four high in the corner of a storeroom.

Mrs. Weaver made a quick move to get in front of the boxes, as if protecting them. "They're fine. Just leave them."

"But banking regulations state we only need to keep records for—"

"I don't care what regulations say!" With a fresh breath, Mrs. Weaver's passion faded. "I'm afraid I'm a bit of a pack rat, though I prefer the title of chronicler." She stroked the top of a box. "These records aren't hurting anything."

They're taking up room. "We could have them scanned and put on CDs if you like. CDs are a more stable form of recording than paper."

Mrs. Weaver headed to the door. "Maybe. But not now." She waited until Patrice was out of the storeroom, then shut off the light and closed the door with a pointed click.

They ended the tour in the largest office. Mrs. Weaver sat behind the massive oak desk, her diminutive size making her appear like a child playing in her daddy's domain. She rocked back in the maroon leather chair, tenting her fingers. "Well, then, do you think you can handle it?"

In many ways it was an insulting question, but Patrice let it pass and affected her own stance of relaxed assurance by taking a seat and crossing her legs. "I have no doubt."

Mrs. Weaver's left eyebrow rose and for a moment Patrice wondered if she'd sounded *too* confident. But then the old woman's laughter calmed her distress. "I knew I liked you," Mrs. Weaver said, sitting forward. "I sense an air of anger in you and—"

Patrice was taken aback. "Anger?"

A flip of her hand signaled that Patrice's concern was unnecessary. "Don't get defensive or take it the wrong way. There are different kinds of anger. There's the anger of disgust and frustration—the kind you have at your husband when he gives you a toaster for your birthday. It's similar to the kind you have when men make wars that we women could avoid if only someone would give us the reins of power."

"And the other type of anger?"

Mrs. Weaver leaned forward on her desk as if taking Patrice into her confidence. "It's the anger borne of confidence and good ideas. It's a fire in your belly that says you simply *have* to take this chance or die trying. It's passion."

Patrice possessed all those feelings. They ruled her. She'd never defined them as anger, and yet . . .

Mrs. Weaver sat back, taking a pen with her to tap on the palm of her hand. "I've made this bank what it is today because of that kind of anger. It grew out of the circumstances of my life. A married woman sixty years ago was expected to be a stay-at-home wife and mother." She cocked her head. "Being pretty brainless was good too. Barefoot and pregnant. That type of thing."

"But certainly as a Weaver . . . they were an educated family. Surely they didn't have such antiquated ideas."

Mrs. Weaver smiled and raised a finger to make a point. "Ah.

But I was not always a Weaver. I was a McHenry, from the poor part of town. I lived on Martha Lane in a white clapboard house and wore hand-me-down clothes. I used to lie in bed and pretend it was a mansion. . . ." Her eyes were in the past, then with a blink returned to the present. "I hated the name of my street. Martha. How boring. If only it were Marguerite Boulevard. Something regal sounding."

"So your family wasn't well-off?"

She laughed. "My father worked at the feed store. Loading trucks."

Patrice nodded. Her own father had been a janitor at a grade school.

Mrs. Weaver slapped the table. "But enough about my BA years."

"BA?"

"Before Augustus." She gave a sly smile. "My marriage to Augustus gave me everything I wanted in life—and more."

Somehow Patrice sensed Mrs. Weaver wasn't talking about finding a soul mate or feeling contented satisfaction in the marriage. Maybe satisfaction *because* of the marriage . . .

Mrs. Weaver sat back, regaining her initial position. "I thank God every day that Augustus was a moron when it came to running this place."

Patrice nearly choked. "What?"

Mrs. Weaver grabbed another laugh. "I love saying that to people. It's payment for all the years I had to pretend he was the one in charge while, in actuality, I was the brains behind the bank. And the brawn. I did the work. I was here every morning by seven-thirty and was the last to leave."

Patrice wondered if this was why she hadn't had any children.

Mrs. Weaver seemed to sense the reason behind her pause. "It's a good thing we didn't have children because there wasn't time for them. Augustus was immature enough in his own right. I didn't need anyone else exhibiting childish behavior." The pen pounded her palm again. "Speaking of . . . has your husband found himself a job yet, or are you still the sole breadwinner?"

Somehow she made it sound like a character flaw—on both their parts. "He's looking. He *does* want to do more with his life than be a househusband."

There went that eyebrow again. "Wanting more isn't a bad thing. Just so *you're* here at the bank concentrating on what needs to be done."

"There's no problem in that," Patrice said.

Mrs. Weaver pushed against the armrests and stood. "Then get to it. Make us some money."

That she could do.

It's not as if Madeline cared what the three employees of the bank thought. She was their boss, their head honcho. And yet, since she'd never closed the door to her office before, to do so now . . . she needed to leave it open.

But it was a risk to get out the records that concerned her, to go through them with the door open and Patrice constantly popping in and out with questions. . . . Patrice was right about all the old files. Why had Madeline kept them? She'd known she could—and even should—dispose of them. Why had she been unable to do so?

Punishment. They are proof of our sin. My sin.

Madeline filed the thought with the other recent intrusions to her conscience and went to the oak file in the corner of her office, near the opened door. She unlocked it and opened the top drawer.

The files in the storeroom were nothing compared to these. Here were the documents that must remain secret. She pulled a specific manila file out of its bed—a file from 1946. With a glance to the lobby, she set it on top of the opened drawer and looked inside. It was full of yellowed pages and notes written in her own elegant cursive. *Check stock certificates* was the top memo to herself.

Odd how she remembered writing that note while she'd been seated at the desk that held court behind her now—though it had been her father-in-law's desk at the time. On that particular morning he'd been out of the office and had asked his son, Augustus, to find a solution to a delicate situation. Augustus had responded to the challenge by taking an early lunch, leaving Madeline alone— in charge of their future.

It hadn't been the first time her husband had been worthless in regard to finding a solution to a tough situation. Though she *had* loved Augustus in her own way, he hadn't been able to make a decision of what tie to wear to the bank every day without her laying it out for him, much less be able to deal with interest rates, closing costs, and banking regulations. And as far as coming up with the inventive procedures that were often needed to solve sensitive problems? Forget it.

Dealing with this file had been the first time Madeline had taken the control away from her dear but dumb hubby. She remembered how surprised she'd been that she hadn't felt guilty about it. Why should she? There was a limit to how long she could sit in the background of the Weaver dynasty, pretend to have no opinion, and nod agreeably to everything the Weavers wanted to do. Besides, she'd seen the frustration on her father-in-law's face as he'd tried to teach Augustus gumption and business sense, tried to get him to see that sometimes corners had to be cut for the good of the bank and the family. She'd suffered her own frustration as her husband had turned away from such instruction, either unwilling or unable to understand. If he wouldn't step forward to get the approval of the family patriarch—Walden Weaver—she'd do it for him. Walden wouldn't condone failure, and neither would Madeline.

Failure in itself was not acceptable then and was not acceptable now. But what had riled Madeline was that Augustus didn't even try. It was as if his brain had been capable of learning only a few dozen tasks, and since he'd learned those by the age of twelve, there wasn't room in his memory banks to learn any more. Or the inclination. Truth was, her husband was a boring man with the personality of a chair and the vision of a blind man on a moonless night.

The result was that Augustus's *non*potential had made her own *untapped* potential churn. She'd felt like a boiling pot whose lid had been clamped shut. If she hadn't found the valve to release the pressure, she would have blown.

Madeline scanned the pages of the file, remembering the exhilaration when her ambition and drive had finally been allowed release. In response to her husband's ineptitude and her father-in-law's adamancy that something be done with this file, she'd found a way to propel herself from mere employee and daughter-in-law into a force to be reckoned with.

From the file she retrieved a photo of the property in question: the Weaver Mercantile. It wasn't that the store itself had been the problem. Or that it hadn't been a success. The problem had lain in who was running it. The family. Who they were. What they were. It wasn't that Madeline necessarily agreed with Walden Weaver's prejudices, but since he'd wanted the family out, she'd found a way to make it—

"Mrs. Weaver?"

At the sound of Patrice's voice Madeline slapped the file closed, sending the photo sailing to the carpet.

Patrice picked it up. "My. This is an oldie." She brought it closer to her face. "Is this Joan Goldberg's store?"

With careful restraint, Madeline took the photo back. "Yes, I believe it is. A long, long time ago."

Patrice nodded toward the file cabinet. "Are those more old files?"

Madeline shoved the file back in its place and slammed the drawer shut. "You have a question?"

It took Madeline's heart a good five minutes to calm down. Stress. The doctor had said to avoid stress.

Not in this lifetime.

They'd been working all morning at the clinic. If Kathy never had to unpack another box . . . unfortunately there were still plenty more waiting in her studio. She stopped and arched her back, groaning. "I think I need a doctor."

She hoped Roy would stop organizing the medicine cabinet and come to her, pull her arms around his neck, nuzzle into her hair, and say, "You've got one. Your very own personal doctor, at your service."

Nice fantasy.

In reality, Roy said, "There's some ibuprofen on the counter. Help yourself."

"You need to work on your bedside manner, Doc."

Her tone made him glance in her direction. Glance, not look. "Give me a break, Kath. I'll be charming after I get this place in order."

"Until then you'll be cold, brusque, and unappreciative?" She knew she was being unfair—and a bit of a baby—but the very fact that he'd forced her into helping him fix up *his* office when she had her own studio to organize . . .

Okay, maybe *forced* was too strong a word. He'd asked her to come. More than once. He'd probably even said please. Too bad Ryan was off somewhere or *he* could be here helping, and she could be home.

Kathy got herself some medicine. The existing paper-cup dispenser was empty, so she cupped a hand and drank, jerking her head back to get the pills down.

"That wasn't very sanitary," Roy said.

She shrugged, happy he'd noticed. Lately, she'd take what she could get attentionwise. Ever since they'd won this contest—probably before then, actually—Roy had been preoccupied. Distant. Weary even. It wasn't anything blatant, but his usual zest had fizzled. She'd often caught him just sitting, looking at air. Or rubbing his temples as if life were a headache and there wasn't enough medicine in the world to ease the pain.

Yes, he *had* admitted coming here was for the best, for Ryan's best anyway. Sacrifices had to be made for one's children—especially such an exceptional child as Ryan. And certainly leaving his practice in Eureka Springs to start over here hadn't been *that* hard. There were sick people everywhere, though Kathy did admit that adapting his practice from obstetrics and pediatrics to general medicine would be a continuing challenge. Yet Roy seemed willing. He'd said so and had been studying to get caught up on the newest treatments—in between selling their house, moving, and dealing with Ryan's objections.

Hmm. On a stress meter good ol' Roy would probably be in the red zone. She studied him a moment as he continued his work

stocking the medicine cabinet. His forehead was knotted in con-
centration, his shoulders taut. On impulse she slid in behind him,
wrapped her arms around his torso, and leaned her cheek between
his shoulder blades.

He stopped his work, but did not lower his arms. She waited for
words, and for him to turn around and pull her into a hug. But as
one moment passed into two, then three . . .

Suddenly, she heard the door to the clinic open. "Hello? I need
help here!"

They both ran to the lobby. Lavon Newsom was holding his son
who was wheezing, his head back. Two little girls—twins—ran in
with them, holding hands.

"He has chronic asthma," Lavon said. "We were outside. I was
raking some old leaves from under the shrubs and from the flower
beds when he had an attack. The inhaler didn't work. He needs a
breathing treatment."

"Bring him back here." Roy showed the way to a just-cleaned
examination room. His voice was calm, but his movements were
deliberate and quick. In the room, he washed his hands and smiled
at the boy while talking to the father. "I'm sorry; what's his name
again?"

"Malachi."

Roy winked at the child while he readied an oxygen mask.
"Malachi. What a strong name that is. You're going to be just fine,
Malachi. I promise." Roy patted the examination table and Lavon
laid his son down.

Suddenly Kathy realized she was needed. The little girls hung
back in the doorway. They shouldn't be there. "I'll take the girls
into the waiting room," she said.

"They are Paulina and Constanza Lopez," Lavon said. "Their
parents run the diner. They're three. I've started to babysit them."

Kathy took the twins away, glad to be separated from the horrible raspy sound of the boy's breathing. She found some kids' books under the counter and got the girls settled, both in one chair.

A half hour later, Roy came out.

"How is he?"

"He'll be fine. They'll be out in a minute."

With a glance to the examination room, Kathy leaned toward her husband. "You don't have the computer set up yet—insurance stuff. What are you going to do about payment?"

"Don't worry about it."

"But . . ."

"Don't worry about it." Roy returned to his patient.

Images of small-town doctors being paid with chickens and sacks of grain entered her mind.

Lavon came out of the room, holding the boy. He smiled at her and reached for his wallet. "Your husband told me no charge, but that won't do." He pulled out three tens and two fives, then looked in his wallet as if searching for more. "I know this isn't much, but it's a start. I really appreciate you taking care of my boy like this."

Kathy set the bills on the counter as Lavon gathered up the little girls and was on his way.

Roy joined her up front. "Well then, my first patient, successfully handled."

Kathy patted the money. "He paid. Sort of."

Roy picked up the bills as if they were something unique to be studied.

"It's not much, is it?" Kathy said.

He placed the money back on the counter in a short stack and gave it a pat. "Actually, it's perfect." He smiled broadly.

It had been a long while since Kathy had seen his smile so bright. She'd have to work on that.

"Knock, knock?"

Kathy looked up from the shelf she was putting together in her studio and found Lavon standing at the opened door, holding a plate of cookies in one hand and Malachi's hand in the other.

He lifted the plate as an offering. "We come bearing gifts. Chocolate-chip cookies. Just out of the oven. Have one."

Kathy got to her feet. "How did you know chocolate-chip cookies are my favorite indulgence?"

"They are everybody's favorite indulgence."

She wiped her hands on her denim capris, took a cookie, and ate half in the first bite. It was still warm and melted in her mouth. She moaned. "Now *this* hits the spot."

"Malachi and I made the cookies for you and your husband as a special thanks for taking care of him today. To have us burst in there, when you were busy setting up . . . it was my own fault. Being from a city apartment without a yard, I never even thought about the allergens stirred up by raking old leaves. I'll know better next time." He nodded once with emphasis. "At any rate, many thanks."

"You're welcome." The cookie gone, Kathy licked her fingers. She winked at Malachi. "Do you like to draw?"

He nodded, so she got out some paper and colored pencils. She set them on a box, using it as a table. "Have a seat, young Malachi," she told the boy. He sat on the floor and started drawing immediately.

Lavon strolled to the canvases stacked against the wall. "Is this your work?"

"Yes. I paint children. Close-ups of children in action."

He pulled one out of the stack that showed the hands of a child coloring in a coloring book. "I like how they are so focused, like you've zoomed into the act itself, the moment."

No one had ever described her style better. "Thank you, Lavon. I appreciate the compliment."

He left the canvases behind and looked around. "So. This is your new studio?"

"It will be."

He pointed to the window. "North light. That's the best, isn't it?"

"Always indirect. Always subtle. No harsh shadows."

Lavon picked up a paintbrush and swiped it against his palm. "I wish I had a talent like this. It must be such a blessing."

"It can be."

He put the brush down. "What's the downside of being artistic?"

Kathy blinked at the question. No one had ever asked her that.

Then suddenly, Lavon pointed at the shelf. "We're keeping you from your work. . . ."

"No, no. I'm all thumbs with a screwdriver anyway. I'll let Roy do it later."

Lavon got to his knees. "Nonsense. You answer my question while I put the shelf together." He took up the screwdriver and pointed toward a stool. "Sit and talk to me."

It felt odd to have someone else working while she watched, but she enjoyed the break. "The downside to being artistic . . ." She took a fresh breath. "I suppose the hardest thing, besides the uncertainty of sales and showings, and critics—"

He laughed. "As if that isn't hard enough?"

"You got that right." She continued, "Beyond the business side is the difficulty of being creative on demand."

He looked up from installing the first shelf. "Explain."

She stood and strolled through the room as she talked. "When

I was just starting out, before I'd really sold much, I could work whenever I felt like it. If a painting took months, so be it. But for a while there, when things started to pop, I suddenly had deadlines to meet and other people to appease. I *had* to work every day whether I felt like it or not, whether I felt inspired or not."

"How do you do that?"

She stopped at the box of paints and began taking the tubes out, dividing them into color families. She didn't want to look at him when she attempted to explain the unexplainable. Especially when it was something she'd ignored for many months. *Why have I ignored it?* That was a question she'd have to answer later. "This will sound dumb, and I'm afraid I'm a bit out of practice, but . . . but I pray."

"For inspiration?"

She was encouraged he hadn't shut her down by saying something flip. "For that, but also . . ." She wasn't sure how much she could say without turning him off.

"But also what?" he asked.

She might as well go for it. "I pray that my eyes are opened to see what he wants me to see so I can paint what he wants me to paint."

"He?"

Uh-oh. "You know . . . God."

Lavon stopped his work, his head nodding slightly, pensively, as if she'd said something profound. "Actually, I do. Know God."

She let out the breath she'd been saving. "You do?"

He nodded. "Does it work? Are your eyes opened?"

"Most of the time."

"So your work is inspired by—" he grinned, cupped a hand around his mouth, and whispered—"you know . . . God."

She smiled back. "I wouldn't say that, but—"

"Why not say it?" Lavon screwed the second shelf into place.

"He gave you the gift in the first place, so the fact you're still in touch with him during the entire process has got to please him. And I'm sure he rewards your obedience with inspiration."

She laughed. "I hardly think obedience is involved. *Desperation* is a better term."

Lavon's face was serious. "Wanting to do things God's way is obedience, plain and simple. It's high living."

She found herself looking at him with new eyes. "You have a strong faith." It was a question, as well as an observation.

"I try."

"Only to fail and try again." She suddenly looked away. Why had she put it that way? "Sorry. I was talking about me. I didn't mean to imply—"

"No offense taken at all. Failure is inevitable, and it's obvious by your words you know that."

She shook her head. "Oh, yes, I know that." *Do I ever. Let me count the ways.* . . . Kathy had an odd thought, knew she shouldn't say it aloud, but suddenly found the words coming out anyway. "I really like talking to you, Lavon. You make it easy to talk about things I rarely discuss. I'm really glad you're here in Weaver." It was too direct. Too aggressive. She tried to backtrack. "Sorry. That probably makes me sound like a desperate housewife, making overtures that may seem . . . truly, I'm not trying to flirt. I'm not implying in any—"

His smile was genuine and made his eyes sparkle. "I like talking with you too. With our spouses working so hard and being so totally consumed with their new jobs . . ." His eyes suddenly looked down, and he went back to the shelves. "Now I'm . . . sorry."

In spite of the knowledge they were skirting the edge of forbidden ground, Kathy felt her stomach stitch in a way she found quite pleasant. She looked toward the boy, reluctantly seeking a diversion. "What are you drawing, Malachi?"

The little boy popped to his feet, displaying his picture. "It's a dog."

"A nice one too," Lavon said.

"I like the purple eyes," Kathy said.

Lavon hurried with the last screw on the last shelf. "There. I'm done." He set the completed shelf upright. "Ready to go."

"Thanks so much. One less thing to do." She wanted to shake his hand, or touch his shoulder. . . . Kathy could tell he was avoiding her eyes. She would have liked for them to share another look.

But suddenly in a hurry, Lavon took Malachi's hand, headed toward the door, and gave her a quick salute. "Thanks for the conversation. We'll have to continue it another time."

"I'll look forward to it."

And he was gone. They were gone.

Kathy went back to her organizing work, but her mind was on Lavon. Which led to thoughts of God. And failures of faith. She'd really enjoyed their talk. Too much. She used to have such talks with Ryan and Roy. But lately . . . speaking of failures of faith . . .

She put the shelf in place and filled it with the tools of her trade.

SEVEN

Do not be afraid or discouraged,
for the LORD is the one who goes before you.
He will be with you;
he will neither fail you nor forsake you.

DEUTERONOMY 31:8

Ryan had never been to the Weaver home. He wished Web were with him. But when Mrs. Weaver had called wanting a couple chairs moved to somebody's house, Web had told Ryan to take the city truck and get it done.

There was something about Mrs. Weaver that scared Ryan. She intimidated him—which he found odd considering she was five foot nothing and he was nearly six foot last time he checked. Yet Ryan was smart enough to know that size was only one factor in a person's power over others. Lisa had wielded plenty of power over him and she'd only come up to his shoulder.

For a moment, he realized that if she'd still been alive, she might have been standing on this porch with him. They'd often been sent on errands and chores together. The Dynamic Duo.

He rang the doorbell. Forget that. They wouldn't even be in Weaver if Lisa was still alive.

But then he never would have met Web, and *that* thought saddened him. He was glad Web was in his life. Web was a perk that made the move easier to take.

The door opened but it wasn't the intimidating Mrs. Weaver. It was a pretty girl with short dark hair. She was small, even frail-looking, like she didn't eat enough. "Yes?" she said.

"I'm Ryan Bauer. I've come to get some furniture?"

It was obvious by the look on her face that she knew nothing about it. Ryan tried to remember the details of Web's instructions. "Web said Mrs. Weaver was going to leave a list of furniture for me to bring to Mrs. Osgood's house."

"She didn't tell me, but come in. I'm Jenna. I'm her great-niece. I'm just visiting."

Ryan was immediately struck by the grandeur of the home. The front staircase was massive, almost sculptural. He was used to stairs being stairs, not a work of art.

Jenna had moved into the parlor to the right, to a small desk that was covered with piles of papers. "Auntie has so many projects going I have no idea how she keeps them straight." She stopped looking with a start, as if remembering something. "Let me go check her bedroom. I've noticed she often has slips of paper by her bedside."

She headed for the stairs. Ryan realized he should have mentioned chairs, that the list would have something to do with chairs—two walnut chairs to be exact—but it was too late. Jenna was gone.

He spotted two matching armchairs that had walnut arms and backs. Noting their red-striped cushions, another word from Web's instructions came to mind: *striped*. These must be the ones. He felt bad for making Jenna go all the way upstairs. If only he hadn't been so intimidated by being in the Weaver house, he would have remembered the instructions better. In fact, he didn't need a *list* of the chairs; he was supposed to get a piece of paper with an address on it, showing him where the chairs were supposed to go.

Jenna was going to think he was the stupidest kid. She was looking for a list while she should be looking for an address.

Nothing you can do about that now. Get organized so you can get out of here fast and quit bothering her.

He moved the first chair to the front hall and went back for the second one. It had a box of pictures on it and as he was transferring the box to the couch, he noticed the top one was a head shot of a man in uniform. Black and white. Old-time stuff, but it was definitely, undeniably Web.

Ryan smiled and picked up the photo. Web was handsome, his face unlined, and he had a twinkle in his eyes. Ryan turned the picture over to see if it noted the year. It did. And so much more: *1943: To Maddy, the love of my life. We'll be together soon.*

Web and Mrs. Weaver had been in love? Serious love from the sounds of it. But they'd never married. Had they? From what Ryan knew Web had never married anyone. So what had come between them to change "love of my life" to friend?

The next picture in the pile was of Web—still in uniform— with another man of about the same age, and a younger Mrs. Weaver standing between them. Ryan could see that each man had a hand around her waist, and she was smiling proudly as if she liked being the filling in their sandwich. The other man was wearing a business suit and represented the halfway point between Web's tall and Mrs. Weaver's short. Ryan noticed she wasn't directly in the middle of the sandwich, but was decidedly closer to Web than she was to the other man.

"Found it!" Jenna called. Ryan heard her feet on the stairs, quickly set the box aside, and picked up the second chair.

She came past the chair in the foyer, touching it as she passed. "I see you found them." She pointed to a piece of paper. "*Two red-striped chairs to Agnes Osgood, 387 Chester Street.* I have no idea why she wants these brought there, but I think it's best to not wonder about the whys. 'Just do it' seems to be my aunt's motto. There *is* this card to bring. It says *Agnes Osgood* on the front. I'm assuming you're supposed to give it to her. Do you want some help with these?"

He shook his head, not comfortable with the idea of this weak-looking girl carrying anything of substance. "You could hold the door."

"That, I can do." Jenna followed him outside, carrying the card and the slip of paper with the address on it. "Sorry I can't tell you where Chester Street is. Not that you can get too lost in Weaver."

"You from a big city?"

"Minneapolis. You?"

"Not so big. Eureka Springs, Arkansas."

Her face lit up, changing her from cute to pretty, as her smile filled out her features. "I've been there! I was little, but I've been there. Lots of trees, winding streets . . . my parents and I stayed in a bed-and-breakfast."

"Plenty of all those things there."

She folded the paper in half. "What made you come here? I mean, what made you want to enter the contest in the first place?"

"My younger sister died in a car crash."

"Oh. I'm so sorry."

He shrugged. He never knew what to say.

"So you're here starting over?"

"My parents are."

"And you?"

"I'm along for the ride."

She tapped the paper against her chin, then seemed to remember she still had it. "Here. The card and address."

"Right." He went around to the driver's side of the truck, but stopped to call after her. "You sticking around Weaver for a while?"

"Maybe."

"Maybe we could hang out some time."

She cocked her head. "I'm too old for you, Ryan."

"I'm sixteen."

"And I'm not."

Her age was hard to gauge. Twenty? Maybe up to twenty-three. He'd never been good at such things. "So we can't be friends?"

"If you're looking for a friend, I'm game. Otherwise . . . not to be rude, but I beg you to take your hormones somewhere else. Agreed?"

"Agreed." Actually, he was more than a little relieved.

Within minutes Ryan found Mrs. Osgood's address on Chester Street. He parked out front of the run-down clapboard house that had yellow peeling paint. The chairs seemed much too elegant to belong inside, yet as Jenna said, it was best not to ask why. Just do it.

He went up to the front door, chairless, with just the card. He knocked and a very old woman with stooped shoulders came to the door. She looked at him warily through the screen and didn't even say hello but let him speak first.

"I'm Ryan Bauer. Mrs. Weaver sent me over here with two chairs." He motioned to the truck beyond, then remembered the card. "And this."

"What's Madeline up to this time?"

Until now Ryan had assumed the transfer of the chairs was

planned—and mutually agreed upon, but it was clear Mrs. Osgood knew nothing about it.

She pushed the screen door open enough for Ryan to stand in its wake, holding it open with his back. Then she opened the card, handed him the empty envelope, adjusted her glasses, and read.

She laughed and shook her head, then walked past Ryan to the edge of the porch, peering up at the sky. Then she turned back to Ryan. "Just checking to see if there were any pigs flying around out here."

"Excuse me?"

The woman slipped the card in the pocket of her housedress and patted it. "Never mind, boy. Go get those chairs. It's about time they sat in their proper place, with their rightful owner again."

"They were your chairs?"

"My mother's chairs, sent over from Germany as a wedding present when she and my daddy were married back in 1873."

"How did Mrs. Weaver get them?"

"Oh there's a lot of things the Weaver family *got* from the rest of us. Bad times come, people die, money is needed to survive, and sacrifices have to be made. Nearly killed me auctioning off all my mother's good things, but I had no choice. Always galled me that Madeline ended up with 'em. Them that has gets more, eh, boy?"

"Yes, ma'am."

She seemed to realize she was talking to an innocent. "Sorry to spit my venom on you, Mr. Ryan Bauer. Old feelings fade but never die. But can you tell me why she's suddenly gained a con-science and is giving me back what she got for mere pennies?"

"No, ma'am."

"Guess it doesn't matter. What's mine is mine again. Bring 'em up here, boy. I know the perfect place for 'em."

Joan entered her living room, tossed the junk mail on the couch, and kicked off her shoes, accidentally turning them into missiles. One bounced off the china cabinet, tipping over a vase and making the dishes rattle, and the other narrowly missed the brass lamp on the end table. She checked on the vase and found it broken.

Ira came in from the kitchen and headed upstairs. "The groceries are put away. I'm going to go work."

On what? was her first response, but before she could say something nice, she noticed a small red *S* on the floor near the coffee table.

Joan heard the door of Ira's office click shut.

Confront him. March up those stairs and ask him what in blue blazes it all means.

Though never one to shrink from confrontation, Joan found that today she had no energy for it. Instead, she sank onto the couch and held the *S* with two hands, even though it was no larger than a fingernail. Cutout *S*s. Whatever could it—?

The doorbell rang and Joan regretted not having had time to install curtains on the front windows. With their veil of cover she might have been able to feign invisibility until the visitor went away. But since she could see out and Web Stoddard could see in, and since he waved . . .

Joan answered the door. "Hi, Web."

"Joan. I saw your car. Have you seen the progress at the shop today?"

"Not yet. We just got back from getting groceries." With the sweep of an arm she offered him a chair before plopping onto the couch. "You'll have to excuse me for needing to sit, but my brain and body are oddly fried and frazzled. Still fabulous, but frazzled just the same."

Joan had expected to hear a chuckle and, at Web's silence, looked at him.

He sat. "What's wrong, Joan?"

Her laugh sounded as forced as it was. "Not a thing."

Web gave her the look of a man who'd heard this answer many a time, and knew it was often a lie. "Can I help?" he asked.

His interest was both disconcerting and touching. "No, no. It'll be all right."

He ran his hands up and down his skinny thighs and studied her. "It's said that 'if one person falls, the other can reach out and help. But people who are alone when they fall are in real trouble.'" He nodded once. "I'm here, Joan."

"I'm not falling."

His look was steady.

She made herself more presentable on the couch and realized she was shoeless. Oh well, too late now. She wanted the subject changed. "So. To what do I owe the honor of this visit?"

"Church," Web said. "I've come to invite you to church on Sunday."

"Uh . . . we don't do church. We're Jewish."

"I know. But since we don't have a synagogue in town I thought you might like to come anyway. God is God. And worship is worship. We all have some thanksgiving to do for even being here in Weaver. Yes?"

True, but . . . "Of course, I mean, Ira and I are very grateful to Mrs. Weaver for choosing——"

Web stood. "I'm all for being grateful to Maddy, but I think it's important we get together and thank the one who's really responsible for pulling this off. None of you got here by coincidence, you know. There's no such thing."

She didn't know, but didn't dare ask.

Web put his hands in his pockets. He had such an innocent, unassuming way about him. "We aren't going to shove our beliefs down your throat, Joan. But coming together under God, loving him, turning to him in times of trouble as well as thanksgiving, each in our own way . . . that's a good thing, don't you think?"

He kept asking her questions that shouldn't be hard to answer, but were. "We'll think about it," she said.

"Sounds like a plan." He turned toward the door. "By the way, are you going to celebrate Rosh Hashanah?"

She was shocked.

"It's the Jewish new year coming up in September, isn't it?"

"Well, yes. I'm just surprised you know about it."

"We come from the same roots, Joan. Your Abraham and Moses is our Abraham and Moses."

She didn't know that.

He headed toward the door and she rose to let him out. "I didn't know we had a preacher in town," she said.

"We don't. I'll do the talking until we get someone proper."

Joan couldn't imagine anyone more proper than Web Stoddard, and the thought of hearing a bit of his wisdom was actually quite enticing. But she and Ira in a Christian church? She and Ira having *any* contact with God?

Both were long shots.

After seeing him out, Joan hesitated between couch and stairs. A nap sounded really good. And yet . . . would she be able to rest until the S mystery was solved?

Probably not. Now was the time for answers. No more Mrs. Nice Guy.

But on the stairs, Joan found herself tiptoeing, once again masking her approach. The door to the home office was closed. And worse, latched. There was no reason to close that door. Ever. She heard Ira talking.

Joan put her ear to the door.

"But I have to see you."

See who?

"Please, Sally. I'm not taking no for an answer. I have to see you. If you want me to quit calling then say yes."

Her heart stopped. Sally? The only Sally Joan knew was Sally Burnstein who used to work for Ira at the store in California. He was talking to Sally?

"Great! I knew you'd give in! How about a week from today? Thursday? Joan will probably be at the shop, getting it ready."

At the pointed mention of her absence, Joan put a hand to her chest. She was going to have a heart attack right there in the hall. Her husband would open the door and find her dead body.

And step over it to go get something to eat for dinner.

"One o'clock would be great. I live at—" Sally must have interrupted him because he stopped talking. "No, I don't want to see you in a public place. I wouldn't feel comfortable there. I just wouldn't. Certainly you're not afraid of me?"

She must have agreed because Ira said, "Good, good. The address is 284 Lawrence Lane. I'm so excited to see you. It will be just like old times."

Joan's legs felt like Jell-O. She stepped away from the door so she wouldn't fall against it. *Old times?* The implications were sickening, yet her mind swam with images from the past, trying to link moments and conversations, trying to put two and two together. Hoping it was nothing, yet wondering . . .

She'd never had to pursue it before because Sally had quit and moved away to some place in the Midwest.

Midwest.

Kansas. Topeka.

Joan gasped, and smacked her hand over her mouth to prevent further noise. Sally Burnstein had moved to Topeka, Kansas, which was now one hour away. Ira was on the phone with her. Sally . . . *S*. Sally . . . *S*.

The *S*s stood for Sally?

It was too sickening, too awful to even grasp. Her husband was interested in someone else and they were going to meet in a week and—

She heard noise inside the room and hurried toward the stairs. She descended quickly and quietly, and dove onto the couch just as she heard the door to the office open.

"Joan?"

She pulled the pillow to her cheek, wanting to bite it. "I'm down here."

For now. *You two-timing, unfaithful, conniving . . .*

Yes indeed, her freeloading days were long gone. Jenna's aunt had kept her busy all day, every day, with lists of things to do for the Founders Day event. Her latest assignment had Jenna paused at an intersection, trying to remember her aunt's directions to the police station. *"Turn right at Roscoe Road."* Sure enough, there it was on the right, two blocks up.

It was a one-story structure with a row of yews planted out front. The venetian blinds hung off-kilter in one of the windows. The parking lot could hold only five cars. Two slots were taken by a police cruiser and a silver SUV. Her own car was an eighty-pound weakling compared to this bully.

Jenna pulled into the farthest parking space and got out. She smoothed her khaki skirt and checked that the back of her peach polo shirt was tucked in. In many ways it was silly she'd had to change to do one errand, and her aunt's excuse that she couldn't wear jeans because she was representing the Weaver name didn't ring as true as her comment that this Seth fellow was cute. The last thing Jenna needed was to have a cute guy in her life. A single cute guy. She wasn't interested. Not now or ever. And though she used to be good at fending off the charming ones, she wasn't confident her abilities were still intact. So her plan was to slip in, slip out, and zip home where she could report to Auntie that she'd successfully completed her task.

A tinkling bell on the front door announced her arrival into an oblong room that held two desks and a few file cabinets. A coffee-maker brewed its wares atop a rolling stand. An orange vinyl chair sat next to a small table holding copies of *Field and Stream* and a *Newsweek* that sported Bill Clinton on the cover.

A man in his midtwenties popped out of an office doorway. His surprised, befuddled look made her think of the British actor Hugh Grant. Even his smile . . . "Well now. My first customer. What can I do for you?"

Jenna took a step closer. "I've come to find out how the arrangements for the tables and chairs are going for Founders Day."

"And you are?"

"Oh. So sorry. I'm Jenna Camden. Madeline Weaver's great-niece."

"Great niece, huh? Not just good? Great?"

Jenna couldn't help but laugh. "Great-niece does sound strange, doesn't it?"

"Grandniece wouldn't be any better. I just have one question. . . ."

Her spine stiffened. "What?"

"Where have you been hiding?"

"What?"

"I haven't seen you around—which considering Weaver is only yea big . . ." He spread his arms from here to there.

"I just came into town Sunday. Early."

"Were you at the Meet 'n' Greet?"

She looked out the window where she could see the corner of her car. Her escape. "I was tired. Besides, I'm just visiting."

"So where's real life?"

Since he was a cop she didn't want to say. "Up north."

"Ah. Big place, up north."

Fine. She'd narrow it down a little bit. "Minnesota."

"Swede or Norwegian?"

"Scottish."

"A foreigner. I'm surprised they let you stay."

She didn't want to talk about home anymore.

"So what brings you to Weaver?"

"Like I said, I'm just visiting."

"Seems you have that answer down pat." He nodded toward the coffeepot, which had gone silent but was emitting a wonderful aroma. "Pot's done."

Before she could respond, he was pouring the brew into two mugs. He shook a paper canister. It made chunking sounds. "Powdered, fossilized cream? Sugar?"

"Black is fine."

He handed her a purple mug emblazoned with *Go Wildcats!* "Pure and leaded. That's how I like it too." He headed down a short hall. "Let me show you the heart of this teeming base of operations, where life-and-death decisions are made every day."

"Life-and-death decisions such as . . . ?"

He stood beside his office doorway and let her enter first.

"You are very demanding, Ms. Camden. I'll have to think on that one. Have a chair."

She sat in the seat facing his desk and he sat behind it, holding his coffee with two hands. "Well. This is it. Pretty exciting, don't you think?"

The room was painted off-white with a poster of a mountain range on one wall. A dusty fake ficus tree stood in the corner near the window. "Riveting."

"Yeah, well . . ." He adjusted the shoulders of his police shirt, pushing them back.

"You need a different shirt. That one's too big."

He pulled it out from his chest, accentuating that it was indeed many sizes too large. "Found it in the coat closet. Guess the prior police chief shopped in the big-and-tall department. I have a new one on order." He lifted up one leg revealing his own well-fitting but nonregulation Dockers. "Getting matching pants too."

"Do you get a hat?"

"Could've, but I opted for mirrored sunglasses instead. Do you think that will make me intimidating to the bad guys?"

Her stomach clenched. "What bad guys?"

He sat back in his chair, making it rock. "If you know of any, send them in. It would sure make my job more interesting."

The image of dark eyes too close came to mind. She wanted to go. "Do you have the info about the chairs?"

He pulled out a piece of paper. "The rental and delivery are all set. Here's the agreement."

She looked it over. He'd done his job. And since her job was done, she rose to leave. "I'll be going then."

The bell on the front door tinkled, and she heard Web's voice. "Seth? You here?"

Seth got up and they both went out in the hall. "Back here, Mr. Stoddard."

The old man smiled when he saw them. "Morning, Jenna. Glad to see you out and about."

"Auntie sent me over."

Seth cupped his mouth. "To check up on me. To see if I was keeping the peace properly."

"So?" Web said. "Is the peace kept?"

"So far. Mr. Stoddard, so far."

"You've been here two weeks so the mister stuff has got to go. I'm plain ol' Web—in every sense of the word. Far as I can see, the only mister and missus around here is Madeline."

"Mrs. Weaver to me," Seth said.

"And to everyone," Web said.

"Except you," Jenna said. "You call her Maddy."

He blushed. "She hates that."

"Then why do you do it?" Seth asked.

He peeked at them, then winked. "Because she hates that."

Jenna was amazed that two old people could tease each other like teenagers. Yet there was something poignant about it too.

"So, Web. What's up?"

Web nodded, visibly going through the act of remembering. "Church. I'm going around to personally invite everyone to a service at the Good Shepherd Church on Mavis Street, Sunday at ten."

"We have a pastor?" Seth asked.

"Not exactly. But I've been known to put a few words together—when I feel called to do so."

"You're feeling called?" Jenna asked.

He looked to the ceiling, then nodded. "'Pears so." He turned toward the door. "Love to see you both there. We've got some praising to do; don't you think?"

"Absolutely," Seth said.

Jenna didn't feel much like praising.

"Why don't you two come together, eh?"

Jenna noticed the slightest hint of hesitation before Seth answered. "Sure. Fine by me. Care for a little churchgoing, Ms. Camden?" he asked.

Before she could respond Web said, "That's what I like to see. The fellowship is starting already." He gave them a two-finger salute. "See you there."

As soon as Web left, Jenna instigated her own exit. "I have to go."

Seth stopped the swing of the door with a hand. "You don't mind me asking you to go to church, do you? I haven't gone for a while, and it might be nice to go back."

She couldn't admit her "while" was eons. Her memories encompassed black patent-leather shoes, a white Easter hat, and sitting between her parents with legs dangling from a pew.

Another lifetime. Another Jenna. Another world.

"Come on." His smile was quite convincing. "It'll be fun."

She'd have to take his word on that one. But in spite of her reservations, she nodded. "I'll meet you there."

A little church never hurt anyone. Did it?

Madeline had just gotten out the Cominsky file dating from 1963 when Seth knocked on the doorjamb of her office.

"Officer Olsen. How nice to see you." She closed the file as he entered.

"Sorry to bother you, but I had a call from the rental company for the tables and chairs and there's been a change and I wanted you—"

"Jenna's handling that now. She was over to see you, yes?"

"Yes. This has happened since."

"What do you think of my great-niece?"

He grinned. "She's . . . great."

"Very funny."

He ran the list between two fingers. "She's nice, but seems a bit . . . nervous perhaps?"

Madeline didn't want to go into any details of Jenna's personal business—not that she knew many. "She's having family issues right now."

"I've had a few of those in my day."

Madeline nodded. She'd found the elder Olsens nice enough, though the father, Larry, had been a bit odd for her taste. "How's your mother?"

"Doing okay. I talked to her the other day. She's really excited about me being back in Weaver."

Patrice appeared at the door. "Excuse me, Mrs. Weaver, but a Bennie Davison is here to see you. He says he works for you?"

Madeline stifled a gasp, then looked at Patrice and Seth. Their curiosity was evident.

"I was just leaving," Seth said, turning toward the door.

Madeline forced normalcy into her voice. "Show Mr. Davison in."

Patrice had just turned around to go get the man, when she nearly collided with him. "You can see her now," she said.

"Thanks. 'Preciate it."

With a final glance at Madeline, Patrice went back to work.

Bennie entered, giving Seth a look.

"I'll talk to you soon, Mrs. Weaver," Seth said.

Madeline regained her senses and pointed to the paper in his hand. "You take that over to the house and let Jenna see it, all right?"

"It will be my pleasure."

From the glint in his eye, she wondered just how well her niece and Seth *had* hit it off this morning. Or was Seth such a charmer his eyes sparkled at the opportunity of being with any pretty woman? She found she didn't object to the notion but had other things to worry about at the moment.

"Hold it there, Officer." Bennie turned to Madeline. "Aren't you going to introduce us, Madeline?"

Madeline skipped over the point that she did not approve of this man calling her by her first name, and let her mind focus on the fact that she did not want the entire world to even know of his existence—especially his profession. But there was no way out. "Officer Seth Olsen, meet Bennie Davison. Bennie, Seth."

Bennie gave Seth a business card and shook his hand vigorously. "Nice to meet ya. I used to be a cop. Of sorts."

Seth glanced at the card. "Really?"

"You bet. It was years ago, but——"

Madeline interrupted Bennie. "Compare holster notches on your own time, gentlemen. Personally, I have work to do."

Seth exited, and when Bennie started to sit, Madeline stood. "Let's take a walk."

His eyebrows rose. "Walk? Sure. Whatever you want."

She wanted him out of there. She led him to the exit, telling Patrice she'd be back in ten minutes.

Madeline started to cross the intersection but had to stop for a car that had the green light. Traffic. So much had changed in the last two weeks. Her anger made her breathing labored, but she waited until they were safely in the gazebo to do anything about it. Then she turned on Bennie, her finger pointing. "First, don't ever call me Madeline. It's Mrs. Weaver."

His hands waved her off. "Whoa there. Fine. Whatever you say, Mrs. Weaver."

With the initial outburst released, she glanced around to make sure no one else was within earshot. The park was theirs. She lowered her voice. "Second, I resent your coming into the bank and announcing to the world that you work for me."

He looked toward the bank as if replaying his actions. "But I do. I've done work for the bank for years. For your husband and your father-in-law. We go way back."

"Yes, yes, that was then; this is now."

Bennie still looked confused. "But I've been here before. Recently. I helped investigate the finalists. We've talked in your office."

"That was before people moved in, when it was only myself and a stray teller. That was before I'd hired someone to run the place."

He pinched his nostrils. "Oh. Yeah. I get it. Sorry 'bout that."

What did apologies matter? The damage was done. She was suddenly tired. The weariness was coming more often lately. . . . "I need to sit." They settled on the bench that rimmed the inner edge of the gazebo. "What do you have for me?"

He reached into the inner pocket of his dirt-colored suit and pulled out a notepad. "I've got the address of the Flemings. They're retired in Florida now. Living in a double-wide, though it isn't as bad as it sounds. But it *was* damaged in hurricane Frances, and insurance paid for only part of it. Mrs. Fleming's in a wheelchair as of late, and I found out they're looking to put in a ramp, but if you ask me, there's not much room inside for her to maneuver around in that contraption. The husband must be thinking the same thing because last Saturday, he went to a retirement home and talked to them a long time."

"Is it a nice home?"

He hesitated a moment. "I wouldn't want anyone I knew to live there."

Madeline looked out over the park. "Is there a nicer facility close by? One of those retirement places that have a pretty dining room, planned activities, and a shuttle bus that takes residents around town?"

"Sounds like you've looked into such a place. Surely, not for yourself?"

"Heavens no. But I've had plenty of friends buy into such establishments. I don't want a nursing home for the Flemings. I want a nice residential atmosphere. Well decorated. Airy. Clean. Fun even."

Bennie cleaned one fingernail with another. "There is such a place," he said, looking up, "but it's expensive."

Expense did not matter when it came to paying off one's sins. "Do it."

He raised an eyebrow. "You got it." He put the pages away. "How long do you want to pay for?"

She had sudden thoughts of decades of fees, but forged ahead. "How old are the Flemings?"

"They're both eighty-six."

"Then arrange to get them in and have their fees paid for life."

"That's mighty generous. Probably the most generous situation you've had me handle."

"Yes, well . . ." *Some sins cost more than others.* "I can't take it with me, can I? Just handle it."

He stood. "Anonymously."

"Of course anonymously. You can have the monthly fees taken from the Regrets Only account."

He chuckled. "I still can't get over that name. Real cute."

She flashed him a look. "Just do it."

He licked the tip of his pencil. "And when they ask who's doing this, you want me to give the standard nonanswer?"

"I do."

She needed to get back to the bank. So much to do. So little time.

Bennie flipped his notepad to a fresh page. "You got anything else for me?"

"That's about it. For today and forever, actually."

His head jerked back. "What?"

She'd meant to tell him later, but might as well tell him now. "Very soon our business will be complete and I will no longer need your services."

"What do you mean?"

She stood. "I mean our affiliation is coming to an end."

When he stood he loomed over her. She could smell coffee on his breath. "But I've been working for the Weaver family for decades."

"Every good thing must come to an end."

"But I depend on the income and—"

"You're a resourceful man, Mr. Davison. You'll come up with something. Surely you have numerous clients."

"Of course, but . . ." He shook his head. "You should have told me."

"I think I just did."

"You should have told me sooner. I turned down other opportunities. I—"

"Get them back." She held out a hand, even though the thought of shaking hands with this man was distasteful. "I wish you the best, Mr. Davison."

She walked down the gazebo steps, back toward the bank. When she didn't hear footsteps she turned around to see if he was following.

He was not. He was still in the gazebo but had a cell phone to his ear.

For some reason her stomach grabbed.

Patrice knew she shouldn't snoop, and in all honesty, she hadn't planned on it. But within minutes of Mrs. Weaver's leaving with that overweight man wearing the cheap suit, there had been a legitimate reason to go into her superior's office. And when she'd noticed the file drawer near the door was not only unlocked but standing open a couple inches . . .

She looked into the bank lobby and saw the two tellers chatting about their plans for the weekend. There were no customers to catch her looking in the drawer—though they'd never know she wasn't supposed to be there unless she acted suspicious.

Be confident. Move with authority.

With a final look through the front window where she could see Mrs. Weaver and the man walking toward the gazebo, she opened the drawer farther. Immediately she noted files that spanned many years, many decades. The differences in office supplies—the manila folders and the style of file labels—were subtle but distinctive. Each file had a name on it, and a year: *Anderson 1962, Berchtold 1958, Fleming 1974, Stein 1946.*

With a second glance out the window to check on Mrs. Weaver, she pulled one out.

Stein.

Patrice expected loan papers or account information. But from her quick glance through, the file contained information about a will and stocks. A trust. And the people involved were named Levi and Esther Stein. Address: 284 Lawrence Lane.

Didn't Ira and Joan Goldberg live at that address? Two Jewish families living in the same house in a very non-Jewish town. Interesting.

She checked the gazebo. Mrs. Weaver was coming back.

Patrice ruffled through the papers to make them neat, but paused a moment when her eyes caught sight of some old foreclosure papers. Next was a newspaper clipping, listing the Weaver Mercantile for sale. And then a copy of a sizeable check from the bank written to Levi Stein. Had they defaulted on their loan and the bank bought them out?

And now, once again, a Jewish family owned the Weaver Mercantile that had been owned by another Jewish family? Decades later? Odd.

She slipped the file back in its place and closed the file drawer so it was open two inches. She left Mrs. Weaver's office behind.

But not the questions.

Ryan heard the pop and saw the car in front of him swerve as a flat tire took control. His first thought was *Poor guy*, his second thought was *I should help*, and his third was *At this rate I'm never going to get back to the soda shop to work*.

But thought number two prevailed and Ryan pulled over behind the car. A heavy man in a suit got out, checked the left rear tire, cussed a bit, then kicked it. He looked up at Ryan. "Stupid tire."

Ryan shrugged. "Need some help changing it?"

The man's relief was plain. "There's ten bucks in it if you do. Hate to get my suit dirty."

Ryan couldn't see how a little dirt and grease would hurt the suit that was brown, looked years old, and was already wrinkled, but he was happy for the ten bucks.

"Pop the trunk," Ryan said. He'd fixed a flat tire before. It wasn't that hard.

The trunk came open and Ryan got out the spare and the jack and set to work.

The man took out a handkerchief and wiped his face. "Sure is hot."

"August is like that."

He stopped wiping. "Don't get cocky on me, kid."

Ryan hadn't meant to be rude, but the guy's comment was dumb. "You live here?" Ryan asked.

The man snickered. "No way. I'm a big-city man. I'm just here doing some work for Mrs. Weaver." He pulled out a cell phone and moved toward the front of the car. "I got some calls to make. Do your stuff, kid."

While Ryan worked on getting the lug nuts loose, the man leaned against the car and talked on the phone. "Hey, Melinda. Just checking to see if you had that check ready. Ha. Checking on the check; aren't I funny?"

Ryan removed the last nut.

"The Stoddard one. The one for twenty-five thou."

Ryan dropped the tire iron.

The man looked in his direction, then went back to his call, angling his body enough that Ryan only heard snatches of the conversation. " . . . get it today . . . hit the fan. Seems we're going to have to find another deep pocket."

He glanced at Ryan, who pretended not to listen.

" . . . Adele Simpson . . . *The Probe* . . . a story . . . set up a time . . . also Belinda Purvis at *Who* . . . highest bidder. . . . On what?"

He turned toward Ryan. "Tell you later." He snapped his phone shut. "How you coming, kid?"

The Probe? Who? Ryan had seen those rags at the checkout lines at the grocery store. Full of gossip and stories about weird stuff. Why would this guy who'd mentioned Mrs. Weaver and Web want to talk to them?

Whatever it was, Ryan hoped it wouldn't mean more press people hanging around town. They'd pestered his family for interviews back in Arkansas *and* here in Weaver. His dad had given one and had somehow managed to not even mention Lisa. But more press meant more chances for someone to dredge all that up.

Ryan put the spare tire in place and wiped his dirty hands on his jeans. He wanted to ask the man some questions, but didn't know how to word them. Suddenly, he remembered Web, waiting for him at the soda shop. He looked at his watch. He was late.

"Am I keeping you from something important, kid? Got a girlfriend pining over you somewhere?"

"No," Ryan said. "I just have to get back to my job."

"Then speed it up." The man pulled out a ten and said, "Here's payment. As soon as you finish you can go. I'm heading over to the grocery store for a Coke." He pulled out a business card that said *Bennie Davison Investigations.* "Just in case you ever need my services. Thanks again, kid."

Ryan finished up. Odd. Very odd.

Ryan wasn't completely surprised to see that Web's truck was not parked in front of the soda shop. Ryan was a good half hour later than he'd said he'd be when Web had sent him to the city storage unit for some wood screws. He was wondering what to do when he spotted a note taped to the door. He put the truck in Park and got out to see: *Ryan. Come to the workshop in my garage. Web.*

Luckily, the note didn't sound mad, didn't say *You're late! You're fired!*

Ryan drove to Web's and found him getting his mail out of the mailbox. He immediately thought of the flat-tire man's comment that Web should be getting a check today.

"Hey, young man. Nice of you to join me."

"Sorry. I helped a guy change a flat tire."

Web looked through the mail as he walked to the garage. "No problem. I'm just giving you a hard—" He was looking at a letter.

"What is it?"

"Don't know." He showed it to Ryan. "But it looks like a check."

Sure enough, the envelope was one of those with a window in it, indicating a check. Ryan tried to catch a glimpse of the return address, but Web's hand covered it.

He opened it, then gasped. "Oh my. No. This can't be."

"What can't be?"

"It's a check for $25,000." Web shook the envelope, to make sure it was empty. "There's got to be an explanation. Nobody owes me $25,000."

"Obviously somebody does. Maybe you forgot."

"I would not forget $25,000."

"Who sent it?"

Web looked at the check a second time. "Regrets Only, Inc. I have no idea who that is, what they are. No clue."

The entire flat-tire incident played back in Ryan's mind. Even though *he* had no idea what the odd man in the suit meant by what he said, maybe Web would know. Ryan got out the business card. "This guy—the man I helped with the tire—he talked to someone

back at his office about you getting a check today. 'Stoddard.'
He said, 'Stoddard.' He said, 'Twenty-five thou.'"

Web's eyebrows nearly touched each other as he looked at the
card. "A PI?" He looked up. "Why would this man say this? to
you?"

"He wasn't saying it to me. He was talking on the phone to
someone else." He decided to share the rest of it. "It also sounds
like he's going to be talking to some reporters from *The Probe* and
Who magazines."

"About what?"

Ryan shrugged, trying to put together all the snippets he'd
heard. "He mentioned working for Mrs. Weaver, about having to
find someone else with deep pockets. Do you know what all that
means?"

"Nope. But I know someone who might." Web turned around.
"Let's call it quitting time, Ryan. I'll see you tomorrow."

"Where you going?"

But Web was already getting into his truck.

Madeline answered the front door but had her purse in her hand.
"Web. I only stopped home for a minute. Did we have an appointment? I'm just on my way back to the—"

He took her purse away from her.

"Hey!"

Web made a curlicue with his finger, indicating she should turn
around.

"I have things to do, Web."

He put his hands on her shoulders. "Yes, you do. You need to
talk to me. Now."

Web had never spoken to her in that tone, nor even looked at her with such a frowny face. As she went back inside and let him lead her into the parlor, her mind reeled. Something was up.

When Web sat her on the couch she decided to take the offensive by standing right back up. "Excuse me, Web Stoddard, but this is my house and you have no right to come in here and—"

"Rights?"

Just the way Web said it made Madeline shiver. It took all her energy not to sit back down. She glanced toward the stairs and wished Jenna would come interrupt.

"You have some mighty explaining to do, Madeline Weaver."

Now *that* was an understatement. Suddenly, Madeline's body betrayed her and she sank onto the cushion, steadying herself with a hand. So much for strength.

As soon as she physically gave in, Web was suddenly attentive and concerned. He sat beside her, perched on the edge of the couch so his right leg touched her left one. He put a hand on her knee. "Maddy?"

She pushed her way to standing again, moving to a wing chair, putting a coffee table between them. "What do you want, old man?"

"Are you okay? You looked a bit weak right then."

She snickered. "Me? Weak? Surely you jest."

He looked skeptical but went on. "What do you know about a company called Regrets Only?"

Madeline's heart flipped. "Dumb name."

"We're not discussing the name, but who they are."

"I—"

"And what connection they have to you."

This was it. Out of the blue, on an ordinary afternoon, a lifetime of careful work would unravel. She'd expected more warning than this. "Web, I really don't—"

He pulled out a check and handed it to her. The check for $25,000—that she had authorized. But how had he found out she was connected to Regrets Only?

She decided to act innocent, something she'd perfected over sixty years of trial and error. "Nice check. What's it for?"

"You tell me."

"How should I know?"

"The existence of a certain man named Bennie Davis implies different."

Pooh. He knew too much to feign ignorance any longer. "Davison."

"What?"

"Bennie Davison."

"So you admit you know him?"

She was too old for this, for thinking fast like this. Yet she knew part of the truth often sufficed for the whole. "Bennie's done odd jobs for the bank for decades. Augustus and his father used him a few times."

"Used him?"

"He's almost a lawyer. Started his own investigation company. They'd have him check people out. Potential customers."

"And he was in town because . . . ?"

She shrugged, trying to act casual. "You know I had the contest winners looked into before I let them win."

"He did that?"

She nodded once. "Just came to be paid."

Web looked down at the check. "He was paid, but why . . . why this?"

Madeline took a deep breath and let it out. "The check came from me, all right?"

"But Regrets Only . . ."

"It's just a name. You knew my mother. She was a stickler for etiquette, so I named a side business Regrets Only as a private joke—in her honor." *Liar, liar, pants on fire.*

Web held the check between his hands. "Side business? As if you don't have enough to do? And why are *you* sending me a check for $25,000?"

Madeline moved to her desk, pretending to organize a few papers. She couldn't look at him for this last lie. "It's a present, plain and simple. Call it a job bonus if you want. I knew you wouldn't take it if you knew it was from me, so I had it sent through the Regrets Only account."

"And you thought I'd actually cash it without knowing where it came from?"

She hadn't thought of that. "I hoped you would."

"Well, I won't."

She looked at him. "But now that you know it's from me . . ."

"I still won't cash it." He crossed the room and put the check on her desk. "I don't need $25,000, Maddy."

"But you deserve it." *And oh so much more.*

He shook his head adamantly. "Give it to charity. Buy the town something special. I'm fine. I have all I need."

They looked at each other, then looked away.

"Almost all I need."

Oh dear. She couldn't deal with *that* right now. She had so much to contend with. Too much. She walked to the foyer. "I'm sorry you don't want the check, Web. I meant well."

His huffing and puffing was over, and he put an arm around her shoulder and kissed the top of her head. "I know you did." When she opened the door he said, "You said you have things to do. Can I drive you somewhere?"

"I'll go later." There was no way she could go anywhere right now.

As soon as she heard the sound of his truck fade away, she slumped onto the front stairs, completely spent.

"Auntie!" Jenna rushed down the stairs.

"Get me upstairs."

"Are you all right?"

"I'm just tired. Get me to bed. I'll be fine."

If only it were true.

Web drove into his driveway and shut off the engine. In the silence that followed, he gripped the steering wheel and leaned his head against his hands.

She's lying. Web didn't know how Maddy was lying, or why, but he knew there was a lot more to the check than a bonus, or even a present. Why now? Why $25,000? Why hide it? Maddy had never been one to do things anonymously. She liked the gratitude that came from giving generously and receiving appreciation.

Something was going on. Something big. Something *not* good. And it went way beyond Maddy being upset that the town of Weaver had nearly died. She'd handled that. The contest was a success. People were adapting, getting along, making new lives. Weaver would come out of this better than it was before. Stronger for the struggle.

Yet he also knew that the more he pushed her into an explanation, the more she'd parry. Whatever was going on was obviously important enough to his dear Maddy to make her keep it from him.

And *that* hurt.

He went inside the house he'd lived in since he was born, the house he'd lived in alone his entire adult life. As the door shut behind him, as the overhead light revealed the wear and tear of an aging bachelor pad, he realized he could have used that $25,000 to make some improvements to this place.

But why? And for whom?

He went to the kitchen to open a can of soup.

Ryan's father met him on the porch. "Where have you been all day?"

Ryan slid past him, went inside. "Out."

His father followed him inside. Ryan smelled meat loaf. "Your mother and I need to know where you are. You can't just be *out*. You have to leave us a number where you can be reached."

They didn't used to ask him where he was going, and Ryan hated the extra scrutiny. "I can't. I move from location to location."

"You what?"

Ryan paused on the stairs. "I wasn't *out*; I was working. Earning money. For college." Even though Ryan wasn't sure he wanted to go to college, he knew his father wouldn't argue because *he* thought college was the most important thing in the world. Typical doctor.

"Working for whom?"

Ryan sighed deeply. He hadn't wanted to play this card yet, but he'd never get upstairs if he didn't calm his dad. "I've been working for Mrs. Weaver, okay? Odd jobs. Wherever she needs me. I'm perfectly safe."

"Oh. Well then . . ."

"Can I go now?"

His father looked at the floor absently and nodded, then suddenly shook his head. "No. Dinner's almost ready. I made meat loaf."

"Where's Mom?"

"In her studio. She's painting. She doesn't want dinner."

Neither did Ryan, but the pitiful look on his father's face made him give in. "What's for dessert?"

His father's face beamed. "Chocolate cake."

Families were too much work.

Kathy stepped back and studied her painting. The little boy hunkered down looking at the caterpillar was nearly finished, though the shadows splaying behind him needed work. Maybe if she conned Ryan into getting into the same position she could get it right. Sure he was much bigger than her subject, but the essence of the shadow would be the same.

She looked outside, checking on the sunlight—and was shocked to see it was dark. When had that happened? She looked at the clock and ended up staring at it. No. It couldn't be 9:50. No way. The last time she'd checked was when Roy had come to tell her he was making dinner.

A dinner she'd declined to attend.

Kathy hurriedly cleaned her brushes, walked the path between studio and house, and slipped in the kitchen door. All was quiet. She spotted Roy sitting at the dining-room table, medical journals spread before him. His head was in his arms, asleep.

She moved to wake him, then stopped herself. He'd get after her not only for skipping dinner but for spending all evening in her studio, oblivious to him and Ryan. A more appealing alternative was to tiptoe upstairs and get into bed. Pretend she'd been there for ages. Talk to him in the morning.

She quietly went upstairs and saw that Ryan's door was closed. And suddenly, the silence of the house was heavy. Kathy never thought she'd miss Lisa's stereo, the sound of her running up and down the stairs, or her constant giggling.

But she did.

She went into the master bedroom and created some noise by turning on the TV. Mindless, mind-numbing noise was better than the convicting thoughts that lived in the silence.

Ryan sat on his window seat and looked out on the night. Though only a thin pane of glass stood between home and the outside, the division seemed far thicker . . . stronger. When he was on his own tooling around town in the city's truck, he was free. He was his own man, and he, Ryan Bauer, was making friends, doing well, and contributing. But here, within the confines of this house, he was a prisoner who could do little more than exist.

The tension that had strangled his family since Lisa's death continued even here in this new house. Conversations were comprised of short sentences, with his dad trying too hard, his mom caught up in her own little world, and himself with little desire to make it any different. The tension had become a habit and even though he knew they'd come to Weaver hoping to break that habit, Ryan couldn't see it happening.

He was living two different lives: one, normal and friendly among the outside world, and the other closed off and sullen in the midst of his family. It wasn't right, but he wasn't sure how to change it.

He turned the wand on the blinds, making the outside disappear, then reappear like a slide show. Blank . . . real life. Blank . . . real life. He left the blinds shut, accepting the inevitable separation from the outside world.

"You have been set apart for God. You have been made right with God because of what the Lord Jesus Christ and the Spirit of our God have done for you."

"First Corinthians six, eleven," Ryan said aloud.

He looked across the room at his books. His well-used Bible lay on the bottom shelf with a snow-globe paperweight of the St. Louis Arch sitting on top. Holding it down. So it didn't go anywhere.

I'm here waiting for you. I didn't leave.

"Yes, you did." Ryan hadn't meant to talk out loud, and when he realized he'd addressed the Bible across the room as if it were God himself . . .

He tossed away the wand from the blinds, making it rattle against the metal slats. He got up from the window seat and went to the shelf, looking down at this book that was supposed to be the instruction book for life.

He lowered his voice to a whisper, but the intensity was still present. "You left Lisa. You made her leave me." He jabbed a finger toward the Good Book. "You don't mention anything about that in there. You never tell people you're going to kill them off when they're young, or rip out the hearts of their family left behind. You talk about love and faith and how good it can be, but . . ."

Ryan hadn't realized he'd started to cry, and he angrily wiped the tears away. The next words were spat through clenched teeth. "You lied!"

Suddenly, he couldn't stand the sight of it. The Bible mocked him by its very presence. He squatted before it with his chest heaving, removed the St. Louis paperweight to clear a path for whatever act of destruction would come next.

If he'd been brave he would have thrown it out.

But he couldn't. He just couldn't.

He didn't want to even touch it.

This life in Weaver was a blank, empty page. Yet, maybe blank was better than the past pages that were full of scrawls, scribbles, and cross outs. Pages ripped and bent. Yellowed. Water stained.

Blank was better than that. The trouble was, he had no idea how to fill the page, and until he did . . .

Ryan went to his dresser and picked up a magazine. He opened the pages wide, then returned to the Bible on the shelf and placed the opened magazine on top of the Bible, with the back half falling down toward the floor creating a curtain, covering the book. He placed the paperweight on top, holding it in place.

He stepped back. It looked ridiculous, yet he felt better now. Safer.

As he got in bed an old Paul Harvey line came to mind: *"You can run, but you can't hide."*

He pulled the covers up under his chin.

EIGHT

Human plans, no matter how wise or well advised,
cannot stand against the LORD.

PROVERBS 21:30

Seth jogged through the rows of corn, the drying stalks cutting at his arms. He wasn't sure Bonnie ran every day, or that his presence would be welcome.

This whole thing was a risk. But one he had to take.

It had taken him all week to get up the nerve to make another early morning appearance through the corn. This morning, to make sure he had no excuse not to go, he set his clock radio to an incredibly loud level, awakening to Elvis singing "Jail House Rock." No one could sleep through Elvis.

Seth saw the opening to the farmyard at the end of the row and slowed his pace, not wanting to appear too winded. Or too eager. He had slowed to a stroll by the time he came through the field into the yard. Bonnie wasn't around. Had he missed her? He glanced at the kitchen window. He didn't want Mrs. Bowden to spot him in her yard again. Not wearing shorts, a Denver Broncos T-shirt, and running shoes. He was prepared to explain his presence to Bonnie but not to her mother.

The door to the kitchen opened and Bonnie came out—wearing running clothes. She smiled. "Well, well. If it isn't Officer Olsen,"

He jogged in place. "I was in the neighborhood."

"Did you think that one up all by yourself?"

He ran toward the main road. "You coming?"

She followed.

Ha.

She followed.

Victory.

Patrice headed downstairs to get some coffee when she heard a quick rap on their front door. But before she could answer it, the door opened and a man came in carrying a baby.

"Oops. Did I scare you?" the man said, nearly running into her.

"Who are you?"

The man blinked. "I'm Brent Martin. This is Wendy. I talked to Lavon yesterday and he agreed to babysit while I'm at work at the grocery store. He said I could just walk in, but maybe I should have—"

Lavon came in from the kitchen and zeroed in on the baby. "Hey, schnookums." The little girl grinned and let Lavon take her.

Brent kissed his baby's hand, then said, "I'll pick her up around six."

"No problem," Lavon said.

According to whom? Patrice moved to get coffee. Malachi pushed past her as if she didn't exist, coming from the kitchen, heading to the baby.

"A new one! Put her down! I want to play with her," he said.

There was another knock and the door opened a second time. It was the woman who ran the café. Some Mexican last name. She had two little girls with her, identical twins, one in a pink sunsuit, the other in green.

"Morning, ladies," Lavon said. He ruffled the hair of both girls at the same time. They were about three. "You ready to play, Paulina? Constanza?" He pointed to the corner by the rocker. "I got out some special blocks just for you."

With one last look at their mother, the twins ran to the blocks, totally at home.

The mother said hello to Brent, then stepped toward Patrice. "I keep meaning to introduce myself. I'm Maria Lopez. I run the café with my husband. You work at the bank, right?"

"I'm the vice president."

"Come over for lunch sometime. Diego makes a great chili relleno that consumes the plate as well as the biggest appetite."

No way. She'd already had enough of the café's constant aromas wafting into the bank. "Thanks, but I usually skip lunch." She caught Lavon's look of disapproval. *Whatever.* "I need to get breakfast."

Malachi jumped up. "Breakfast!" He turned to the three little girls. "Do you want waffles or dirt?" All but the baby rushed past Patrice.

"Dirt?" Brent asked.

"Don't worry. It's an ongoing joke. And no one can resist my waffles." He looked at Patrice. "Right, lovey?"

"If you'll excuse me." She escaped into the kitchen. Which was crowded with children—not her own. She poured herself a mug of coffee and waited for her husband to enter.

He did. Carrying the baby. The three older kids were taking over the booth. Malachi's old high chair sat in the corner.

"There now," Lavon said after getting the baby strapped in. "Waffle time!"

The children squealed and clapped.

Patrice pulled her husband's arm, getting him away from his fans. "What's going on here?"

"I'm making breakfast for the kids."

"Exactly. The kids. I knew you were taking care of twins, but I thought it was temporary. And not first thing in the morning. Now, a baby?"

"Brent needed a sitter so I agreed."

"Without talking to me?"

He opened a cupboard and got out the pancake mix and oil. "You're not home during the day. Why should it matter to you?"

Indeed. "I hate you being stuck here all day. How do you get any work done?"

He put the red mixing bowl on the counter and got out measuring cups. "This *is* my work."

She laughed.

He did not.

"Lavon, you can't be serious."

"Why not?" He measured out three cups of mix. "In case you haven't noticed, I'm good with kids. They like me and I like them."

"But surely this isn't enough."

He put his hands on her shoulders, forcing her to look right at him. "I think we need to reassess our definition of *enough*, Patrice. We have no house payments. You have a good job. Our cost of living is low. Our needs are being met."

"Your needs."

He cocked his head. "What does that mean?"

She pulled away from his grip, running her hands over her hair. "I don't think this is going to work. The town's too small, it's too . . ."

"Perfect?"

She laughed. "Hardly."

"Don't you like your job at the bank?"

"There's not enough work to keep me busy. We have two tellers who stand around talking most of the day; Mrs. Weaver hangs around working on secret files and—"

"Secret files?"

She waved away his words. "The point is . . ." She took a fresh breath, giving herself time to find a way to describe this vague feeling of unease. She thought of something. "We don't belong here."

"Daddy? Waffles?" Malachi said.

He went back to the counter and took up his mixing duties. "Maybe you don't belong here, but we certainly do."

She huffed.

He ignored her and turned to the kids. "Now . . . who can make a sound like a waffle bird?"

Patrice sat at her desk, staring at her trash can—her very full trash can that needed emptying. She tried to remember if she'd seen anyone doing such chores.

She glanced at the carpet nearby. It needed vacuuming.

Certainly they had a cleaning service. Or at the very least, someone assigned to do such things.

You do it.

No way. The vice president of a bank did not empty the trash or vacuum the floor. She didn't even want to think about the restrooms.

Her eyes returned to the trash and a different thought emerged. Patrice thought of Mrs. Weaver's secret files. The older woman was constantly going through that file cabinet by the door. Did she ever throw away anything that might be interesting?

She found herself standing, looking toward Mrs. Weaver's office.

No. If she was too good to empty the trash, she certainly was too good to rifle through it.

However . . .

With a quick check of the time, she walked into her boss's office. She had ten minutes, tops, before Mrs. Weaver showed up for the day. She did not turn on the light. The morning sunshine would have to be enough. Patrice went behind the desk and pulled the black wastebasket from the leg opening. It was plenty full. She placed it on top of the desk and began going through it. She noticed a distinct increase in her heart rate, but wasn't sure if it was because of her gumption or in anticipation of what she might discover.

Her eyes zeroed in on what looked to be a copy of a contract with Hillside Home. In Florida? What was Mrs. Weaver doing with that? Certainly she didn't have real estate in Florida.

Patrice expertly breezed past the nonessential parts and zoned in on the names: Bert and Agnes Fleming. Wasn't that one of the names in the file cabinet behind the door? But the name under the blank sign-on-the-dotted-line said: *Representative, Regrets Only, Inc.* What did any of this have to do with bank business?

The lights turned on. "What are you doing?"

Mrs. Weaver stood in the doorway. How long had she been there? *Calm. Calm.* Patrice let the contract slide back into the trash. "Morning, Mrs. Weaver. I was just emptying the trash cans."

"Hmm."

Patrice carried the wastebasket toward the door. "We don't have a cleaning service, do we?"

"No."

"That's what I thought. That's why I'm doing it." Patrice wanted to leave, but Mrs. Weaver stood in the doorway and didn't seem in any hurry to let her pass. *Please let me go. Please.*

Patrice couldn't look her in the eyes knowing her own were notoriously revealing. She felt Mrs. Weaver's gaze boring into her.

"I think it's time we have a little chat, Patrice."

Uh-oh. Patrice knew from experience what that meant. A dressing-down, a hand slap, or at the very worst, a firing.

But no. She wouldn't be fired. Mrs. Weaver had chosen *her* to be her heir apparent. She'd moved her here, all the way from NYC. And Patrice hadn't really done anything wrong. She was just trying to learn the business.

Mrs. Weaver settled behind her desk, and Patrice sat in one of the guest chairs. "I think we need to address an attitude problem, Patrice."

Patrice felt a surge of relief. Obviously, Madeline hadn't seen her going through the papers. She played the part of the good employee. "Yes, Mrs. Weaver?"

"I sense that something is missing from you."

"Excuse me?"

"You have a position of power here in the bank, Patrice, and ultimately in this town. But with power comes the need for respect."

Patrice nodded, understanding completely. The people of Weaver needed to respect her.

"That's something you've got to earn from them and give to them."

Patrice needed to respect *them?*

Madeline leaned forward on her desk. "It's something you'll never get until you quit treating these people like scum on your shoe because they don't come from the big city *and* they have the gall to be white."

Patrice gasped. "I am not prejudiced and I resent—"

"Resentment. Now, there's another problem." Madeline sat back. "Ever since I first met you you've oozed resentment. You resented entering the contest, you resented being interviewed, you resented Weaver being in the middle of the country, and once you won, you resented moving here."

This is ridiculous. "So why did you let us win?"

Madeline considered this a moment. "I liked your husband. Lavon is a good man, the kind of man we need here in Weaver."

"He babysits." Patrice's voice was thick with disdain.

"For now. And maybe that's all he'll ever do here. But I saw a spark in Lavon's eyes that's totally missing in yours. It's not something I can define, but it tells me he's the kind of person I want around Weaver because he won't let himself fail."

"I won't let myself fail either," Patrice said.

"I'm glad to hear it. And I'm counting on it." She paused just a moment. "Have you made any friends here in Weaver, Patrice?"

Patrice had reached her limit. She stood. "If you'll excuse me? I have work to do."

Madeline's eyes twinkled. "Oh that's right. The trash."

Patrice felt her jaw clench, but retrieved the trash can. She'd started this . . . she headed for the office door.

"And Patrice? Get the trash behind the teller stations too, all right?"

Touché.

It continued to be a bad morning. Patrice got the trash emptied but then Madeline asked if she would vacuum.

Fine. If it would earn her brownie points, she'd do it. She even cleaned the tiny lunch area and the restrooms. One of the tellers had said, "I'll do that, Mrs. Newsom." But Patrice declined the offer. At this point, she had to do it herself. And she had to have Mrs. Weaver see her do it.

Patrice believed she'd earned her way back into Madeline's good graces when Madeline dropped a shopping list on Patrice's desk.

"Just a few needed supplies. Will you take care of it?"

"Sure."

But as she put the list in her purse she noticed the item that was listed first—in letters larger than the rest.

Paper shredder.

It wasn't over.

After his run with Bonnie, Seth was idling on high. Things were progressing nicely and his second trip through the corn had paid off. On their run, Bonnie's wary chip on her shoulder had dislodged and they'd had a good time. She'd even agreed to go out to dinner with him tonight. Unfortunately, she'd rejected his idea of driving an hour into Topeka because she had to get up early tomorrow to help check the irrigation system, so they were only going to the Salida del Sol, but that was better than nothing. One step at a time.

Once at work, feeling quite victorious, Seth decided to delve into the Bennie Davison issue. Although he had nothing to go on besides the odd feeling he'd gotten when they'd met in Madeline's office, Seth had long ago learned to pursue such feelings. He settled in front of the lone computer in the main room and put Bennie's business card front and center. The Internet was an amazing thing, and having police access to some additional sites soon led him to the information he was after.

Not that it pleased him.

Benjamin Davison had been arrested in Illinois for assault, illegal wiretapping, and various lesser offenses. He'd been in jail nine months. As far as Davison Investigations? Seth was slightly surprised to discover that it *was* a legitimate business, registered in Kansas, although Bennie himself was not a registered PI. Yet oddly, the business listed no street address. Just a post office box. At best, it sounded unprofessional. At the worst, shady.

Either way he didn't like having Bennie Davison around town. But what could he do? Davison was doing some work for Mrs. Weaver. Seth was only in Weaver because of her generosity. He couldn't rock that boat.

But he could certainly keep a close watch on it.

I'm doing what I'm supposed to be doing.

Joan sat at her desk in the back office of what soon would be Swenson's Soda Shoppe and checked another item off her to-do list. The morning had been very productive: she'd ordered the tables and chairs, found a source for the food supplies, and had checked on her previous order for the glassware and dishes. None too soon, because Mrs. Weaver wanted all the stores and businesses ready to open in time for the Founders Day celebration—which was in two weeks. It was going to be tight, but Joan would get it done. She actually thrived working under pressure. Which she now had—in spades.

But the challenges of starting a business paled when compared to her newest challenge of facing Ira's infidelity. Considering how much she'd thought about it since overhearing his phone conversation with Sally last night, stewing and worrying had become a full-time job.

In spite of her intense desire to have it out with him in a first-rate ruckus, she'd decided to lay low and pretend everything was normal—until next Thursday at one, when she would hide in the house to witness the secret rendezvous between Sally the floozy and her husband the creep.

Ryan appeared in the doorway, interrupting her plan of revenge. "Mrs. Goldberg?" He held up a stack of photos. "These were stuck in the back of a drawer in the counter."

Joan scanned through the set, which were photographs, black and white with white borders.

"They look really old," Ryan said.

From the fashions and the cars, the photos looked to date back to the thirties and forties. The top photo was immediately recognizable. "Here's the gazebo," Joan said. "And will you look at those dresses. And hats with gloves. It's got to be the forties."

Ryan pointed at the next one. "This one's of the bank. It hasn't changed much at all. But the cars sure have."

This was wonderful. Seeing Weaver at an earlier time was an amazing experience. There was a photo of a band concert in the gazebo, a rose-planting ceremony, and a picture of a manger scene in front of the town hall. She'd have all of them framed. They'd be a perfect addition to the décor of the—

Joan had reached the last photo. It, more than any other,

grabbed her full attention. "Oh my . . ." She held the picture close. It was of the building they were in now. A Weaver Mercantile sign extended across the entire storefront and a sign for Soap 5¢ graced the window. Out front was a gathering of people. The way they had their arms around each other, holding babies and the hands of children, it appeared to be a family. "It's the store!"

As she was looking at it, Ryan lifted the edge. "There's writing on the back."

Joan turned it over. It was a listing of the names of the people in the picture. How nice. Yet it was the heading that caught her attention: *The Steins 1943.*

Her heart skipped. She looked at the picture a second time, alternating between the list of names and the faces. "Levi, Samuel, Mazel, Sadie, Esther . . ." She knew those names. Her eyes were drawn to the white dress of the baby on the front row. It had dark polka dots.

Red polka dots.

Red? It was a black-and-white photo. Why would she think— know—they were red?

Joan looked past the dress and to the child's face. Although it was a little blurry—as if the rambunctious little girl had moved just as the photo was being taken—Joan could see . . . she could tell . . .

She pointed to a child in the front row. "I think this baby is me!"

Ryan moved close and they looked at the picture together. "Are you sure?"

She turned the photo over and found her name. "It is! It says Joan. And Zara . . . she turned the picture around and recognized her mother. "This is my mother! I have this dress in a box of old things my mother gave me. It has red polka dots and smocking at the top." She held the picture up for Ryan to look. "See?"

"Where's your dad?"

Joan scanned the faces. She didn't see him, then remembered. "He fought in the war," she said. "In the Philippines. He didn't come home until 1945. This is 1943."

"So you were here?" Ryan asked. "In Weaver?"

"Apparently." Joan's eyes grazed over the faces of her family. "I obviously don't remember being here for this picture. Actually, I don't remember being here—ever. I grew up in Indiana." She looked at the list of names. "But I know the names are family."

"Wow. You were here. That's weird," Ryan said.

Indeed it was. Joan tried to make one plus one equal two. It was complicated by the fact that there were larger implications than merely finding a family photo. Her extended family had owned the Weaver Mercantile—the store she was sitting in right now. "This is such a bizarre coincidence."

"There's no such thing."

Web had made the same comment. And now, Ryan said it with such certainty, she was forced to look at him. "Of course there is."

Ryan shook his head. "You being here now when your family was here before . . . that's gotta be part of a plan."

"Who says?"

He hesitated, then said, "God."

Joan chuckled and held up the picture. "God arranged this connection?"

"Well, yeah." He looked as if he wanted to say more, but instead started to step toward the door. "I really need to get back to work."

She reached out and snatched the sleeve of his T-shirt. "No you don't, bucko. You don't make a comment like that and leave."

He stayed, but hung near the door, out of reach. "I don't know what you want me to say. It's just something I believe."

"That God brought us here because my family was here before."

He shrugged. "How else do you explain it?"

Joan opened her mouth to speak, but found she had nothing to say. "Why would God want us here?"

"I dunno."

She wagged a finger at him. "Don't hold out on me now, Ryan Bauer. You started this; you finish it."

He shoved his hands in the pockets of his jeans. "I just know he's got a plan and somehow everything fits."

"How?"

"I dunno."

"That's not a good answer."

He shrugged again and looked toward the main room as if he longed for escape. "Just 'cause we don't understand it—or even like it—doesn't mean there's not a plan."

Joan suddenly remembered that Ryan had lost a sister in a car accident. Surely he couldn't think *that* was part of some divine plan. She wanted to ask, but it wasn't something she felt she could bring up.

Ryan crooked a thumb toward the main room. "Web's expecting me to finish putting a coat of varnish on the oak before noon."

"Fine. Go for it. Thanks for bringing me the pictures."

He nodded and was gone.

Joan sat at the desk and stared at the picture of her family. It didn't make sense. Such coincidences did *not* happen. What could it mean?

Yet Ryan's words returned to her: *"How else do you explain it?"* She couldn't.

But as Joan took a second look at the photo of the bank, she thought of someone who could.

"Mrs. Weaver?"

Madeline looked up from her work to find Joan Goldberg standing in the doorway of her office.

"A moment of your time?" Joan asked.

Madeline hated the twitch in her stomach. "Come on in. How's the shop coming?"

"Very well. I had a few doubts about taking on a new enterprise after being retired but—"

"I didn't."

"Excuse me?"

"I had no doubts about you. You're much too young to be retired. It's a waste of talent for women like us to be idle."

Joan smiled. "Women like us?"

A slip of the tongue, but also a truth. Madeline shrugged.

"I assume you're referring to more than our over-fifty status?" Joan asked.

"An inconsequential."

Joan's eyes were bright as if she were deciphering an especially delectable riddle. "I know! You're referring to our vibrant intelligence and our effervescent superiority over all things dull and mundane."

Madeline smiled. She liked this woman. A lot. "Plus our astounding beauty."

"Ah yes. Can't forget that." Joan winked, set her elbows on the armrests, and clasped her hands across her middle. "We Weaver women are really something, aren't we?"

Weaver women. Madeline liked the term. "That's what I was counting on, getting women like you back in town."

"Back in town . . . interesting you should say that because I have something to show you." She reached into her oversized purse, pulled out a black-and-white photo, and handed it to Madeline.

Madeline recognized the Weaver Mercantile immediately. But when she saw who was standing so proudly in front of it . . .

"That's my family," Joan said. "That baby in the polka-dot dress is me. Dredging up other old memories, I think my aunt and uncle owned the store. The Steins?"

Madeline's mind swam. The only comment or question she could think of sharing was "Where did you get this?"

"Ryan found it and some other photos in the back of a drawer."

Madeline nodded. She had no idea where this conversation would—or should—lead. She looked down at her desk. Paperwork. She could use it as an excuse. "I believe the Steins did run that store. Now, if that's all, I'm really busy and—"

"But don't you think it's amazing? That out of all the entrants for the contest I end up being chosen to take over an old family property?"

She wished Joan would leave. "Yes, well . . ."

Joan suddenly clicked her teeth together, then leaned forward. "Ryan said it wasn't a coincidence. I didn't believe him at first, but . . ."

Madeline sat back, creating distance.

"Well?" Joan said.

Madeline sighed. "Women of vibrant intelligence, indeed."

Joan sat back too. "So the kid was right?"

All Madeline had admitted was that she'd chosen the Goldbergs for a reason. With a start she realized she didn't have to *reveal* the reason. She smiled, chose a pencil as a prop, and began the lie. "When I first saw your maiden name on the list and it said your husband was in the retail business, I remembered the Steins and wondered if there was a familial connection." *A familial connection. Good. Good.*

"When did they leave Weaver?"

"A long, long time ago." She gave a cursory glance to the picture. "Soon after that picture was taken, I think."

"Why did they leave?"

Without meaning to, Madeline glanced at the file cabinet by the door. She looked away. "I don't remember." She nearly added that she was too young, but she hadn't been. In fact, she'd been old enough to be a part of . . . it.

Joan looked down at the picture. "It's so amazing to think that somehow we got back here, in the family business."

"In their house too." Madeline hadn't meant to say that, but immediately realized it wouldn't hurt for them to know. Best tell a few available truths so the truth that was unavailable, unsharable . . .

Joan's hand flew to her chest. "We have their house?"

"The very one."

"That is so incredible. Ira will be stunned."

When Joan got up to leave, Madeline nearly congratulated herself on getting safely through the meeting when—

"Did you choose us because you thought we were the best people for the positions or because I was a Stein?"

A loaded question. "Both." Madeline added, "You earned your way here through your essay and the interview, but I will say the possibility that you were related to the previous Steins was a point in your favor."

Joan cocked her head, and Madeline sensed another question coming on. "Why didn't you ask us during the interview if we'd had relatives here? Or tell us, if you knew."

Madeline's incoming breath went out before it achieved fruition and she was forced to take a fresh one. "I wanted it to be a surprise," she finally said. *Lame. Very lame.*

"It is that." Joan shook Madeline's hand across the desk.

"Thanks so much, Mrs. Weaver, for everything, even the extra consideration."

"My pleasure."

At the door Joan paused. "When were you going to tell us?"

For the first time during the entire conversation Madeline found she could be entirely truthful. "I hadn't figured that out yet."

"Actually, it worked out pretty well, don't you think?"

As well as could be expected. Considering.

Joan drove home to tell Ira the amazing news that they'd won the contest because of the Goldberg-Stein link. It made her feel special, as if the roots that had once been yanked out of the Weaver ground could be replanted.

It also might push the Sally issue into the background. Maybe if Ira started to feel as if he belonged here because of some deep historic destiny, he'd let go of this absurd connection he was trying to rekindle with Sally. Not that Joan forgave him his indiscretion— whatever it entailed. If only she knew more details about their past relationship. If only he wasn't acting so odd. So needy.

Although Joan hated sexism in all its forms, she'd discovered through her years of working with kids that a male's ego and self-esteem were every bit as fragile as a female's. Often more so. Luckily, she'd never suffered from lack of self-worth, nor questioned her ability to be what she wanted to be. Not that Ira had filled her boat with compliments and attagirls. After years of trying to shame him into showing interest in the details of her life, she'd decided if she got affirmation from *somebody*, it counted. Even if that *somebody* wasn't her husband. So she'd surrounded herself with a few good women friends who listened and praised and hugged at all the needful moments in her life.

In turn, not wanting Ira to have to look elsewhere for an ego boost, she'd tried to be interested and supportive of him. Tried. But had she failed? Is that why he'd bonded with Sally? Did Sally give him what Joan had not?

Arriving home, she handily put that bit of self-analysis on hold. With the interesting news about the history of the store—and their house—she felt in a giving mood. She'd surprise Ira, cajole him into going out to eat so she could tell him all about it. They hadn't tried the Salida del Sol yet. Maybe this news would be something to bond them together.

She got out of the car and strolled to the front door. But instead of entering in her usual slapdash manner, she sidestepped to the kitchen door and turned the knob quietly, once again in her stealth mode.

She wasn't sure why. It's not like she suspected Ira had Sally hidden up in his office, doing . . . *stuff*. He wasn't doing much of anything lately. As far as she could figure, while she was working at the shop every day, Ira did nothing but sit in his office in front of his computer.

Yet was he having a "virtual" affair with Sally until they met and could have the real thing? Was he conversing with her through extensive e-mails, forming a growing bond that didn't have to deal with the visible realities of expanding waistlines and receding hair?

Before she left the kitchen, Joan slipped off her shoes and set them neatly on the floor. Then she tiptoed upstairs, hating that it had become a habit. The office door was ajar, and she could see that Ira had his feet propped on the desk, his hands behind his head. His eyes were closed and his face was mellow with contentment.

How dare he look content when their marriage was on rocky ground!

The time for subtlety and sneaking was over. She shoved the door all the way open, making it ricochet off the wall.

Ira's feet hit the floor. "What the—?"

"Hello, love. A penny for your thoughts?" Joan noticed a red *S* on the floor and picked it up. "What's this?"

Yet when Ira's glance flickered with fear, she found she couldn't continue, and actually suffered her own stab of anxiety. Did she really want to confront him and have him try to explain? Such an encounter would surely be a crossroads moment in their lives, and she wasn't sure she was ready for it. Obviously, that "ignorance is bliss" saying was based on truth. As well as fear.

"What do you want, Joan?"

World peace, the end of hunger, and a diet that includes Snickers, potato chips, and Alfredo sauce. Barring those miracles she wasn't sure what to say. She pinched the letter into a small ball and slipped it into the pocket of her khaki shorts.

"Here." She gave him the photos.

Ira looked at the top one. "Old pictures. So?"

He had never shared her interest in all things old. He handed them back to her, then stacked some magazines. "I have work to do, Joan. I don't have time for—"

She was just about to make a snide remark regarding his "time" and "work" comment when fatigue and frustration pressed upon her. Joan's desire to share the news about her family and her heritage evaporated, as did her desire to try and make her marriage better.

She gave her husband what he wanted by walking out of the room.

So be it.

Kathy walked up the front sidewalk of Lavon's house carrying the empty cookie plate, knowing there was no need for her to make a special trip, knowing there would surely be a more natural chance for her to return this ordinary Corelle plate.

She went anyway.

Lavon met her at the door. "I thought that was you. What brings you out and about?"

She held up the plate. "All gone. Consumed in way too little time."

"Glad you liked them. But you didn't have to make a special trip for the plate."

Malachi appeared in the doorway. "Daddy, can we go outside and play?"

Lavon put a hand on his son's head. "Don't interrupt, Chi-Chi, and say hello to Mrs. Bauer."

The little boy turned to Kathy. "Hello, Mrs. Bauer."

"Hello, Malachi."

The twins, who were dressed in coordinating sunsuits, pink and green, pressed into the gaggle at the door. "It appears I'm surrounded," Lavon said. He gave the go-ahead and the children burst out like prisoners being set free. "Let me get the baby and we can have a chat on the porch."

Kathy helped one of the little girls get a child-sized shopping cart down the porch steps before taking a seat on the porch swing. There was something perfect about the scene. Children playing in a front yard on a summer day. A breeze cutting through the heat, making the branches of the trees sway as if they approved.

Lavon came out carrying the baby. She was a cutie, with a big grin exposing baby teeth. He set her down and she held on to his leg as he spread a blanket and a few toys on the floor of the porch. She was instantly amused, leaving him free to join Kathy on the swing.

"Phew," he said. "Each change of locale is a production."

"I've forgotten the work but remember the weariness."

He made the swing sway. "It's a good weariness."

They went back and forth a few times. Kathy didn't know what to say. She wasn't sure why she'd come. She barely knew this man.

But I want to know him better.

Having her true motives form into a cognizant thought frightened her. She stood suddenly, sending the swing into gyrations. "I should go."

"Please don't." They shared a moment of awkward silence. Then Lavon said, "It's nice to have an adult to talk to."

She knew it was an excuse, but she grabbed on to it and returned to her seat. She thought of their common ground. "How's Malachi doing since his . . . his episode?"

"All right. Actually we have an appointment with a specialist in St. Louis in a week."

She perked up. "What day?"

"Uh . . . Friday. A week from today I guess."

Kathy stopped the swing to face him. "I'm going to St. Louis in a week to have a meeting with Sandra Perkins, the lady who's arranging a gallery showing of my paintings."

"Next Friday?"

She nodded. "The same. We should caravan or something."

"So Ryan and Roy are going?" Lavon asked.

"No, no. They both have work and will wait for the actual showing. I was going alone."

"Then forget the caravan. Ride with Malachi and me."

Kathy blinked. "Patrice isn't going?"

He shook his head. "Patrice doesn't do well in doctors' offices. And since she's just started at the bank . . . I was going to take him."

"Alone in a car for six hours with a four-year-old? Not an easy undertaking."

His face beamed. "Oh my . . . I see God's hand all over this."

"I hardly think—"

Lavon stopped her words with a lift of his hand. "If either of us had not won this contest and moved to Weaver, if we had not met last weekend at the Meet 'n' Greet, if Malachi had not needed emergency help that brought me to your house with cookies, if you had not stopped by today—" he took a fresh breath—"we would not have compared notes and would have driven to St. Louis separately. Perhaps passing each other on the road."

She laughed. "You do have it figured out, don't you?"

He shrugged. "Try to dispute even one of my points. I dare you."

Kathy replayed them in her mind, then shook her head. "I can't."

"Told ya."

"This *is* amazing."

"You bet it is." He raised his face. "Praise the Lord!"

Kathy should've thought of that, but yes, praise the Lord.

Ryan stood between the flower beds he'd been assigned to weed and the juniper bushes that crowned the corner of the house. He kept slightly behind the bushes, not wanting to be seen.

He watched his mother talk to a man on the porch next door. They sat on the swing together like they were best friends, laughing, smiling, chatting. . . . He couldn't hear what they were talking about, but whatever it was, it had his mother smiling in a way Ryan hadn't seen in months.

It made him mad—and more than a little scared.

He felt his legs twitch and knew his impulse was to storm across the yards, move onto the porch, and demand to know what was going on. Why was his mother enjoying the company of this man? Alone, while his father was at work at the clinic? It wasn't right.

But when his mother started to leave Ryan was relieved he hadn't done any storming. Maybe he was overreacting. Maybe the whole thing was innocent.

Yet, just as the relief was settling over his tense nerves, he saw his mother pause at the top of the porch steps and hug the man. It wasn't a one-second hug either, but a full five seconds. Too long. Way too long.

Ryan pulled farther behind the bushes until his mother's van pulled away. He didn't like this. Not one bit.

Kathy burst into the clinic to share her good news. "Roy! Roy!"

She expected him to come out of the back, but he didn't. She took a few steps down the hall and saw that one of the examination rooms was closed. He had a patient? Of all times . . .

She returned to the waiting room and straightened the front-desk area. He still hadn't gotten the office part of the clinic in order. She'd do a good deed and help him now.

Ten minutes later, when he still hadn't come out, the urge to help faded. She returned down the hall. She could hear him speaking softly to the patient. Would they never get done? She had things to do.

She tapped on the door with a knuckle.

The talking stopped. The door opened a crack. When Roy saw her a crease formed between his eyebrows. "Kath, not now."

Kathy couldn't see past him to tell who it was. "It'll just take a minute."

"Is it an emergency?"

She suddenly wished it was. "No."

"Then I'll talk to you later." He closed the door on her.

Kathy stood in the hall a moment. How dare he not give her the time of day. She had important news she wanted to share and he wouldn't even spare one minute?

She moved her purse to the other shoulder and stomped out. She didn't need him.

Yet halfway home she realized there was no one else in Weaver she wanted to tell. Except Lavon. And he already knew, was part of it, and had helped make it happen.

At least someone cared about her.

Lavon hated when he and Patrice fought like they had this morning. Even if he felt he was in the right taking on more day-care kids, he'd learned after four years of marriage that it was imperative peace be made as quickly as possible. The fact that he was usually the one who had to make the effort could be annoying, but was a necessity. "Blessed are the peacemakers" and all that. Sometimes he didn't feel very blessed, or very much like blessing.

Lavon dug his hands into the ground beef, spices, and bread crumbs, getting ready to form Swedish meatballs. He'd add mushroom gravy, mashed potatoes, a green salad, and angel-food cake for dessert. It was common knowledge that the way to a man's heart was through his stomach, but he'd also found Patrice's heart and taste buds didn't mind the experience either.

He heard Chi-Chi playing with the twins in the living room. He was glad Brent had picked Wendy up early. She was definitely the most work. Maria would be over soon to get the girls.

He glanced at the kitchen table. The roses and daisies picked from the flower bed looked pretty in the vase. He wasn't good at arranging them, but their mere presence should make his wife smile. The table was set—but not with china. And not in the dining room. Both deliberate choices had been Lavon's response to his innocence in regard to their argument. A nice dinner and flowers he could do. But bowing down to the full throttle of a fancy dinner would hint at being a doormat.

At least that's the excuse he'd given himself. He wasn't sure if God agreed with him on that one, but despite a good effort, he just couldn't bring himself to give in completely. Patrice had to assume some responsibility, didn't she?

She wouldn't. But he wished she would. Every argument brought a fresh dose of hope, that *this* time her pride would crack and *she'd* be able to say she was sorry so they could move on. He knew he wasn't perfect, but in regard to this aspect of their marriage, Lavon was the one who handled confrontation with grace.

It was God's doing. Somewhere along the way, probably during their first year of marriage, under the strain of becoming a husband and a father simultaneously, he'd figured out that it helped to surrender each argument to the Lord by asking God, "Help me say only what you want me to say." Strikingly, God's nudges to talk or not talk often led to Lavon's silence. How interesting. To be silent while Patrice went on and on . . .

In all honesty, sometimes it worked and sometimes it didn't, but what was constant was how good Lavon felt afterward. As if he'd truly given it his best shot and hadn't made things worse. It took two to argue. If only Patrice would do a little surrendering too.

He looked up from the meatballs when he heard a car in the drive. She was home early. He really wished the twins were gone but it couldn't be helped. *Make do. Make do.*

Patrice came in the back door and hooked her purse on the coatrack, nearly toppling it.

Warning, warning . . .

"Hey, lovey."

She grunted and walked right past the table toward the stairs, not paying any attention to the pretty setting or the flowers. He tried not to let it get to him. He grabbed a towel for his greasy hands and walked after her.

She was halfway up the stairs. *Stomp. Stomp.* Patrice's frequent admonition to Malachi to not walk like an elephant entered his mind.

"How was your day?" he asked after her. A dumb question, yet he had to start somewhere.

She ignored him. He followed her into the bedroom. She kicked her shoes off. One hit the clock radio.

"Hey!" he said.

"Don't even start!" She got out her jeans. "I've had a horrible day."

"What did you do?"

She froze, the jeans in hand. "What did *I* do? Why do you always assume that I did something bad?"

It was a loaded question. "Fine." He picked up her shoes. "What happened?"

"No, no," she said, drilling her skirt onto the bed. "Let's get to the heart of this. I'm sick of you thinking I'm a horrible person and that *I* cause all the problems in my life."

It was an old argument that led nowhere. If she wasn't willing to see the truth . . . he headed for the door. "I have to get the meatballs in the oven."

She yanked on his arm. "Oh no you don't. You stay here and fight like a man."

He despised that statement because it implied the kind of man he tried hard *not* to be. He looked at her hand and she dropped his arm. "If you would like to start this conversation over . . ."

She put her hands on her hips. "Why? Because you're not winning?"

"There is no winning, Patrice."

"Of course there is."

"Are you going to tell me what happened at work?"

"What *I* did?"

No more. He left the room. "Dinner will be ready in twenty minutes."

After finishing work for the day, Ryan didn't want to go home. He didn't want to sit through the usual awkward silence or inane chitchat of dinner, not after seeing how his mother had come to life in the presence of another man.

Lavon Newsom. After finishing the yard work, Ryan had asked Web about him. The Newsoms were from New York City. One boy, age four. The wife worked at the bank with Mrs. Weaver, and the husband . . . Web wasn't sure what the husband did, but the very fact he was home during the day made it pretty clear he didn't have a job yet.

How handy for secret meetings with his mother.

But just because Ryan didn't want to suffer through dinner at home didn't mean he wanted to go hungry. Physical labor made him famished so he headed toward Salida's. As he cut through the park he heard his name called from behind.

"Ryan!"

He turned and saw Jenna coming from the direction of the Weaver home. "Hey, Jenna."

She caught up with him. "Where you heading?"

He pointed toward the café. "To get dinner. Care to join me?"

"Actually yes. Sort of. I convinced my aunt to let me get take-out. Before I showed up I think she nibbled rather than ate real meals, and since I'm rather worthless in the kitchen, I told her I'd spring for takeout."

Ryan was disappointed she wasn't going to sit and eat. "So you've ordered already?"

"No. We don't have a menu at home. So I'll sit with you while I wait. In fact . . . are you eating alone?"

"That was the plan."

"Then join us. My treat."

"Eat with you and Mrs. Weaver?"

"Neither one of us bites. Promise."

It was definitely better than eating alone.

Seth held Bonnie's chair and they settled in at the table by the window. Maria Lopez handed them menus. "Fresh sopaipillas tonight. And the bean burrito is the special. Rice and beans, with a taco on the side."

"Thanks," Bonnie said. She opened the menu.

"We could have gone into Topeka," Seth said. "When I asked you to dinner, I wanted it to be a little more special than chips and salsa." To emphasize his point, he dipped a chip and ate it. Then immediately reached for his water. The salsa was spicy.

"This is fine," Bonnie said. "Out is out."

After they placed their order, Bonnie nodded toward the entrance. "Isn't that Mrs. Weaver's niece?"

Seth turned around and saw Jenna enter the café with the Bauer kid, Ryan. Their eyes met. He started to wave, then remembered he was on a date with Bonnie and looked away. Immediately, that seemed wrong, and he wished he'd waved, but by then it was too late and . . .

Great. Just great.

The waitress showed Ryan and Jenna to a table where they could look over the menu and wait for their order, *and* where Jenna could see Seth and his date—couldn't help but see Seth and his date. And worse than seeing them was the fact that it bothered Jenna something awful. Why? She wasn't interested in Seth— in any man. So what difference did it make if he was sitting with another girl? They'd just met. They'd only spoken a few times. They had no relationship. Seth was free to date whomever he wanted.

Then why was her stomach tied in knots at the sight of him?

Ryan poked her arm with the corner of a menu. "Earth to Jenna?"

"Oh. Sorry." She tried to concentrate on the listing of enchiladas and tacos.

Ryan looked over his shoulder, then back at her. "You keep looking at Seth and Bonnie. You interested in him or something?"

"No!" Her voice sounded way too forced. She had to change the subject. "Have you eaten here before? What's good?" But she wondered, *Bonnie who?*

"Is he the reason you won't date me?"

Jenna resisted the impulse to look in Seth's direction again, even though she could feel his eyes on *her*. "Very funny. I won't date you because I'm five years older than you are."

"Yeah, right. Whatever you want to believe." He glanced over his shoulder again, and both Bonnie and Seth looked in their direction. Jenna raised the menu to block the view. Order. She needed to order and get out of here.

"Bonnie's not as pretty as you are; that's for sure," Ryan said.

She wouldn't miss the opening a second time. "Bonnie?"

"Bonnie Bowden. They own a farm nearby. Web told me it had been Seth's family farm." He looked over his shoulder a third time, then added, "Yup. You're definitely prettier. Her chin's too soft, and her hair color's nothing special, not dark and pretty like yours."

She appreciated the compliment, but hated that her mind amended Ryan's description by adding that Bonnie's hair was beyond "nothing special" and was an ordinary dishwater blonde—after you'd washed a lot of dishes. Petty. Truly petty.

This was ridiculous. She wasn't interested in Seth Olsen. She wasn't.

The waitress came and took their order. None too soon.

"You're not eating," Seth said to Bonnie.

She set down her fork. "What's all that about?"

He looked at the plate of burritos that had just been served. "What?"

Bonnie nodded in Jenna's direction. "Since she's come in you've looked at her at least a dozen times."

"I have?" *I have!*

"How do you know her?"

"Mrs. Weaver is having her work on some of the Founders Day stuff." He leaned forward as if sharing a secret. "Actually . . . we've had several meetings where we've exchanged sensitive information such as how many tables to rent and what kind of chairs are the most comfortable for the best price." He put a finger to his lips. "Shh. Don't tell. Loose lips sink ships."

"So you know her."

He sat back. So much for humor. "Barely. I've only talked to her a few times."

Bonnie looked at Jenna again. "You could've fooled me."

Time to try physical contact. Seth reached across the table to touch her hand but she pulled it away before contact was made. "I hardly know her, Bonnie. I'm here with you. And she's here with somebody too."

"The guy she's with looks like he's in high school."

Seth was glad for the chance to legitimately look in Jenna's direction one more time. "See? She likes her men younger than springtime. That's Ryan Bauer. He's the son of the new doctor. His mother's an artist."

"So how old is Jenna?"

He took a bite of burrito. "I think she turns fifty next week. The light in here is very complimentary." This was exhausting. He sipped his Dr Pepper. "Enough about them. Tell me how you're going to work the irrigation tomorrow. Your family's methods are so much more advanced that those my family used. My dad always talked down computers and science breakthroughs as if they were the work of the devil."

Thankfully, Bonnie took the bait and the talk turned to farming.

Seth tried to concentrate, but unfortunately his thoughts were permanently locked on Jenna.

This was not good. Not good at all.

"Well, well. Look what the cat dragged in," Madeline said. Ryan and Jenna set the take-out sacks on the kitchen counter. "You a delivery boy on the side, Ryan?"

"No, ma'am." He glanced at Jenna.

"We hooked up in the park, Auntie. Ryan was going to eat alone, so I invited him to join us."

"I hope that's okay," the boy said.

"Fine with me." Madeline got out three plates. "It gives me a chance to hear how your work with Web is going."

Jenna pointed to a drawer, and Ryan got out three forks and set them on the table. "Things are going good. He's keeping me busy."

"I need you to pick up those chairs and bring them to Mrs. Osgood's," Madeline said.

The two young people exchanged a look. "He already did that, Auntie."

"Yesterday," Ryan added.

"Oh, well. I guess I didn't notice they were gone. Good boy." She sat at the table and let Jenna bring the food to her. "Mrs. Osgood didn't give you any flack, did she?"

Ryan hesitated. "No, ma'am . . ."

"What *did* the old bat say to you?"

The boy squirmed in his chair, indicating Agnes must have said something distasteful. "Out with it, boy."

"She said the chairs had belonged to her mother and you got them when they had to sell off her estate. She didn't seem to like that you've had 'em."

Madeline laughed. "No, she wouldn't."

"She wondered what made you give 'em back."

"That's nobody's business but my own. She should be appreciative, but since she isn't, I have a mind to send you over there and snatch them back."

"Auntie!"

Madeline realized she'd gotten worked up. Sometimes this restitution stuff was for the birds. "Oh, don't worry. I won't do it. What's done is done. But she makes me mad—course she always did, so nothing's changed in that."

The food had been distributed and Madeline reached for her fork. But suddenly Ryan bowed his head and started praying, "Bless this food and make us worthy, O Lord. In Jesus' name, amen."

When Ryan looked up it was evident he'd said grace out of habit. "Oh," he said. "Sorry."

"No sorry needed," Jenna said. "That was nice."

Madeline tucked the straying lettuce into her taco. "So you're a good Christian boy; is that it?"

"I . . . I guess so. Or at least I was."

She laughed. "So now you're a straying sinner?"

"Auntie, that's rude."

"He's the one who said he *was*. Past tense."

Ryan cut into his burrito and ate a bite before answering. "I'm taking a break for a while."

"Taking a break from God?" Jenna asked.

Madeline remembered the sister. "Does it have something to do with your sister's death?"

"Auntie, I'm sure Ryan would rather not talk about it."

"Can't get over what you don't talk about." She gave her niece a pointed look, took a bite, then asked the boy, "Was your sister driving?"

He shook his head. "She was only fourteen. But she had a boyfriend who was older. And drunk. Mom liked that she was with the popular kids—didn't like the drunk part, of course, but . . ." He took a fresh breath. "I told Lisa to stay away from the guy, but she didn't listen to me. She laughed at me, squeezed my chin, got right in my face, and said, 'You worry too much, Ry.' I should have protected her better. Stopped her."

Jenna reached across the table and touched his arm. "You tried."

Ryan shook his head. "Lisa always did what Lisa wanted to do. But that night I got this sick feeling and went looking for her. I saw the flashing lights and a crowd and . . ." He ran a hand across his eyebrows. "I can't believe I'm telling you this."

"You found her? At the crash?"

He nodded.

"I'm so sorry, Ryan. I can't imagine."

Madeline didn't like how the moment had turned all touchy-feely. Facts were facts and were best dealt with by using logic instead of emotions. "You and your family moving here . . . that's exactly what you needed. A new start."

"Yes, ma'am."

Jenna squeezed his hand. "But it's hard being strong."

Ryan nodded " 'Be strong and take courage, all you who put your hope in the Lord!'" He looked at Jenna, then at Madeline. "Web told me that one. It's a Bible verse."

"Yes, yes," Madeline said. "Web's full of verses. A regular verse-for-every-occasion man." She was disappointed but not surprised that Web had gotten to this boy already. He'd fill the boy's head with all manner of God stuff. Oh well. That was Web. She pointed across the table. "Enough of all this. Pass the salsa, boy. My taco's getting cold."

Kathy heard footsteps on the porch and sprang from the living-room chair. She'd been waiting for Ryan for over an hour. With Roy working late at the clinic, she'd had to suffer through her fears alone.

As soon as he came in the door, she pounced. "Where have you been?"

"I had dinner at the Weavers'."

Kathy felt a wave of jealousy. "At Madeline Weaver's?"

"Yeah."

"Why didn't you call? I made dinner."

His snicker wounded her. "I thought that was Dad's job."

"Don't talk to me like that. I make my share of the meals."

He headed for the stairs. "Whatever."

She pulled at his shirt, making him stop. "And don't walk away from me! Why didn't you call?"

"I didn't think you'd be here."

"Of course I'd be here. Where else would I be?"

She could tell by the flash in her son's eyes that he wanted to say one thing but said another. "Sorry. I'll call next time." He headed up the stairs.

Kathy called after him. "You can't make us worry like this! You have to let us know where you are and what you're doing. You have to be accountable."

He stopped on the landing and looked down at her. "So do you, Mom."

"What?"

He shook his head and walked away.

She was left at the foot of the stairs totally confused. Unfortunately it was not a new feeling.

Patrice made sure that in spite of the nice dinner—and flowers, as if that would make everything right—it was a silent evening at the Newsom residence. Every time Lavon tried to make conversation, she returned silence. There was such power in silence. It put her in charge.

To accentuate her anger she made sure she was extra sweet to Malachi, reading him *Curious George*, chatting away while she gave him his bath. *See how chatty I can be if you're deserving?*

She had looked forward to bedtime when she'd be able to strike the most poignant blow. When Lavon tried to cuddle, she pulled away and showed him her back. He didn't say anything, but also turned over so his back was to hers.

Message received. A victory logged.

Her mind drifted to thoughts of work: Mrs. Weaver catching her snooping in the trash, and the not-so-subtle hint when she put *paper shredder* on the shopping list. Patrice couldn't give her boss the silent treatment. She couldn't play power games with *her*, which meant she couldn't win.

But then she thought of the secret files. In the business world, anyone with a secret was fair game.

Patrice smiled and dug her cheek deeper into the pillow. She'd win that battle too. Eventually. If she played her cards right.

NINE

We are not like those
who turn their backs on God and seal their fate.
We have faith that assures our salvation.

HEBREWS 10:39

"Answer it, will you, Roy?"

The phone kept ringing. Kathy turned over in bed and saw that Roy wasn't there. And it was light outside.

Of course it was. It was nearly ten on a Saturday morning. She crawled across the bed and got the phone.

"Hello?" Her voice was thick with sleep.

"Oh, Kathy. Did I wake you?"

Lavon. She pushed herself to sitting. "No," she lied. "I just haven't talked much this morning." She cleared her throat and tried to force life into her voice. "What's up?"

"Hopefully dinner. I know it's short notice, but I thought it would be nice if you and Roy came over for dinner tonight. You and I have gotten to know each other, but our spouses have barely met."

Which might be a good thing. "What can I bring?"

"Not a thing."

Super.

"What did Roy think about us carpooling to St. Louis?"

Kathy hesitated. Lying about being lazy on a Saturday morning was one thing but lying about the fact that she hadn't told her husband that detail . . .

"Haven't you told him yet?"

"He was busy yesterday. It wasn't the right time." She turned the tables. "How about you? Did you tell Patrice?"

A pause. "Actually . . . can I just say ditto to your it-wasn't-the-right-time excuse?"

Kathy took comfort in knowing she wasn't the only one having communication issues. "Are we going to tell them tonight at dinner?"

"That's the plan."

It was good to plan.

Roy parked the car in front of the Newsoms'. He'd agreed to go to dinner, but Kathy could have done without his attitude. He shut off the car as if his arm could barely manage the effort, sighed, then closed his eyes.

Kathy held in what she really wanted to say and said instead, "It *can* be an early night—if it's really necessary."

He did not open his eyes and rubbed the back of his neck. "That would be good."

"But you're not going to act all tired and boring, are you?"

His eyes opened and his head slowly turned toward her.

Oops. "Sorry," she said. "But this is the first dinner we've gone to and I don't want people thinking you're a sludge."

"A what?"

A better description failed her. She opened her door. "Let's go."

Lavon met them at the door with a welcoming smile. "Come in, come in." The men shook hands. Patrice was in the dining room, where the table was beautifully set. Although she said hello she seemed no more friendly than she had at the Meet 'n' Greet.

"What a lovely table," Kathy said.

"It's my husband's doing." Patrice straightened a knife. "He's the domestic god around here. I just make the money."

Kathy was taken aback and checked on Lavon's reaction. He chose that moment to turn toward the kitchen. "Make our guests comfortable, lovey. I'll get the munchies." He stopped in the doorway. "Would anyone like a soda? Or I've made some raspberry iced tea?"

"The tea sounds fine," Kathy said.

"Make it two," Roy said.

"You got it," Lavon said. "And for my wife a Diet Coke. It'll be right out."

"Do you need any help?" Kathy asked.

His smile was genuine and seemed to be a Band-Aid on the awkwardness of the past few moments. "No thanks. I've got it covered."

Kathy was disappointed. The thought of having to make small talk with Patrice, sans Lavon, was not appealing. "Where's Malachi?" Kathy asked as she sat on the couch.

"He's at the Lopezes'," Patrice said, taking a seat on a modern leather-and-chrome chair. "Since their girls are over here every day till all hours, she owes us."

What an interesting way to put it.

Roy got comfortable amid all the pillows at the other end of the couch. "How's your new job at the bank, Patrice?"

"Though Mrs. Weaver *is* still around, I run things day to day."

"That's a lot of responsibility," Kathy said.

"Not really. I used to be at a bank in Manhattan, so I—"

"Manhattan, Kansas?" Roy asked.

Patrice looked horrified. "Heavens no. New York City."

"That's right. I knew that. Weaver must be quite a change for you," he said.

She snickered, making it clear what she thought of Weaver.

Then why did you come? Kathy knew Lavon loved it here and Malachi seemed content, so maybe *their* happiness was the reason. Yet, even from their short contact, she didn't think Patrice was the type who would make such a large sacrifice for anyone. There had to be more to that story.

Kathy was relieved when Lavon came in with a tray of drinks and appetizers. He passed them around. Patrice remained seated.

Lavon ended up near the fireplace, holding his glass of tea. "Well, now, I think it's time to share the main reason for this evening's gathering." He smiled at Kathy. "Would you like to do the honors?"

Although Kathy had longed to tell Roy her news yesterday, now, with this audience, she was suddenly wary. But everyone was waiting.

She set her glass on the coffee table, glanced at Lavon, then at Roy, and took a fresh breath. "You know that I have a gallery showing coming up next month in St. Louis."

Roy did a double take, obviously not expecting this topic. "At Sandra's new gallery. Yes, of course I knew that."

"I set up a meeting with her next weekend to go over the logistics and also to bring along a few of the paintings."

Roy turned his body toward hers. "Next week? When was this decided?"

She'd told him. More than once. "It's been planned since before we moved here. Remember we talked about the six-hour drive I'd have to make by myself for this meeting?" Surely, he'd remember that.

Patrice interrupted. "What does this have to do with anything?"

Kathy swept her hand toward Lavon. "You can tell this part."

Patrice's eyebrows rose.

Lavon began his explanation. "It just so happens that next Friday I have—or rather Chi-Chi has—a doctor's appointment with a specialist about his asthma. In St. Louis." His eyes looked as his wife, then moved to Roy. "Since we're going to the same city on the same weekend, instead of taking two cars we can drive together."

"Share the driving," Kathy said. "I remember what it's like traveling with a four-year-old."

"It's quite amazing when you think about it," Lavon said quickly. "Both of us making appointments in St. Louis for the same weekend?"

"Then getting to know each other . . ."

Lavon nodded. "It's pretty apparent God's hand is in this."

Kathy heard a soft expulsion of air from Patrice. All talking stopped. Patrice met everyone's eyes. "Oh, don't mind me. You have to understand my husband can identify God's hand in finding fresh tomatoes at the grocery store."

"Patrice . . ."

She gave him the slightest glance, then continued. "Fine. So maybe that's a *slight* exaggeration. But it's not that far off." She took a sip of her pop. The ice cubes clattered.

Kathy thought of the roll call of noncoincidences that Lavon had listed and wished he would list them now. That would show his wife what was what. But he was silent . . . and took a sip of tea.

Thankfully, Roy filled in the dead air. "It does seem convenient."

Kathy wanted to give Patrice a so-there nod but didn't. "I'd planned to leave Friday and come home Sunday, but since Malachi's appointment is Friday, I'm going to move it up a day. Thursday through Saturday."

"Kathy's been very accommodating," Lavon said.

"Apparently," Patrice said.

There was a moment of awkward silence and Kathy's stomach tightened.

Lavon set his drink on the mantel. "As far as the kids I babysit . . ."

"Yes," Patrice said. "What about the little darlings?"

Lavon cleared his throat. "When Maria first started bringing the twins, she told me that her mother moved here with them and if I ever couldn't babysit, it wasn't a worry. The grandmother could do it—would love to do it. The grandmother just didn't want to be tied down every day. I even met her one time when she came to pick up the girls. She's a nice lady." He looked to his wife. Patrice's left eyebrow was raised. Lavon picked up his glass and fueled himself with another sip. "The grandmother will take the baby too. It's just for a couple days." He headed toward the kitchen and Kathy wanted nothing more than to follow him.

Patrice's words stopped him. "All tied up neat with a bow, isn't it?"

He turned to look at her. "It is working out well."

A challenge was being played out between them. Finally Patrice set her Diet Coke on the coffee table, breaking the moment. "Where are you staying?"

Kathy chimed in. "I'm staying with Sandra—my friend who runs the gallery." She nodded at Lavon.

"And Malachi and I will stay at a hotel at Union Station. The old train station has been renovated with shops and restaurants. I've heard it's very nice. I'd like Chi-Chi to have a bit of fun amid all the doctor stuff."

Patrice crossed her legs. "Which leaves the other question of when all this scheming came about."

Kathy resented the word *scheming*. She looked at Roy. He hadn't said much. What did he think about all this? But Roy's face was unreadable. In fact, he'd angled away from her and was facing the room again, sipping his tea as if he had no interest.

But Kathy hurried to explain. "I stopped over the other day to return the plate from the cookies Lavon brought over."

"He brought you cookies?"

Oh dear. Kathy glanced at Roy, hoping he'd answer. He didn't. "It was a gesture of thanks—a delicious gesture of thanks—for Roy's help during Malachi's asthma attack."

"Do you normally get paid in cookies, Dr. Bauer?"

Roy moved, proving he was paying attention after all. He balanced his drink on the palm of his hand. "The clinic wasn't set up for payments and insurance yet."

Kathy mentally added these additional noncoincidences to Lavon's list of how God's hand was in all this.

Lavon clapped his hands once. "Well then. It's all set. The trip's a go."

Yes, it was. With or without their spouses' support.

"Too bad we had to leave so early," Kathy said, as they pulled away from the Newsom home.

"I've had a long day, Kath. My head is splitting."

Is it? Or are you faking?

They drove a block in silence. Roy had been quiet all through dinner. But it didn't matter. Patrice had been more than happy to fill the dead air talking about herself.

"That Patrice . . . do you realize she never once asked anything about our lives? She never asked about the clinic, or my art, or Ryan. For all I know she doesn't even know we had a daughter. She was me-me-me, all the time."

Roy kept driving. If only he'd say something. Yet Kathy knew the silence was preferable to his saying something negative about the showing, or the trip, or—

"This isn't right, Kathy."

"What isn't right?"

"You going to St. Louis with a man."

"I'm not going *with* him. We'll share the driving. He's a friend."

"Whom you've only known a few days."

She attempted a laugh. "He's not a serial killer or anything. He babysits, for goodness' sake."

Roy took a breath, let it out, then took another one. "But he's a *man*. And you're a woman. It isn't right."

"Excuse me? We'll have a four-year-old, rambunctious little boy with us."

He didn't say anything.

"If you don't want Lavon to go with me, then I *can* go alone—though considering Lavon is heading in the same direction, it would be terribly dumb. Or if you're worried about the drive, you go with me."

"I can't. You know that."

"You could. Weaver's been without a doctor for over a year. You could go if you wanted to."

"No, I couldn't. Mrs. Hutchinson is expecting a baby any day and it's going to be a difficult birth. She came to me because she doesn't like the doctor she's been seeing in Emporia. She likes me. She trusts me. She expects me to be there for the birth."

"So you're choosing her over me." Two could play at this game.

He looked at her for the first time. "Don't even start."

"Then don't you," Kathy said. "Lavon and I are friends. More than likely when I'm driving he'll sleep or be occupied with Malachi, and vice versa. And we're not even staying at the same place. Except for the driving part we won't see each other. And remember, this is a working trip. Once we get to St. Louis, I won't have a moment to breathe—and Lavon will be consumed with making his son breathe easier." *Good one, Kathy.*

"I still don't like it."

Yet by his tone she knew she'd won. As he pulled into their driveway she reached over and touched his cheek. "It's the logical thing to do, Roy. It'll be fine."

But the excitement brewing in Kathy's stomach proved her true expectations were way beyond *fine.*

Patrice got a dish towel. She hated that they didn't have a dishwasher. Who didn't have a dishwasher? Lavon washed the glassware first. He was so meticulous, it drove her crazy. He hadn't said much since the Bauers left—blessedly early. *Headache, my foot.*

She started out with a huge sigh. "Boy, am I glad that's over. That woman is a bore. Me-me-me. It's all about her."

"What?"

"All she talked about was herself."

Lavon shook his head. "I didn't hear that at all. You seemed to be doing most of the talking."

"Only because I took charge and grabbed the conversation away from her. Kathy acts like being an artist makes her God's gift to humanity. So she slaps a little paint on a canvas? Big whoop." She

set a dried glass on the counter and waited for another one. A wet
spot remained deep inside the glass, but she let it be.

"I've seen her work. It's good."

"I'm not sure I like your being at her house—and her being over
here."

"We're neighbors. Neighbors visit each other." He handed her
a goblet.

"Do neighbors take six-hour trips together—for three days?"

"We're taking separate trips—together, for convenience's sake,
Patrice."

"Roy should be the one going with her."

"Kathy doesn't need anyone to go with her. She's fine going
alone. I'm the one benefiting by having another adult in the car
with Chi-Chi. Besides, Roy's a doctor. He has responsibilities."

"He's a wimp. Barely said a word all night."

"You did enough talking for all of us."

She shoved him sideways, making him fling sudsy water across
the floor. "What's that supposed to mean?" she asked.

He cleaned up the splatters with a paper towel, then took the
dish towel away from her. "Go on. I'll finish up. Even though
I cooked and cleaned all day."

"Are you saying I didn't help?"

He tossed the towel over his shoulder and went back to washing
goblets. "Go pick up Malachi, Patrice."

Fine. Whatever.

Ryan heard the family van drive up. He looked away from the TV
and checked the time. They were home way early. Which was fine
by him. The fact his parents were having dinner at the Newsoms'

hadn't pleased him. The only reason he hadn't said anything was because his dad was going to be there too. And Mrs. Newsom. Chaperones.

And maybe the vibes he'd gotten when he'd seen his mom and Lavon on the porch were all wrong. After all, what did he know about man-woman stuff? He'd never had a real girlfriend, though he *had* taken Abigail Oswald to homecoming last year. They hadn't talked much after the dance—or even at the dance—which was fine by him. Abigail had spent the majority of her time giggling with her girlfriends and flirting with Tony Randolph. It wasn't as if he'd seen his mom and Lavon kiss or anything. Just laughing and talking.

And the one lingering hug.

His parents came in the kitchen door and he heard keys being tossed on the counter. His dad entered the living room first, heading for the stairs. He didn't even say hello.

"Aren't you home early?" Ryan asked him.

"Headache."

"You seem mad."

"I'm not."

He disappeared upstairs. Ryan's mom stood in the doorway to the kitchen, taking off her earrings.

"What's Dad mad about?"

"Oh nothing. He's . . ." She palmed her earrings. "Did you remember I'm going to St. Louis next Thursday to meet with Sandra about my showing?"

"When did this happen?"

She sighed deeply. "You men. Don't you listen? It was arranged months ago."

Ryan looked at the TV. His mom was leaving. That was fine by him. One less parent to deal with.

"The thing is," she said, "Lavon Newsom has to take his son to a doctor's appointment in St. Louis at the same time, so we're going to carpool."

Ryan bolted from the couch pushing the ottoman across the rug to form a path. "You can't go with *him*!"

His mother pushed the ottoman back where it belonged. "Why ever not?"

"Because . . . uh, because . . ." His mind was blank. "I'll drive you."

"Oh no you won't. You just got your license. I will not have you taking the responsibility of both our lives—"

"I'm a good driver. I drive a city truck all the time. Web trusts me. You have to give me a chance. Just because Lisa died in a car crash doesn't mean—"

"No." Her voice was adamant. "You don't have highway experience, nor experience driving in a big city like St. Louis. I'd be a wreck worrying, and besides, I don't need a driver. Lavon does. By going together I'll be able to help with Malachi. It's a six-hour trip, which is a long time for a little boy."

He knew she was right on every point, but he couldn't have her go with Mr. Newsom. He just couldn't.

She moved toward the stairs. "Don't worry so much. I appreciate the offer, but this is the best solution. The two of us will be fine."

Exactly. Two of them. That was the problem.

He shut off the TV and headed for the front door.

"Ryan? Where are you going?"

"Out."

"It's nearly dark. What are you going to do?"

He shut the door against her questions. Against her.

Ryan was glad to see Web's garage door open, the fluorescent light making it glow like a beacon in the deepening dark. There was a massive workbench inside, and Web was looking through some tiny drawers, talking to himself. Ryan walked quietly, not wanting to scare him, but was unsure how to do anything but.

"Faith," Web suddenly said in a louder voice. "'What is faith? It is the assurance that—'"

Ryan stepped forward. "Actually, I think it's 'confident assurance.'"

Web smiled. "Hi there, young man."

"Hi."

"Are you sure it's 'confident assurance'?"

Ryan nodded. "'What is faith? It is the confident assurance that what we hope for is going to happen. It is the evidence of things we cannot yet see.' Hebrews 11:1, right?"

Web smiled. "I'm impressed."

"Don't be." He picked up two fallen screws. "You going to be the preacher tomorrow?"

"I'm going to talk. I'm not a preacher. Just the resident fix-it man."

"You're more than that."

"Why, thank you, young man." Web looked pleased. "I was working on my talk when you caught me in the error."

"You had it right," Ryan said. "You were just missing a word."

"An important word."

Ryan shrugged.

Web dug through a drawer of screws, trying to find one to match the one in the palm of his hand. "What's brought you out tonight?"

At that moment, Ryan realized that even though he'd come to

Web's because he was upset, he couldn't say anything, couldn't share his fears about his mother and Mr. Newsom. "I'd better go."

"Suit yourself. But you're doing me a favor sticking around. An old guy like me likes having young'uns around."

The old-fashioned term made Ryan smile. Although he thought he knew the answer, he asked the question anyway. "You sound like a grandpa. You have grandkids?"

"Nope. No kids either. Never married."

Ryan remembered the picture of Web in uniform at Mrs. Weaver's, with the special inscription on the back: *To Maddy, the love of my life. We'll be together soon.* "Why didn't you marry?"

"Things got in the way. The war. Other things."

"Mrs. Weaver?"

Web gave Ryan a pointed look and Ryan held it a long moment. "How did you know?" Web asked.

"I saw an old picture of you in uniform." He looked away, suddenly feeling as if he'd intruded. "And another of you and her."

He looked toward his house. "Where?"

"At her house. At Mrs. Weaver's."

Web went back to digging in the drawer. "Maddy has pictures of us?"

"Did she love you like you . . . did she love you?"

He rested his hand on the drawer. "Yes."

"Then why didn't you get married?"

"She married someone else."

Ryan wondered if the "someone else" was the other man in the picture. "But if she loved you . . ."

"Sometimes other things seem more important than love."

"Like what?"

Web shut the drawer. Hard. His head drooped. "I don't want to talk about this, Ryan."

It still hurts him.

Ryan thought of his mom and dad. Was his mom going to hurt his dad like this?

He hadn't realized he'd been staring into space until he felt Web's hand on his shoulder. "What's wrong, boy?"

Ryan stepped away and shook his head. "Nothing."

"Something."

Ryan risked a glance. "It *might* be something . . ."

"Maybe I can help." Web pulled a metal stool close and slapped the top of it, then leaned against the workbench. "What's said here stays here, Ryan. Promise. A worry shared is a worry halved."

It took him a moment to figure out the saying. "Did you make that up?"

"Believe it or not, that saying is older than me."

Ryan dangled his legs from the stool, put his heels on the rung, then let his toes skim the floor. He wanted to tell Web about his suspicions, but he didn't know how to word it. Besides, it was family business.

He stood. "I really need to go."

Web pursed his lips and nodded. "You do what you have to. Just know I'm here."

"I know. I do know that."

Web leaned close, pointing upward. "And he's here. Anytime you need him."

Ryan headed for the door.

"You'll be coming to church tomorrow? I need someone to check for omitted words. You can keep a running tab if you'd like."

He looked at the ground. "I don't think so."

"Why not?"

"I don't do church right now." That sounded bad. "I'm taking a breather. A time-out. Even a sabbatical. That's what people take when they need a break, isn't it? A sabbatical?"

Web put his hands in the pockets of his overalls. "Some people use sabbaticals to have a little conference between themselves and God, to get renewed, to be restored."

Some people. Not me. "See ya."

Ryan was glad his parents weren't hanging around the living room waiting for him—though he bet his mom had wanted to be there and had been called off by the cooler head of his father.

Ryan slipped upstairs, being as quiet as possible. There was a light under the door of his parents' room. He didn't knock. He was home safe. Wasn't that all that mattered?

He was safe. Yet his mother's safety was another matter. If the connection he saw between her and Mr. Newsom was real . . .

Once in his room, he kept the lights out, fell onto the window seat, and looked outside through the slats of the blinds. The moonlight was strong tonight, making horizontal bands across his room.

His worry didn't come from nowhere. His parents hadn't been getting along for some time now. Although his dad tried to be the solid rock he'd always been, Ryan had witnessed a chipping away since Lisa died. Not a total crumbling—as yet—but definitely a chink in the fortress. The chisel was the fact that his father blamed his mom for Lisa's being out with the fast crowd in the first place.

Ryan agreed with him there. His mother's utter glee when Lisa had made the middle school cheerleading squad, her encouragement—and open checkbook—when Lisa wanted to wear the

clothes the popular kids wore . . . it was as if Kathy Bauer the mom
was creating a Kathy Bauer the teenager through Lisa Bauer the
child.

Ryan knew his mom had given up the fun of her teenage years
because of him, because he was born. But she'd never guilted him
out about it. She'd never said anything blatant like "Because of
you I never got to have fun." Yet over the years—especially before
Roy had come into their lives—Ryan had figured out how things
had been. He wasn't dumb.

So when Lisa had become a teenager and had exhibited all the
appropriate pop-tart traits like being cute, peppy, giggly, and all
that, a light had turned on behind his mother's eyes. She'd gotten
a second chance with Lisa.

So it's her fault Lisa died.

Ryan shook his head against the hate that always accompanied
that thought. He wasn't supposed to hate his mother.

Or hate himself for not protecting Lisa.

I tried.

A little. But not enough. Most of the time it was Lisa who protected *him* while he lived in his separate world of Jesus, thinking
he was hot stuff for having a special *in* with God.

A lot of good it did me.

There were just the three of them now. A family of three. Barely
a family at all. And yet . . . if his mom and dad broke up . . .

"No!" His exclamation came out as a whisper but there was the
power of fear behind it. He could not let his family fall apart. He
hadn't been able to protect Lisa, but he *would* protect his family.
He would not fail this time. He couldn't.

But how could he make things better? How could he stop things
from falling apart?

Renew. Restore.

Web's words.

The words expanded into a familiar phrase: *"Renew a right spirit within me."*

It was a verse from Psalms. Ryan liked the Psalms, even identified with them, because most of the verses were written by King David, who was a guy who'd been hurt and done some mighty hurting of his own. A complex guy. Imperfect. But still "a man after God's own heart." That phrase had always intrigued Ryan and as a kid, he'd ached to have those words apply to himself. He'd been on the right road for a long time and sometimes he knew—he *knew*—God approved of him. *"Well done, my good and faithful servant."*

Was God proud of him now?

He glanced toward his magazine-veiled Bible on the shelf. He hadn't touched it since that one day when—

He did a double take. Even in the moonlight he could see that the magazine was on the floor, neatly closed. And the St. Louis snow globe that had been holding it in place? It was also on the floor, sitting erect on top of the magazine—as if it had been placed there on purpose.

Ryan crossed the room and flipped on the light. He stared at the scene. It didn't make sense. Earlier today he'd seen the magazine in place.

Hadn't he?

He tried to remember for sure but couldn't.

Then he started at the realization that if the magazine and snow globe *had* been in their present position earlier, he *would* have noticed.

He wrapped his arms around his torso. The snow globe wasn't toppled on its side as if it had fallen off, free to roll a few inches. It was erect. Neat. Deliberate.

Mom?

He looked toward the door and wondered if this was his mother's doing. Was she messing with him for being rude to her? for walking out earlier? Had she removed the barriers Ryan had erected between himself and the Good Book? Was it her not-so-subtle hint to read it?

He sank onto the bed. Somehow knowing a logical explanation was possible made him relax. It was just his mom. No big deal.

"Renew a right spirit within me."

Suddenly, he got up, crossed the room, and snatched the Bible from the shelf. He took it to his desk and sat with a slam and a bang. Only then did he take a breath and wonder what he was doing.

Yet amid the heavy breathing and the anger, there existed a hint of contentedness with being at this desk with this particular book in front of him. He'd been in this position countless times. Sometimes he read and didn't get much out of it. Other times he got so involved it was like reading a novel he couldn't put down. And occasionally he was moved to tears, ending up on his knees with his face to the carpet, totally humbled—whether in awe or shame. At those times it was as if heaven and earth were one and the same and God was his alone.

I miss that. And with his next breath he knew God did too.

Renew, restore.

Ryan placed his fingers on the book, closed his eyes, and whispered, "I give up. Show me what you want to show me. Show me how I can protect my family."

He opened to the Psalms, knowing he *would* find the passage that had been dogging him.

And he did. Psalm 51, verses 10 through 12:

Create in me a clean heart, O God.
Renew a right spirit within me.
Do not banish me from your presence,
and don't take your Holy Spirit from me.
Restore to me again the joy of your salvation,
and make me willing to obey you.

Renew and *restore*. Right there. Front and center as if Web had known exactly which verses Ryan needed—which passage Ryan would turn to.

He couldn't know.

But God knew.

Ryan laughed softly, admitting defeat. Then he read the verses again, as if *he'd* written them. As if he truly were King David, a flawed but faithful man after God's own heart.

Renew, restore.

Obey?

He'd work on it.

Seth was watching the evening news when he heard footsteps on the porch. Then a knock.

Who would be coming over this late? He opened the door.

"Hi." Bonnie smiled tentatively and put her hands in the pockets of her shorts.

"Hi, yourself."

"Sorry it's so late, but . . ."

Seth looked at his watch. "Actually I have twenty-eight minutes before I turn into a pumpkin. Want to come inside and be my witness?"

She hesitated. "Can we sit on the porch?"

"Absolutely. Let me turn off the TV."

He came outside and found her already on the porch swing. Wonderful inventions, porch swings. He sat beside her and they began to rock. "How'd the farming go today?"

"Fine. But I . . ."

They swang up and back. When she didn't continue her sentence, he prodded. "You . . . ?"

"I thought about you while I was working."

Victory is mine! "I thought about you today too." He bumped shoulders with her. "Two minds with but a single thought."

She glanced at him, then away. "I had a good time at dinner last night. I like talking with you, being with you. I just had to come over and tell you that."

He took a chance and linked his fingers through hers. Her hand was strong, capable, and she did not withdraw it. "I'm glad you did." The sound of cicadas swelled around them. "The moon's so full tonight," Seth said. "It's—"

She let go of his hand and angled to face him. "I came to invite you to go to church with me and my family tomorrow."

He laughed at the way she'd blurted it out, as if it had taken all her courage. But it was perfect. Bonnie and the family. Church. Sitting shoulder to shoulder. Sharing a hymnbook. Good stuff. "Sure. That would be nice—as long as you don't make fun of my singing."

"You don't sing well?"

"Ever heard a dog baying at the moon?"

"Yes."

"That was me."

She stood but did not laugh. He wished he could make her laugh, but it seemed sense of humor was not a Bowden trait.

"I'll see you tomorrow then. I'll meet you there," she said. With a wave, she left.

Meet you there . . . as Seth went inside, the words sounded familiar. Then, with the door halfway closed, he stopped cold. They sounded familiar because he'd heard another woman say them a few days previous.

Jenna.

He closed the door then banged his head against it. He had two dates for church.

God would get him for this. In fact, God would have a front-row seat.

TEN

As a face is reflected in water,
so the heart reflects the person.

PROVERBS 27:19

Who could be knocking at the door this early—on a Sunday?

Madeline pulled her pink robe close and answered it. "Web? What in the name of mornings are you doing here?" She gave him a half-eyed once-over.

"I've come to take you to church."

She started to close the door but he stopped it with a hand. "Leave me alone, old man."

"I will not. This is the first worship service we've had since the new people have moved in. As the matriarch of Weaver you need to be there."

"You won't miss me."

"Of course I will. And so will everyone else."

"I haven't gone to church in years. So why would I go now?"

"Everyone in Weaver is starting over, starting better. Why don't you do the same?"

"Because I don't want to."

He tossed his hands in the air. "Heaven forbid Madeline Weaver does anything she doesn't want to do."

"Don't be mean. And don't make me out to be one of those Pharisees you've told me about. A hypocrite. I'm not going to pretend to be someone I'm not. Going through the ceremonies, thinking highly of myself because everyone can see me."

"If you come, you might like it."

"Dream on."

"You need to go, Maddy."

"Says who?"

He pointed upward.

She crossed her arms. "Are you saying God will strike me down if I don't go?"

With a sigh of exasperation he turned to leave, dismissing her with a hand. "If only he would."

She called after him. "That's not very Christian of you, Web Stoddard."

Kathy poured herself a second cup of coffee, then returned to the table to read the Sunday paper. She was surprised to hear Ryan's footfalls on the front stairs, and even more surprised to see him come into the kitchen dressed in khakis and a red polo shirt.

"What are you all dressed up for?" she asked.

"Church."

Kathy's coffee slurped over the edge of her mug onto the front page. "You're going to church?"

He checked his watch. "Gotta go. Don't want to be late."

"But—"

And he was gone.

Kathy looked at Roy, who sat across the table from her. "What was all that about? He hasn't wanted to go to church since Lisa died."

Roy closed his newspaper. "You want to go too?"

"We don't even know which church he's going to."

"I could guess. Web came by the clinic and said he was preaching today. I bet Ryan's going to his church."

Kathy hated to admit it, but she'd come to like their lazy Sunday mornings. The thought of getting dressed and putting on makeup . . . she ran a hand through her hair. "We don't have time. I'd need to take a shower, dry my hair. There's no way we could make it in time."

"We could if you wanted to."

"Don't put it all on me. You're not dressed either."

He folded the paper in half and looked at her expectantly.

"What if we go next Sunday when we have a little more warning about it?" she asked.

"Next Sunday you'll be tired from being in St. Louis."

Probably. She got up to freshen her already-hot coffee. "God's waited for us this long; a couple more weeks won't matter."

"That sounds as awful as it is."

"*You* could go," she said.

He opened the newspaper and hid behind it.

He was doomed. It was a fact Seth acknowledged as he sat in his car and watched Jenna enter the church. She looked very pretty in a blue-flowered dress and sandals. The way the fabric moved around her legs as she walked up the steps made her look ethereal.

Delicate. And a bit vulnerable. There was something about that girl that made him want to hold her close to keep her safe.

She was far different from the solid, able Bonnie with the college degree and athletic build. As usual, thoughts of Bonnie brought along visions of the farm. Seth's mother was going to be thrilled when his plan was complete. The look on her face, the way she'd take his hand and squeeze it. *"Oh, honey. There is nothing you could have done that could have made me happier than getting the family farm back. Your father would have been so proud. All is forgiven. You're such a good son."*

The sound of a car driving into the parking lot shoved the dream away. In order to create the future he had to get through the *now*.

When the car pulled past, he was glad to see it wasn't Bonnie. It would not do to have her find him outside where they'd make an entrance together. He had to get to Jenna first.

And do what? Tell her what?

The questions had kept him awake much of the night. If only he'd come up with some answers. As it was, he'd have to wing it and hope God would take pity on him and make things turn out well.

Unfortunately, Seth wasn't even sure what he defined as "well." He only hoped it didn't involve being decked, dissected, or decimated by two angry women. He hurried toward the church.

Web was at the door, shaking hands. "Nice to see you, Seth. Jenna's waiting inside for you."

Seth nodded.

Web put a hand on his shoulder. "You look nervous. Is everything all right?"

"Peachy." He moved inside, but within seconds nearly backtracked to hide behind Web. For standing in the narthex talking with Jenna were Bonnie and her family.

Halt! Desist! Retreat while you still can!

Bonnie saw him before he had time to act and, worse, came toward him. "Seth. Good morning."

"Morning." He looked past Bonnie at Jenna. He smiled, trying to show her that she was included in the greeting.

"Hello, Seth," Jenna said.

The Bowden parents chimed in with their own hellos. So far it was very generic. Doable. Safe. After all, what was safer than a church lobby?

Home. Being home alone would be good.

The thought was reinforced when Bonnie linked her arm in his. "Let's go inside and sit. I'll lead you to the family pew."

If only he hadn't asked Jenna to meet him here, he could have enjoyed the victory of being included with the Bowden family. As they walked toward the entrance to the sanctuary, Seth longed to extend his hand to Jenna, to include her. Yet how . . . ?

Mr. Bowden did it for him. "Come on, Jenna. Join us."

The way things worked out Seth sat between Bonnie and Jenna, perhaps, all things considered, the most ideal solution to a very nonideal situation. As everyone settled in, he tried to calm his heart, just certain its beating showed through his shirt.

But then a window of opportunity opened. Bonnie leaned forward to chat with her parents seated to her right, giving Seth a chance to speak to Jenna to his left. He tried to think of something witty to say, but his mind was blank.

"You look pretty this morning," he said, giving her his most charming smile. "Like a vision in blue."

She nodded, but there was a crease between her eyebrows.

Seth tried again. "The Bowdens . . . they're nice people, yes? Letting us invade the family pew? They took over my family's farm. I represent the *before,* while they're doing quite well creating an *after.*"

"That's nice."

He nodded, then glanced toward Bonnie, hoping she was still talking to her parents, giving him more time to—

No such luck. She was looking right at him. He flashed a smile in her direction. Then back at Jenna. *Smile here, smile there, just keep smiling.*

Bonnie put a hand on his arm. "I was just talking to Mom and Dad and we wondered if you'd like to come to dinner after church," she said.

Seth started to look toward Jenna, but then Bonnie added, "Oh, yes . . . Jenna, you're welcome too."

Seth let out the breath he'd been saving. Problem solved. "That would be nice," he said. He turned his full attention to Jenna, waiting for her to accept.

She fumbled with words. "I . . . I don't—"

Suddenly Bonnie heard her name and turned toward a young woman in the side aisle who beckoned her over. "Excuse me," she said, sliding past her parents to get out.

Finally. Real time alone.

"You'll come, won't you?" Seth asked Jenna.

Her head shook no. A definite no.

"Why not?"

"I can't do this."

"Go to dinner?"

Another shake no. "I just . . ."

Seth felt true disappointment at her refusal. "It's just a dinner. I wish you'd come. I'd really like to spend more time—"

"I'm back," Bonnie whispered as she returned to her seat.

A man started playing the piano up front. The service was beginning. Yet all Seth could think about was the woman who wouldn't be coming to dinner.

Madeline knew Web would be mad that she didn't show up in church. Yet she'd often told him that making him mad was her goal in life. For what else gave spice to Web's existence? What else got his blood pumping? She was actually doing him a favor by riling him.

She nodded at her point and allowed her confidence to lengthen her stride down the driveway. A brisk walk through the park on a Sunday morning. Now *that* was the way to worship.

Madeline crossed the street and entered the park—which she had to herself. Fine with her. Madeline didn't mind being alone. She was strong in her convictions and if everyone else wanted to be a weak lamb, blindly following some shepherd in a toga, she couldn't stop them. That didn't mean she'd succumb.

She looked down as she walked, concentrating on the cracks in the sidewalk. *Step on a crack; break your mother's back.*

"Madeline?"

She looked up and saw Joan Goldberg. Joan was wearing a red jogging suit. Why wasn't she at church? Then she remembered the Goldbergs were Jewish. Wasn't Saturday their Sabbath? "Good morning, Joan."

"I thought you'd be in church with the others," Joan said.

"I'm quite content being a heathen. How about you?"

Joan looked appalled. "I'm Jewish."

One had nothing to do with the other. Did it? "Are you a practicing Jew?"

Joan laughed. "Practicing till I get it right. Ha-ha." She scuffed the toe of her Reeboks against the edge of the walk. "Actually . . . I don't even practice much."

"Why not?"

"If I answer, will *you* answer the same question?"

"Turnabout, fair play, and all that?"

"You bet."

They started walking and Joan talked. "Ira and I used to be faithful, but then life intervened and we got wrapped up in other things. I guess we put God on the back burner and just haven't had the time or inclination to take him off." She glanced at Madeline. "How 'bout you?"

"Truth is, the Weavers were into church for show more than substance. After Augustus died, I even let the show part slide. I mean, what's the use? Besides, I'm too old to change my ways."

"But your friend Web is preaching today. He must be very religious."

Madeline stifled a laugh, then crossed her fingers. "Web and God are this close. He's spent his entire life trying to get me to join in—accept Jesus." She waved her hands by her head. "'Ask Jesus into your heart, Maddy.'" She let her hands drop. "I get tired of it. If believing in Jesus is the way to heaven, well . . . I'll find my own way, thank you very much."

"You're pretty gutsy," Joan said.

She was surprised by Joan's objection. "You certainly can't believe that Jesus stuff? About him being the way to eternal life and all that?"

"No, no," Joan said. "Of course not. But . . . I do like the idea of heaven. I hope there is one."

They found themselves at the gate to the Weaver Garden, which made Madeline think of something else Web always said. "According to Web Jesus is the gate. And those who go through him will be saved. Speaking of gates . . ." She tried to open the iron one in front of her and found her way barred. "This stupid thing!"

"Let me try," Joan said. But in spite of her shaking and cajoling, the gate remained closed.

Madeline rattled it like a prisoner wanting to be set free. "*Uggghh.* I wash my hands of this. It's got to be the most temperamental piece of metal in the world. Now, if Web were here, he'd walk right up and get it open—without a struggle."

"That doesn't make sense," Joan said.

"No, it doesn't. But it's a fact. Web has a way with things like no man I've ever known."

Joan smiled. "I've wanted to ask, and now that you've opened *that* gate . . ."

"Were we lovers?"

Joan chuckled. "Were you?"

"No. But we have loved each other forever. If I hadn't married Augustus I would've married Web." She left out the part about actually being engaged to him.

"You'd have been the wife of a fix-it man." Joan put a hand to her chest. "That sounded awful. He's a very nice man, but considering you became a Weaver by marriage and gained a boatload of status and position . . ."

Madeline waved Joan's distress away. "Don't bother yourself feeling bad about stating facts. I've thought the same thought a hundred times."

"Was Augustus a good man?"

Madeline shrugged. "Good enough."

Joan nodded, but looked away.

"How about your Ira? Is he a good man?"

Joan took hold of the wrought-iron spikes that topped the fence. "He has his moments."

"Which means he also has his moments being a pill. Am I right?"

Joan looked across the garden and didn't say anything.

"Come on. Talk to me, Joan. We're two of the most mature women in Weaver, by age *and* by the fact we're here instead of with the weaker set this morning. I'm not going to condemn you— or him."

Joan let go of the fence and pointed to a bench nearby. They sat. "I'm worried about Ira's health."

"I didn't know he was sick."

Joan hesitated. "Not sick, sick. I'm worried about his mental health. Emotional health."

Madeline let an eyebrow rise. "Really."

"Ira spends an inordinate amount of time at the computer doing who knows what. And the rest of his time daydreaming."

"About what?"

Joan's lips opened, then closed.

"Spill it, heathen."

Joan's smile was fleeting. "Years ago there was another woman in his life and now . . . she lives close by."

My, my . . . "Do you think they're seeing each other?"

Suddenly, the words spilled out. "I'm beginning to think the main reason he agreed to enter this contest was so he could be near her. Sally lives in Topeka and used to work for him in the store, and I guess I knew he was infatuated with her, but when she quit and moved away, I thought that was that. But now it's clear he's never forgotten her and it sounds like there *was* something going on back then and . . ." Joan seemed to realize she was rambling. "She's agreed to meet him on Thursday, at our home, and . . . I don't know what to do."

Madeline fought back memories of finding Augustus in the bed of another woman. That scene, and the confrontation that followed, still played out in excruciating slow motion in her memories. "You stop it. You stop him. Now."

"How?"

"Call him on it."

"But he hasn't done anything."

"That you know of." Madeline patted Joan's back when her shoulders slumped. "Don't let this slide, Joan. You take hold of this situation and bring it to a head. You don't need the past sticking its foot in the door, ruining things."

"No, I don't."

"Then fix it."

Joan pinched a piece of lint from her jogging pants. "I plan to be home Thursday when they have their rendezvous."

"Skulking in a closet?"

Joan looked up. "Does that sound horrid?"

"Sounds smart to me. A woman's got to do what a woman's got to do." Even if it meant forcing the other woman out of town and using her husband's guilt to gain *herself* more power at the bank. Madeline knew from that experience—and others—that consequences were either costly or profitable, depending on which end of judgment's scale one was sitting upon.

Suddenly, Joan stood and looked down at Madeline. "Stand up, heathen. I feel a hug coming on."

Madeline stood and accepted Joan's gratitude. It was awkward.

Joan pulled back. "Thank you. I'm glad we ran into each other this morning. It was a nice coincidence."

"Web says there's no such thing."

Joan cocked her head, considering. "He told me that too."

Madeline was suddenly beyond weary. Her legs felt weak and she sat again. All these thoughts of consequences and judgment . . .

Joan touched her arm. "Are you all right? You look pale."

"I'm fine. Like I told you, get it settled. Life's too short to leave loose ends."

Joan looked at her oddly, then said her good-bye and walked off.

Madeline sat on the bench awhile, the thoughts of unfaithful husbands and mutinous bodies killing the joy of the morning.

Web was glad it was over. Many churchgoers had come up to him afterward, shaken his hand, and said nice things, but he would have rather slipped out the back and gone home without the to-do. He was satisfied with how the talk went, but he knew his limitations. He was no preacher and didn't want these people to start thinking he was.

He saw the last person out. "Bye, Mrs. McKenna. Have a good one."

Web closed the door of the church and leaned against it. The silence was a balm to his nerves. He hadn't thought he was so tense, but now that it was over and he was alone . . .

"Web?"

Web started. He looked to the left and saw Ryan Bauer coming out of the sanctuary. "Ryan, you startled me."

"Sorry." He nodded to the inside of the church. "I was just waiting in there until everybody left."

Interesting. Web walked toward him. "May I ask the reason for this waiting?"

Ryan shoved his hands in his pockets and grinned. "You clean up good."

"You don't look bad yourself, young man." He waited for the real talking to begin.

"I just . . ." Ryan looked at the wall to his left, to the photos of past pastors. "I just wanted to tell you that I'm back."

"Back?"

"The sabbatical's over." He eyed Web, as if waiting for him to get it.

"Oh . . . all renewed and restored?"

"Getting there."

He gave Ryan a slap to his back. "Good for you." They headed toward the front doors.

"But can I ask you one thing?" Ryan said.

"Sure."

"Did you know that Psalm 51 had the words *restore* and *renew* in it when you said them to me?"

"Psalm what?"

"Never mind." Ryan opened the door. "I'll see you tomorrow at work."

Web watched him go, then locked up, feeling quite content.

"Would you like some more mashed potatoes, Seth?"

Seth sat back and patted his stomach. "No thanks, Mrs. Bowden. You've got me stuffed and happy. I couldn't eat another thing."

She frowned. "Not even apple crisp?"

He loved apple crisp. He took an exaggerated breath. "Maybe just a little."

Amelia Bowden got up to get the dessert. Seth's brownie points were earned and cataloged. He was in. The family liked him. Bonnie liked him. And he liked them. Before he knew it he'd be back on this farm, making the Olsen name one with the earth once more.

As Mr. Bowden—"Call me Bill"—and Bonnie talked about their schedule for the next week, Seth looked around the dining room. He'd spent the first eighteen years of his life in this house, eating many meals in this room, though honestly, none as good as the one he'd just eaten. But it looked different with the Bowden oak furniture in place of his parents' walnut dining-room set with the striped, olive-and-orange upholstered seats. Only the shell was the same.

How much the same?

He looked to his left, toward the ceiling in the corner. Yup. There was the crack he'd often stared at when his mom had made him sit at the table and finish every bite of a meal because children were starving in Timbuktu. Oddly, seeing it was still there was like finding a long-lost treasure from his childhood. Maybe someday his own children would sit at this table and he could point to that crack and tell them the story of trying to choke down lima beans and liver. His wife would come in from the kitchen and say, "Stop it, honey; you've told that story a thousand times."

Bonnie laughed at something her father said, and Seth's attention was drawn back to the here and now. He was getting ahead of himself thinking of marriage and children. Yet, that *is* where he needed all this to end up.

When Amelia came through the door carrying apple crisp, Seth suddenly realized that the wife he'd just fantasized about, coming through that same door, was a wispy brunette with porcelain skin.

Wearing a flowing blue dress.

He punished himself for the thought by eating two helpings of dessert.

Jenna sat in the wing chair in Madeline's parlor, her knees drawn to her chest. She stared at nothing. If only she could think of nothing.

Her mind teemed with thoughts of Seth Olsen. She hated the jealousy that had grabbed her when she'd seen Bonnie take his arm at church. There was no reason for her to have such a feeling. She barely knew the man. She'd sworn off men. On his part, sure, he'd been nice to her, talked to her, smiled at her, made her laugh. But that shouldn't have caused her to feel jealous if he did the same with someone else. She wasn't that needy—or easy.

She was smarter now. Wary. Hopefully on the edge of wise. She couldn't risk trusting a man now or ever. Besides, she didn't deserve a guy like Seth anymore—and chances are, would never have a chance with a guy like him. So why dream? Life had thrown her a curveball and she had to deal with it. Somehow. Some way.

"My, my, child, Web's sermon wasn't that bad, was it?"

Jenna looked up to see her aunt in the foyer. It took her a moment to change the direction of her thoughts. "Web did great. He was quite inspiring. You should've been there."

"Hmm." Madeline came in the room and put a finger on Jenna's upraised knee. "You don't look very inspired. You look depressed."

Jenna forced a smile. "Pensive. I'm pensive."

"Good try, young lady. But that wrinkle in your brow speaks otherwise."

They held each other's gaze a few seconds. Jenna tried to look strong, tried to make her aunt understand that she would *not* talk about it.

Finally Auntie sighed. "Well, then."

Jenna put her feet on the floor. "So. What do you need me to do today for the Founders celebration?"

Madeline started to answer, but was distracted by the sound of a car in the drive. She went to the window, pulling the curtain aside. "Do you know anyone who drives a baby blue Beetle?"

Oh no . . . Jenna was at the window in seconds. "It's Mother!"

They watched as Barb Camden started for the front door. "Well, well," Madeline said. "Is mama hen coming to collect her baby chick?"

Jenna ran up the stairs. "Tell her I'm not here."

Madeline went into the foyer, her voice demanding. "You get down here this minute, Jenna Camden! I will not allow you to hide. It's time you two had this out. You came here because of a disagreement; now fix it."

"So you can get rid of me?"

Madeline pointed at her. "You're welcome here as long as you want—you know that. But now it's time to make nicey-nice to your mother."

"Even if she doesn't deserve it?"

"Even if."

The doorbell rang. Jenna found a spot to stand on the third step from the bottom. Her insides clenched as if the boogeyman stood on the other side of the door, ready to burst in and do his worst. It was a ridiculous feeling.

It was just her mother. *Ha*. Barb Camden could be called many things, but *mother* was not one of them.

Her aunt answered the door. "Looky here. Another relative come to visit," Madeline said. "But what have you done to your hair, Barb? It's practically pumpkin."

Jenna's mother came inside, patting her short shag. "It's called Hibiscus."

"It's quite . . . tropical," Madeline said.

Barb's eyes found Jenna. "I've been looking all over for you, girl. And after checking with all your friends, I find you here?"

Jenna had been gone from home six weeks and her mother was only now trying to find her? And how did she know who her friends were anyway? She'd never paid any attention to Jenna's life beyond the necessary. Her mother was lying. She hadn't called anyone.

Madeline shut the door.

Silence. Prolonged silence.

Suddenly, Madeline opened the door wide. "Out! Both of you."

The force in her aunt's voice caused Jenna to bobble on the step. She grabbed the railing for support. What was Auntie so upset about?

"Come on, you two. I said get out! I will not tolerate stubbornness in my house—not by anyone but me. So if you want to do the silence game, instigate the thrust and parry, or play dodgeball with each other, I don't care. Just do it outside. I have things to do."

"That's the welcome I get?" Barb asked.

"Take it or leave it."

Jenna decided to grab the upper hand by being generous. "Hello, Mother."

"See?" Madeline said, taking her hand off the doorknob. "Jenna's willing to be civil. Now both of you, come into the parlor."

Said the spider to the fly. Jenna sought the stability of a seated position, returning to the chair she'd been sitting in. She was glad her mother took the far end of the couch. Her aunt sat on the couch, between them.

"Well then," Madeline said, slapping her thighs, "who wants to go first?"

Barb's breathing was heavy. "I'll go."

"Good for—"

"It's all Jenna's fault!"

Jenna recoiled at the frenzy in her mother's face as much as at her words. If anyone was to blame for the current situation it was her mother. "You're one to talk," Jenna said. She purposely kept her voice low. Jenna was determined to counter whatever over-the-top emotion her mother displayed with calm. Auntie respected calm.

"You think any of this is my doing?" Barb said.

"Absolutely," Jenna said.

Her mother's jaw dropped. "I did everything I could to keep Rex with me. He only started acting strange when you left, so it's obvious you're the one who caused the prob—"

It took Jenna a moment. "Rex left you?"

"Moved out yesterday."

She popped out of her chair, her plan for calm forgotten. "I have to go."

"Go?" Madeline said. "Don't be ridiculous."

Jenna rushed to the stairs. It wouldn't take her long to pack. She had to get farther away. States and states away.

"Jenna! Stop!"

Jenna paused on the top stair and looked down at her aunt. There was no way to explain. No way her aunt would understand. "I have to go, Auntie. I have to."

Her mother appeared in the foyer. "I knew you were guilty, and now you're proving it. Guilty as sin."

Madeline flashed a look at Barb. "Hush, Barb. Jenna . . . you need to explain yourself."

"I can't." If she said the words out loud nothing would ever be the same. She couldn't do it. She couldn't.

"You can explain and you will," Barb said. "Now get down here and tell me what you did to make Rex leave, because I know it's your fault. And he was the best thing that's happened to me since the divorce."

Her mother's eyes got misty. She was sincere. She actually

believed what she said. It was preposterous. Jenna let out an expulsion of air. "Are you totally blind?"

Her mother blinked up at her. "He was good to me, took care of me—until you drove him away."

Her mother's total ignorance and gall lured Jenna back down the stairs. "I left because of that man—that awful, horrible, nasty, evil—"

Madeline applauded. "Good, good. Now we're getting somewhere. Let's sit and finish this thing."

Barb didn't budge. "You're being hateful, Jenna. He's none of those things. It's because of you treating him so badly . . . he said *that's* why he couldn't stick around."

Madeline raised a finger along with her point. "Hold up a minute. Jenna's here. She left. If what he's saying is true . . . with her gone, he'd have no reason to leave."

Barb hesitated, but only for a moment. "He loves me. I know he loves me." She backtracked to the parlor, sat on the couch, pulled her purse to her lap, and got out a Kleenex. Madeline returned to her place on the couch, but Jenna remained standing near the foyer, wanting to keep her options open.

Barb dabbed at the corner of her eyes even though Jenna hadn't seen any real tears materialize. Once her theatrics were complete, Barb put her hands in her lap. "What *did* you do to him to drive him away?"

This was ridiculous. "Do to him? What did *I* do to him? Do? I do?"

Barb nodded, waiting like the ignorant, overly trusting, needy woman she was. Rex wasn't the first boyfriend her mother had lived with since the divorce. But he was certainly the worst.

Barb turned to Madeline. "Rex is such a kind man. He was always doing things for us, taking care—"

Jenna had heard enough. "Oh, he took care of us all right. He *did* for us, all right." Jenna looked toward the stairs, toward escape. Yet where could she run to? This wasn't going to go away. Ever.

Barb spoke to Madeline again. "She's always been jealous of my boyfriends, and since Rex was by far the handsomest one of the lot—"

Jenna sucked in a breath and used the fuel to propel her next words into the air. "He raped me!"

Madeline gasped.

But Jenna's mother just sat there, her mouth slightly open, her forehead furrowed as if she were contemplating a difficult math problem—like one plus one. Surely she was going to react. Surely she would show some hint of outrage or compassion.

Barb snapped out of it, but her features did not soften into those of a mother ready to comfort her child. Instead they pulled into odd angles, her eyes small, her nose scrunched in disgust.

Suddenly, she sprang from the couch, and before Jenna could retreat, Barb took hold of Jenna's upper arms and shook her. "You lying, filthy, ungrateful girl. How dare you say—"

Madeline's hands got into the mix and managed to pull Barb away. "Barb! Enough!"

Madeline kept her at bay by putting a hand to Barb's chest. Jenna was amazed by her aunt's strength, but knew her mother was the strongest of the bunch. If she came at her again . . .

Forget her mother's physical outburst. Jenna was sobered by the hatred in her eyes. She'd seen many emotions in those eyes through the years but up until now, she'd never seen hatred. And at this new revelation, she realized there would be no sympathy and no apologies for bringing Rex into their lives. In this one crossing of the room Barb Camden had taken sides, leaving Jenna alone. To deal with *everything*.

But not completely alone.

For Madeline was leading Barb back to the couch, telling her to calm down. Her aunt might be on Jenna's side. Might.

Madeline turned to Jenna. "You, child. You come over here and sit." When Jenna shook her head, Madeline pointed at the chair. "It's my house. My rules. Sit."

Jenna sat and was again glad for the stability of the chair beneath her.

Madeline took her place between them. "Now then. Let's sort through this."

"There's nothing to sort through," Barb said. "She's lying!"

Jenna slowly shook her head from side to side. No, she wasn't lying. No, this would never work out. No, her mother would never listen. No, there was no hope.

"Barb," Madeline said, "you *will* be still and let your daughter talk."

"But if she's going to repeat the lie—"

Jenna felt hollow, as if the breath of her mother's words could make her disintegrate, to be dust for the cleaning woman to sweep up and discard.

Madeline pointed at Barb. "Shh! Not another word."

Barb closed her mouth with a tap of her teeth.

Madeline turned to Jenna. "Now. Calmly, tell us what happened."

Jenna nodded toward her mother. "She doesn't care," Jenna managed. "It's obvious no matter what I say she'll blame me."

Madeline turned to Barb. "You will listen with an open mind, won't you, Barb?"

At first Barb didn't answer, but when Madeline didn't look away, she finally nodded.

"Go on. Tell us," Madeline said softly.

Jenna fingered the fabric of her dress, finding comfort in its silky texture. She allowed herself two deep breaths, and with the new air seemed to find a modicum of energy. Oddly, once she began to speak, she discovered the story wasn't hesitant to come out, as if it had been patiently waiting in the wings for its cue. "One evening, about six weeks ago when Mother was out, Rex——" she let the next words pour out in a rush, afraid of being interrupted——"Rex had come onto me a few times before then, but I'd always been able to tell him to back off. Honestly, I just thought he was one of those guys who liked flirting. I didn't think he was dangerous and——"

"He's not!"

"Barb . . . ," Madeline warned.

Jenna smoothed her skirt over her legs. "But on that night he wouldn't stop. He wouldn't back down. I moved from room to room trying to avoid him, but he followed me, trying to touch me, teasing, getting too close, saying suggestive things. I decided it was best to leave and was getting my car keys and purse when he cornered me in the kitchen, grabbed me hard, and kissed . . ."

Her hand shook as she put it to her mouth and her next breaths were taken with difficulty. "I . . . I tried to get away, but he . . . but he chased . . . chased me down, and forced me . . ." She looked at her mother, then at her aunt. "He raped me."

There. It was out. The deed was done. It was now a reality for all to acknowledge.

Barb's head was caught in a pendulum swing. "I don't believe you."

Jenna glared, her anger rose, and with it, a surge of energy. "Do you want details, Mother? I can give you plenty of details to prove that I've seen what only you——no, I take that back——what probably too many women have seen regarding your boyfriend's anatomy."

"Shh! Both of you." Madeline turned to Jenna. "I can't tell you how sorry I am, Jenna. Did you go to the police?"

Barb popped out of her seat. "Police? Is that why Rex left?"

"No, I didn't report it."

"You should have," Madeline said. "The man needs to be arrested and brought to—"

Barb's arms flailed. "Oh no you don't. You aren't going to arrest Rex for any such thing. He's innocent."

Jenna began to cry. To have her mother take that cretin's side over her own . . . *she* was the victim. Her mother should be comforting *her*.

"You really should have reported it," Madeline said softly. "Now, it's going to be hard to prove—"

Barb's smile was full of victory. "Exactly. She can't prove anything!"

"That doesn't mean it didn't happen, Barb."

"It *didn't* happen," she said. "And since she has no proof, it's just her word against his."

With effort Jenna stood, then slowly stepped toward her mother, needing to be close when she dropped the bomb. Needing to see her face. Wanting to witness the shock in her eyes. "You want proof?" She put her hands over her abdomen. "I have the ultimate proof."

Her aunt understood first and whispered the words. "You're pregnant?"

Jenna nodded.

Barb's head shook vehemently. "It could be anybody's child."

The threat of tears evaporated at the coldness of her mother's words. "It's his."

Barb stared at Jenna, her chest heaving. Moments passed. "Get an abortion and be done with it."

Jenna wished she could act aghast at her mother's suggestion, but in truth she'd thought of it—thought of it enough, was desperate enough, to go to Dr. Bauer at the clinic the other day and ask him to do it. He'd refused. And though Jenna hadn't made a definite decision either way, the fact that her mother wanted her to have the abortion was a vote in favor of having the baby.

"No abortion. She will do no such thing," Madeline said.

Her aunt's words surprised her. She'd always thought of Madeline Weaver as a modern woman, up-to-date in every way. Jenna often felt conservative compared to her feisty auntie.

"You want me to have the baby?" Jenna asked.

"I want you to have no regrets."

"But I have huge regrets," Jenna said. "If only none of this had—"

"But it did happen, Jenna. Now you have to deal with it the best you can."

"Exactly," her mother said. "Get an abortion."

"Quiet!" Madeline said. She came to Jenna's side and put an arm around her shoulders. Her eyes pinned her down with their intensity. "I was pregnant once."

"What?" Barb said. "You never had any children."

Madeline kept her eyes on Jenna. "I was pregnant, but because it happened when I'd just started to work at the bank, when I'd just started getting my father-in-law to accept me as a working equal, I decided I couldn't have a baby and let him fall back into seeing me as *just* a woman. So I got rid of it."

"Why didn't you have another one?"

For the first time ever Jenna saw tears in her aunt's eyes. Madeline let go and walked a few steps away. "I couldn't. The procedure was botched and I never got pregnant again." She faced them, her eyes on fire again. "God punished me, but you . . . you will not have the same thing happen to you. You will have this baby and have no regrets."

Jenna was touched that her aunt had shared such a hard secret.

She moved close and pulled her into a hug. "Thank you for telling me. It means—"

"Well, well," Barb said. "Who'da thought the high-and-mighty Madeline Weaver had an abortion? An illegal one, no doubt, considering the times."

Suddenly, Madeline grabbed hold of Barb's arm and, showing amazing strength, pulled her toward the door. "We've had enough of you." With her free hand she yanked the door open. "Out. And away."

"You can't kick me out."

"Wanna bet?" Madeline shoved Barb over the threshold and closed the door.

Barb screamed, "Good riddance! Who needs you anyway? You're both trouble. I'm glad to be rid of you." Barb stormed off the porch.

Jenna heard the car start and back out of the driveway with squealing tires. She found she'd been holding her breath. She let it out and looked at her aunt. Where could they go from here?

Madeline shook her head slowly. "Why didn't you tell me?"

A million reasons, and none at all. All she could offer was a shrug. Luckily, it was good enough, and her aunt slipped her arm through hers and led her back into the parlor, to the desk where Madeline took a seat. Then she took up the phone and dialed.

Who was she calling?

Too soon, Jenna found out.

"Seth? This is Madeline Weaver. Would you please come to the house immediately? Jenna needs your services. Now." She hung up. "He'll be right over."

"I don't want Seth to know. I don't want anyone to know."

"So you want a rapist to get off scot-free, so he can rape again?"

"Of course not."

"Then stand tall and do the right thing."

"But we just said it's too late."

"Maybe. Maybe not. The point is, Officer Olsen will know what to do."

Seth returned his cell phone to the holder on his waist. "I have to leave."

"What's going on?" Bonnie asked.

"Mrs. Weaver needs me at her house. She didn't say why. But it sounds serious." He felt a bit guilty for not mentioning that Mrs. Weaver had specifically stated that it was Jenna who needed his services, but that fact *did* add urgency to the situation. He turned around from their stroll down the lane and started back to the Bowden house.

Bonnie sighed. "We've barely started our walk. We were having such a lovely afternoon."

And they were. Seth couldn't deny it. He enjoyed Bonnie's company. But that didn't stop him from nearly jogging to get back to his car.

So he could get to Jenna.

"We want you to arrest the slimeball," Mrs. Weaver said after she and Jenna had told Seth about Jenna's rape.

"I'm afraid it's not that easy." He glanced at Jenna. Her eyes were red from the crying that had come with having to relive the whole thing again. She sat across the dining-room table, but he longed to close the distance between them. If only he could reach across and take her hand, offer comfort in some way.

But Jenna held her aunt's hand. There was her comfort. They'd brought him over in a professional capacity, not as a friend. And certainly not as someone who felt the emotion of deep empathy that went beyond the normal compassion of a police officer for a victim. And then there were the emotions of hatred and anger that made him want to hunt down Rex Mennard and make him pay. And the emotion of confusion because he knew he shouldn't be feeling such ownership in the situation, as if it affected him personally. Not when he was setting his heart on Bonnie Bowden and seeking hers.

"Certainly you can do something," Mrs. Weaver said.

He shook his head. "We need evidence. At the time it happened, if she'd reported it and had a rape kit done, we would have been able . . ." He wished he had better news. "I'm truly sorry."

Mrs. Weaver slapped her hand on the table. "Bring the guy in! Make him confess."

This brought a small smile to Jenna's face. "I'm afraid my aunt has been watching too many cop shows. Even if they brought him in, Auntie, even if he admitted sex had occurred, he'd deny it was rape. He'd say I seduced him."

"DNA!" Mrs. Weaver said. "When the baby is born you can prove it's his child through the DNA."

Jenna shook her head. "At that point I wouldn't want to prove he's the father. I don't want him in my life. I don't want him to even know there is a baby."

"Good point," Seth said. "He doesn't know you're pregnant?"

Jenna pulled her hand from her aunt's grip and gasped. "Mother! Mother knows! She might tell him."

Mrs. Weaver took her hand back. "Maybe. *If* Barb ever finds him, which I doubt she will. He's the one who left, and if your mother's charming behavior today was any indication of what she's like to live with, I think we can safely assume he's long gone."

"I hope so," Jenna said. She looked at Seth. "I should have reported it. I admit that. But now, since it'll do no good, I never want to think of him again. I want to move on."

Seth was greatly impressed. How could this delicate being harbor such an inner strength? "You're a very strong woman."

She smiled at her aunt. "Stronger now than I was yesterday. What doesn't kill us makes us stronger, right?"

"That's my girl." Madeline rose from the table and Seth stood. "No, no. You sit. I'm going to get us each a huge piece of chocolate cake and some coffee. How does that sound?"

Though he was still stuffed from the Bowden dinner he couldn't refuse. He wouldn't. "That'd be nice," he said.

Seth entered his house and slammed the front door. A framed black-and-white photo of Long's Peak fell to the floor. He let it be and threw his keys on the couch where they bounced, hit a vase of flowers he'd picked from the yard, and knocked them to the floor.

He couldn't ignore the seeping water like he'd ignored the picture. He righted the vase and rushed to the kitchen for a towel. What a mess—in regard to the flowers and his love life.

He'd just spent time with two wonderful women. Both were pretty, both were good conversationalists, both brought out the best of his charm and witty nature. But as far as what they could offer him . . .

The family farm loomed behind any thought of Bonnie like a

prize hung just out of reach. His whole reason for entering the contest culminated in what perks came out of their relationship.

Then there was Jenna.

He brought the wet towel back to the kitchen and dropped it in the sink. He leaned against the counter, his head low between his shoulders. *Jenna, Jenna, Jenna.* Delicate, soft, lovely Jenna with the shy smile and gentle laugh. What did she have to offer him?

She was pregnant by a rapist. She was a victim. She was needy.

He didn't want to be needed. He liked strong women who took life as it came.

Yet she was doing just that—she was getting through this horrible time. Dealing. Surviving.

But a baby. Jenna had never said if she was going to keep it. He had no trouble picturing her with a child. But picturing himself beside her, as she held a baby—another man's baby?

He lifted his head and looked at his reflection in the window. Confused eyes stared back at him.

What a mess.

ELEVEN

Whenever trouble comes your way,
let it be an opportunity for joy.
For when your faith is tested,
your endurance has a chance to grow.
So let it grow, for when your endurance is fully developed,
you will be strong in character and ready for anything.

JAMES 1:2-4

Kathy stuffed her makeup bag into the suitcase. Her mind was full of lists. Did she have everything? Navy pants, white shirt, flats, belt . . .

"Mom?"

She spun around to see Ryan standing in the bedroom doorway. "What are you doing up so early?"

"I wanted to talk to you before you left."

Ryan? Talk? She attempted to keep her eyebrows in their nonsurprised position, but couldn't be sure how successful she was. "Come in."

He took one step forward, then stopped. The old gym shorts and wrinkled T-shirt he slept in matched the tousled condition of his hair. He wrapped his arms around himself. He didn't talk.

The to-dos nudged her, urging her to hurry. Lavon was waiting for her to pick him up. "You had something to say?"

His weight shifted. "Just be careful, okay?"

She was a little confused by the seriousness in his voice. He sounded more like a father than a son. It must be the highway trip that was worrying him. The driving. None of them got in a car anymore without thinking about Lisa's fate.

Kathy put her hands on his upper arms. "I'll be fine. We'll be fine."

His eyebrows dipped and his eyes flitted across hers. "Just be careful. About everything. Not just the driving."

She pulled him into a hug. "You be careful too, okay?"

Ryan went back to bed. Kathy went back to her packing. Lavon was waiting.

Roy helped Kathy slip the last of the paintings into the back of the van.

"Watch the corner," she said.

"Yeah, yeah."

Kathy looked over her checklist—again. "I think I have everything."

"I've heard they do have general living supplies in St. Louis."

His mood was hard to read. He seemed peeved one minute but solicitous the next. He followed Kathy to the driver's side, where she opened the door and faced him for their final good-bye. It was hard not to let her excitement show. Seeing Sandra again, planning the showing . . . it would be a fun weekend. And perhaps her career would take off again. Plus, the added anticipation of good company on the trip there and back. She bounced twice on her toes but forced herself to stop. "Well then, here I go. Say a prayer that everything goes great."

With a sigh, Roy pulled her into his arms. "I do, Kath. I hope everything is wonderful." He kissed her once, then added, "Say hi to Sandra for me. Safe journey. Call me."

She nodded, but suddenly felt tears threaten and couldn't look at him. "I'll miss you. I love you, you know."

"I know. I love you too."

She felt really bad—for about a block. Then she let her excitement take over.

Joan's mind was mush. Spy would never be a suggested vocation for her. Even though she'd tried to work on soda-fountain stuff all morning, her mind had rebelled by zeroing in on thoughts of Ira and Sally and their meeting at one o'clock. The images of what might transpire intertwined with the details of her plan to be there as a witness.

When she went home for lunch at eleven-thirty, she was appalled by what a good actor Ira was. If she hadn't known what was about to transpire she wouldn't have guessed he had any plans beyond the norm. He was totally calm and composed as he ate his tuna sandwich and Cheetos.

Which ticked her off because it made her question other times in their past when he had obviously applied the calm façade while he was messing around. The least the man could do was act guilty.

Toward that end, Joan considered blowing his cool by telling him she was going to stay home this afternoon and work around the house. *Deal with that, bucko.* But in truth, she wanted this whole thing done. And so at twelve-fifteen, she put her plate in the dishwasher and headed back to the store.

"Have a good afternoon, honey," he said.

You too, honey bunny.

However, instead of driving back to the shop, Joan parked a block away and ran back to the house. Getting inside without being seen might be difficult, but she counted on Ira's obsession with the computer to lure him upstairs for one more hit before Sally's arrival. Or maybe he'd go upstairs to comb his four hairs over the top of his bald spot in an attempt to get pretty for the bimbo.

She peered in the kitchen window. He wasn't there, and she didn't see any movement in the living room beyond.

She backed up a few steps in order to check the window of his office. As expected, the light was on. Perfect. She slipped in the back door, turning the knob and holding it so she could close it without a click.

Then she moved to her hiding place. Since there was no hiding place that would *not* be dramatic, she'd decided to go for the full effect by taking up residence in the entry closet. Although she wasn't sure she'd do it, popping out at the appropriate time yelling, "Surprise!" had a certain appeal. Or, if she chickened out, hunkering down between the folds of their coats until it was safe to come out had its own tragic feel.

She moved to the closet, but when she opened it, she found the floor filled with boxes. Ira must have stuffed them in there.

She heard movement upstairs.

Without time to waste, she shoved the boxes to the back, got inside, and closed the door.

Her right leg was skewed oddly. She needed to rearrange, but wasn't sure there was enough room. The drape of the coats pressed around her face, making it hard to—

Suddenly, she heard Ira coming down the stairs.

She held her breath. She heard him move into the kitchen. There was the clink of the coffeepot against its maker, then water running. He was making coffee for his rendezvous. Since when was he a good host?

Joan was forced to push such thoughts aside as her body rebelled at its cramped quarters. There was no way she would be able to sit quietly for any length of time in this stifling prison.

Knowing time was ticking away, she made a bold decision. She opened the door, climbed out, closed it, then ran up the stairs on her toes. Into the office she went. As soon as Sally came she'd go out into the hall and listen. She checked the computer. It was off. Ira would not be back before Sally's visit. Yes, this would be better. At least she could breathe up here.

Joan positioned herself behind the door, still leaving it wide for appearance's sake.

But then she saw something very odd. She closed the door more, creating some distance so she could see better. But seeing did not help her understand.

The entire back of the door was covered with *S*s. They assaulted her like a slug in the gut. Thousands of *S*s, some as small as a quarter-inch high, covered the door. The collage must have taken hours to create. Previously, she'd guessed the few *S*s she'd seen him cut out stood for Sally. Odd, but harmless. Yet this door was above and beyond . . . this door was evidence of obsession. Fixation. Even madness?

She heard the doorbell and was hurled back to the moment. Joan put a hand to her chest, attempting to calm her breathing. At the rate her heart was pounding in her ears, she'd never be able to hear a word.

Then the voices began.

First, Ira's. "Hello, Sally. It's so good to see you."

"Nice to see you again too, Ira."

"I've made coffee. I remember the way you like it. Cream, two sugars."

"You have a good memory," Sally said.

"I remember everything, my dear. Everything."

Though Joan's stomach felt as if she should consider a dash to the bathroom, she moved out of her hiding place behind the door, into the hallway at the top of the stairs. Good or bad, she had to hear.

"Ira, you promised."

"I promised to behave myself, and I will," he said. "But that doesn't mean I can't bring up our past."

"*Our* past? We don't have a past."

"Don't be mean, Sally."

Her voice rose. "I'm not, or I'm trying not to be. But you make it very difficult." Joan heard her walk across the room, her heels loud on the oak floor. She stopped walking. "You have to quit pretending there was more to our relationship than there was."

"Oh, my dear, denying what was is an insult to both of us."

"What *was*?"

"Our love for each other."

There was a moment's pause; then Sally stroked each word: "I have never loved you, Ira."

He didn't miss a beat. "Of course you did. And it scares you. I understand that. That's why you felt the need to run away. I was married and you respected that and—"

"I quit because you were making my life uncomfortable."

"Love is often uncomfortable."

Her laugh was cruel. "Don't flatter yourself. I have never loved you. Never. Ever."

Joan put a hand to her mouth. This didn't make sense. Maybe Sally was in a state of denial. Maybe she knew she was being over-heard and was covering herself.

Yet as Sally continued with her harangue, with her denial of any connection beyond business, Joan knew what she said was the truth. There'd never been an affair. The romantic relationship between her husband and this woman was one-sided.

Oddly, she found herself sad. Yes, it was good to find out that Ira had not been physically unfaithful, but the fact that he'd thought there was love where there'd been none, that he'd imag-ined intimacy, that he'd longed for it, that he'd moved halfway across the country for it . . .

Joan imagined the hurt on his face, the way his jowls must be sagging in despair, the way a cupped crease would have formed in the space between his eyes.

His voice was unsteady. "You . . . you're just protecting yourself from being hurt a second time, Sally. But I assure you, I would never hurt you. In fact I've moved here to be close to you, and I'm willing to totally commit to you and—"

Her voice was incredulous. "But I'm married! I have a child."

Silence. Then Ira said, "I can love your child as my own. I promise."

"Ira . . . you're crazy."

"Yes, I admit it. I'm crazy in love with you, dearest Sally."

Movement.

Then, "Get away from me! Don't you dare touch me!" Heels on the floor. Then the sound of the front door opening. "You stay away from me, Ira Goldberg, or I'll call the police. You're a sick, demented man. Get out of my life! No more calls. No more letters. No more presents. I never want to see you again. Ever!"

The door slammed. The house filled with silence. Joan held her breath. The silence continued. Had Ira left? Had he gone after Sally, taking his humiliation into the town where people might see?

Joan was just about to check when she heard a loud thump and bang on the floor. She ran onto the stairs and saw Ira in a crumpled heap next to a toppled coffee table. She rushed down to him and lifted his head onto her arm. "Ira? Are you okay? Ira?"

He opened his eyes and looked up at her. At first it was as if he didn't recognize her. Then his eyes cleared slightly. "Joan?"

"I'm here. Shh. I'm here."

Suddenly, with the panic of a drowning man, he grabbed her and pulled himself up into her arms. He sobbed against her shoulder.

And she comforted him.

Ira had to be helped onto the couch. He acted like a zombie—unseeing, uncaring. To her initial question of "Want to tell me what all that was about?" he didn't answer. Not even a shrug. He slumped onto the cushions as responsive as a sack of potatoes.

She tried to shock him into a reply. "You say there was an affair; Sally denies it. Who's lying?"

He stared into the space between his knees and the coffee table. His right hand stroked his left as if it needed comfort. There was no indication he'd even heard her.

It wasn't fair. How could she have a decent fight when he wouldn't cooperate? And fight she must, because that's what one did with an unfaithful husband.

If he actually was unfaithful.

Her next thought formed into words, as much for her benefit as his. "You know, Ira, it doesn't really matter if anything happened or not because it's clear you pulled a Jimmy Carter, committing adultery in your rotten, two-timing heart."

He sniffed.

Joan wanted to insist he defend himself. Anything to prove he was alive, aware of what was going on, capable of cognizant thought, capable of acting at all like the Ira she knew.

But he gave her nothing. And in his nothingness, her heart melted.

She patted the throw pillow, getting it into position against the couch's arm. "Why don't you lie down." When he didn't move, she took his legs and swung them onto the couch, forcing his torso to pivot with them. She was relieved when he leaned against the pillow on his own.

Joan opened an afghan and covered him, manually lifting his arms to tuck it underneath. She righted the coffee table and sat on it. Who was this man? She'd noticed he'd been a little spacey during the past few years, but to jump from that to this . . . this broken *child* of a man?

She put a hand on top of his. "Can I get you anything?"

He looked right at her. Then he fumbled until he held her hands. *Finally! He's coming out of it.* "You had me scared there, old man. You rest now and when you wake up we can talk all about—"

His face suddenly brightened. "She still loves me, doesn't she?"

Joan's heart stopped and a surge of sorrow sped through her body, baring ragged teeth and biting open a gaping wound. Right behind it was the salt of fear.

He was waiting.

She squeezed his hands. "Of course she loves you. What's not to love?"

He smiled, nodded, and closed his eyes to sleep, content in his own little world.

Oblivious that Joan's had just been destroyed.

Can I leave him alone?

Joan stood at the front door and looked back at her husband, asleep on the couch. It was an odd thought to have about a grown man—a man she'd been married to for decades. Yet *that* Ira and *this* Ira were as different as a live bear and a stuffed one. She wanted her bear back—growls and all.

His snore told her he was in deep sleep. She could leave. She had to leave. Get fresh air. Remove herself from the confines of the place where her world had been blown apart. If she didn't, she'd find herself babbling and yanking out clumps of hair.

Joan locked the door with her key—locking him in?—and drove away. Where? She hadn't a clue.

Her mind swam with questions that had no answers. Was Ira really crazy? Or was he faking his confusion, embarrassed by the Sally incident? Either way, it left her in a predicament. Should she—could she—stay with him? Or should she just keep driving and leave Weaver entirely? She'd proven she could start over, so should she do it again, somewhere else? Alone?

She spotted Web changing the lettering on the sign outside the church. Without exactly knowing why, she stopped and got out of her car.

Web stood up from his work. "Nice to see you, Joan. How are you this fine day?"

She found herself stammering. "I . . . uh, I was just . . ." She laughed and offered a shrug. "I'm not very eloquent today."

"Luckily, eloquence has never been a prerequisite for neighborly conversation." He gathered the box of white letters and closed the glass front on the sign that said God Answers Knee-Mail. "Come inside. I'm ready for a sit and a chat."

Inside? A church?

Her face must have revealed her panic because he laughed. "It's perfectly safe. I promise."

What could she say? She followed his lead and went up the steps into a red-carpeted lobby. An office sat to the right. It looked a lot like the synagogue she and Ira had occasionally attended back in California. But when Web went through some double doors and entered the sanctuary, Joan balked.

"We can be comfortable in—" He looked back at her, hesitated, then moved to the very last pew in the back. "How about this? Close to the door."

Again, she had no defense for why she didn't want to come inside, so she slipped in as quickly as possible and sat on the edge of the cushioned seat hoping Jesus wouldn't notice.

Web sank beside her with a groan. "Ah. Now that's the ticket. Sometimes I get going on to-dos and forget I also need time for nothing to do."

Joan made an attempt at levity. "All work and no play makes Jack . . ."

"'Come to me, all of you who are weary and carry heavy burdens, and I will give you rest.'"

Weary, carrying heavy burdens. It was a good summation.

"Care to share?" Web asked.

Joan shook her head incredulously. "I have got to get myself a new face. It seems I can't keep a single emotion secret."

"Do you want to keep them secret?"

"I don't necessarily want the entire world to know."

"Then how 'bout just me?"

How about just him? Joan ran a hand along the top of the pew in front of them, the cool smoothness of the oak a comfort. Her eyes strayed to the large cross that hung on the front wall behind the altar. So strong. So imposing. So . . .

He patted her arm. "We have the same God, Joan, the same roots. We Christians just celebrate where you Jews left off."

She wasn't sure what he meant by that but took heart in the calm assurance of his tone. "I'm having some trouble with Ira." She hadn't meant to tell Web the details. She'd meant to give him a condensed version. But once the words started flowing, they didn't stop. Not until she was done and the story was complete, down to every last *S*.

Complete except for an answer as to what to do next.

"I'm so sorry, Joan."

"I don't know what to do."

He nodded, and she thought, *He doesn't either.* But then he surprised her by saying, "Here's what you do. You go home, give Ira a hug, tell him you love him, and—"

She scooted away. "Hug him? Love him? He's in love with another woman!"

"Maybe. But obviously he's mentally confused right now."

Joan snickered. "*Crazy* is the word I'd use."

"He needs help. Professional help."

Her defenses rose. "And what am I supposed to do while he's getting this help?"

"Stick by him. 'In sickness and in health,' right?"

"Jews don't say that when they get married," Joan said.

Web nodded. "I bet you say something similar."

In truth, Joan couldn't remember what had been said at their wedding; she wasn't sure what had been promised. But certainly,

God wouldn't expect her to hang around with a husband who'd been pulling away from her for years, and who—at least mentally—was unfaithful.

"Ira needs you, Joan."

"He's hurt me."

"Indeed he has. And it will probably get worse before it gets better."

She let out a huff. "This is your idea of encouragement?"

"It's a truth and 'the truth will set you free.'"

"At what cost?"

Web nodded toward the cross up front. "Doing the right thing is always worth the cost—even if it's hard."

"I'll have to take your word on that."

He smiled. "You have it. Mine—" he nodded again toward the cross—"and his." Web stood and offered her his hand.

She rose—reluctantly. "Thank you for talking with me."

He shrugged. "So . . . what *are* you going to do now?"

Her thoughts refused to move past the immediate. "I guess I'll go home and see if Ira's awake."

"And the hug and the I love you?"

"We'll see."

Web pulled her into a hug of her own. "God be with you, Joan. And with Ira."

As Joan left the sanctuary she glanced over her shoulder toward the cross. Odd how it didn't scare her anymore.

When Joan opened the front door, she panicked. Ira wasn't on the couch. The afghan lay in a heap on the floor. She ran inside. "Ira?"

No answer.

She moved to the bottom of the stairs. "Ira?"

No answer.

She was heading to the kitchen when he appeared in the doorway holding an apple. "What are you yelling about?"

She flung her arms around him—and it had nothing to do with Web's suggestion. But just as he started to hug her back, she pulled away and smacked him in the arm. "You scared me!"

He chewed as he talked. "For going into the kitchen and getting an apple?"

Of course not. That would be silly.

He sidled past her and sat in his recliner. Up went the footrest with a clank. He opened a copy of *Newsweek*. "What's gotten into you, Joan? You're acting weird."

She let her jaw drop to its proper gawk position. "What's got into *me*? *I'm* acting weird?"

He held the apple in his jaws while he folded the magazine to the page he wanted. When he removed it he said, "What's for dinner tonight?"

Had she missed something? She felt as though she'd read the first part of a book, then skipped to the last page. The getting from point B to point Z was missing.

When he looked at her expectantly—for the menu—she knew she had two choices. She could call a time-out, bring up the whole Sally thing, the Ss-on-the-door thing, and duke it out. Or she could tell him "meat loaf and corn" and escape to the kitchen like a good wife.

He crunched another bite of apple. "This won't hold me. Let's eat early. I'm really hungry."

Just the way he said it, as if this was truly the most important thing on his mind, made her realize that the key to any decision had to be based on whether her husband was avoiding the Sally incident on purpose, whether he was in complete denial as a mode of self-preservation, or whether he was totally clueless about what had just transpired an hour before. One implied arrogance, the second guilt, and the last, illness. She had to know the answer before she could proceed.

Joan pushed the rolling ottoman to the foot of the recliner and put a hand on his outstretched leg. "Ira, we need to talk."

"Can't it wait until dinner?"

"No, it can't." She pulled the fabric of his pant leg taut, smoothing away the wrinkles. She chose her words very carefully. "I . . . I want you to tell me your feelings about Sally."

"Who?" There was no complicity in his eyes.

"Sally Burnstein, your old employee."

He cocked his head. "She quit years ago, Joan. You know that." The impatience in his voice seemed genuine.

She sat back. "But she lives in Topeka now. An hour away."

He turned the page of the magazine, scanning the articles. "Small world."

"Would you ever want to see her? invite her down?"

He made a face. "Oh, I don't know. I suppose it would be the polite thing to do, but it seems rather awkward after all these years. I'd rather not."

Joan's mouth was dry. "You'd rather not?"

He shrugged. "I'll leave it up to you, but I'm fine with leaving things the way they are." He started to read.

Leave things the way they are. . . . She stood and pushed the ottoman away. "How do meat loaf and corn sound?"

"Got any peas?"

"I think so."

"Make it peas then."

Peas she could handle.

At the police station, Seth sat at the computer and studied the rap sheet for Rex Mennard. It was lengthy. Burglary, assault, resisting arrest.

Bottom line? Rex was a bully who took what he wanted.

Like he took my Jenna.

He blinked. *My* Jenna? Seth had hoped that four days away from her presence would cleanse all thoughts of her from his system. But if anything, the absence had made his heart grow fonder.

Too fond, considering he'd spent the last three evenings with Bonnie. Bonnie was such a nice girl, and it was clear she thought of Seth in a way similar to how *he* thought of Jenna. It was very complicated. And not good.

Yet it *was* advantageous as far as his plan went. And the plan was everything. It was the essence of his being, the focus, the higher goal.

At what cost?

The cost of not getting the farm back would be his mother's broken heart. Maybe even her health. She hadn't been the same since he'd left home. And though it was his father who'd died soon after, his mother was not exactly well. Since she'd moved to Kansas City there was something wistful about her. She didn't call as much and often wasn't home when he called her. He imagined her wasting away, a woman without a purpose. Although she'd gotten a job at the phone company, Seth knew it couldn't fill her up. Fulfill her. Not in the way the farm had. He owed her so much. It was a debt he had to pay.

His father's admonition retuned: *"Be a man, Seth! Be a man."*

Getting the farm back was the one way he could please both parents.

On impulse, he picked up the phone and dialed his mother's number.

There was no answer.

But as it rang, he realized it was a weekday. She was at work. When the answering machine came on, he left a message. "Hiya, Mom. Hope things are going all right. I'm doing okay here. In fact, I may have some very good news for both of us soon. I'll call again. Bye."

There. He'd done his duty and called his mother. And he was going beyond the call of duty with his plan for getting the farm back for her. For him. For his dad. There were rewards for doing one's duty.

And costs.

As he hung up, he heard a car and saw Bonnie drive into the station's parking lot. His stomach suffered a guilty lurch. She got out, carrying a plate of something. He bet a hundred bucks it was piled with oatmeal-raisin cookies. He'd made a comment the night before that those were his favorite and she'd bumped her shoulder against his and smiled a smile he'd already come to recognize as her I-have-a-surprise smile. She was such a giving person. His wish was her command.

You have her right where you want her.

He stood to greet her as she came through the door, bringing with her a burst of hot summer air. She went to him and kissed his cheek. "Afternoon, baby."

Baby. He wasn't sure he liked that particular term of endearment that had first popped into their conversation two days previous, but he hadn't called her on it. "Afternoon yourself. And what do we have here?"

She presented the plate as if it were a platter of gold. "For your eating pleasure. Oatmeal raisin."

He kissed her lightly on the lips. "You're too good to me. Thank you."

"You're welcome. Glad to do it." Her hands unencumbered, she put them in the back pockets of her jean shorts. She looked toward the computer. "Whatcha doing?"

He was glad the screen was facing away from her. Not that she'd know who Rex Mennard was, or why Seth was interested in him. "Just getting some area updates."

"In case a crime spree sneaks up on Weaver?"

"You never know. There could be criminals lurking outside the city limits."

"Maybe we should erect a scarecrow to keep them away."

"I'll put it in the suggestion box."

She moved close, setting her hands on his waist. "Instead, think about this . . . Mom and Dad want you to come to dinner tonight. They're in Emporia now, bringing Grandma Bowden for a visit. I want you to meet her."

Meeting the extended family. He knew what that meant.

Bonnie snuggled against his chest. "I've told Grandma everything about us."

Us. Seth put a hand on her back and hoped she hadn't heard the skip of his heart.

There was no reason for Seth to bring the list to the Weaver home, and there was a good chance both female residents would see the errand for what it was—an excuse to see Jenna. But he had to chance it.

"Well, well," Madeline said after opening the door, "who have we here?"

Seth held up the list. "I made a list of all the citizens of Weaver, their street addresses, phone numbers, and e-mail addresses."

She looked at the list, then up at him. "Too much time on your hands, Officer Olsen?"

He shrugged. What could he say?

"Since you're here you might as well come in and say hello to Jenna. I know she'd strangle me if I let you leave without seeing her."

"Auntie!"

Madeline stood aside, and Seth saw Jenna come through the foyer from the kitchen. He wished she could give him the same greeting Bonnie had given him. Instead she gestured toward the back of the house. "I'm trying out different punch combinations for Founders Day. You can vote."

"Don't get tipsy, you two," Madeline said, moving toward her desk.

"There's no alcohol in any of them, Auntie."

"Mores the pity. Have at it."

The kitchen table was covered with five pitchers of pastel-colored liquids and three two-liter bottles, along with glasses, measuring cups, and mixing bowls. "Here's what we have to work with." Jenna pointed as she spoke. "We have orange juice, cranberry juice, lemonade, pink lemonade, limeade, and the requisite Sprite, Squirt, or 7-Up."

"You're going to use all of them?"

"No, no, silly. Some of them. That's what I'm trying to figure out." She handed him a glass. "Try this one."

He took a sip and made a face. "Too sour."

"That's what I thought. Too much lime. Just a minute." Using a series of measuring cups she poured three liquids into a bowl. She stirred, then dipped a glass for a taste.

He took one, then two sips. "I like this one."

She took the glass away from him and tried it herself. "Mmm. This is definitely a finalist." She set it on the counter where Seth saw two other filled glasses. Other finalists? Jenna took a sticky note and pen and wrote down the three ingredients she'd used. She stuck it on the glass. "There."

"You're very organized."

"To appease Auntie I do my best to *appear* organized. Little does she know I often prefer to wing it." He loved the way she swung back and forth to some inner rhythm as she talked. "Shall we try again?"

"Absolutely. I'm sure we can do better." His words surprised himself. What did he care for punch recipes? Yet as Jenna moved to the table and began her work, he knew she could have involved him in gutting a chicken and he would have been willing to watch. Just to be there.

"So . . . I haven't seen you in a few days." She hesitated, then began again. "I really want to apologize for the other day. The whole thing with . . ." She shook her head, covering her abdomen with her hand. "Just forget about it, will you?"

He wished he could. He thought about telling her what he'd found out about Rex's background, but wanted to abide by her wishes. She seemed happy today dealing with all this punch stuff. He liked seeing her happy. "It's forgotten—unless you ever want to talk about it."

"I don't."

"Okay then."

She took a deep breath. "What have you been up to all week?"

He spread his arms to encompass the messy table. "I'm afraid this is the highlight."

"Pretty pitiful, Officer. You need to get out more." She looked at her watch. "In fact, how'd you like to go have dinner at the Salida? It's enchilada night. Two for one."

If only Seth could replay the last ten minutes. How stupid he'd been to come see Jenna when he wasn't free to stay, wasn't free to spend a decent amount of time with her.

He moved a pitcher of orange juice an inch to the right. "I'm sorry; I have other plans."

Her smile died, making him want to do the same. "Oh," she said.

Seth thought fast, figuring part of the truth was safer than saying nothing. "The Bowdens' grandmother is in town and they want me to meet her."

"You're meeting the extended family."

"Well, yeah, but only because my family used to own the farm." The excuse sounded more lame with every use, but he had nothing else to give her. "My mother's heart was broken when she lost the farm and—"

Jenna took a measuring cup to the sink and rinsed it under a rush of water that could have cleaned a food-encrusted bowl. "Tell Bonnie hi for me."

Seth sensed that if he said more he'd only make it worse, so he headed for the door. "Remember, I like that second one the best."

"I'll remember." She didn't look up from the torrent of water.

He let himself out.

Jenna emptied all the glasses of punch into the sink. The pitchers of perfectly good juice went next. She turned on the water, watching the last of the pastel liquids wash away.

That was dumb.

She shut off the water. Yes, it was. And it went far beyond wasting good food.

She moved to the kitchen table and let a chair catch the slump of

her body. She was falling for Seth Olsen. She hadn't meant for
it to happen, but it had.

And he was interested in her.

Why else had he stopped over? Why else did he smile in a way
that lit up his face? Why else did he let his eyes linger on hers?
Why else did he stay and vote on a stupid punch recipe when he
had a thousand better things to do?

Like have dinner with Bonnie.

He was pursuing Bonnie. That was clear. And yet, there was
a reluctance there. He seemed apologetic, as if he was seeing her
against his will, as if something was forcing them together and—

She gasped as the last puzzle piece slipped firmly into place.

The farm was Seth's passion. It was the reason he'd entered the
contest. It wasn't Weaver that had lured him home; it was the farm.
All were facts he'd made clear from day one.

But what Jenna hadn't allowed herself to see was the full plan.
Bonnie owned the farm. If Seth married Bonnie he'd gain that farm.

It was a horrible plan—cold, even deceitful.

"My mother's heart was broken when she lost the farm."

Oh my. Could it be that he wasn't doing it for himself, but was
doing it for his mother? He was willing to pursue and even marry
Bonnie in order to mend his mother's broken heart?

Jenna couldn't imagine doing such a thing for her own mother.
Did Barb Camden even have a heart to be broken? Jenna shook
her head at the unkind thought. But still . . . to imagine the kind of
love and concern Seth must have for his mom . . . it was something
Jenna had never experienced. And probably never would. That
kind of love, loyalty, unselfishness . . .

And he is interested in me. He is. I'm not imagining it.

But he couldn't choose Jenna. Not while his higher plan was
falling into place. Besides, Bonnie was a catch in other ways

beyond the farm. She was a college graduate; she came from a good, stable family.

And she wasn't pregnant with a rapist's child.

Forget the farm. Seth couldn't choose Jenna because his mother would never approve of her. Jenna was white trash. Seth would never be truly happy with her. He *had* to choose Bonnie. It was the best thing for him, for who he was, for who he could be. Bonnie and the farm would make him happy—and his mother happy.

And Jenna sad.

She pushed away from the table to finish cleaning up.

So be it. If she cared at all for Seth Olsen, she had to let him go.

"Mother Bowden, your food is getting cold." Amelia Bowden offered a plaintive glance to her husband across the dining-room table.

Bill put down his forkful of green-bean casserole to address his mother. She sat at the table, her arms crossed. "Is there something wrong, Mother?"

She didn't answer, but her eyes were locked on Seth, forcing him to look away. What was this woman's problem?

When the silence lingered, he finally looked up. *Then* she spoke.

"I wondered if you'd ever get around to looking at me, eye to eye."

"Excuse me?" Seth said.

"I don't trust anyone who can't look me in the eye."

"Mother! Don't be rude. Seth is our guest," Bill said.

She snickered and put her cloth napkin beside her spoon. "He's much more than that. He's *after* much more than that."

Bonnie dropped her fork with a clatter. "Grandma, Seth is a dear, dear friend. He's not after anything."

Mother Bowden once again crossed her arms over her nonexistent breast. "'Cept you. And this farm." She pointed at each of the Bowdens one by one. "It was *his* family's farm. Remember that. He's here to get it back."

Even as his insides constricted in full panic mode, Seth said, "I can assure you, Mrs. Bowden, I have no intention of going into farming again. I'm a police officer. I like being a police officer."

She fingered the top edge of her place mat and squinted at him. "You hoping to find some loophole in the law so you can grab the farm back and take possession again?"

Seth's protests were joined by others from the three Bowdens, all talking at once. Yet the fear that this old woman had ignited in his belly flamed. Were his intentions so obvious?

As the protests died, Mother Bowden put a finger to her lips, nodding. "Ah, I see now. I see how you're doing it. You're courting Bonnie hoping to *marry* into the farm, aren't you?"

Bonnie pushed her chair back, making it teeter. "Grandma, stop it! I will not have you talking about my boyfriend like . . . like he's a . . . a male gold digger."

"*Lothario* is the term."

"Mother!"

She wasn't fazed. "I'm just trying to get things clear in my mind. First Bonnie says he's merely a friend, but now she says he's a boyfriend." Her eyes were suspicious. "I think it's important we get to the truth."

Bonnie grabbed his arm and pulled him up and away from the table. "Let's go, Seth."

He was happy to follow.

Bonnie stormed outside, heading toward the lane, ranting the entire way. "I can't believe she'd say such a thing. She's always been opinionated. She's never liked anyone I've brought home. She's just a—"

"Bonnie, it's raining."

She looked up and the drops hit her face, but she kept walking. "I can't go back there. Not while *she's* there."

Seth had to jog to keep up with her. He took her arm to get her to slow down to a fast walk and they found a common step. Seth tried to think of something to say, but he couldn't, not without lying. Yet the truth would mark the end of their relationship. And he didn't want that. Farm or no farm.

Their feet crunched on the mixture of wet dirt and gravel. Seth wiped the rain off his face and shielded his eyes. The rain got heavier.

Bonnie was oblivious. Her hair was soon soaked and hung in wet strands skimming her shoulders "Grandma thinks just because she's old she can be rude and blunt and—" she took a fresh breath—"you should have heard what my parents went through when they decided to buy this place."

"She was against it?"

"Big time. It didn't matter that one of the reasons they were doing it was so Dad could be closer to her in her final years." She snickered. "As if she'll ever have any final years."

Seth stopped walking, forcing Bonnie to do the same. He had to squint against the raindrops. "Don't say things like that. People can die way too soon."

"Oh." She touched a finger to her lips. Rain trickled down her hand. "I'm so sorry. Your dad." She pulled him into a rain-soaked hug. "Please forgive me. Please?"

It was easy for Seth to forgive, but much harder for him to accept that he was the one who needed the forgiveness.

"Here is your room key, Ms. Bauer," the desk clerk said. "Room 345. I hope you enjoy your stay."

Kathy and Lavon walked toward the elevators and pointed at the UP button. Malachi pushed it. Twice.

"Sandra feels bad that I couldn't stay at her house, but with the pipes breaking . . ." Kathy spread her arms to include the lush interior of the lobby. "I hope you don't mind me calling you, joining you here. Intruding." She looked around the lobby. "This is a beautiful hotel."

The elevator came and she wheeled her suitcase inside.

"What floor is Kathy, Daddy?"

"Three," he said. "Same as ours." He glanced at Kathy. "Next to ours."

Malachi pushed the button for the third floor. Twice.

The doors closed and they looked at the numbers above the door. "I'm really beat," she said.

"Us too. We played hard this afternoon."

"I got a caramel apple *and* popcorn *and* got to ride a horse thingy," Malachi said.

"A carousel."

"I haven't been on one of those for ages," Kathy said.

"Actually, we went more than once," Lavon said. "With the hundreds of miles we drove in the van today, plus the half-dozen trips round and round on the carousel, I figure milewise we're halfway through Illinois."

Kathy laughed. The doors opened on their floor and they followed the arrows toward 345.

"Here you are," Lavon said.

She unlocked the door. He held it open while she wheeled her suitcase inside.

He retreated into the hall as she took possession of the opened door. "We've eaten so much junk all day, we haven't had a real dinner yet. You want to grab a bite?"

"I don't think so," Kathy said. "I think I'll crash."

He nodded. "Maybe we can have breakfast together."

"That would be nice."

"Eight o'clock?"

"Eight it is. Night."

Kathy closed the door and put on the safety latch. She peeked in the bathroom and strolled to the bed, where she sat. It was a beautiful room with furniture worthy of an expensive home. She and Roy had rented such a nice room one time when they'd gone to a medical convention in Chicago. But Kathy had never been in one alone.

She heard the muffled sounds of a TV next door. In Lavon's room.

To think that this morning they'd gotten in the van as mere acquaintances. Now, twelve hours later, it was as if they'd known each other all their lives. Of course having six hours to talk did the trick. Luckily, Lavon was a good conversationalist. Such a long trip with a less-able person would have been excruciating. As it was, the miles and hours flew by and Kathy ended the day liking and respecting Lavon Newsom more than she had to start with. He was a good man. And Malachi was a bright, well-behaved child.

Speaking of good man . . . she looked at the phone and gasped. *I never called Roy!*

She started to dig her cell phone out of her purse when she felt something odd in the purse's pocket. An envelope.

She took it out. It had her name on it, in Roy's handwriting. She opened it and found a floral-covered note card. A photo fell out, a photo of the three of them in front of their old house. A neighbor had taken it just before they pulled away for the move to Weaver. Their smiles were weak, but at least they were smiling. They'd moved to Weaver with such hope.

She propped the photo against the table lamp and opened the card to read the note: *Dear Kath, Always remember I love you. Roy.*

The awkwardness and tension of the past weeks fell away. She got out her phone. Its display indicated she'd missed two calls. From Roy. Had she been so busy with Sandra at the gallery that she hadn't even heard the phone ring? Apparently.

She dialed and he answered. "Roy. Hi, hon. I'm here."

"How would I know?"

Uh-oh. "Sorry. I should have called to tell you I got here safely, but we got busy and—"

"I'm in the middle of a pile of paperwork, Kath."

She glanced at the note and picture. His written words of love clashed with his tone. "Don't you want to hear about my day?" she asked. "A lot happened. There were problems with Sandra's plumbing and—"

"I'm not up to this. Call me tomorrow—when you can fit me in." He hung up.

Kathy stared at the phone, incredulous. She talked to the dead line. "You didn't even let me tell you that I'm not staying at Sandra's. I'm in a—"

Never mind. It was probably best he didn't know.

Besides, since he'd made it clear he didn't want to know the details of her day, why should she tell him?

Case closed.

"I was taking a bath, Lavon." Patrice's voice sounded tired.

He stood between the parted curtains, looking out on the lights of the night. "Did you have a hard day at work?" he asked.

"The usual. How goes the art queen?"

"Patrice . . ."

"I don't have to like this situation, Lavon. She's with you and I'm not."

Lavon realized he needed to tell her about Kathy being at the hotel. A piece of information like that, coming out accidentally, would take on a life of its own. "There was a change of plans. Kathy's friend, Sandra? Where she was going to stay? Her house flooded. Broken plumbing. So she's staying at Union Station with us. It's a beautiful renovated—"

"You and Kathy are staying in a hotel together?"

He didn't like her emphasis on the word *together* but thought it safer to ignore it. "The rooms are very elegant."

She snickered. "Come on. St. Louis? Elegant?"

"Very."

Silence.

Lavon put his forehead against the glass. It was cold. "It couldn't be helped, lovey." He noticed she hadn't asked about their son. "Malachi and I had a great afternoon. We hung out around here awhile, then went down to the Arch. Even went inside. Quite amazing how they have an elevator going up the legs of—"

"Can I talk to him?"

"He's in the tub for a quick soak before dinner and bed." Lavon paused and heard Malachi singing "I've Been Working on the Railroad." "We've ordered burgers from room service."

"Is Kathy joining you?"

"No."

A pause. "She does have a separate room, doesn't she?"

At least she'd come out and said it plain. "I'm insulted you would think otherwise."

"You, I trust, but her . . ."

"What has Kathy ever done to make you not trust her?"

"She likes you. I can tell."

"I hope she likes me. We live in the same, very small town." He wanted to ask how Patrice could tell Kathy liked him, but knew that would get him into more trouble. "I better check on Chi-Chi. I'll call you tomorrow after we've been to the doctor's. Love you."

"I don't like this, Lavon."

"I know. But it'll be fine."

He hung up hoping he was right.

TWELVE

Oh, do not hold us guilty for our former sins!
Let your tenderhearted mercies quickly meet our needs,
for we are brought low to the dust.

PSALM 79:8

The pain made Madeline squirm in the bed, trying to find some corner of comfortable. It was evasive. And pesky. She had work to do. She couldn't give in to this sickness.

Not yet.

And maybe she could just stay in bed one day . . . everybody did that occasionally. She didn't have to tell anyone why. She could say she had the flu. People would leave her alone if she had the flu.

She reached for the bedside phone to call in to the bank, when Jenna knocked on her door. Madeline withdrew her hand. "Come in."

"Morning, Auntie. I'm—"

With one look at her niece, Madeline forgot her own pain. "You look awful, child. What's wrong?"

"It's either morning sickness or the flu. I'm going down to get some crackers and 7-Up."

Pooh. If Jenna used the flu excuse, Madeline couldn't use it too. Or could she?

The pain reminded her she might not have a choice.

"You coming down for breakfast?" Jenna asked.

"No. I'm going back to bed for a little bit."

"Is something wrong?"

Madeline frowned. "Can't an old woman take a morning off once in a while without getting the third degree?"

"Of course you can. Let me know if you need anything."

There was no rest for the weary.

Or the dying.

As Seth walked up to the Weaver house, he knew he should stop thinking of reasons to stop by, but he couldn't stop himself. He hated how they'd left things yesterday, with Jenna asking him to dinner and his having to decline, saying he was eating with the Bowdens.

What a dinner that had been, with Mother Bowden pinning him to the wall regarding his intentions and motives. Bonnie had passed it off as the ranting of a cantankerous old woman. Bonnie was too good, too trusting.

The act of ringing the doorbell cut off any further self-condemnation. He forced himself to think of the excuse he'd come up with for this visit: would there be any need of special traffic signs and parking for the Founders Day event? He put the question foremost in his mind, but immediately let it fall away when Jenna answered the door.

She looked green and haggard. She leaned her cheek against the opened door. "We gave at the office."

He noticed she was wearing pajama pants and a T-shirt. "Did I wake you?"

"I'm slow getting started this morning."

"Are you all right?"

She shrugged. "My aunt's resting."

"Actually, I didn't come to see *her*." So much for carefully created excuses.

Jenna's eyes met his. After a pause she asked, "How was your dinner with Bonnie?"

"And her family. Fine."

Instead of asking more questions, she said, "I'm glad."

"Glad?"

She nodded to the porch swing. "Want to sit? I need to talk to you."

His stomach grabbed. Something in her voice . . . "Sure."

"It's cool this morning; let me get a sweater."

Seth positioned himself on the far side of the swing, both eager and fearful of where the conversation would go. Jenna came outside wearing an olive green sweater overlapped tightly around her torso, her arms holding it in place. She sat beside him. He had no idea what to say.

Her first question did not alter that condition. "Are you and Bonnie serious?"

If he said yes, it would hurt Jenna. He couldn't bear the thought. But if he said no and it turned out he and Bonnie got engaged, she'd still be hurt and would brand him a liar.

You are *a liar. You're lying to yourself more than anyone.*

They rocked up and back in the swing. After a few passes, Jenna pulled her knees to her chest and let Seth do the work.

"Your nonanswer is your answer," she said.

"I'm just . . . confused," he finally said.

She kept her eyes straight ahead. "Let me preface my next words by telling you I am as surprised as anyone for what I'm about to say. I never intended . . ." She dug her chin into her knees a moment, then began again. "I'm skipping past what is and jumping directly to the what could be, which is silly and schoolgirlish, and . . ." She took a fresh breath. "I like you a lot, Seth. But I don't have a thing to offer you. I'm unemployed and pregnant. I don't have a degree or a career." She looked at him. "I don't have a strong family like Bonnie; I'm not close to my mother like you are; I don't even know where my dad lives anymore. I have nothing to offer."

"Jenna, don't—"

"I have to say it. Say it all. And that includes stating the fact that I've been raped. I'm tainted, ruined. Soiled."

He was appalled. "Don't you dare say such a thing about yourself. Don't even think it. You're the victim. Rex Mennard is the one who's tainted, ruined, and soiled."

She didn't say anything for a moment. "I wasn't a virgin."

"So?"

Her glance in his direction was quick before she looked away. "So . . . I wasn't an innocent."

"Maybe you weren't an innocent, but you *were* innocent. Rex is the guilty one. He's at fault, not you. You said no. He ignored it."

"But—" she let out a sigh—"everything's changed because of that one act. The baby . . ."

He wasn't sure he should ask, but he did anyway. "Are you keeping it?"

"Yes." As soon as she said it, she put a hand to her neck. "Until just this minute I wasn't sure, but now that I've said it . . . yes, I'm keeping it. The baby's the true innocent in all this."

So that was that. Jenna and the baby were a pair. A duo. A package deal. He wasn't sure how he felt about that.

But Bonnie and the farm are a package deal too.

Jenna was looking at him. Studying him. "Because I'm having feelings for you and because it can't ever be, you need to quit coming around here, Seth. You need to concentrate on what's best for you. And that's pleasing your mother and gaining back the family legacy. I don't have a family legacy, and never will. That's an important thing, Seth. It's worth fighting for—even sacrificing for. That's why I want you to quit teasing me—teasing us—with this . . . this whatever it is we're doing and concentrate on finding happiness with Bonnie and the farm."

His mouth moved but he didn't say anything. Somehow she knew everything, every motive, every outcome he'd planned.

"Don't look at me that way," she said. "You know I'm right. No matter what I feel for you, or even you for me, you can't be happy with me. You need that farm. It's a deep-down part of you. So go get it."

She stood and moved to the door, then paused with a hand on the handle. "I've just made your life easier, Seth Olsen. Go to Bonnie. She's the one for you."

The door closed. Seth remained on the swing, knowing his legs would not support him enough to stand. The whole Jenna-and-Bonnie situation had just been taken out of his hands. The way to get the farm had been cleared. He should be happy.

But he wasn't.

Jenna closed the door, then leaned her back against it, letting it guide her to the floor. She pressed the tears away with the palms of her hands.

Seth was gone. She'd shoved him away.

You've just sacrificed your own happiness for his.

It was a noble thought that didn't lessen the pain.

She put a hand to her abdomen. The baby. The baby was her happiness now. She spread her fingers and wondered what it would be like to feel the baby move. Soon. Soon her son or daughter would be big and strong. She'd make sure of it. She'd be a good mother. A great mother.

With her next thought her hand stopped its movement. One reason she'd given up Seth was because she had no family legacy. Yet she and the baby were already a family. The two of them would give the Camden line a fresh start. They'd make their own legacy.

"Thank you, God," she said aloud.

As the prayer filled the air around her, she realized how far she'd come. The horror of the rape had transformed into a prayer of thanks. How could that be?

And Jenna knew the prayer was heartfelt. Sincere. For no matter how her current situation had come about, the baby was good. And it was hers. And God's. And he'd be with them both through it all.

As she got to her feet, there was no question that Jenna Camden felt a little more whole than she had a moment before.

Praise the Lord.

As soon as Bennie Davison came into the bank, Patrice suffered a shiver. There was something about the man that made her radar kick into a high shriek.

Gone was the cheap brown suit she'd seen him in before. Today his ivory-colored suit reminded her of the attire one might see in Key West. Lightweight. Linen. And horribly wrinkled. It was out of place in Kansas.

Oblivious, he flashed her a wide smile, revealing a silver crown on a lower molar. "Morning, Miss Patrice. And how are you today?"

"Fine." She kept her voice even. Uninterested but polite. "Mrs. Weaver isn't here this morning."

He looked toward Madeline's office. "Will she be in later?"

She hesitated. "It was implied."

"Then I'll wait."

He started to walk toward Madeline's office. Patrice didn't want him hanging around all morning. She stood quickly. "Perhaps it would be better if you waited in the park? or at the Salida?"

He looked over his shoulder toward the exit. "They have good food?"

I wouldn't know. "Excellent."

"I'll be over there then." He pulled a cell phone from his pocket, then slipped it back inside. "Stupid thing. Out of juice. I meant to recharge it last night. I was going to have you call me but . . . will you come get me when she comes in?"

As if Patrice had nothing better to do? "Sure." She watched him walk catty-corner across the street.

Fifteen minutes later, another outsider came into the bank. Not that Patrice knew all the citizens of Weaver as yet, but like Bennie, this woman stood out. The skirt of her black suit was a good foot above her not-so-skinny knees, her orange blouse revealed too much cleavage, and her heels were appropriate for any Times Square hooker. She was too much. Her cup runneth over. Literally.

"May I help you?" Patrice asked.

"I'm looking for someone who works here? Bennie Davison?"

Patrice felt her eyebrows raise. "And you are?"

The woman produced a business card. "Adele Simpson from *The Probe.*"

The Probe was a gossip rag. Celebrities were constantly suing it for one reason or another. What would this reporter want with Bennie? He was as far from celebrity as Miss D-Cup was to being a Weight Watchers' spokeswoman.

Yet Patrice wanted to know more. "Mr. Davison is not here right now, but I'm his associate. He said you might be coming. Can I help you?"

Adele's look held a tinge of suspicion. "Do you work for that Mrs. Weaver woman too?"

Mrs. Weaver woman? With a wayward glance at the tellers—who were watching the exchange—Patrice leaned forward confidentially. She sensed now was the time to take sides—or at least appear to take sides. And for some reason Patrice also sensed that Adele was anti-Madeline. Patrice chose her words carefully. "Let's just say I've had my share of dealings with Mrs. Weaver." She shrugged, letting Adele come to her own conclusion.

"Well then—" Adele looked around the bank—"is there a place we can talk privately? I just have a few more questions for Bennie, but I've been unable to reach him. I've left six messages."

Thank heaven for dead cell phones.

Patrice led the way to the conference room. Adele declined her offer of coffee. "So," Patrice said upon closing the door, "how can I help you?"

Adele retrieved a notebook and pen from her purse. She turned the pages until she found the right one. "I need to check some facts. Bennie told me that Madeline Weaver and the Weaver family arranged for some Jewish family to be kicked out of town back in the forties?"

Patrice's heart skipped a beat, but she played along. "Yes . . ."

"And now, one of the winners of the land contest is a relative of that family? They're even living in the old family house and are taking over the old family business location?" Adele pointed toward the front door. "Is it that empty space that has the Swenson's Soda Shoppe Coming Soon sign in the window?"

Jewish. Soda shop. The Goldbergs?

"That's the Goldbergs' business."

Adele used her pen to point at her notes. "That's where I got confused. The original family was named Stein and the contest family is named Goldberg, and the store has Swenson in the name. Swenson's hardly a Jewish name."

Patrice had heard the reason for that. "It was a name from Joan's youth. From the town she grew up in. Something like that."

Adele made a note. "So the Goldbergs and the Steins *are* the same family?"

Patrice didn't like where this was going. "I believe so, but . . . what's the title of your article going to be?"

Adele smiled proudly. "I'm trying to choose between 'Contest Covers Up Past Sins' and 'The Sins of a Matriarch Revealed.' I like the first one best."

Patrice thought of all the old files. Did they hold evidence of the sins of the matriarch? of Madeline's sins?

"There's one more question I had about an SUV that Regrets Only, Inc. purchased for a family who lived here in the sixties? Apparently there was a little trouble with that bit of restitution. The family wouldn't take the vehicle without knowing the reason behind the gift. They sent it back. I was wondering if that had ever been cleared up."

"I don't know." It felt good to say something completely truthful. "In fact, I'm not sure I can be of any more help to you after all. Perhaps you'll have to keep trying to get ahold of Bennie."

Adele sighed. "Oh dear. I suppose." She stood to leave. "When is the article going to be published?"

"I've got to talk to Bennie about that one too. We've tentatively agreed to wait for his go-ahead—apparently there are still a few things he wants to clear up. But my bosses will not wait forever."

Patrice showed her out, hoping that Bennie was well into his breakfast burrito or huevos rancheros and he and Adele would not bump into each other on the street. She stood at the door and felt better when Adele's car pulled away.

"Mrs. Newsom?" asked a teller. "Who was that—" she made a face—"that person?"

"Just someone passing through." Patrice made a decision. "I'm going over to the Salida for a bit. Will you get the phones, please?"

"Okay, but you hate the Sali—"

Patrice strode across the street.

Bennie sat at a table under a garish sombrero hanging on the wall. His plate was smeared with egg yolk, hash browns, and the crusts of two slices of bread. Apparently he wasn't keen on Mexican food either.

He smiled and waved. "Hey, Miss Patrice. Has Mrs. Weaver showed up, or have you come over to join me?"

Maria—the mother of the twins—beamed as she picked up a menu. "It's so nice to see you here, Patrice. Can I bring you some coffee to start?"

"No. Nothing, thanks," Patrice said. "I just need to see Mr. Davison."

Bennie raised his eyebrows suggestively. "Woo-hoo. I like the sounds of that."

She moved to the edge of his table and, though she hated to lean close, did so in order to keep her words between the two of them. "I've just had a nice talk with an Adele Simpson from *The Probe*."

Bennie's already pasty complexion added another layer of paste. He slapped some bills on the table, made a good show of saying a happy good-bye to his chat mates in the café, and led Patrice outside.

On the sidewalk, he took her arm roughly. "What's going on?"

She shook his grip away. "That's what I want to know. Let's walk." She nodded toward the park.

They crossed the street and gained some privacy.

"How did you end up talking with Adele?" he asked.

"She came to the bank asking for you, acting like you worked there."

He dug a toothpick into his teeth as he walked. "I told her I worked for the Weavers and the bank, but I never implied I worked in the building. She misunderstood."

"She had a few questions about an article she's writing about restitution? The sins of a matriarch?"

Bennie stopped on the path and shoved his finger in Patrice's face. "This is none of your business. I've been working for the Weavers and the bank for decades. Don't think because you won any dumb contest you can come in and condemn me—"

Patrice saw a new avenue open up. Although it disgusted her to do so, she pressed his hand down. Gently. And offered him a smile. "I'm not condemning you, Mr. Davison. I'm thanking you."

"What?"

She started walking again, needing the movement to fuel her lies. "Frankly, the state of the Weaver National Bank is appalling. I left an important position at a bank in New York City for this?" She let out a laugh. "And I'm more than a little annoyed that Mrs. Weaver still comes into work. That wasn't part of the deal. I thought I was coming to Weaver to run things as the bank's vice president, not as some peon answering phones and mopping the restroom."

"So this article could help you?"

"I believe it could. At the very least, it would hurry along the inevitable."

"But if the reputation of the bank is ruined . . ."

Patrice shook her head and took a chance. "The bank as an institution is not involved. The administration is. And since I'm new . . . I'm in the clear. I came here on faith. So it's natural when it all comes down, I'll be viewed as the innocent, poised to take over and rebuild the bank for the good of the town."

Bennie walked up the steps of the gazebo and took a seat on a bench. "If you're wanting a cut of my payment from *The Probe*, forget it. I'm the one who's done all the work and taken all the risk."

She wondered how much he was getting. Probably in the five figures. "I'm not interested in cutting in on your money. My reward will come later."

His shoulders relaxed.

"But I am curious . . . if you've worked for the bank for decades, why do this? Why now? Why cut your ties?"

"Madeline's cutting my ties. She told me last time I was here that my work for her was through. She's been a cash cow. I've depended on this income and was not prepared for it to dry up. She forced me to be creative and come up with some other revenue."

"Is your name going to be used in the article?"

He waved his hands. "No, no. Adele promised me. I'm just 'a source.'" He grinned. "Always wanted to be 'a source.'" Bennie stood and looked at his watch. "When do you think Mrs. Weaver will be in? I can't wait all day."

Patrice thought up another lie. "Actually, that's another reason I sought you out at the Salida. Mrs. Weaver called in, saying she was sick. She won't be in at all today."

Bennie cussed and headed down the gazebo steps. "If you ask me, I can't be done with this job too soon."

"Should I tell her you were here?"

He turned to face her. "Nah. What she doesn't know won't hurt her." He laughed. "Actually, it will hurt her, but—" he chuckled— "I'll be talking to you, Patrice." Suddenly, he turned serious. "You aren't going to say anything to her—or to anyone—are you?"

"Why would I?"

He laughed again. "It's never good to bite the hand that feeds you, right?"

Exactly.

Patrice sank onto a bench in the gazebo, purposely choosing a spot on the opposite side from where Bennie had parked his deceitful self.

What an odd conversation. Two odd conversations. What bothered her the most was that the words she'd said had come so easily, as if she'd been thinking about them a long time. As if she was happy with Bennie's deception. As if it was only logical for her to remain silent and let things play out for her own benefit.

Actually, it *was* the logical thing to do.

Everything she'd said to Bennie about her position at the bank and her opinions of Mrs. Weaver were frosted with an element of truth. She did want to take over and do things her way ASAP.

But the question remained: was this the way to go about it?

Yet how could she stop what was already in motion? The secrets were out. The article was being written. The money—or at least part of it—was probably in Bennie's grimy hands. So what choice did she have but to let things proceed of their own accord?

She looked across the park to the Weaver mansion. Madeline was home. She had not called in a second time. As far as Patrice knew, Madeline would be in this afternoon.

I can tell her then.

But no.

Patrice had the feeling if she didn't talk to Madeline now, she never would.

Tell her? When did I ever start thinking about telling her?

Patrice took a deep breath. She'd always thought about telling Madeline. Always. Greed, ambition, pride, and curiosity had grabbed their moments, but in the end, Patrice knew Madeline had to know what was going on.

Don't bite the hand that feeds you, indeed. The bottom line was: who did Patrice want feeding her? Bennie Davison or Madeline Weaver?

She headed to the mansion.

Patrice was surprised when Web answered the door. "Morning, Patrice." He looked over her shoulder. "Bank burn down?"

She suddenly realized she'd already been gone a long time. But it couldn't be helped. "I need to talk to Mrs. Weaver." *Alone.*

"She hasn't been feeling up to par this morning." He glanced inside to his left. "She's up but—"

"Oh, let her in, Web. I'm fine."

He opened the door wide.

Patrice walked into the foyer and was immediately impressed.

The place oozed old-world money. It was indeed a mansion. In New York it would cost millions.

Mrs. Weaver sat at her desk in the parlor. "Get in here and tell me what's wrong enough to get you to leave the bank."

A knot formed in Patrice's throat. She took a seat on the couch. Mrs. Weaver remained at her desk. Web stood in the doorway. Was he going to stay? She glanced in his direction. "I'm afraid it's a bit sensitive. . . ."

Web made no move to leave.

"Web can be here. Go ahead."

Patrice felt her heart beating in her already blocked throat. The only way to ease her discomfort was to say it. Now. New Yorkers were known for their bluntness. So be it. "Bennie Davison stopped in today."

Mrs. Weaver blinked, then seemed to regroup. "We didn't have an appointment."

Patrice shook her head. "The problem is not in *his* showing up, but with another person showing up, namely a reporter from *The Probe*."

Web raised his right hand. "There are no alien babies in Weaver. I promise."

Patrice dove to the punch line. "The reporter asked for Bennie—who'd obviously made her think he worked at the bank. He's sold a story to them. About you, Mrs. Weaver. About the bank. About what he's been doing for you all these years."

Silence.

"The reporter told me some of the details," Patrice said delicately.

Mrs. Weaver gripped the armrests of her chair. She blinked. She looked at Web. Then at Patrice. "This can't happen. He wouldn't be dumb enough to betray . . ."

"What is she talking about, Maddy?" Web asked.

"He doesn't know?" Patrice had assumed . . .

Mrs. Weaver put a hand to her head as if feeling pain. She looked to Web. "Water please?"

He left the room.

Mrs. Weaver leaned forward and lowered her voice. "What did Bennie tell you?"

"The reporter did most of the talking. She said something about the Goldbergs, and some Jews being kicked out of town. And there was an SUV given to another family?"

Mrs. Weaver groaned. Web came back and she greedily drank the water. She handed him the empty glass, then said, "Web, this is bank business. There's no reason for you to be here."

"Sounds like I need to be here."

She gave him a scathing look. "I can function without you, old man. I know that's hard to believe."

"I'm staying. And you can't make me go."

"Just because you're bigger than me . . . ,"

"Maddy, my gut says it's serious. You'll need me in the end, so just let me stay." Web looked at Patrice. "Go on, Patrice. Pretend I'm a bug on the wall."

"If only I could swat you down," Mrs. Weaver murmured.

Patrice wasn't sure what to do. It was clear Mrs. Weaver did not want him present, but it was also clear he wasn't going to leave.

Mrs. Weaver sighed deeply. "Gracious day, take a seat, Web. I'm too tired to argue with you. But if you're going to be here I won't have you hovering over me like a vulture waiting to pick me apart."

"I would do no such thing, and you know it."

She waved a concession at him while he sat in a wing chair close by. Then she took a cleansing breath, which seemed to add to her strength, allowing her to sit more erect. It was at this time Patrice could see how Mrs. Weaver had gotten through sixty years in the banking business. The woman could rise to any occasion. She was a survivor.

"How much does the reporter know?" Mrs. Weaver asked.

"Know about what?" Web asked.

Mrs. Weaver pointed at him. "Bug on a wall, remember?"

"If I'm here, I have to know what's been said."

With an exaggerated sigh, Mrs. Weaver filled him in on the basics. Only then did she turn back to Patrice. "So, I ask again. How much does the reporter know?"

"Quite a bit. She knew a lot of details," Patrice said. "It's enough to do damage."

"Who exactly is this man Bennie?" Web asked.

Mrs. Weaver hesitated just a moment. "He's done work for the Weaver family, for the bank, for years. My father-in-law used him. Introduced me to his type of services."

"Which is?"

"He makes things happen."

"That's pretty vague . . . ," Web said.

She ignored him and fingered some papers on the desk. "Oh, pooh. Like I said, I'm too tired to care. You want the truth, Web? The truth is, Bennie was used to cover up indiscretions the bank committed in its own interest."

"Such as?" Patrice said.

Mrs. Weaver's hand stopped its movement. "The business world can be cutthroat, Patrice. You know that. And our bank was not just *a* bank; it was *the* bank, *the* cornerstone, run by the founding family of Weaver. We constantly had to look toward the greater good. We had to be a godfather to the people of Weaver. Father confessor—or mother confessor, as the case may be."

Web shook his head. "Maddy, what did you do?"

She raised a hand. "I refuse to go into more details. Just know that I'm in the process of making amends, making restitution." She glanced at him. "In spite of what you may think, I do have a conscience, Web Stoddard, and if you must know, it kicked into high gear this last year. Bennie has been doing good things for me since then. Righting past wrongs. Truth be told, I'm doing my best to be the woman you think I am."

He reached for her, but she did not take his hand. "Ah, Maddy . . ."

"Well, I am trying, you old coot," she said.

In the moment that followed, the connection Patrice saw between the two octogenarians made her heart ache for its own deficiency.

Mrs. Weaver pulled her eyes away from Web's and looked to Patrice. "So. When is the article coming out?"

"That's not decided. It sounds like Bennie is going to give the reporter the go-ahead at some future date. I'm not sure when, but he implied it was under his control."

"And he believes them?" Web asked. "Believes the press?"

Patrice shrugged. "Apparently."

Mrs. Weaver shook her head. "That rag will print the article when it benefits them. They won't wait forever."

"I have a question," Web said. "If this man has worked for the bank for so long, why would he betray you now?"

"I know exactly why," Mrs. Weaver said. "We're wrapping things up. His services are no longer needed. I told him as much."

"So it's money," Web said.

Mrs. Weaver shrugged. "Money makes the world go round. He's probably waiting until he's received final payment before publicly stabbing me in the back."

"He implied as much," Patrice said.

"The article will hurt your reputation, Maddy."

"It will hurt the bank," Patrice said.

Mrs. Weaver shook her head. "It will hurt the town." She sighed and looked out the window. "To think that all of this that was done to help Weaver thrive can bring it to its knees. After Weaver's gotten its second wind too."

Web stood. "You sound like you're giving up."

She pointed at him. "I most certainly am not! Sit down."

He sat.

"I'll pay him off," Mrs. Weaver said matter-of-factly.

"That won't stop the article," Patrice said. "The reporter already knows the details."

Web nodded. "If the paper doesn't get a go-ahead from Bennie, they'll run with it on their own."

Mrs. Weaver pursed her lips and stared into space, her mind clearly at work. Then suddenly her chin quivered and her forehead furrowed. Her head shook in short movements. "Then it's over, and it's all been for nothing." She looked at Web angrily. "It's all your fault!"

Web moved to her side, kneeling beside her. "Maddy . . ."

She pushed against his shoulders, but he remained firmly in place. "All your talk about God and love and doing the right thing and making him proud. See what good it's done me?"

He ran a hand over her arm. "It has done good. It has."

Patrice felt guilty being a witness. Should she leave?

But as soon as she stood, Web held his hand toward her. "There's no certain solution to this. Except one. We need to pray about it."

Pray? With her boss? About shady things, guilty things? Things Patrice wouldn't want God to even know about?

Web's hand remained extended. "Come on, Patrice." He took

Mrs. Weaver's hand, and Patrice was surprised when she did not object.

It was awkward with him on his knees beside Mrs. Weaver's chair. But what choice did she have? Patrice got down on her knees on Mrs. Weaver's other side and took their hands. Her boss's head was bowed, though Patrice couldn't tell whether it was from piety or embarrassment.

Web closed his eyes and began. "Father, take this mess. Make it work out according to your plan. Amen."

Patrice waited for more. But there wasn't any. "That's it?" she asked.

"That's it," Web said, awkwardly getting to his feet. He helped the ladies up.

Patrice let out a laugh. Maybe she and Lavon should have gone to church last Sunday. This man's sermons would certainly be short enough for her taste.

Mrs. Weaver tugged at her arm. "Don't you dare laugh at Web. If he says that's it, then that's it. Nobody has a better in with God than Web does. I trust him completely."

Web put a calming hand on her shoulder. "I'm glad you trust me, Maddy, but you'd do even better trusting him yourself. He's got the ball now."

Web reminded Patrice a lot of Lavon. Such a simple faith. Naïve and innocent. And ever present.

Mrs. Weaver looked at her watch. "Enough of all this. Shouldn't you be getting back to work, Patrice?"

"Yes, ma'am." As Mrs. Weaver showed her the door, Patrice asked, "But what should I do if Bennie——?"

"Refer him to me," Mrs. Weaver said. "I'll take care of him."

"And God'll take care of you," Web said.

Mrs. Weaver shrugged. "It appears I'm surrounded. Now back to work. But thanks for coming over. I never forget loyalty."

Patrice was counting on it.

Madeline parted the curtains and watched Patrice walk down the driveway. "That took guts," she said.

"Yes it did. I think you have a good one there."

"Yes, I do." She let the curtain fall and went back to her desk. "That praying stuff, Web . . . that *was* taking it a bit far."

"Why do you say that?"

"Mixing business with God?" She shook her head. "It's not done."

"It's done much more than you think, Maddy. God's the God of every part of our lives. There's no corner that isn't his."

There was odd comfort in that—but also fear. She wasn't sure she liked the idea of God seeing into the dark corners of her soul—places even she didn't want to visit.

She picked up the list they'd been going over when Patrice had arrived. "I will admit it gives me peace to know the article isn't going to come out."

"What?"

"Now that we've prayed . . ."

"That doesn't mean the article isn't going to be published."

She threw the list on the desk. "Then what did we just pray for?"

"That God would handle it—according to his plan."

"But certainly he wouldn't want the article to come out and ruin everything."

Web shrugged. "Greater good, Maddy. You said it yourself. You constantly had to look to the greater good. So does God."

"But I want—"

"I know what you want. And so does he. But consequences aren't wiped out when we pray. Consequences are inevitable."

"This is not what I want to hear right now, Web."

"But that doesn't make it any less true. The article may come out. But since we've given it up to God, we can be assured that in the end, good will come from it."

"All for the best? That rot?"

He nodded. "God knows what he's doing, Maddy."

She'd believe it when she saw it.

Ryan watched his father stir the spaghetti sauce. And stir it. And stir it. "I think you got it covered, Dad," Ryan said.

Roy looked up. "What?"

"The stirring. You're going to wear a hole in the bottom of the pan."

Roy looked at the spoon as if seeing it for the first time. He put it on the counter. He stared at it, once again lost in thought. This wasn't like him.

"Have you heard from Mom?" Ryan asked.

Roy picked up the spoon, the tomato sauce dripping from it. "Last night. Late."

"Is she okay?"

He looked at Ryan. "Why shouldn't she be okay?"

The way his father's forehead was furrowed spoke volumes. His dad knew. His dad suspected.

"We should have gone with Mom this weekend," Ryan said.

"Why do you say that?"

He hesitated. "I just . . . her going with . . ." He shrugged.

Roy put the spoon back in the pot and resumed stirring. "It's a meeting with Sandra. We'll go when she has the actual showing. She's fine. Just fine."

But was she? Suddenly, Ryan had to say it, had to speak out. "She's interested in Lavon, Dad."

His father just stood there with the stupid spoon in his hand. He blinked. "Don't be ridiculous."

"I saw them talking on his porch. Mom was practically . . . giddy. Like a teenager, giggling, flirting . . ."

Roy removed the spoon from the pot, took it to the sink, and rinsed it. And rinsed it. "It was just a coincidence they went together," he said over the sound of the rushing water. "It wasn't planned. Your mother's meeting and Malachi's doctor appointment . . . it was logical they carpooled."

Ryan snickered. "It certainly worked into their plans well."

Roy shut off the water. He set the spoon in the sink. Then he faced his son. "I trust your mother, Ryan. She would never do anything to hurt our marriage. She and Lavon are just friends. We're all trying to make new friends here." After a pause he added, "Right?"

The hopeful look in his father's eyes was pitiful. Ryan had always thought of his dad as a practical man, a man of science. Of facts. Yet, by the way he stood at the sink with his shoulders slumped and his will apparently broken, it was clear that in regard to this issue, Dr. Roy Bauer was choosing ignorance.

"Whatever you want to believe, Dad." Ryan left the house.

Ryan walked. And walked.

He had no destination in mind. He just wanted to feel better. His dad had been so certain nothing was wrong—that nothing *could* be wrong between his mother and Mr. Newsom.

Ryan called out to his other Father. *God? Help me. I hope I'm wrong. Please make me wrong.*

Ryan suddenly realized he was on the Newsoms' street and their house was just ahead. Without knowing why, he walked faster.

Too late he saw Mr. Newsom's wife on the porch, reading. He pulled up short, but not short enough.

She looked up.

He couldn't turn and walk away. "Hi," he said.

"Hi." Her eyes suddenly showed recognition and she sat upright. The swing stopped its movement. "You're Kathy's son, aren't you?"

He went up the front walk tentatively. "I'm Ryan."

"Have you heard from your mother?"

"No . . . I mean, my dad has, but I . . ." He shrugged, then realized he had an opening. "Have you heard from your husband?"

"He's safely there. He and our son had the doctor's appointment today. I'm hoping to hear how it went any minute now."

The kid was along. That made things a little better. But . . . "Why didn't you go with them?"

She seemed offended. "I work at the bank. I couldn't get away. Why didn't you or your father go?"

"I . . ." Ryan took a fresh breath and was appalled when his fears came tumbling out. "They shouldn't have gone away together." There. He'd said it.

It seemed to take her a moment to define *they*. "I don't know what you mean."

Might as well finish it. "Your husband and my mom. They shouldn't have gone. Together. Out of town. On such a long trip."

Mrs. Newsom moved to the railing. "What are you implying, kid?"

He'd gone too far. He had no proof. She looked mad and he didn't even know her.

"I gotta go. My dad's waiting dinner."

He ran back the way he'd come.

"Hey!" she called after him.

He ran faster.

What had he done?

Patrice read the same page for the second time. Her thoughts kept returning to Ryan's implication about Kathy and Lavon. Not that her husband had ever done anything to make her mistrust him. On the contrary, he was the most trustworthy man she knew. So much so, it drove her crazy sometimes.

Lavon was nothing if not honest. The first year of their marriage, when they'd been figuring out their taxes, Patrice had suggested they fudge a few figures. After all, everybody did it. Lavon had emphatically declined. "Fudge on one thing, fudge on another. I can't do it, Patrice." She'd admired him for that—even while it made her feel unworthy.

She still felt unworthy. Every day, in a dozen different ways, Lavon revealed himself to be a shining example of manhood. Husbandhood. Fatherhood. Yet he never held her in contempt or lifted himself up as some bastion of perfection. He didn't need to. She was an eyewitness.

Sometimes, his goodness disgusted her. The higher he raised himself by good example the lower she sank in comparison until the idea of ever catching up seemed impossible.

"They shouldn't have gone away together. Your husband and my mom."

Any thought of being inferior vanished as jealousy grabbed hold. The emotion grew quickly, and within minutes, it spurred her on, insisting she know the truth.

She went inside to call Lavon. To catch him? Why would she want to catch him?

And yet she called.

His cell phone rang. And rang. Three rings. Four. His answering service came on. *I can't talk right now, leave a message.*

Hi, this is your wife. Remember me?

But instead of leaving a message, she hung up. The Ryan kid didn't know what he was talking about. Everything was fine. Patrice was not going to let some kid complicate an already complicated day.

She went back to the porch, opened her book, and read the same page for the third—and final—time.

The bell above the door to the gallery jingled, announcing a customer.

Sandra Perkins looked up from the slide viewer she was holding. "Go see who it is, will you, Kath?" She checked her watch. "It might be your friends."

Kathy hadn't realized it was that late. She stopped writing on the clipboard and wove her way through the gallery exhibits toward the front door. She spotted Malachi first. "Hey, kiddo."

The boy held up two suckers, one in use. "Look what I got at the doctor's!"

"Two of them. You're some lucky boy. But save room for dinner, okay?"

Lavon smiled. "He conned me into eating one of them now and one later."

"How did the appointment go?"

"Very well," Lavon said. "Chi-Chi had a bunch of tests and we'll get the results next week. We like the doctor a lot, don't we, bud?"

"He has a funny mustache."

Lavon made a sweeping movement downward, as if the doctor sported an old-fashioned handlebar style. "Thanks for inviting us for dinner. I'm glad to get a chance to see the gallery."

"And meet me," Sandra said, coming out from the back. "You're glad to meet me, I'm sure."

They shook hands and Kathy made the official introductions. "Sandra's been with me since the beginning."

Sandra affected a low European accent and bowed gallantly, "I alone made her who she is-s-s today."

"It's more true than not," Kathy said. "Sandra had a gallery in Eureka Springs and when I wanted to churn out the quick and easy paintings, she helped me focus on finding my artistic voice."

"Wow," Sandra said. "I did that?"

They all laughed.

Lavon walked toward some of the hanging pieces. "Did you get done what you needed to get done this weekend?" he asked.

"Just finishing up," Sandra said. "I'm going through the rest of her slides, making the final choices." She put a hand on Malachi's head. "I bet you're hungry, aren't you, young man?"

Malachi nodded even though he had a sucker in his mouth.

"Do you like Chinese food?" she asked him.

He nodded again.

"A kid after my own stomach." She looked at Lavon and Kathy. "Chinese okay with you two?"

It was.

Sandra raised a finger dramatically. "But first! I want to show this young artist a special place."

Kathy looked at Lavon. "You'll love this."

Sandra led them to a room with a sign above the door: Budding Artists' Studio. The walls and shelves inside were lined with kids' paintings and sculptures. Kid-sized tables and chairs were fitted with all sorts of art supplies.

"Voila!" Sandra said. She held out a chair for Malachi and set a piece of paper before him. "Have at it."

Malachi looked up at Lavon. "I can paint?"

"It appears so. Go ahead."

Malachi looked across the pots of paint, the cups of colored pencils, and the trays of crayons and markers like a chocoholic in a Godiva shop.

Sandra sank into a kid-sized chair to help him get started. She looked up at Lavon and Kathy. "I thought we'd have a picnic right here, if that's okay." She pointed to her office. "Kathy, grab a fifty out of my purse; then you two walk down to Bao Ching's and order what you want. Get me cashew chicken and crab rangoon." She shooed them away. "Two blocks to the left. Now go. We're busy."

"Will you be okay, Chi-Chi?" Lavon asked.

It was a dumb question and received no answer, because Malachi was already picking out his paint.

Kathy and Lavon easily found the restaurant, ordered, and were told it would be twenty minutes. Instead of waiting inside, they decided to wait in a small park across the street. They had the place to themselves.

Kathy fell onto a bench. "What a day."

Lavon stood in front of her. "But good, yes?"

"Good. Yes." She closed her eyes a moment and listened to the cicadas droning in the canopy of trees overhead. "But sometimes I feel selfish."

"For what?"

"For enjoying the whole art thing so much. For letting it take over so I think of nothing else. I mean, I know I'm selfish. I admit I'm selfish—as if that will somehow make it better—but the point remains that I'm way too capable of letting all thoughts *but* art fall away. I've barely thought of Roy and Ryan today. And that's wrong. Isn't it?" She realized how bad that sounded and spread her arms wide, face to the sky. "There. Crucify me on the cross of my iniquity."

Lavon laughed softly and sat beside her. "Down, woman. I'm sure you're not that bad. And isn't extreme focus normal for creative types?"

"Probably. But don't tell me it is, or I'll rationalize that if Michelangelo and Monet could be me-oriented and moody, so can I."

"But your art is important to you."

"To *me*. It's important to me. A long time ago, I even dedicated my art to God and felt that *it* was what he wanted me to bring to the world."

"It sounds like there's a story there."

There was. But it was a story she didn't share often anymore. Why didn't she share it more often? Yet, Lavon . . . she knew he'd understand. "You really want to hear?"

He made a show of getting comfortable. "Absolutely." He checked his watch. "What else am I going to do with the next eighteen minutes of my life?"

It was wonderful to have a willing audience. Kathy began.
"Twelve years ago, when my first husband, Lenny, was alive, when
Ryan was only four and Lisa two, I got an anonymous invitation to
go to Haven, Nebraska."

"What for?"

"That was the clincher. The invitation didn't say. But it had this
wonderful verse on it." She dipped deep into her memory and
retrieved it. "'If you had faith as small as a mustard seed, you could
say to this mountain, "Move from here to there," and it would
move. Nothing would be impossible.'"

"Cool verse."

"Exactly. It was all about possibilities. At the time, my marriage
to my first husband was in trouble, I was floundering about almost
everything, plus I had two little kids. I was desperate to find my
purpose."

"Did you?"

"I think so . . . thought so. I took the kids and drove six hundred
miles. There were four other people in Haven who'd received invi-
tations. Some amazing things happened, and—" she decided to get
to the point—"at the end of it all, we dedicated our lives to God in
very specific ways. I dedicated my art to him."

"And you've been working on it ever since."

She shrugged. "With varying degrees of success, and through
many bouts of doubt."

"Doubt about what?"

She'd never even voiced this one aloud. "Do I love it too much?
I've been given a family yet I often resent their presence." She covered her eyes with a hand. "That sounds horrible. I love them, but
sometimes having to share my time between my passion and my
family has been tough. Almost impossible."

"Most people are torn between how they want to—and how

they should—spend their time. We're a busy society. Priorities get skewed."

She sighed. "But by doing so many things at once, do we end up not doing anything well?"

He didn't answer for a moment. "That's a good one."

"Do you have an answer for me?"

"No. But it's a good question."

She laughed. It felt so good to laugh. It felt so good to talk about how she really felt. In spite of her flaws, she felt appreciated. And happy. Suddenly, she leaned over and kissed Lavon's cheek.

His head moved back enough to look at her. Then, he took her face in his hands and kissed her back. On the lips.

All logic died and they locked in an embrace, in a deserted park, in a town where no one knew them.

These weak rationalizations flashed through Kathy's mind as she let herself consume and be consumed by the moment. She couldn't breathe. She didn't need to breathe. Lavon would breathe for her.

It was wonderful. It was the most exciting thing that had ever happened to her. She wanted more. But she knew it should stop.

She wanted more.

Someone cleared a throat.

They stopped kissing and looked toward the sound. A sixty-something couple walked on the path nearby. Their faces were stern with disapproval. At the kiss? Or because she was white and Lavon was black?

Kathy scooted away from him. "Evening," she said.

The couple moved on.

Lavon stood. "Oh my . . . I'm so sorry, Kathy."

She also stood and smoothed her dress. "I'm the one who's sorry. I started it. I don't know what came over me."

Lavon looked at anything but her. "We were just caught up in a happy moment. We weren't thinking."

But we were feeling. Oh, what a feeling.

"We need to get going," he said. "I can't believe I . . . we need to get going."

But she didn't want to go. She wanted to sit back down on that bench and . . .

Lavon walked across the street as if trying to escape her presence.

What a disaster.

All evening Patrice had made a valiant attempt at acting nonchalant, at giving self-indulgence a good shot. After finishing a chapter in her book, she'd left the porch, made a dinner of microwave popcorn and a diet Dr Pepper, and watched part of *Finding Neverland* on DVD— she never missed a Johnny Depp movie. Then she'd given herself a facial and pruned in a tub until the heat of the water lost its bite.

She rarely had the luxury of an evening alone. She deserved an evening alone.

But now, her self-indulgence complete, the jealousy of the afternoon returned, as if it had been waiting for its turn. *You deserve an answer to what's bugging you. You deserve to know the truth about your husband and Kathy.*

The feigned nonchalance surrendered. Dressed in her favorite sweats, Patrice sat on the bed and stared at the phone. She hadn't tried calling Lavon again. And worse, he hadn't called her.

She dialed.

He picked up on the second ring. "Hello?"

Patrice heard Malachi's laughter in the background. And more horrifyingly, Kathy's.

Lavon's muffled voice came through a hand-covered phone. "Shh, bud! You're having way too much fun. I can't hear." He returned to the phone. "Sorry. Hello?"

Patrice hung up, then unplugged the phone, severing all communication.

Her husband and son didn't want to talk to her.

They were having way too much fun.

Without her.

She shivered. And though she knew the shiver didn't come from cold, she went to the closet. Comfort was important. She needed comfort above all else.

After finding her favorite slippers, she noticed a drawing on the opened closet door. It was one that Malachi had made for Lavon, a big red heart that had DADDY drawn in big kid-sized letters. It had been on the refrigerator back in New York, and once in Weaver, Lavon had started to put it back on the fridge, but Patrice had stopped him. She didn't want the kitchen cluttered up with odd papers. She was going for the clean look.

And so . . . Lavon had found a place for it here. And alongside the drawing, he'd put a snapshot of himself and Malachi, cheek to cheek, grinning. And another one of Patrice.

Patrice, alone.

She dropped a slipper but let it lie. The contrast stunned her. The two men in her life together. And her alone.

Doubt swooped in, nudged jealousy aside, and brought fear on its tail. Her entire adult life rushed before her. Days and weeks and months of Lavon and Malachi bonding together and her going on . . . alone.

By choice.

What had she done? Had she been too standoffish? Had she been wrong to encourage the attachment between her husband and her boy? Had she been so desperate for relief from her single-mother status that she'd virtually relinquished her rights to her own son? Now Malachi and Lavon were off on a trip to St. Louis, having fun with Kathy—a woman who was talented, pretty, domestic, and good with kids. They'd never even asked Patrice to come along. It probably had never really entered their minds.

Or hers.

Had she lost Malachi to Lavon? And was she losing Lavon to Kathy?

If so, she'd done it to herself. In ways too numerous to count she'd separated herself from her family. Why would they need her? want her? How many times had Patrice shooed Malachi away because she was busy with something more important? More important than her son?

And Lavon . . . when was the last time she'd given him a compliment? The only things she brought to the marriage were complaints, belittling comments, and demands. Meanwhile Lavon and Malachi were creating a life without her, excluding her because she'd virtually asked to be removed, and had approached mothering and being a wife as annoying items on her to-do list.

Patrice clamped a hand over her mouth, stifling a sob. She was a horrible mother, a horrible wife, a horrible person.

She was nothing.

She threw the slipper back in the closet and kicked the other one out of the way so she could close the door against the condemning evidence.

Then, in panic, she escaped the bedroom and ran down the stairs, outside, onto the front porch. She stopped at the railing, letting it be a barrier between home and away. A streetlight cast a glow across a corner of the grass, sharing its light with the neighbor's house. The house was empty at the moment, but someday, someone would live there again.

It was so quiet. Was that another part of her most recent attitude problem? Did she miss the constant sounds of New York City?

She held her breath and listened again. The streetlight hummed. A cricket chirped in the bushes to her right. That was it. In the city who knew if streetlights hummed or crickets chirped? A dog barked in the distance, proof she was not alone. Alone, yet not alone.

In the big city she had never been alone. Even when they'd gone out on the balcony of their apartment they could see the windows of hundreds of other people, some lit, some dark; but all with the promise—or curse—of people inside. And on the sidewalk below there'd always been a bustle. And cars . . . the traffic never ceased. She remembered looking up at the sky once and being shocked by its expanse skimming the top of her world. She had rarely looked up in New York. Her entire world was spent looking down or across. Not up.

Needing to find the sky now, she hurried down the porch steps into the middle of the street. She looked up and shielded her eyes from the streetlight. Hundreds of stars greeted her.

Where's the moon? Patrice turned around in the middle of the street, searching for it. There it was, low, hidden behind the house. She ran into the backyard and found it. And laughed. One odd victory in a day full of odd emotions.

Suddenly, Mrs. Weaver's voice sounded in her ears: *"I'm doing my best to be the woman you think I am."*

Perhaps Patrice wasn't so different from her employer. Both were strong, independent women. Both had men in their lives who stuck with them, no matter what; men who had a vision of the woman they could be.

Patrice sank into the grass, finding it soft yet cold in spite of the summer heat. Being a better woman was too high a goal, too high a bar. Lavon was too good for her. He was everything she was not. He gave and she took.

Then give. Give it up. Surrender.

She raked her fingers through her hair. "I won't."

You must.

"I can't."

You can. With my help.

With a start Patrice realized that something beyond the norm had just occurred. The reality of sitting in the grass in the dark melded with an inconceivable, untouchable conversation going on in her mind. *You can, with my help* was not her own thought, but . . .

God's?

She trembled and hugged herself.

No. It couldn't be. She'd never given God much notice. Lavon prayed enough for both of them. For the Almighty to bother with her now was ridiculous.

And yet . . .

She sat still, holding her breath. Maybe if she was very quiet he'd tell her more.

But there was no more. Her disappointment surprised her. Since when did she care what God had to say?

Since now.

The ride back to the hotel was completely silent. For her own part, Kathy was mentally exhausted from putting up a happy social façade. Dinner had been excruciating. Malachi had been oblivious, but only *his* laughter had been real. Afterward, Sandra had asked what was wrong.

"Nothing," Kathy had said.

"You're a liar," Sandra had said.

A liar, and worse.

But soon Kathy could lock herself in her room and wait it out until tomorrow—when they'd have to endure yet another awkward time together. Six hours' worth.

They parked and Lavon carried a dozing Malachi into the hotel lobby. As they waited for the elevator, Kathy realized she hadn't called Roy since their tense conversation the night before. She'd hoped he would call. But he hadn't. And now . . . another day had gone by with no communication. An eventful day.

She dialed him now, needing to hear his voice.

"Hi," she said when he answered.

"Hi." His voice sounded hollow.

"We're done for the day."

"We?"

Oh, dear. "How are you? How's Ryan?" The elevator doors opened and she hurried to add, "I'm getting into an elevator to go to my room so I may lose the signal, but if I do—"

"You're in a hotel?"

Kathy stifled a gasp. How could she have been so careless? She motioned for Lavon to go on up and walked toward the lobby, seeking privacy. She stood near a potted tree, her face toward the wall. "Sandra's house had plumbing problems so I had to go to a hotel."

"Did you stay in the hotel last night too?"

"Well . . . yes. It's a real nice one attached to Union Station. Remember seeing it when we walked around the shops on that trip we took to the Arch?"

"I don't care how nice it is. Is Lavon staying there too?"

Her defenses rose higher. "Sure. Lavon and Malachi. We only have our van, you know."

"Why didn't you tell me you were staying in a hotel?"

Kathy tried to distract from the issue. "Why does it matter? You had my cell number. I've been available all day. You could have called me anytime."

It didn't work. "We're not talking about calling; we're talking about sleeping. Lodging. Letting your husband know that you're staying in a hotel with a man you barely know."

I'm not staying with *him.* "Don't you trust me?" *Not that you should . . .*

"Should I?"

"Roy!" Her objection sounded as false and contrived as it was.

She could hear him breathing. "Kath . . . two people of the opposite sex staying in a hotel . . . it's not a good idea."

"You didn't mind me driving six hours with him."

"Actually, I did mind, and now I wish I'd gone with you."

"But you didn't."

He hesitated. "I have to go. Ryan needs me. At least somebody does."

He hung up and Kathy stared at the phone, incredulous. Everything was falling apart. It wasn't just this trip. It had been coming on for a long time. And though she was quick to blame Lisa's death, she feared it was more than that—as if anything could be more than that. How she longed for the old Roy. He was always the loving one, the patient one, the forgiving one. Did he long for the old Kathy? She was the . . . the . . .

Impatient, selfish, bickering one.

She caught the next elevator, hoping a change of location would offer a change of thoughts.

Back in her room, Kathy did not turn on the TV. She did not even take off her shoes. The moment she closed the door, she unexpectedly fell to the floor, resting her head on her hands. "What have I done?"

It came out as a prayer, a plea, a confession, a boast.

For unwillingly, even amid her regrets, her thoughts slipped back to the passion on the bench.

"No!"

She scrambled to her feet, trying to get away from the memories. How could she long for something that was so wrong?

Kathy sat on the bed and extricated a pillow from under the bedspread. She hugged it tight, but instead of the motion forcing the memories away, the contact brought them back. With a vengeance. She closed her eyes . . . and let the memories take over. She didn't say no this time. She didn't flee from them, but embraced them for the delicious feelings they rekindled. In response to a sudden stab of guilt, she reminded herself they were just thoughts. Images of something that was past. It wasn't like she'd do it again.

Though she'd like to.

She threw the pillow across the room.

Lavon had the phone in his hand, ready to call home.

He looked at the clock. It was nearly ten. After Patrice had called while they were eating dinner at the gallery, he'd seen her number and called back. But the phone was off the hook or something. He'd tried her cell phone too, but she wasn't answering.

As if she knew.

Perhaps it was best they didn't talk tonight. He shouldn't call when his soul was so troubled, so much at war with his mind and his body. He might not be able to hide it from his wife and might even end up confessing. Knowing her as he did, he wasn't sure that was the wisest choice. He liked being the rational one, the capable one, the one who could handle every situation and every role. Patrice embraced anger often enough; Lavon certainly didn't need to add to her attitude.

He set the phone on the nightstand and sat on the edge of the bed. Within seconds, his hands found each other and he started praying. "'Though the spirit is willing enough, the body is weak.'" He snickered. "I sure proved that one right, didn't I, Father?"

His thoughts sped to memories of Kathy. Nice memories.

Lavon began to pace. "Help me *not* think of her. It never should've happened."

But it did.

Lavon stopped pacing and bowed his head. "I'm sorry. So sorry. It was wrong." When he opened his eyes, he noticed the bedside table. There was usually a Bible inside. He needed a Bible.

He found it in the bottom drawer. *God bless the Gideons!* He didn't even know where to start, but suddenly a word popped into his head: *flee.*

He looked it up in the concordance and turned to the book of James. He immediately knew this was God's word to him at this specific moment in his life. He read the words once, then read them out loud as an epitaph for all that had gone before. "'Humble yourselves before God. Resist the Devil, and he will flee from you. Draw close to God, and God will draw close to you. Wash your hands, you sinners; purify your hearts, you hypocrites. Let there be tears for the wrong things you have done. Let there be sorrow and deep grief. Let there be sadness instead of laughter, and gloom instead of joy. When you bow down before the Lord and admit your dependence on him, he will lift you up and give you honor.'"

Lavon closed the book and continued his prayers, utilizing a hefty dose of bowing and depending—and promising, that with God's help, it would never happen again.

The house was quiet—too quiet. Ryan had heard his dad talking on the phone with his mom, but hadn't heard what he'd said. The fact that Dad hadn't come out of the master bedroom since then was a good clue it hadn't gone well.

Did that mean Ryan's suspicions were true? Was something going on between his mom and Mr. Newsom? He stood in the hall outside the master bedroom and listened.

Hearing nothing was almost more disturbing than hearing something. He knocked. "Dad?"

He heard his father clear his throat. Then, "Yes?"

"Can I talk to you?"

The door opened. His father looked horrible, his face drawn. He only met Ryan's eyes for an instant before looking away. "What?"

"Are you okay?"

He retreated to the chair by the window. "No. Actually I'm not."

Ryan's stomach rolled. "Did you talk to Mom? Is she . . . I mean . . ."

His father's jaw tightened. "I don't know how she is because I didn't let her tell me anything about her day. I was too busy being a suspicious creep."

Because of me.

"So she and Mr. Newsom—" Ryan shook his head vigorously—"I'm sorry. I shouldn't have said anything. It was dumb. What do I know?"

His father stood and put his hand on Ryan's shoulder. "It's good you said what you said, because it's made me realize I need to appreciate your mother more. I need to show her I love her. I need to quit taking her for granted. We need to talk like we used to."

Ryan blinked. It was not the reaction he'd expected. "Wow."

Roy laughed. "Actually, you know what we need to do? Something we haven't done together in a long while?" He got to his knees.

Ryan nodded. God appreciated joint efforts. Especially ones that involved prayer.

THIRTEEN

Those who lead blameless lives
and do what is right,
speaking the truth from sincere hearts.
Such people will stand firm forever.

PSALM 15:2, 5

It's time to see Lavon again!

Kathy snuggled into the covers, letting that luscious first thought meld with her dreams. Such nice dreams.

The clock radio buzzed. Annoyed, she slapped it into submission, and within moments realized that the Lavon of reality and the Lavon of her dreams were two different men. And they did *not* meld together nicely no matter how hard she tried.

She sat up and took a deep breath. The foggy feelings of half sleep faded, and reluctantly she let them go. It was Saturday. It was the day she was going home, returning to real life. The world of galleries, praise, perks, and passion was over. By this evening she'd be entrenched in her mundane life in small-town America, where she'd deal with domestic duties, a moody son, and a husband she'd grown away from.

She shouldn't feel this way. These were the feelings of a bad mother, a bad wife. *Bad Kathy*.

In a way it made her mad that it was Lavon's strength and discretion that had caused her to behave. Once they'd kissed, he'd been the one to flee. She'd never considered herself a woman who would succumb to temptation, and the kisses and the accompanying emotions had shocked her as much as they had thrilled her. So had the fact that she'd held on to and willingly replayed the memory of her indiscretion. As a good, Christian, married woman, shouldn't she have been quick to confess, to beg God's forgiveness, and ask for his help in keeping the memories at bay, vowing to never even consider such a thing again? "Thou shalt not commit adultery" and all that.

But in spite of knowing what she should be doing, thinking, and feeling, she hadn't sought out God at all. And Lavon's coolness the rest of the evening, the way he'd avoided her eyes . . . message received. There would be no more kisses. Even if she wasn't strong enough to resist him, he was obviously strong enough to resist her.

She'd gone to sleep last night mad at his rejection, mad that he'd caused her mind to be consumed with *him*. To escape her anger, she'd greedily sought sleep and the dreams of another Kathy and another Lavon. Two people free to do whatever they wanted to do.

Enough of this. She rubbed her face roughly, knowing that she *had* to stop this private argument and face up to what happened.

What *had* happened? An impulsive kiss had turned into a few moments of passion. Lust. But beyond that . . . *if only there had been something beyond that*.

Round and round Kathy went. She lay back down in defeat. She noticed the photograph propped against the table lamp: she, Ryan, and Roy, smiling hesitantly at the camera. Hesitant like she was now. Yet together through everything. She spotted Roy's note, tossed carelessly nearby. She picked it up. *Dear Kath, Always remember I love you. Roy.*

They were words of love. Plain, simple, and full of power.

Suddenly, the memories of her ardent kisses with Lavon ceased to bring pleasure, and a different emotion took over. Shame. Kathy stood, her head shaking back and forth. "I kissed him. *I* kissed him first."

How had it happened? Had she wanted it to happen? Even subtly arranged for it to happen?

She moved to the window and pulled the curtains aside, hoping the sunlight would finish the mind-clearing process. As if on cue her thoughts leaped back to when she'd first talked with Lavon at the Meet 'n' Greet; the time in her studio when he'd brought cookies and put the shelf together; the conversation on the porch that had led them to this place; a dinner with their spouses . . . how had these few times of contact progressed to a kiss? Yes, Lavon was a handsome man, but Kathy had been around handsome men before. What made him different?

He listens to me. He shows interest in my art. He allows me to think of myself and forget about my troubles.

He let her be selfish.

"I have to get home. Now!"

She spun toward the clock. Last night, she and Lavon had agreed to leave at eight. In an hour. Would he think she was crazy if she called and asked—

She picked up the phone.

"Sure. Ten minutes. No problem. See you then." Lavon hung up the phone, trying to decipher Kathy's urgent request to go home immediately. Now, not an hour from now. It wasn't that hard. He felt the same urgency to be away from this place and back to some roots. Back to his root: Patrice.

It was odd to think of her that way. She wasn't the strong one. She was the feisty one with a zest that often caused more trouble than stability. Like a thunderstorm that brought blessed rain, Patrice's blessings were often accompanied by thunder and lightning. And sometimes flooding.

You're no better. You're different but no better.

If Patrice was the rain, he was the sun. He was the warm one.

But I can also burn. And like a sunburn, sometimes the damage and the sting didn't show up right away.

He remembered the kiss. *He'd* burn for that.

No. That wasn't true. He'd confessed that sin. It was washed away. Jesus had done that for him.

Yet the fact that he'd kissed Kathy in the first place bothered him. Though Kathy had made the first move, he knew he was just as much to blame. From their first conversation at the Meet 'n' Greet, Lavon had sensed Kathy was desperate for someone to care about her art, and so, he'd become that someone. And when she'd shown herself to be a little needy emotionally? Lavon to the rescue, becoming all things to all people, proving he could be successful at any vocation, any emotion, that no situation was beyond his control.

Except the kiss. His lack of control about that situation had ruffled him more than he liked to admit.

"Lead me not into temptation" needed to be his mantra today. Though he intended to be strong, though he'd promised himself and God it would never happen again, he also knew it could. He was not Superman. He was human. Oh so human.

Kathy wanted to get home sooner rather than later?

That sounded like a good idea.

He woke up his son.

They got on the interstate heading west. Malachi sang to himself in the back of the van. Lavon's stomach pulled with nerves. How were he and Kathy ever going to endure six hours together?

Kathy made the first move. She spoke to him softly, for his ears alone. "I'm sorry, Lavon. For . . . all of it. I'm really sorry."

Relief flooded over him. "Me too. It never should have happened. In fact, I never should have offered to carpool. It was dangerous."

"That's what Roy said."

"That's what we both knew." He glanced at her. "Didn't we?"

Kathy nodded. "I liked you, Lavon. I like you. I like being with you. I thought all this would be okay, and . . . fun."

"Me too. But we can't . . ."

"I know. And we won't."

Good. At least they were agreed.

"Are you . . . are you going to tell Patrice?"

That was a toughie. "I don't know. You?"

"I don't know either," Kathy said. "I hate keeping secrets, but isn't there a time when total honesty can do more harm than good?"

"That's what I was thinking," he said. Or was he just being chicken?

"If you do end up telling her, let me know, okay?"

"Agreed."

She sighed, then adjusted a pillow between her head and the car door. "I'm going to nap, but let me know when you want me to drive."

"Will do."

Silence was good. Silence was best. Silence was safe. He'd take silence.

Sift together dry ingredients.

Patrice looked up from the cookbook. "Sift? What's *sift?*"

She'd awakened this morning to sunshine and chirping birds. When she'd taken her coffee onto the porch, a neighbor had jogged by and called out, "Good morning!"

And it was. A feeling of renewal had grabbed hold of her. Life could be good—if she let it be.

She'd gone into the house with an absurd goal—to make her family cookies. She didn't know how to make cookies. That was Lavon's thing.

Not anymore. Today it would be her thing. Sift or no sift.

The phone rang. She wiped her hands on her shorts and answered.

"Hey, lovey."

"Lavon!" Her insides tensed.

"We're on our way home. We missed you."

"I missed you too." And she meant it. "How did everything go?"

"I like the doctor. He says our little boy should be feeling a lot better soon."

Our little boy.

There was a pause. "I love you, Patrice."

Just the way he said it . . . her throat tightened. "I love you too."

"See you soon."

Patrice hung up and pressed a hand to her chest. They were coming home to her. She had another chance.

She would not blow it.

Joan spread her arms and did a three-sixty turn in the middle of Swenson's Soda Shoppe. "Isn't it beautiful, Ira?"

He looked around, his face befuddled. "Where are we?"

During the past three days, when he'd made such odd comments, she'd thought he was acting, keeping up the part he'd started when she'd caught him with Sally.

But after the comments kept coming, she'd come to realize he wasn't acting. He truly couldn't remember. He truly was clueless.

After talking with Roy yesterday, she'd made a doctor's appointment for Ira in Topeka. A neurologist. She hoped it wasn't Alzheimer's.

She ignored Ira's latest "Where are we?" question and slipped her arm through his, leading him behind the soda fountain. She took out a spoon and pushed the plunger on the container of butterscotch, filling it to the edge of overflowing. She handed it to him. "Here. Taste. It's your favorite."

He was skeptical, like a child being asked to take medicine. But as soon as the topping met his taste buds he smiled. "Butterscotch!"

"The ice cream's coming in tomorrow. We'll be all ready for Founders Day next weekend. Then I'll make you a huge sundae with butterscotch, nuts, and a cherry on top."

"Two cherries," he said.

She kissed his cheek. Two cherries. She'd give him anything. If only . . .

Madeline answered the phone, "Hello?" But at that same moment, the doorbell rang. She went to answer it, taking the telephone with her.

The person on the line said, "Is this Madeline Weaver?"

"Yes. Who's this?"

"This is Thomas Brown from the *Washington Post* and . . ."

The Washington Post? *Why would they be calling me?*

"Hold on a minute." She covered the phone with a hand and opened the door. Web was there, displaying a copy of *The Probe*. "The article?" she asked.

"Yup."

"Is it bad?"

He opened his mouth to speak, closed it, then tried again. "Yup."

Without warning, Madeline's legs buckled, but Web caught her and helped her into the parlor, onto the couch. This was it. The end. All her hard work trying to make restitution through Regrets Only was blown to bits.

She still had the phone in her hands. She handed it to Web. "Hello?"

"Yes, I was speaking with Madeline Weaver. I'm from the *Washington Post* and I wanted to ask her about the allegations—"

"No comment."

Web hung up and set the phone on the coffee table. He looked at Madeline. "You want to read it?"

Did she have a choice? "Read it to me."

Web read her the article, which detailed many of the indiscretions of the Weaver National Bank, naming names, dates, and details.

Finally, she'd had enough and interrupted. "This is God's idea of handling it?"

"Just wait, Maddy. He's not done yet."

"Seems done enough to me. I'm through. Finished. A lifetime of work ruined." She leaned back, letting the cushions of the couch catch her. "It's over, Web. I tried to make things right but it didn't work."

"You can keep going, keep making things right."

She wasn't sure about that. For two reasons. She was literally running out of time; plus she was weary. Exceptionally weary.

Madeline heard footsteps on the porch. Many footsteps. Then the doorbell rang. Voices. A knock on the door.

Web was at the window. "It's a bunch of people. Strangers. Five or six. There's a camera." He looked at Madeline. "Looks like they're reporters."

Madeline let out a little laugh when she realized the first thought that came to mind—*I feel like crawling into a hole to die*—was far too apropos.

Web went to the door to handle the reporters, and Madeline was glad to let him do it. But when she heard them all talk at once, when she heard Web get flustered, she knew she had to go. Weary, dying or not, all this was the result of her sin. And *she* needed to handle it.

She closed her eyes a moment and found herself offering a prayer. Short, but a prayer nonetheless: *God, help. Please help.*

As she neared the door, Web was making a good stab at saving her reputation. " . . . made restitution to these people. You need to ask them what she's done for them through a company called Regrets Only, Inc. You ask them if you want to witness the kind of heart this woman really—"

Web glanced her way, cutting off his own sentence. The reporters saw her and yelled out fresh questions.

Madeline put a hand on Web's arm. "You did good, Web. Now, it's my turn."

"Are you sure?"

"The piper has to be paid." For the first time she looked at the reporters. Eye contact only spurred them into a louder feeding frenzy. Their pressing bodies made her want to retreat. She couldn't proceed like this. There had to be order. She raised her hands, asking for silence.

Surprisingly, she got it. "I am Madeline Weaver. I will answer your questions, *if* you pull back off the porch and behave yourselves. The way this is going to work is that I will make a statement first and then I will answer a few questions. I will remind you this is private property, ladies and gentlemen, and I *will* do this my way."

They exchanged looks, but quickly fell back, like hungry troops retreating in order to be fed. There weren't "five or six" like Web had originally reported, but ten. Why hadn't they had this kind of coverage for the contest?

Simple. Because scandal sells.

She went all the way outside onto the porch, and took up a position at the center of the top step. Web stood a short way behind her, on the edge of her peripheral vision. There, ready to help. As he'd always been.

When the reporters were settled and looking up at her with expectant faces, she began a statement. "I am guilty."

They yelled out questions, but she felled them with a look. "A statement, remember?"

"Shh." The crowd chastened itself.

"I am a Weaver. I worked at the Weaver National Bank. When I worked there, I went along with various indiscretions in regard to bank business. Most were carefully orchestrated to skirt the law, never break it." She sighed and thought of the deceit she'd propagated against Web. Withholding his inheritance was against the law. He could press charges if he wanted, if he knew the real truth about the $25,000 check she'd given him.

She looked back at him and he offered her a smile, ever supportive. He was unaware of her true character and the wrong she had
done against him.

"Who leaked the story?"

She'd obviously paused too long. They would not observe her
rules forever. Besides, this question she wanted to answer. "His
name is Bennie Davison. He has his own PI company. My father-
in-law and my husband used his services for decades to facilitate
our plans. And recently I used him to—"

"What's this about restitution?" a reporter asked.

She also didn't mind this question. "A year or so ago, I began to
feel remorse. I decided to make things right—as much as I could.
I went through old files, had Mr. Davison do some checking,
found out what the victims of the bank needed, and arranged to fill
those needs through a company called Regrets Only."

"Why now? After all these years, why a year ago?"

That question she could not answer. She shifted her weight to
the other foot. Her initial surge of adrenaline was depleted. She
was spent. She couldn't do this much longer.

Web slipped up behind her, a hand to her elbow. "You okay?"
he asked.

The questioner persisted. "Mrs. Weaver, why the rush for restitution now?"

Rush for restitution. A good phrase. And suddenly, a new need
arose in Madeline Weaver. The need for closure.

She shrugged away from Web's contact and took a step toward
this audience who would spread the word . . . and spread her secret
into the world.

"Why now? Because I'm dying."

With that, she turned and went inside.

As soon as she escaped into the house, a sharp pain made her gasp. She pushed a hand against it and sucked in a slow breath.

Web was right behind her, closing the door. "Maddy, what was all that?" As soon as he saw her, he was at her side. "Maddy?"

"Get away from me, old man. I'm fine."

"You're not fine."

"It's no worse than the rest."

"What's all this about dying? You're not dying, are you?"

"That's what I said, wasn't it?" She moved into the living room, taking a place on the couch again. She needed cushions. She needed comfort.

He sat beside her. "What kind of sick are you?"

Madeline didn't want to put a name to it. Call it denial or just plain stubbornness. Sick was sick. Dying was dying. "Sick enough to know time is short."

He swallowed. "How short?"

"You know that Calvin and Hobbes saying, 'God put me on Earth to accomplish a certain number of things. Right now I am so far behind, I will never die'? I think this article coming out when we'd prayed for it not to is a good sign that God's had enough of my work. He's telling me the gig's up, game's over. The work of Madeline Weaver is done."

Web's face was stricken, pulled. He looked every one of his eighty-two years. He picked up the phone. She heard a dial tone. "What's Dr. Bauer's number?" he asked her.

She took the phone away and silenced it before taking his big hands in her small ones. "Dr. Bauer can't help. No one can."

He yanked his hands away. "Who says?"

"Four doctors say." In response to his shocked look, she contin-

ued. "I've been to four different doctors to make sure. Two in
Topeka and two in Kansas City. I spared no expense, Web. But
money and determination can't buy me a miracle, and that's what
I need. If I'd gone in earlier, maybe, but you know me: too busy,
too stubborn, and too ornery to abide by preventative tests and
checkups. I'm paying for that now. It's my own fault. Too little
too late—in a lot of ways regarding a lot of things."

Web was crying now, and Madeline realized she hadn't seen him
cry since he was a boy. He was always so strong, so immovable in
his strength. She wiped away a tear with her thumb. "Stop that,"
she said. "It makes you look old."

"I am old."

"So am I. And you'd think it would make this dying stuff easier
to take, but it doesn't. 'She lived a long life' is a bunch of bun-
kum." She stroked his arm. "I want to live, Web. You know that.
I have so much more I want to do. I was trying so hard to be good
enough, Web. So hard."

He wiped another tear away. "Good enough for what?"

He would make her talk about that. It. Yet maybe it was time . . .
"Good enough for that heaven you've kept dangling like a carrot
in front of me all these years."

"You aren't good enough, Maddy."

She stifled a laugh. "Thanks a lot."

He shook his head. "No one is. That's the point. As I've been
trying to tell you, you don't have to *be* good enough. And though
making restitution is fine, you'll never be able to pay for your sins.
Not completely."

"What happened to Web-the-encourager?"

"I'm Web-the-truth-teller. You don't get to heaven by working
for it, Maddy; you get there by faith. By believing in Jesus."

"So all my work has been for nothing?"

"Of course not. But if you're doing it to earn heaven . . . it doesn't work that way."

Her mind couldn't handle another thought. "I can't do this right now, Web." She sighed deeply. "I'm drained. Spent."

"Don't give up, Maddy. You're a fighter. So fight."

He was right about that. She offered him a smile. "I do like a fight."

The relief in his face was plain. But suddenly she realized she'd revealed only one of her secrets. There was one more. If the frequency and intensity of the pain were any indication of the time she had left, she'd better get on with it. "There's one more thing I need to tell you."

Web used his handkerchief, then stuffed it into the pocket of his overalls. "Luckily, it can't be any worse than that last one."

She made a teetering motion with her hand.

"It is worse?"

"Depends on your attitude."

He shook his head. "No more, Maddy. Not now."

"Sorry. No can do."

He ran his hands over his face and through his hair, holding on to his head a long moment.

She knew this was hard for him. Hard for her too, but it couldn't be helped. When she died, she wanted to go with a clean slate. "You ready yet?" she asked.

"You don't give a fellow much choice, do you?"

"Sue me." Her own words made her laugh because they were inadvertently appropriate. "Actually you could sue me for what I did to you."

"Maddy . . . I'm not sure I want to hear this."

"You're the one who's always talking about the truth setting a person free. You really believe that twaddle, or have you been doing a bit of false preaching?"

"Of course I believe it. And I can take whatever you have to say. If you need to tell me some truth in order to be free, go for it."

"So I have your permission?"

"Maddy!"

She took a breath from her innermost regions, ignoring the pain it brought with it. "Remember when your mother died?"

"That's going a ways back. Fifty-some years . . ."

"You thought she left you nothing other than the house and a few knickknacks."

He paused. "Yes, that's what I thought . . . Maddy . . ."

She held up a hand, needing to get this all out at once instead of in little pieces. "Your mother left you $500 in some bonds kept at the bank. They're worth $25,000 now. . . ." She waited for him to get the connection.

"The check you gave me? As a bonus?"

"The very one. A little payback for the money I kept from you back in 1952."

"You *kept* from me?"

She nodded once. "I kept from you. I didn't want you to leave Weaver, and since you'd come home after the war to find me married to Augustus, I was pretty sure that given a little spending money, you'd get out of town. Literally."

"You *stole* from me?"

"I kept money from you—in trust, you might say. I gave it back."

"Over fifty years later."

She shrugged. "You and your Jesus are big into forgiveness, right?"

"He is. At the moment, I'm not too sure about me."

She leaned back. "You're going to hold a lousy $500 against me?"

"Twenty-five thousand dollars."

"I paid you back. And you said you didn't want it. Don't be a hypocrite."

"Me?"

Okay, so she'd blown it with the hypocrite line. . . .

"You kept my money because of totally selfish motives."

She flipped a hand at him. "You want to move away? Move away."

"It's been fifty years!"

"I told you I'm sorry," she said. "At the time it seemed very logical. I wanted you here so I made it happen."

"But I wouldn't have left."

"Why?"

"You know very well why. When we were twelve I promised I'd stay in Weaver. You promised. Augustus promised. A promise is a promise."

"I . . . I forgot," she said. Her tone softened. "I should have known you wouldn't."

He snickered sarcastically. "That's me. Good old reliable Web." He rubbed the space between his eyebrows. "But let me get this straight. You weren't content having one man; you needed to have me around too?"

"Can I help it if I loved two men?"

"But you married Augustus."

"That doesn't mean I didn't love you."

They stared at each other. They were at an impasse.

Finally Web spoke. "You love me?"

She had to roll her eyes. "Of course I do. I adore you, you old coot. And since we're talking truth here, I will admit that I'm sorry I married Augustus while you were off to war."

"You're sorry you married Augustus?"

His eyes were disgustingly hopeful, and she nearly countered with something snide like *I'm sorry I didn't wait for you to get back so you could have been at the wedding,* but that wasn't the truth.

She might as well finish this.

"I . . . I am sorry I married Augustus. I married him for his money and his family's position in the community. I should have married you. I loved you more." She studied him. "Much more."

At that moment she hated his face. He'd never been one to hide emotion, and in the seconds that followed this last declaration Web's face visited joy, frustration, anger, and regret. She'd suffered more than enough of those emotions on her own.

"Remember the name of my company? Regrets Only? The name had nothing to do with etiquette—me, care about etiquette? Pooh to that. The company name came out of my realizing my mistakes and wishing I'd never made them. And—" she cleared her throat— "and never marrying you, my dear man, is my biggest regret."

There. She'd said it. All of it. She waited for him to say something.

He sniffed and used the handkerchief again. He stuffed it back into his pocket. Then with moans and groans, he got down on one knee.

"What are you doing?"

He took her hand. "You know very well what I'm doing."

"Oh no . . . you're not. You're not."

"You shush. I am." He cleared his throat. "Maddy—Madeline, will you marry me?"

"But—"

"No *but*s. And no more regrets."

Suddenly, perhaps for the first time in her life, Madeline felt completely undeserving. How could this man love her in spite of

everything? Why had he stood by her all these years? How could
he have endured seeing her married to another man? How could he
have stuck by her when all she did was shoo him away, perplex and
vex him?

Tears came, surprising her. She was not a crier, for what good
did tears do? And yet . . . she could do nothing to stop them.
"Why, Web? Why do you love me? I've done nothing but take, yet
you give and give and give. . . . Why do you love me?"

He rubbed a tear from her cheek with his thumb in the same way
she had done for him earlier. He smiled at her, the wrinkles around
his eyes deep and intricate. "I just do, Maddy. I admit it doesn't
make sense. Yet even when I didn't want to love you, I did. You've
always had my heart, Maddy, even when you've broken mine."

The thought of such unconditional love was too much. She
began to sob. She didn't deserve him. Not even a little bit.

He kissed her hand. "I'm just loving you like Jesus loves you,
Maddy."

A window in her mind opened, and soon after, her heart. All that
Web had said about Jesus . . . years and years of words she'd ignored.
Suddenly, it made sense. It fit. Through Web's unconditional love
she had a new inkling into what Jesus was all about. It wasn't fully
formed yet, but she felt fuller inside, as if something had been added.

"So?" Web said. "Will you marry me?"

What could she say but, "Yes. Yes, I'll marry you."

They hugged like they hadn't hugged in over sixty years. And
kissed for the first time since October 22, 1942.

When they released from the embrace they both laughed. "Not
bad for two eightysomethings," she said.

"Not bad at all." He stood and pulled her to her feet. "Come on."

"Come on where?"

"We're going to get married. Now."

"Don't be ridiculous."

He pulled her toward the door. "I've waited sixty years for this. I'm not waiting another minute. We're going to the church."

With difficulty, she stopped him. "We don't have a pastor in town. You're the acting pastor."

He looked to the ceiling for just a moment. "Then I'll do it myself." He led her through the front door and down the porch steps toward his truck.

"But we don't have a license. We don't have witnesses. It won't be legal."

He stopped with the truck's passenger door open. "Time's short, Maddy. You, who have pressed the edge of legalities for decades, are going to press them once more—for love. God knows our hearts, and the paperwork will follow. For now we'll have him officiate and the angels themselves will be our witnesses."

"You're crazy."

He kissed her. "Crazy in love."

It had been years since Madeline Weaver had been in church and she expected to feel awkward there. Unwelcome.

Yet with Web by her side she felt at home. As if she'd come home.

It was odd standing near the altar with the big cross on the wall behind it. But facing Web, having her hands held in his, just the breadth of them keeping their bodies apart . . . looking into his eyes and seeing them sparkle in a way they had never sparkled . . .

With a look to the cross, Web began, speaking to the cross as if Jesus himself were there. "Jesus? God? We stand here before you wanting to be married. We love each other. We want to spend the rest of our lives together."

When Web looked down at her, Madeline felt her throat tighten. How she wished she had fifty more years.

He looked up at the cross. "We've made plenty of mistakes, Lord, and we're both mighty sorry for them. You know our hearts. You know where we stand with you, Lord. And I trust you to bless what we're doing here today. Because you're all about love, Lord. All about love."

Web took a deep breath and looked at Madeline. "I, Web, take you, Maddy—Madeline—as my lawfully wedded wife. I promise to love, honor, and cherish you all the rest of my days." He nodded to her.

"I, Maddy—" She gave him a special smile. For she was his Maddy. "I take you, Web, as my lawfully wedded husband. I promise to love, honor, and cherish you all the rest of my days—and may there be many of those."

"Amen," Web said.

"Amen," Madeline said.

Web took a deep breath. "Can I kiss you now?"

"Absolutely."

After they kissed, Web pumped his fist in the air and yelled, "Yee-haw!"

Madeline laughed and tugged his arm. "Is it proper to yell yee-haw in church?"

He kissed her again.

Seth hadn't planned to drive to Kansas City, but when he'd gotten up this morning, his first thought was of Jenna and their talk on the swing when she'd given him up.

"Don't look at me that way, Seth. You know I'm right. You can't be

happy with me. You need that farm. It's a deep-down part of you. So go get it. I've just made your life easier, Seth Olsen. Go to Bonnie. She's the one for you."

His way was clear. He didn't have to worry about hurting Jenna. She'd pulled herself out of the picture. She'd cleared the way. She'd virtually given him her blessing.

The thing was, he didn't want her blessing.

"I want her."

His words had echoed earlier in his empty bedroom. Those three words said it all.

Seth had laughed and bounded out of bed. He would go to Jenna. He'd make her understand that he didn't care about any farm. Not if it meant he couldn't have her.

But there was one thing he had to do first. One other person he had to see.

For Sale by Owner

For sale? Seth parked in front of his mother's house in Kansas City and hurried up the front walk, all thoughts of his own predicament gone. He rang the doorbell.

She appeared shortly, waving at him through the glass. "Seth! What a pleasant surprise."

They exchanged the requisite hug and he jumped in with his question. "You're selling the house?"

She drew her shoulders back and grinned. "I am. I told you that."

He vaguely remembered her saying something about it. "Why?"

Grin still in place, she slipped her arm through his and led him to the living-room couch. "I have some news for you. I've had some news that I've repeatedly tried to tell you, but you've been so obsessed with this Weaver thing that you—"

"I have some news for you too."

Her grin faded. "There you go again, Seth. Interrupting just as I'm about to tell you . . . besides being annoying, it's impolite and—" Eyes on him, she cocked her head. "Oh my. Seth, you look so serious. I guess you'd better tell me your news first."

He couldn't sit for the telling, so he moved to the middle of the room, letting the coffee table come between them. "You know I entered the Weaver land contest because I wanted to move back home."

"*Had* to move back home, the way you told it. So, how is it? Is Weaver fulfilling your every fantasy?"

He hated when she made fun of him, even when he deserved it. "What you didn't know is that I had an ulterior motive for all this."

Her chin jutted back. "That sounds ominous."

"Not really. Actually, not at all. The fact was, I was doing it all for you."

"Me?" She scooted forward on the cushion. "You certainly have me curious."

He returned to his seat, needing to match this present reality with at least the physical portion of his daydream about the moment when he'd tell her the news. Only now . . . the news had changed a bit. He'd failed in his attempt to make her happy and proud of him.

"My, my, Seth. You look so solemn, as if your entire world has been blown apart."

"It has . . . in a way." He took one of her hands. "My plan—once I moved back to Weaver—was to get the farm back. Reclaim the family farm."

Her eyebrows dipped. "Why would you want to do that? I thought you were glad to be away from the place." She was talking about his leaving eight years ago.

"I was. At first. But when I left, I was just a punk kid. I didn't know what was important. I thought farming was too much work."

"It was."

"What?"

His mother sighed. "It *was* too much work. My job working forty hours a week for the telephone company is a cinch compared to the constant to-dos and worries on the farm."

"I . . . I thought you loved farming."

She straightened the magazines on the table. "I loved the idea of it. And I loved being in the country. We never see sunsets like that in the city. But as far as the work . . ." She shook her head. "Certainly you remember how much your father and I argued about it."

Thinking back, he did remember. Why hadn't he remembered before?

"Of course, things would have been a lot easier if your father had been any good at farming. His skills were pathetic. Pitiful. We would have lost the place eventually. His death just hurried it along."

Seth didn't know which point to address first. "Dad would have lost the farm because he wasn't good at it?"

His mother looked confused. "The man refused to enter the twenty-first century, Seth. You know that. He resisted anything new and technical." She snickered. "Actually, he wasn't doing that well with twentieth-century methods either. There was no way we could compete with other operations that were modernized."

"But I thought . . . when I left and wasn't there to help, I thought you lost the farm because . . ."

"Because you weren't there?" She laughed. "Honey, like me,

you may like the idea of being a farmer, but like your father, you don't have the talent or the gift of being a man of the earth."

Seth didn't know what to say.

She put a hand on his knee. "You haven't been harboring some guilt trip, have you?"

He looked down at her hand. The veins were prominent. "I thought the reason Dad got sick and lost the farm was because I abandoned him. You. It."

She took both his hands in hers. "Oh my, the misconceptions of youth. First off, you didn't abandon us. You grew up and left home to be on your own, to become a policeman. You like police work, don't you?"

"Yeah, I do."

"See? And as far as your dad's getting sick? He smoked three packs a day his entire life. That's what killed him. Actually, when he got sick and we had to sell the farm it was a relief—selling the farm, that is. Your dad's sickness was another matter. Stupid smoking. But nobody could ever tell Larry Olsen anything he didn't want to hear, or get him to do anything he didn't want to do. You know that."

She'd said those last three words repeatedly, and they were completely true. He knew that. He knew much more than he'd let himself acknowledge. How stupid and blind was that?

A strong memory returned and needed to be addressed. "On the day I left, you said I was breaking your heart."

She looked across the room a moment, then back at him. "I probably did. And I probably felt that way—at that particular moment." She fidgeted, as if something else was trying to work itself out into the open. "Another truth is . . ." She shook her head. "Never mind."

"Oh no you don't. Tell me."

"It's not something a son needs to know."

His thoughts flew with awful possibilities. Now he *had* to know. Seth took her hand. "We're getting things up front now, Mom. Everything. Just tell me."

She gently pulled her hand away as if she couldn't say anything while there was contact between them. She took a fresh breath. "When you told us you were moving out, moving far away, my first reaction was panic—and it had nothing to do with the farm."

He waited.

She glanced at him, then away. "You were my buffer, Seth. My buffer between your father and me."

"Buffer? I don't under—"

"Your presence made my life easier." She expelled her air and closed her eyes. When she opened them again, the words came out in a rush. "Your father and I hadn't been getting along for years. He was a failure at farming and it made him frustrated, which made him mean. I tried to think of something else we could do to make a living, anything to get us away where we'd have a chance to live a more normal life. If your father could have been good at something he might have been nicer and—"

"Did he hit you?"

She shook her head. "He shoved me a few times. He yelled— a lot. But mostly it was horrible tirades against me, against the world, that made me afraid."

"Afraid of him."

She blinked. "Afraid *for* him."

Seth absorbed her words. "Suicide?"

She moved from the couch to the mantel, fingering its edge. "He threatened repeatedly. It was exhausting to try to buoy him up, talk him out of it, encourage him—especially when my words sounded hollow even to me."

"Did he ever try to kill himself?"

She let go of the mantel. "No. Soon after you left he got sick. And then he panicked, realizing death *was* coming close and . . ." She shrugged. He knew the rest. "When you were around, when you were in the house, I was safe from the tirades. I used to hate when you and your friends would go out on the weekends. I didn't even like being alone with him for that short time. So when you announced you were moving away . . . I panicked. And I said you were breaking my heart." She took a step toward him. "I didn't mean for you to be haunted by those words all these years."

Seth leaned forward, his elbows on his thighs. He ran his fingers through his hair and over his face. He hadn't known any of this. Why hadn't he known any of this?

His mother sat beside him, rubbing a hand across his shoulders. "So, you're getting the old farm back, are you? Who'da thought?"

Seth's mind zoomed back to the present. "Actually, I'm *not* getting the farm back." He pinched the corner of a magazine and moved it a quarter inch to the left. "I'd planned to. In fact I'd started dating the daughter of the new owner with that goal in mind."

She lowered her chin. "You were using a girl's affections to get the farm?"

He couldn't answer.

Her hand stopped its comfort and slapped him between the shoulder blades. "Seth Olsen! I raised you better than that. You don't mess with the heart of a woman. No good comes of such a thing. For her—or you."

"I feel like such a fool. There I was, trying to get the farm back for you, not knowing you were glad to be away. You're so sentimental; I thought you'd be pleased to be back on the family place. And when you complained about your job at the phone company . . ."

"Everybody complains about their job. It doesn't mean they

want to quit." She drew him into a hug. "Oh, Seth, I'm sorry you had to go through this, thinking things that weren't true, taking blame that wasn't yours. If I'd known, I would have set you straight in a flat-out, double-timed minute."

He pulled away and started to stand. "I need to go."

"Oh no you don't." She pulled him down beside her again. "I've been trying to tell you what's been going on in my life for months. Now that I have you here, you're going to listen."

He suddenly noticed that his mother's cheeks were rosy. And was she wearing eye makeup?

She held out her left hand and for the first time, he noticed a ring. "I'm getting married. His name is Jeffrey Carter. I met him at dance class."

"Dance class?"

"I've been taking salsa lessons." She moved her torso and arms in a Latin motion.

Seth tried not to gawk.

His mother continued. "Jeffrey is fifty-two, divorced years and years ago, has a grown daughter, works for an insurance company, and has a wonderful house in Prairie Village. That's why I'm selling. We're going to live in his place—after our December wedding, of course."

"Isn't this kind of sudden?"

"Not at all. Like I said, I've been trying to tell you . . . besides, we first met in college, but lost touch. We've been dating four months now."

Seth shook his head. The idea of his mother married to another man . . . to think of his mother finding romance . . .

She slipped her arm through his and bumped shoulder to shoulder. "Ain't life grand, Seth? Simply grand?"

It did have its moments. Even for stupid fools.

Telling Bonnie wasn't easy, and it was hard to suffer through her tears, and would continue to be hard dealing with her anger when their paths crossed in the future. And what about the Weaver grapevine? Would everyone find out about his mercenary motives?

Seth knew the answer to that, and would have to play the part of the contrite rogue for months to come. Yet, better a few tears now than many tears—or even a divorce—later. Getting a stern glare from Bill Bowden on his way out of the Bowden home didn't ease the knot in his stomach. Yet he knew in the place deeper inside, behind the knot, that he'd done the right thing breaking it off. For everyone involved.

Did that everyone include Jenna?

He was about to find out.

Seth pulled into the driveway of the Weaver mansion and was relieved to see her car out front. On the way to the door he regretted not bringing flowers or some other peace offering. The last time they'd talked, they hadn't parted on good terms. He just hoped what he had to say would be enough. Didn't good intentions—pure intentions—count for something?

Before he could knock, Jenna opened the door. "What do you want?"

With only a moment's hesitation he said, "You. The farm's not a deep-down part of me. You are."

She cocked her head and stared at him. "I don't understand."

"I want you, Jenna. You."

She looked past him, then back at him. "What happened?"

"A lot. I have a lot to tell you."

She lifted her chin. "Maybe I don't want to hear."

"I'm betting you do. Hoping you do."

Seth won the bet. She let him in.

After dropping Lavon off at home, Kathy sped through the streets of Weaver, challenging any traffic—scant though it was—to get out of her way. She'd been gone only three days. Yet how often had she longed for three days away, on her own, heralding the idea of such solitude as akin to heaven?

Foolish, foolish woman, thinking she could handle temptation . . . playing with it . . . teasing it. She thanked God it hadn't been any worse. How easily it could have been worse.

She pulled into the driveway and shut off the van. She paused a moment in the silence and said a prayer for help, the right words, and the right attitude.

"Kathy!" Roy was on the front stoop, waving at her. He was smiling.

Was he really happy to see her? She burst out of the car and met him halfway. The cocoon of his arms made anything seem possible.

She pulled away, "You smell like . . . like Mr. Clean."

He laughed and led her toward the house. "I have been Mr. Clean. You should see the place. Spic and span."

"I know I left things in kind of a mess. You didn't have to do that. I would've—"

"No problem," he said. Kathy felt guilty because it wasn't a problem for Roy to do nice things for her. The opposite however . . .

No. She couldn't get down on herself. She was going to do better.

Ryan was at the door. "Hi, Mom." She hugged the other man in her life. "I'll get your suitcase."

Kathy hid her surprise that Ryan was actually offering to help and pulled Roy inside, wanting to have a moment to talk to him out of Ryan's presence. "I need to tell you something, Roy. Right away."

His brow creased in worry. "What?"

"I . . ." She almost confessed the kiss, then detoured to a safer confession. "I shouldn't have gone without you. We need to do more together."

Ryan came in with her suitcase and Kathy found herself glad to have him there. She sat on the middle of the couch and patted the places on either side. After they settled in, she put a hand on their knees. "I'm so glad to be home."

"We're glad to have you home," Roy said. "But I have a confession to make."

Confession? Kathy's throat was dry. She let him continue.

"I need to support your art more, Kath. I've been lax about that."

He was apologizing to her? Where had the bitter man of last night's phone call gone?

"Back in Haven you dedicated your art to God. Sometimes I forget that," Roy said.

"I remember Haven," Ryan said. "I told God that I'd always be a good brother to Lisa." Suddenly, his eyebrows dipped. "Oh." He sucked in a breath. "I'd forgotten about that. I . . . I didn't do very well keeping that promise, did I?"

Kathy pulled in a breath. The progression of the conversation shocked her. She didn't want Ryan to feel bad about himself. "Stop it, Ryan. You were an awesome brother to Lisa. Lisa made a choice to get in that car."

Ryan stared at the floor. "I should have made her listen."

Roy reached behind Kathy and put a hand on his shoulder. "Lisa only heard what she wanted to hear. She wanted to be with Matt." When he looked at Kathy, she knew what he was thinking.

"I'm the one who encouraged her to be with that group. If anyone's to blame, it's me," Kathy admitted.

Roy put his hand on hers. "But Lisa knew all the warnings about alcohol and driving. She wasn't ignorant. In the end the responsibility for her death—" he took a fresh breath—"fell on Lisa herself."

The room echoed with the words.

"We've never said that out loud," Kathy said.

"We should have. A long time ago." Roy looked at Ryan and waited until Ryan met his gaze. "You're not to blame. Do you understand that?"

Ryan's eyebrows nearly touched and his chin quivered. He nodded. Kathy pulled him into a hug. "I'm so sorry we didn't set you straight from the beginning. You are the most important person in our lives." She pulled back and looked at his wonderful hazel eyes with their ridiculously thick lashes. "I promise from this day forward to show you that. In fact . . ." She stopped and allowed a new idea to materialize.

"Kath?"

She stood, stepping away from both of them. The thought that had intruded on this moment was so simple yet so profound. Why had she never thought of it before? Finally, when she felt able, she faced them, looking directly at her son. "I shouldn't have dedicated my art to God back in Haven. My art is miniscule in importance when compared to my family. If I had been any kind of mother I would have known that and dedicated my motherhood to God. I should have left Haven vowing to bring you and Lisa up the best I could, not vowing to be successful with some silly paintings."

"Your paintings aren't silly," Ryan said.

"But I've made them too important. I've made *me* too important. I haven't thought enough about any of you. In fact, if I hadn't tried to live vicariously through Lisa, she would never have been with that group, never would have been in the car with Matt, never—"

Roy was at her side, pulling her close. "Stop," he said. "Stop."

But she couldn't. A ticker tape of her past filed by, each act of selfishness a horrid piece of evidence damning her. Another thought overwhelmed her. "Ryan was the one God wanted to go to Haven! The invitation was meant for him, not me. He's the one who's led the godly life since then. He's the one who can change the world." She looked at her son. "It wasn't about me. It was about you!"

"Mom, don't. Please don't."

Kathy sank to the floor, surprisingly spent. She'd come home ready to be a better wife and mother, ready to make such a declaration to her family. Yet far beyond her initial objective, these revelations had come into her consciousness like bolts out of the blue, electrifying and shocking. And with their arrival her simple intent had turned more complex.

Yet . . . the essence was the same. She needed to love her family better and put them first. It's what God had wanted all along, through all that *had* gone before, *was* now, and *would* be in the future.

Roy knelt beside her, stroking her back, and Ryan joined them, his arms spanning his mother and father. They cried with her. For her. For them. Eventually their tears turned into quiet prayers, and only after they'd been cleansed by both did they stand again.

But this time it was different, because the Bauer family wasn't standing alone anymore.

Never again would they stand alone.

Patrice pulled the curtains to the side. Lavon was on his way up the front walk, led by Malachi, skipping.

She held a plate of cookies. "Here we go," she told the empty house.

Lavon opened the door and Malachi slipped in beneath his arm. "Surprise!" she yelled.

He grinned. "Wow. What a homecoming!"

Patrice kissed him, then Malachi. She hugged them close with her free arm.

The boy noticed the plate. "Are those cookies?"

She gave him one, then held the plate like a treasure. "They're made from scratch."

Lavon took one and examined it, front to back. "You made these?"

"I even sifted."

He laughed and took a bite. "Delicious."

Malachi reached for another one, but somehow the plate tipped and the cookies fell to the floor. He looked up at his mother, ready to cry. "I'm sorry, Mama. I'm sorry."

The old Patrice would have yelled at him and reminded him that he should be more careful. But the new Patrice kept the scolding at bay—with difficulty—and reached down, picked up a cookie, and took a bite. "Five-second rule!"

After a few more minutes of chitchat, Malachi grew bored with the homecoming and started playing with his Legos in the corner of the living room.

Patrice drew her husband toward the kitchen. They stood facing each other; it was distressingly awkward. Patrice knew the reason for her own awkwardness, but had no idea why Lavon was acting so strange.

The ice was broken when they each took a deep breath at the same time. "So," Lavon said with a laugh.

"So," Patrice said.

He kissed her cheek, then drew her into a hug. But it still felt odd. Something wasn't right.

She pulled back. "How was the trip?"

Lavon ran a finger along the edge of her cheek. "Enlightening."

I've had my own moments of enlightenment. "In what way?" she asked.

He looked her in the eye. "In the way that . . . I love you. I adore you. And I need to appreciate you more."

That's exactly what I decided. How odd they'd come to the same conclusion—apart. Her suspicions filed by but did not veer into her thoughts. Her husband and son were back home. She was not alone any longer. Her husband and son loved her and were giving her another chance to be a better woman. She hugged him tight. "I love you too."

She wouldn't let them down. It was a promise.

Madeline had never been so content. Lounging on the couch, using Web's torso as a pillow, was a comfort she'd never missed because it was a comfort she'd never dared to imagine.

She'd been held by strong arms in her time. She'd even been loved. But Web offered her something she'd never experienced.

Acceptance.

In a way beyond her ken, she was beginning to recognize that having one special person accept her for who she was—flaws, foibles, and all—made her the recipient of a level of love far higher than hugs or even kisses.

"You've always had my heart, Maddy, even when you broke mine." She sighed at the memory of Web's words.

"What's the sigh for?" Web asked.

"For you. Because of you." She sat up and offered him her best smile, then stood and extended her hand. "But what I want to know is why we're cuddling on the couch when we could be more comfortable upstairs?" She leaned close and whispered. "After all, we *are* man and wife and this *is* our wedding night."

Web slowly moved from reclining to sitting upright. His hands hung between his knees, keeping each other company. "I've been thinking about that, Maddy . . . and . . . well . . . I don't think we oughta go upstairs."

She couldn't believe her ears. "But we're married. In a church. Before God."

He risked a glance. "But not legally. Not completely."

She pointed a finger at him. "Who's the one who told *me* she needed to press the edge of legalities for love?"

His head shook back and forth. "I know. Guilty as charged. You just got me worked up." He smiled. "You do that to me, you know."

She put her hands on her hips. "Oh, I get it. You're getting cold feet. You don't *want* to marry me."

He stood and took her hands. "Of course I do. I just want to do it right. In fact, I have a plan. Tomorrow, you and I will go to Topeka and get a marriage license. If we have to wait a few days to have the real ceremony with a real preacher, we'll do it. We'll do whatever it takes."

"Sounds like a bunch of red-tape bother to me."

Web pulled her hands to his chest and forced her to look in his eyes. "I promise you, Maddy Weaver, by next Saturday, by Founders Day, you will be my bride in every sense of the word."

His eyes were intense, and oh so blue. How had she resisted him so long?

"Do you really promise?" she asked. Why did she feel like a teenager?

He kissed her hand. "I promise."

With a burst of energy, she shoved him away. "So. I suppose you're wanting to go back to your house now, to climb into your own bed."

He gave her a sly smile. "That's not what I want at all." He returned to the couch and resumed his position. He patted his chest. "Who needs a bed anyway? Come cuddle, old woman."

"Who you calling old?"

Madeline returned to the place she belonged.

FOURTEEN

Where two or three gather together
because they are mine,
I am there among them.

MATTHEW 18:20

Madeline sat at the kitchen table with the final to-do list. Jenna stood at the stove and stirred the oatmeal.

Today was Founders Day. Today was the culmination of all her hard work. "Did you finalize the program yesterday?" she asked Jenna.

"It's all taken care of." Jenna glanced toward the kitchen door and lowered her voice. "Web's barbershop quartet wanted to do six songs, but I got them down to four."

"Good for you. We don't want too much of a good thing."

Jenna looked shocked. "So they're good?"

"They are. Web's got a beautiful baritone."

"I didn't know. I just assumed . . ."

"People never believe other local people are good. Fact of life." Madeline went back to her list. "Did you call——?"

Web burst through the kitchen door, waving the newspaper. "Eureka! Praise be to God!" He slapped the paper on the table on top of Madeline's list. "Looky there."

The headline read "Matriarch's Restitution Changes Lives." Madeline started skimming the article, but Web gave her a synopsis.

"Reporters found some of the people you helped, Maddy. And they interviewed them and found out the good things you'd done." He pointed at the second paragraph. "Here they mention a couple in Chicago who's had a handicap ramp put on their house, plus received a handicapped-retrofitted car as a gift from Regrets Only."

"You did that, Auntie?" Jenna asked.

"Oh, she did much more than that. Dozens and dozens of good deeds. And the press is picking up on it." He turned back to Madeline. "Read the last line."

She adjusted her glasses. *"Rising above the indiscretions of the past, Madeline Weaver proves that it's never too late to make things right."*

Jenna clapped. "Bravo, Auntie!"

Madeline felt herself blush. Who would have guessed it would all turn out all right?

Web took a seat at the table and pointed over the top of the paper. "Look to the right. There's a companion article about a whole bunch of people making amends for past wrongs. Kentucky, Maryland, Maine . . . it names people from three or four states. It's catching on, Maddy! You've started a trend."

Jenna laughed. "My aunt, the trendsetter."

"Oh pooh," Madeline said. But she was pleased.

"I told you God wasn't done with this yet," Web said.

Madeline opened her mouth to argue, then closed it. "I guess you're right."

Web raised his hands to the sky. "Glory, glory hallelujah!"

"Stop that," she said, even as she held in a smile. "Jenna? Where's that oatmeal? We have work to do."

Joan sat next to Ira. He ate his barbeque, coleslaw, and orange Jell-O slowly, deliberately, as if he had to think about every bite. Gone was the man who used to wolf down his food so fast Joan had to get after him.

She put a hand on his forearm. "Would you like some pie? I saw pumpkin, cherry, and apple crumb over there."

He looked up. "Sure."

She waited for him to specify which one, but when he didn't . . . "I'll take care of it," she said.

She was taking care of a lot of things lately. And most disturbingly, Ira seemed happy to let her take over as if he were a child. And to think that Joan had complained for years about his bickering, domineering nature. She could do with a smidge of that stronger attitude now, anything to prove he was her Ira again.

They'd gone to the neurologist last week and were waiting for the tests. But the doctor had hinted that the initial signs indicated Alzheimer's—a diagnosis that scared Joan more than the word *cancer* would have scared her. Cancer was treatable . . . there was so little known about Alzheimer's.

At the dessert table she ran into Ryan. "Hey, Mrs. Goldberg. I loved the banana split you made me at Swenson's this morning. I'm trying a root-beer float next."

"I'll fatten you up yet, Ryan Bauer. And I'll see you Monday after school."

"Do you have to call me a soda jerk?" he asked. "That's weird."

"You is what you is, kid." Joan chose a slice of pumpkin pie.

Ryan glanced in Ira's direction. "Is he okay?"

"He will be." As she took the pie back to Ira, she wondered about her answer. Would Ira get better? They'd have to take it one day at a time.

For better or worse.

In sickness and in health.

Madeline felt a hand on her shoulder. "It's time for your speech, Auntie."

She looked back and nodded. Jenna looked stunning in a turn-of-the-century pink dress with a lace bodice and oversleeves. And with her hair dressed over pads in an upsweep, she looked like many a picture in the Weaver attic—which is where they'd found the dress.

Madeline winked at the ever present Seth standing beside her great-niece. He'd rented a three-piece suit—more 1920s than 1906, but Madeline appreciated the effort. Then she looked across the table at the Newsoms. "Now comes the boring part," she warned.

"I'm sure that's not true," Patrice said.

"Are you trying to earn brownie points with me, young lady?"

Patrice nodded. She'd been quite solicitous lately. For whatever reason, it was as if she'd had a complete attitude makeover.

Madeline looked down at her apple pie that was still untouched. Though Lavon had brought it over for her, she wasn't hungry, which was a pity considering the immense amount of food present. She leaned her head low and looked directly at the little boy across the table. "Malachi? Can you eat another piece of pie?"

He nodded excitedly, a dab of Cool Whip from the pumpkin pie he was devouring dabbling his chin.

"It's yours." She pushed it toward him then stood as Seth pulled out her chair. The three of them walked toward the gazebo, with

Jenna babbling on about logistics and Madeline smoothing the line of her long blue dress and adjusting the angle of her flower-trimmed hat.

"There's a microphone and Web's going to introduce you—if that's okay."

"Can't think of anyone else I'd rather have do it."

Web was waiting for her in the gazebo, which had been decorated with sprigs of fall-colored leaves, pumpkins, and mums, announcing the arrival of fall. It was Madeline's favorite time of year. How appropriate.

Web, looking dapper in his brown suit, starched collar, black tie, and derby hat, met her at the top of the steps. It was odd seeing him dressed up, but she found him quite handsome—for an old coot.

My old coot. Just yesterday they'd gotten married in a church in Topeka. Some pastor friend of Web's had done the honors. And last night, just as he'd promised, she had become his bride in every sense of the word. As yet, only Jenna knew their secret.

"Are you ready, Maddy?" Web asked.

"As I'll ever be." She gestured toward the lectern. "Let's get this wrapped up before they finish their dessert and scatter. I like 'em fat and sassy."

He kissed her cheek. "This is your moment. Enjoy it. I'm very proud of you."

She blushed and felt ridiculous. Eighty-two-year-old women did not blush.

Web went to the lectern and tapped on the mike. "Ladies and gentlemen, may I have your attention?" People looked in his direction and quieted. "As you may know I'm Web Stoddard, and I have the honor of being the oldest resident of Weaver." He looked toward Madeline and gave her a wink. "Though only by six weeks."

Madeline raised her chin. "I have no idea what you're talking about."

"Methinks the lady protests too much, but I'll let it go, because I don't want to rile the lady in question, and lady she is. She and I have known each other our entire lives, and in many ways each of us takes up where the other lets off. Actually, it was in this very spot back in 1936 that she, myself, and another friend, Augustus Weaver, made a pact to never leave this town. A pact we kept. Although it's just Maddy and me now, we've taken our childhood vow seriously. We've not let the outside world tempt us away from this place that is good and wholesome and . . . right." Web's eyes scanned the crowd. "Weaver is a *right* place and now it's *your* place, and we hope that today you too make a pact with your loved ones to never leave."

Madeline noticed many nods and was heartened by it. Maybe, just maybe . . .

"But enough from me," Web said. He beamed at Madeline. "I now present to you the woman who made this day possible, the woman who had the gumption and vision to see a way to get people back in Weaver, and most importantly, the woman who, as of yesterday, became my wife."

The crowd was silent for a moment. People exchanged glances. Jenna beamed and whispered in Seth's ear. And then they were all on their feet, applauding. Web held out his hand to Madeline and she joined him.

She motioned to the audience to quiet down. "Oh pooh. Enough already," she said into the microphone.

"Kiss! Kiss! Kiss!"

Jenna's chant was soon universal. Joan Goldberg was actually hopping up and down in anticipation.

Web whispered in her ear. "Shall we?"

She whispered back. "Why not? Let's give 'em a thrill."

With that, Web leaned her back ever so slightly and kissed her.
The crowd roared its approval.

He helped her upright and Madeline fanned herself. This was
rather fun. Web withdrew with a smile, tipping his hat.

"Go get 'em, Mrs. Weaver!"

Madeline pointed at Seth. "That's exactly what I intend to do,
Officer Olsen. But it's Mrs. Stoddard now." She waited for them to
quiet down again. It was time to get to the point of the day—the
point of everything.

"In fact, go get 'em is exactly what I *did*." Madeline looked out
over the crowd. There were over three hundred by Jenna's esti-
mate. Ex-Weaverites and their families had come back home—at
least for the celebration. And who knew? Maybe after today they'd
want to move back for good. That was her highest hope.

When Madeline had their attention she began—by repeating her
last line. "Indeed, that's what I did. I figured out a way to go get
'em—to go get *you* so this town I love would have a chance to be
reborn. We nearly died—" she raised a gloved fist—"but we didn't!"

There were cheers and her heart was full. To her surprise her
throat constricted and she felt tears threaten. *No! No. Don't you
dare cry. Madeline Weaver Stoddard does not cry in public.* Out of the
corner of her eye she saw Web take a half step toward her and she
shook her head. He returned to his place.

Madeline cleared her throat. She would finish this with dignity.
It was imperative. She would not get another—

She shoved that thought aside because she knew it would only
add another burden to this emotional moment. She couldn't think
about that now. She had to focus on the here and now, with all
these people gathered, waiting for her. She applied a smile and
within seconds, it became genuine. "When our ancestors came to
this country, they came as Swedes, Irish, Chinese, Germans,

Africans, Czechs . . . that was their main identity—at first. But as they formed communities like Weaver, what they *had been* slipped away and was replaced with what they were now: Americans. Kansans. Weaverites. With great courage and determination they let the past pass, took the present by the shoulders, and gave it a mighty shove toward the future. They did not look back at what was, but looked forward to what could be.

"That's what we're doing once again on this day, the one-hundredth birthday of Weaver. We've come together at this crossroads to start over and build something great. We are family, and as family we must accept the ways we are different but grab on to the ways we are the same." She held her hands in front of her, fingers splayed. "We must take who we are as individuals, and weave it together to form something stronger than the one." She intertwined her fingers, forming a two-handed fist of strength. She took a deep breath to make her final proclamation. "We are the weave of the world, and we must continue to be united so we can meet back here in another hundred years."

Web led the applause. People cheered and patted each other on the back.

Madeline acknowledged their recognition with a nod, then stepped away from the lectern.

Web pulled her into a hug. "That was wonderful, Maddy."

"Was it?"

"You know it was."

And she did know it. She'd said what she had to say. What more could she ask for?

As Web helped her negotiate the steps in her long dress and high-button shoes, she was swarmed by well-wishers, people wanting to shake her hand. People lauding her words.

It didn't get much better than this.

The barbershop quartet was finishing their first song—Web singing his mellow baritone—when the pain attacked.

Madeline was sitting with a group at a table, but the pain caused her to miss the end of Ed Renner's story about how he'd moved to New Jersey as a boy, but was thinking of coming back to Weaver now that he had two boys of his own. She tried to smile and nod to give him encouragement, but her thoughts were consumed with *This is a bad one. I have to get home.*

"What do you think, Madeline?" Joan asked. "Ed would fit right in, wouldn't he?"

She gave an answer she hoped would be appropriate. "We'd love to have everyone move home." She glanced at Joan, then said, "If you'll excuse me?"

Madeline rose and took a step away from the group.

Immediately Joan was at her side, a hand on her arm. "You okay?"

"No."

"You want to sit down?"

"I want home. Stay with me, Joan. Get me home."

Joan's eyes got wide. Madeline looked toward Web. *I need him. Now.* But seeing how his face lit up when he sang, knowing how long he and the others had practiced, she didn't want to disturb him. Let him stay and revel in the festivities. Home was just across the square. She could slip away . . .

Not a chance. The pain came in for a second volley.

She collapsed.

She opened her eyes to see faces above her—but not the one face she wanted to see. "Web. Get Web."

As soon as she saw him, she let herself sleep.

Joan had rarely prayed, but she prayed now as she sat beside
Madeline's bed in the Weaver mansion.

Suddenly, Madeline opened her eyes and looked around.
"Where's Web?"

"He's out talking with Roy and Jenna." She started to stand.
"I'll get—"

Madeline shook her head. "Not yet. You . . . heathen . . ."

Joan smiled. "Me heathen. But I must admit being a heathen is
kind of scary in times of crisis."

"I'm scared."

"You'll be fine." Joan leaned close and whispered, "I've been
praying. God is probably so shocked he's going to give me everything I ask for."

Madeline smiled, then shook her head slightly. "I'm still . . . I'm
scared of what's *after*, Joan."

Joan was suddenly overwhelmed. The woman wanted reassur-
ance of heaven? She was *not* the one to ask. "There's heaven. You
go to heaven."

Madeline's head still shook. "Not so simple. Web says . . .
narrow gate."

This was not how Joan always thought of it. *If* there was a
heaven, she imagined a huge gate with God letting everybody in—
everybody who'd led a good life. And surely Madeline Weaver
qualified. Look at what she'd done for the town. "How's this?"
Joan offered. "When you get to heaven, you send me a sign that
you're there. Then we'll both know."

"Jesus . . . I must . . . must . . ."

Now Joan was really out of her element. *Web! Get in here!*

As if hearing her command, the bedroom door opened and Web

came in with the others. Joan willingly relinquished her position at the bedside.

Web took Madeline's hand, leaned down, and kissed it.

Madeline smiled. "Time's up, old man."

He shook his head, but he did not argue with her—which surprised Joan. Shouldn't a person argue with such a statement?

"She's been asking about heaven," Joan whispered. "She said something about a narrow gate?"

Web nodded once, then said, "'You can enter God's kingdom only through the narrow gate. The highway to hell is broad, and its gate is wide for the many who choose the easy way. But the gateway to life is small, and the road is narrow, and only a few ever find it.'" He pulled her hand to his cheek. "We've been together since we were born, Maddy my love. I will not go through eternity without you. I won't."

She pulled his hand to her lips and managed a small kiss. "Jesus?"

"Yes, Maddy. Jesus. Like I've told you before. He's the gate."

She smiled and nodded, then opened her eyes and met his. "Jesus. *My Jesus.*"

Web sucked in a sob. "Yes, Maddy. Your Jesus. Always yours now. Always."

Her face softened as if all stress was gone. "You're a good husband, Web. You've always been a good husband."

He nodded. "I'll love you always, Maddy. Always. Always."

"Love you. Always," she said. There was a small intake of breath. Then she let it out, and there was no more.

Joan held her own breath, unsure.

But when Web leaned forward and kissed Madeline, when he awkwardly wrapped his arms around her and held her while he sobbed, she knew her friend was gone. She stepped back toward

the center of the room, shaking her head. Jenna hugged her as Roy
went to the bed.

Web's face was wet with tears and he kept one hand on
Madeline's shoulder as Roy used his stethoscope, then looked up
at Web with a nod. He put a hand on Web's arm. "You okay?"

Web sniffed, but said, "I will be."

Jenna hugged him. "I'm so sorry."

He nodded. "We're all sorry for her passing. And yet . . ." He
looked back at Madeline, wiped an eye, then took a ragged breath.
"Think of this: she had her Founders Day. She accomplished what
she wanted to accomplish. And she accepted Jesus so I know I'll
see her again. In not too many years, we'll be together as we've
always been together."

See her again? Joan began to cry fresh tears and brushed them
away. "But how do you know? How do you *know*?"

Web went to her and pulled her into a hug. "Because God said
so," he whispered.

She pushed away from him feeling slightly angry at his calm.
"Said what?"

He captured her right hand in his. "I'll share everything I know
with you, Joan. All of it. Whenever you're ready."

She had no idea what he was talking about, but only knew she
wasn't ready to hear much of anything right now. Life wasn't fair.
Not fair at all.

Joan walked toward the park. The Founders Day celebration
had ended with Madeline's collapse and only a few small groups
still milled around, most likely waiting for word about their
matriarch.

Joan didn't plan on telling them anything. There was another place in the park she felt compelled to visit.

The Weaver Garden was where she and Madeline had first met and where they'd met every Sunday since. And though neither one of them had ever been able to get inside, the atmosphere was still calm and quiet, the bench outside serving as almost-as-good a spot to roost and rest.

Joan was glad the Weaver Garden was in a far corner of the park, away from the gazebo and the tables. Birds felt safe hopping from fence finial to flower to branch. It was a peaceful oasis. A place to think. And grieve.

She stood at the fence and looked inside, holding tight to the cold wrought iron. She was so confused. Madeline's death was not as much of a shock as the way she had moved from confusion about heaven to peace once Web said a few short words about Jesus. Just like that? Panic to peace? How could that be? And *was* Madeline in heaven right now? Had something happened in those few short minutes to make *that* her reality?

"Show me a sign you're there, Madeline. Show me a sign there's *something* there."

Joan retreated to the bench and found herself sitting to one side, as if any moment Madeline would come and join her.

I'm so alone.

She thought of Ira and had the vague recollection of asking Ryan to take care of him in the hubbub of getting Madeline to the Weaver house. Ira was probably at home now, waiting for her. The thought did not bring her comfort nor make her feel any less alone. For in his own way, her husband had left her too. Not in the way she'd worried about him leaving, but in a way far worse. Would he get better? Would things ever be the same again?

I'm so alone.

But maybe not completely. Swenson's Soda Shoppe was open, and if this morning's grand opening was any indication, she would meet many new friends there and soon know them by name. Actually, she wasn't the sort to need a big circle of friends. Just a few would do. A few people to really talk to and confide in.

Web.

She liked the idea of having him as a friend. And oddly, the idea of future discussions about heaven and God was intriguing. Scary too. But intriguing nonetheless. As a former teacher, she had a mind that sought knowledge. She was open to it, open to a lot of things since they'd moved to Weaver.

She glanced back toward the garden, but then—

She turned around completely. Toward it. The gate. It was open.

Joan rushed toward it and put a hand on top, needing to prove it was real.

It had been closed, but now it was open?

Show me a sign you're there, Madeline. Show me a sign there's something there.

Joan's laughter turned to tears. She'd done it! Madeline was in heaven! Meaning there *was* a heaven. There was a life *after* . . .

Joan opened the gate all the way, ready to go inside.

But then . . . she stopped short and slowly pulled it closed. In time she might pass through the gate. But not yet.

Not yet.

Yes, I am the gate. Those who come in through me will be saved.
Wherever they go, they will find green pastures.

JOHN 10:9

A Note from the Author

Dear Readers:

Change. Can't live with it; can't live without it. We have a love-hate relationship with change. I'm as guilty as anyone. I want things to be different, but when they get different, I long for them to be the way they were.

Fickle, fickle, fickle.

And yet I've always been fascinated with people who are willing to attempt the big changes—the starting over, pull-up-roots-and-plant-new-ones kind of changes. That's what got me thinking about the initial concept for *Crossroads*. That, and my anger and sorrow at the fact that small-town America is suffering a slow death.

But you've never lived in a small town, Nancy. Why should you care?

We all should care. Because even if we're from the biggest big city, if we're honest with ourselves and dig deep into our hearts and souls, we all long for the essence of small-town life: the safe streets canopied with trees, the city park with a gazebo where band concerts are held on summer nights, stores where the clerks know us by name and order Necco wafers just for us, and big front porches with swings where we sit and chat with neighbors as we watch the kids play ball in the street. Don't lie and say that doesn't appeal to you on some level.

"But I can't move there," you say.

But what if you could? What if someone offered you a free house and a free business, thus taking away the biggest excuses for not exploring that place in your heart? What if someone ignited your pioneer spirit? What if you had the guts to just do it?

I've always been fascinated with the pioneer mentality. Living in Kansas, I wouldn't even be here if one hundred and seventy years ago some brave people hadn't left what they knew and headed west to start over. I think the hardest part must have been knowing when to stop. Obviously some didn't (hello, California!), but many did. Whether it was due to exhaustion, a gut feeling that this was the place, or an act of God, the middle of our country was populated. One family, two . . . a town was born. Then another and another.

Have you ever looked at the names of small towns? Some are named after a geographical feature: Conway Springs, Mound City. Others are obviously named after one of the initial settlers: Aliceville, Laurie, and Beatrice. And still others must have reminded the settlers of where they'd come from: Mexico, Prague, and Versailles.

But the bottom line is: America was born in small towns. They are our roots. And they deserve to live.

Recently I've even heard of some real-life land giveaways. Life becomes art becomes life. Go for it, small towns! Do whatever it takes to survive and thrive. Actually, the lure of free land has been around a long time. My own family immigrated to the United States from Sweden because of the lure of free land. The fascination with the concept must be in my genes.

An aside for those of you who are familiar with my Mustard Seed series (*The Invitation, The Quest, The Temptation*): Originally, there was going to be a fourth book in that series (*The Inheritance*) but it didn't happen. So to appease those of you who've written asking about that book (who *still* write and ask for that book) I give you a compromise. Within the pages of *Crossroads* I have placed a few familiar faces: the Bauer family from the Mustard Seed series. As you know, once a book is completed the characters' lives continue (you did know that, didn't you?). So Kathy, Roy, Ryan, and Lisa have not remained stagnant since the last sentence of *The Temptation* got its period. I will say it was nice to see them again and catch up. It was like a family reunion. And they were happy I contacted them. For even characters need a chance to start over.

We all do.

Happy reading and God bless us every one.

Nancy Moser

ABOUT THE AUTHOR

NANCY MOSER is the best-selling author of three books of inspirational humor and 13 novels, including *The Seat Beside Me,* the Mustard Seed series, and the Christy Award–winning *Time Lottery.* She also coauthored the Sister Circle series with Campus Crusade cofounder Vonette Bright. Nancy and her husband, Mark, have three children and live in the Midwest—but alas, not in Weaver.

Scripture Verses in Crossroads

CHAPTER	TOPIC	VERSE
Prologue	Unity	Ecclesiastes 4:12
Chapter 1	Work	1 Chronicles 28:10
	Surrender	Luke 18:18-22 (paraphrased)
Chapter 2	Purpose	Habakkuk 1:5
Chapter 3	Hope	Psalm 94:19
Chapter 4	Trust	Proverbs 3:5-6
	Work	1 Chronicles 28:10
	Peace	Luke 6:27-29
	Justice	Matthew 5:6
	Purpose	Jeremiah 1:5
Chapter 5	Plans	Proverbs 19:21
	Burden	Matthew 11:30
Chapter 6	Arguing	Philippians 2:14-15
Chapter 7	Encouragement	Deuteronomy 31:8
	Helping	Ecclesiastes 4:10
	Purpose	1 Corinthians 6:11
Chapter 8	Plans	Proverbs 21:30
	Peacemaker	Matthew 5:9
	Strength	Psalm 31:24
Chapter 9	Faith	Hebrews 10:39
	Faith	Hebrews 11:1
	Renewal	Psalm 51:10
	Loyalty	1 Samuel 13:14 (paraphrased)
	Obedience	Matthew 25:21
	Renewal	Psalm 51:10-12
Chapter 10	Heart	Proverbs 27:19
	Salvation	John 10:9 (paraphrased)